MARIANNE A. SCOTT

OF ICE AND HEARTBREAK

A FAE ROMANCE NOVEL

Editor: Samantha Reads Spicy

Cover Design: Moonlit Town End Art & Design

Fantasy Map: Eternal Geekery

For those who aren't afraid to take fate into their own hands

Content Warning

Your mental health is important! Please be aware of the following situations in this book:

Alcoholism/using alcohol to cope with trauma

Loss of a spouse (told in flashbacks)

Rejected mates (told in flashbacks)

Explicit Sex (M/F)

Erotic Asphyxiation

On-page sex between multiple partners (not including the main characters)

Mild Voyeurism

Of Ice and Heartbreak is a stand-alone in the *Fae Romance Series* and has a Happily Ever After.

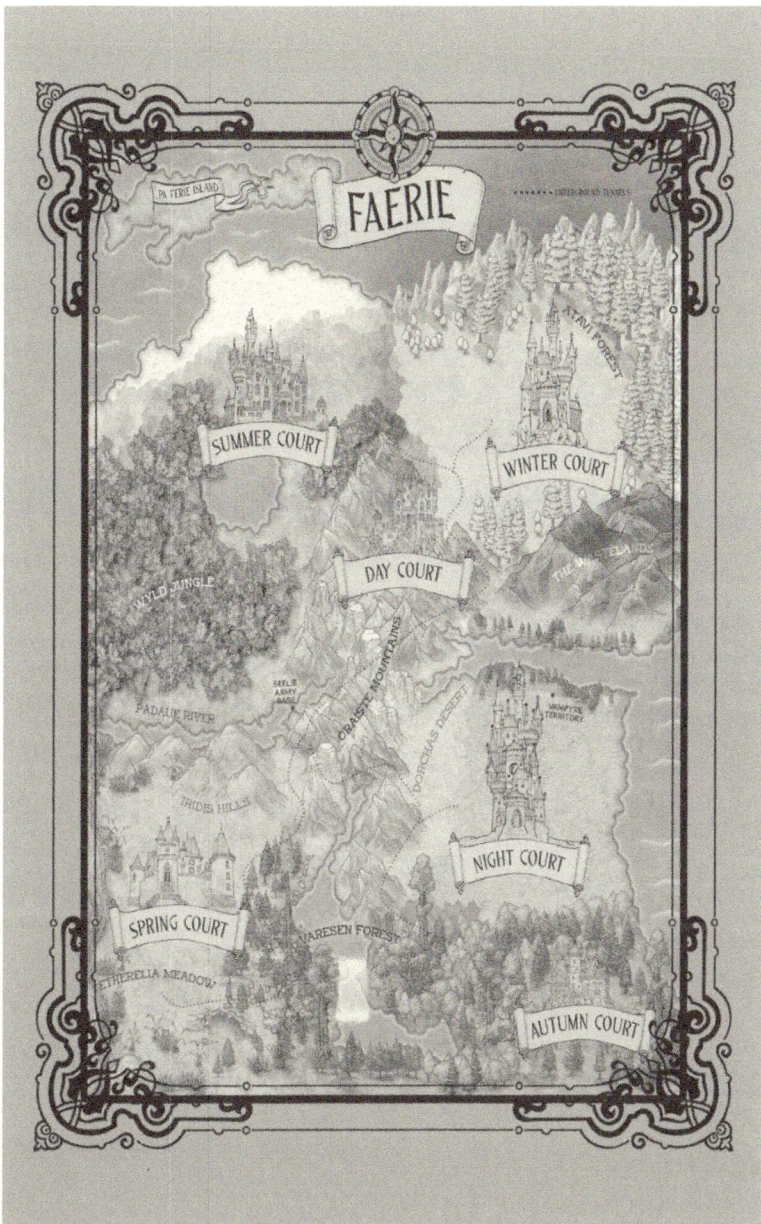

Chapter One
Edina

Two Mortal Years Ago (Mortal Realm)

"Fuck me, it's cold."

The winter wind threw the door open, rattling the bell above it as I stumbled inside *The Cracked Chalice*, a dive bar down the road from my school and the only place I could conceivably get to in this weather. Though, in hindsight, I should have changed into jeans rather than the mini-dress I wore. Even with the thigh-high boots I chose for the weather, I still had a lot of skin showing. Skin that was now all pink and wind burnt.

It took me shoving my weight into the door to get it to shut again, and when I turned back to the interior of the bar, the patrons, all three of them, were staring. "Hey, boys," I wiggled my fingers in their direction while I knocked the toe of my boots against the floor to clear the excess snow that accumulated. I shucked off my puffy coat and hood, and shook out my hair, running fingers through my long blonde waves to untangle the knots. The scarf came next as I shoved it in my jacket pocket and hung it all on a coat rack in the corner beside the door.

"Didn't think you'd make it." I looked up across the dimly lit space and found Joe, the owner and bartender, lounging on a lawn chair behind the bar. He was a middle-aged man who had lost most of his brown hair, though he tried to make up for it with the scraggly graying beard he rocked. I grinned when I saw him wearing the flannel I'd bought him for Christmas last year, the red marginally less faded than the ones he usually wore.

"Don't lie. I'm the whole reason you opened tonight," I laughed, making my way through empty wooden tables and approaching the bar. The other customers went back to whatever game they were watching, the lights of the flatscreen competing with a few neon signs that showcased the beer and liquor offerings alongside a large, red neon sign that read *BAR* directly over the liquor.

Joe shook his head and stood, making me a drink before I even got to the forest-green leather stools. I loved this place. I loved the worn wooden floors that always had a fine coating of peanut shells, even on slow nights. I loved that I could still spot the abnormally large scuff on one of the tables from when my best friend and I discovered tequila and table dancing. And I loved that it was just clean enough that I wasn't afraid to put my head down on the shiny varnished bar top.

Joe set my vodka soda on the bar by my preferred stool, tossing in an extra lime with a wink before logging the drink into the computer. I left my parents' black card here years ago. It was easier, and I trusted Joe. I checked the statement once and found out he wasn't leaving himself tips on the tab. When I asked him about it, he said, "You're not supposed to tip the owner." So, I started bringing cash.

I sipped my drink and sighed. The bitterness from the soda cut the citrus of the lime so perfectly that I took another large gulp. I didn't even taste the vodka tonight, which usually spelled trouble, but felt fantastic.

"Long week?" Joe asked, sitting back in his chair with a little grunt as he sank.

"Finals," I said around the straw, taking another gulp.

"Should I just leave you the bottle?" he chuckled. Without taking my eyes off him, I abandoned my straw and chugged the rest of my drink. When I slammed the glass back on the counter, he was belly-laughing as he put another drink in front of me. "I was gonna drink this one but looks like you need it more than me."

"You're too good to me." I slid him the empty glass.

"Which final was it today?" he asked, and I noticed he kept the bottle within arm's reach that time.

"Battle Magic."

That was one of the other reasons I liked it here. Joe, like me, was a witch. As were most of the regulars. I know, witches in Salem, Massachusetts. Stereotypical. But sometimes myths were born from just enough reality that they're conceivable. Salem happened to be a major hub of witches in the Kingdom of Magic since one of the best magical academies and a magical military base were here. Not that any of the mortals— non-magic-using folk— knew we existed, living right alongside them. They explained away the extraordinary, and we did our best to keep our magic hidden. It's why places like *The Cracked Chalice* were so great. We were able to let ourselves relax.

"Any more?" Joe asked, and I shook my head. My Battle Magic final was my last one, which meant I had only one semester left at Salem Academy of Magical Arts. *Thank fucking god.* I got it, witches needed to learn to control their magic so we could blend into the mortal world, but I've had a pretty solid handle on my magic for years. I just wanted to be done and move to London to be near my best friend and set up a wedding planning business that used actual magic to make mortal weddings...well magical.

"Headed to the island for the break?" Joe asked as I stirred my drink. My parents...owned an island, which I didn't tell many people because they automatically assumed things, only some of which were true.

"Nah, London," I beamed, and Joe instantly caught my meaning.

"How is Katie? I miss her."

"Promoted again." I bragged like it was my accomplishment. My best friend was an overachiever like that. "In another high-profile relationship. Overall, killing it."

Joe laughed heartily. He got a kick out of our dating lives, mainly because I think it reminded him of the glory days. "I almost forgot," he said and pointed to something over the cash register covered in brown paper. "Wanna see your birthday present?"

"Is this what I think it is?" I squealed, standing on the footrest of my stool and leaning as far over the bar as I could. He got up and ripped the paper down, revealing a picture of me, Joe, and Katie from my eighteenth birthday. We'd had another blizzard like this, so we couldn't go into the city. Katie and I talked to Joe until he finally kicked us out, but not before I forced him to take the picture and promised I'd be his favorite customer one day. *"Joe!"*

"It's an incentive to keep drinking here even though you can be served anywhere now," he said, rubbing the back of his neck. I beckoned him closer and pulled him into a half hug over the bar. When Katie left for London, Joe sort of became my best friend here.

"It's cute that you think I don't get served everywhere," I whispered, and when he pulled away, I gave him a flirty wink and a shrug of my shoulder. His laugh boomed through the empty space.

My phone buzzed in my bra, and I turned away to fish it out to spare poor Joe like he didn't accidentally witness my nip slip a year ago. My good mood deflated when I saw the name on my screen.

Mia

Heyyyyyy.

Mia

Soooo, Brett just texted and asked if I was going to Mikayla's party...and he seemed so sad when I said I wasn't.

I scoffed. Brett was her on-again-off-again situationship.

Mia

So, I'm gonna go there. Are you mad?

Mia

Don't be mad.

"Get stood up?" Joe asked. I rolled my eyes.

"It's impossible to find a decent wing-woman, Joe." I texted Mia back and told her to stop being a whipped little bitch. The three dots appeared and disappeared about five times before I gave in and told her it was okay.

"I don't think you'll have much luck in here tonight," Joe said, setting a fresh drink in front of me. I groaned and flopped dramatically on the bar. I really needed to blow off some steam and was hoping I could find someone to do that with.

I bailed on Mikayla's party because I'd already slept with the people I found attractive from my school. And I didn't do repeats.

Mia

So I just walked in...

Damn, that girl worked fast.

Mia

And Mark is asking for you.

Mia

Laura too. And she's super drunk...Cinco de Mayo in Cabo, drunk. She keeps screaming that she wants to make out with a girl before we leave school.

I was not in the mood to be someone's first tonight, but Mark was promising. He wasn't really my type, he had the whole cute-nerdy thing going on, but I'd heard he at least knew how to find a clit. One more drink, two max. Then I'd be drunk enough to have some bad sex with a college student. That was the problem, once you started fucking people in their late twenties/early thirties. Anyone younger just...lacked.

The bell on the door tinkled as I shelled a peanut and discarded the remnants on the floor. "Maybe not," Joe muttered under his breath, as he stood and straightened his flannel. I popped another peanut into my mouth as the stool next to mine slid back.

"Scotch, neat," the voice next to me said to Joe. His voice wasn't deep, per se, but it had a faint accent that was intriguing. Not quite British, but close...like maybe he lived there for a bit.

I could feel his eyes on me, but instead, I made eye contact with Joe, who nodded, telling me the guy next to me was worth my time. I chuckled into my drink. *Maybe Joe is the wing-woman I've been searching for.* I turned over my shoulder slightly and scanned the body of the man beside me.

He was wearing dark denim, and a black button-down shirt rolled up to his elbows, exposing pale skin. He didn't look super muscular, but that slim kind of toned. Finally, I looked at his face and my mouth parted. His hair was brownish red, and he had a smattering of freckles over the bridge of his nose, but his eyes were what kept me captivated. They were so green it was almost otherworldly. He definitely had some kind of magic; I could practically feel it wafting off him.

His stare was intent, not even the slightest bit ashamed that I caught him looking at me as much as I was looking at him. "Do you come here often?" he asked, and I scoffed.

"*That's* your opening line?" I asked, unable to keep myself from laughing.

His flirty smile was crooked and all kinds of disarming. "Yeah, I fucked that up," he laughed.

"You wanna give it another go?"

Joe set his drink down. The man picked it up and downed the contents in one gulp. He cleared his throat, and in the most serious voice said, "What's your sign?" I cackled, the earlier drinks making my laugh easy and loud, and he lit up at the sound. "I'm Puck," he said, sticking out his hand.

"As in hockey?"

"As in Shakespeare. My mother was a tad obsessed with *A Midsummer Night's Dream.*" I placed my hand in his. His grip was tight, but his skin was soft, so definitely not someone who worked with his hands. His thumb brushed against my palm in a way that made my core tighten.

"I'm Edina."

"Can I buy you a drink, Edina?" The sound of my name in his accent had my stomach flipping. I bit my lower lip and watched as he tracked the movement.

"Hmm." I playfully tapped my finger on my chin. "I'm not sure you moved past the first round. Those opening lines..." I clucked my tongue.

Somehow, I ended up spinning toward him, which wasn't noticeable until he placed one foot between mine on the footrest and his thigh brushed against mine. He leaned forward, and I fought the urge to mimic his movements. In a low, rough voice he murmured, "Don't worry. I *excel* at the next part."

A slow smirk spread across my face. "Prove it."

THE NEXT HOUR WENT by in a flurry of flirting, drinks, and subtle touches. I knew in the first thirty seconds of seeing Puck that I was going to sleep with him, but it was a dance. I enjoyed the art of picking up someone almost as much as I liked the actual sex. Sometimes even more...see previous note on the college students I slept with.

The other patrons left even though the storm outside had quieted, and Joe moved his chair to the other end, keeping an eye out but not intruding. I had him switch me to straight seltzer a few drinks ago. My magic worked better when my mind was clear, and I wouldn't go home with a stranger if I was unable to defend myself. The last thing I wanted was to find myself in a sticky situation and not be able to focus enough to cast a simple spell. As it was, my wand would take some maneuvering to get out of this dress.

I laughed at whatever joke Puck was telling, more focused on the way his fingers absently toyed with the ends of my hair. He was so close we were basically sharing a stool, but he wasn't as drunk as I'd expect him to be after downing most of a bottle of scotch. If anything, he seemed clearer than when he walked in. I was puzzling over that mystery when his hand fell away, and he sighed heavily.

"I should probably head home," Puck said, signaling to Joe to close out his tab.

I wasn't the kind of person who cared enough to keep my emotions off my face, especially when I'd been drinking, so I imagined I looked at Puck like he lost his damn mind. I also wasn't the kind of person to beg.

"Right," I murmured over my straw, loudly sucking on the melted icy, soda mix at the bottom of the glass. "Well, it was nice meeting you, I guess." There was a little extra bite to my words, but fuck him for wasting my time.

Puck chuckled, low and deep, and slowly stepped off his stool. I didn't realize how tall he was until he was standing. I'm tall... but he dwarfed me. *Damn, I love that.*

He leaned into my ear, his warm breath tickling my skin and making me shiver. "I misspoke. I meant *we* should probably get out of here."

Everything tightened. My skin felt too hot inside my clothes. "That's presumptuous," I purred, my voice turning husky.

"Is it?" He leaned impossibly closer while still not touching me. "Edina—" *Fuck I like the way he says my name,* "—would you like to come home with me so I can spend the night buried between your legs?"

"Yes, please," I blurted, all pretense of hard-to-get completely gone.

"Good, I already called a rideshare." He smirked as he signed his receipt.

I hopped off my stool and walked back to the coat rack to grab my stuff. "Night, Joe."

"See you next year," Joe called. "And happy birthday."

"It's your birthday?" Puck asked, a slight edge to the question that I was sure I was imagining.

"Next week. I'm a Christmas Eve baby."

"Happy early birthday," he said, helping me into my coat and holding the door open for me as we stepped into the cold.

The wind stopped, leaving light flurries that drifted onto the existing snowbanks that grew even larger as a plow haphazardly cleared the roads. I scowled at the drift that was blocking the street.

"Use your magic," Puck said, and I froze. Just because I met Puck in *The Cracked Chalice* didn't mean he was a witch. I racked my brain trying to figure out what I said that would make him think I had magic.

"You added ice to your drink earlier," he clarified. *Shit, I don't even remember doing that.* My raw magic, the magic that wasn't funneled into my wand to be used in a spell, was Water Magic. Most witches had some form of elemental magic, except for the few that had Light or Dark Magic. I rarely used my raw magic since spells were more efficient, except for adding ice to my drink, apparently.

"You're a witch too then?" I asked.

"I have earth magic." *That's a weird way of putting it.* I shrugged it off and used my magic to push enough snow aside to form a path.

Not two seconds later, a black car with a sign on the windshield appeared. With one hand on my back, Puck guided me into the car. We got situated in the backseat, and Puck's hand started drawing idle lines around my knee making me squirm. His hand slipped to my inner thigh, and I inhaled sharply.

"You're killing me," I murmured. Our eyes connected.

The next thing I knew I was in his lap, our tongues tangled. One of his hands gripped my ass while the other threaded in my hair, tilting me so he had the perfect access. He swore as I rolled my hips against his already rock-hard cock. The kiss was frantic. Desperate. And fuck, it was a good kiss.

"Edina," he rasped. I took his bottom lip between my teeth, and his groan had my clit throbbing. "There's one thing I need to tell you about where I live."

"You're here," the driver barked. We pulled away, breathless, lips swollen. Puck's eyes were hooded with desire as he opened the door and I managed to clamber off him. He threw a fifty at the driver and gave a half-assed apology before he was out of the door and pulling me back into him.

I gave him my cheek so I could see where we were, and realized I knew the place. The gray building was squat and surrounded by a thick stone wall with barbed wire atop it. I'm pretty sure mortals thought it was a jail or a police precinct, and they were close. "You're a soldier?" I asked. We were right outside the Dragons Compound. The Dragons were the magical military, and Salem was one of their strongholds. I'd been here enough to know it well.

"Not exactly." He took both my hands. "Don't freak out." My hackles rose, and the magic within me rushed to the surface, ready to be used in a pinch.

Magic shimmered over his skin. It looked like he was pulling away a filter that dulled his appearance. His eyes somehow became greener, his jaw more defined. But that's not what made me gasp. His ears lengthened to points and brown wings that seemed to be etched with vines emerged from his back. They were taller than he was, and the edges were rounded.

"You're Fae," I breathed.

This is way outside my kink zone. Fae were not welcome in this realm, because when they were, they would rape and pillage and cause enough fucking chaos that mortals started noticing and writing about it.

My mother was a tad obsessed with Shakespeare my ass. The Fae were immortal. I bet this Puck was the one that *A Midsummer Night's Dream* was based on.

"Yes," he said, his hands still holding mine. "I know they teach you to fear us, but we're not monsters. *I'm* not a monster."

"I could get in trouble for just talking to you." I looked around frantically and saw the shadowy figure of a Dragons officer walking the perimeter. "Why the hell would you walk into a military stronghold? If they see you—"

"I'm glamoured to anyone but you," he said. His thumb made a soothing swipe over the back of my hand. "And we're here because there's a portal."

The world was spinning. I didn't know how to process any of this. "You want me to come with you—"

"To Faerie, yes." Puck looked hopeful. He wanted me to go to another realm, to leave this world and go to Faerie, which was incredibly dangerous for a human in the best of circumstances. Time worked differently in Faerie, I could go for a week and miss months here.

"One night," he vowed. "Then I'll bring you right back here or to any other portal in this realm. You'd be back before your birthday."

One night in Faerie was one week in our realm. One week where I had no responsibilities or obligations anyway. I was supposed to swing by my home in Manhattan and go to my parents' Solstice party, but I wasn't entirely sure they'd notice if I didn't show.

I could die.

But fucking hell, it would make a great story.

"Okay," I said, and Puck's face brightened.

"Okay?" He pulled me in for a searing kiss that had my toes curling and left me breathless. "You're going to love Faerie."

"I guess we'll see."

Chapter Two
Edina

Two Mortal Years Ago (Mortal Realm)

PUCK DIDN'T GIVE ME a minute to second-guess my answer. He scooped me into his arms, bridal style, smiling widely as I yelped. "I've got you, gorgeous." He winked, and then we disappeared. His body was solid against mine, but we were completely invisible. I lifted my hand, studying the air where it should be as Puck started to move into the compound.

"Normally, I'd teleport us," he said conversationally like that wasn't a ridiculous notion. Witches couldn't teleport, at least not elemental witches. I'd heard tales that dark witches could, but I never met one to ask. "But they have some safeguards set up. We'll have to fly."

Is that what we're doing? All I could tell was that we were moving quickly through the gate of the compound and towards the thick concrete doors which swung open upon our arrival. Unlike witch magic, Puck didn't need a wand to channel a spell. He didn't even need to lift his hands, they both stayed on me the entire time. He just opened the door.

As if he could see me gaping at him, invisible lips pressed against the tip of my nose. We flew—apparently—through the darkened halls, expertly avoiding the handful of soldiers making their rounds, until we reached a door that was surrounded by four very official-looking men.

"Hang tight, gorgeous," Puck murmured, setting me down and turning visible. The men's heads snapped to him, and he gave them a playful smile. "Evening, gentlemen." His eyes glowed electric and their jaws went slack. "We're just heading in the portal; you won't have any memory of this. Sound good?"

They nodded in scary synchronicity and stepped out of the way. Puck was before me again in a flash, removing the spell that made me invisible and scooping me into his arms again. "Shall we?"

I was without words, a rare occurrence. I was simultaneously terrified and so turned on I couldn't think straight. *This is a bad idea. I should run.*

Puck wrapped his hand possessively around the small of my back and pulled me into another mind-melting kiss. My hands fisted in his hair, and he gripped my ass with enough force to lift me off the ground. "Say yes, Edina," he growled into my mouth. "Come with me."

"Yes," I breathed, and we strode through the doorway without breaking our kiss. I pulled away for one second, enough to see that we were on some kind of moving walkway shrouded in a periwinkle mist. We hurtled forward so fast it made my head spin.

"Eyes on mine," Puck said, capturing my attention. "Portal travel takes some getting used to. Focus on me."

Well, I can do that. I closed my eyes and kissed and bit along his jaw, relishing his groans as I reached his neck. I blew into his ear before sinking my teeth into his lobe and licking away the hurt.

"Goddess," he swore.

"Mmm, I've been called that before." His chuckle was warm and lit up my insides.

The weather shifted, no longer the frigid cold of a New England winter, nor was it the weird misty feeling of the portal. It was warm. Balmy. And it smelled like it had just rained.

"You can open your eyes now." Puck set me down and I turned, opening my eyes. "Welcome to the Spring Court."

I wasn't sure I'd ever be able to accurately describe my first glimpse of Faerie. It was the most beautiful place I'd ever seen. More beautiful than my parents' house in the Maldives. The sun was setting, but the sky wasn't just soft, wispy colors. It was vibrant sherbet orange, rose pink, and lilac that gave way to an indigo blue so deep it felt like you could touch it.

We were in a forest where each tree was more idyllic than the next. The leaves were green and full and hung just low enough to provide shade without obstructing the perfect sky. There were patches of vermillion spotted toadstools interspersed around thick grasses that were high enough to tickle your ankles.

And the *flowers*. They were every color in the rainbow and some that weren't. There was one lily that was literally glowing like it was coated in bioluminescence. They grew wild, popping up in multicolored patches with no rhyme or reason, and yet they were perfectly placed. Dragonfly-type insects flitted from flower to flower before returning to a knot in the bark of a tree.

I kicked off my boots and socks so I could feel the grass beneath my toes, reveling in the cool feel of the soil. Puck removed my heavy coat and unwound my scarf, stooping to kiss the juncture of my neck and shoulder. A breath escaped my lungs, and my body arched into him instinctively.

"You like it?" he asked, his voice soft and unsure.

"It's a dream." I couldn't stop looking, taking in everything. I popped up on my tiptoes and realized we were at the edge of the forest, and off in the distance were rolling hills that should have some nun singing about how they were alive with the sound of music.

"We should get inside before the sun sets," Puck murmured and once again scooped me into his arms. He looked different here too. Even after he revealed himself to me, I could tell he had dampened his shine. Here, it was unrestrained, and he was even more beautiful. Mythical. His smile was still easy and wide, but his teeth were whiter, his lips pinker. It made me want to run my tongue along them, which was exactly what I did. "I hope you're not afraid of heights."

"Nope." I popped the 'p,' drawing his attention to my mouth. He swore again and bent his legs. My stomach bottomed out, stealing my scream as we shot straight into the cotton candy-colored sky. The higher we went, the more the colors deepened into a mix of indigo and violet that were interspersed with stars that looked close enough to touch.

"You can," Puck said, reading my mind. "Not here, but in the Night Court, they turn stardust into jewelry."

"It's official, I'm never leaving," I proclaimed, and something in Puck's chest stuttered. "Relax, I'm kidding. One night, remember?"

"Right." He angled us back toward the ground. While we were amongst the stars we must have flown laterally over the center of the forest. Below us, the greenery was lush and so close together that you couldn't see the grass below.

Puck swooped beneath the canopy and pulled up just before we reached a giant limb. "You live in a treehouse?" I asked as he touched down on a balcony made of the same rich auburn color as the trunk of the tree. He carried me through a sliding glass door, throwing magical lights into the room to illuminate his home.

The raw grain of the wooden floorboards was so natural I'd be convinced they were untouched if it wasn't for the smooth texture I felt as Puck set me down. The walls were also wooden, but not in a dingy-seventies-cabin way. In an I-hollowed-out-the-trunk-of-this-tree-and-used-all-the-parts way. You'd think the cream sofa and glass coffee table would be out of place, but it worked in the odd mix of treehouse and bachelor pad.

The living room area was massive, and while there was no electricity, there was a small kitchenette with a farmhouse sink that had an old-fashioned pump. Puck sauntered behind the island and pulled a bottle of wine from a lower cabinet.

"Haven't you heard the stories about humans eating or drinking in Faerie?" I teased as he poured two glasses.

"This is from your realm," he said, crossing back to me and extending the red liquid. "I wouldn't serve you Faerie wine."

"Why's that?"

"I prefer my lovers conscious."

I took the glass and clinked it against his before turning my back on him and walking to the glass door, which took up most of the wall. The stars were out in full force now, twinkling mischievously, like they were ready for a show.

Puck stepped up behind me and brushed the hair off my shoulder. I took a large gulp of the wine as his lips ghosted along the slope of my neck. "Is this okay?" he asked, his breath hot against my skin.

"Yes."

He connected with my skin, kissing and biting and licking down my shoulder. I arched into him, my head hitting his hard chest while my ass ground into his very prominent erection. My blood was boiling, the heat radiating from his lips directly to my core. I needed more, but he was taking it slow, savoring every inch of my skin. "I hope you don't expect me to beg."

His chuckle was so deep I felt it everywhere, and my body instinctively sought his. I couldn't help but whimper when his hand wrapped around my waist and pulled me closer to him. I worked my hips, rolling and teasing him as much as he teased me. My breath mimicked his, heavy and strained.

I'd had enough. I turned in his hold, took both of our glasses, and slipped away to place them on the coffee table. He tracked me like a predator. And maybe he was. Maybe I should have been afraid of being with someone so much more powerful than I was. But it only made this entire experience hotter.

Slowly, I slipped one strap off my shoulder, following it with the other. "I should be doing that," Puck said, but he was rooted to his spot by the door. I reached behind me to slide the zipper of the dress down, allowing it to fall from my body in a pool of fabric at my feet.

When I stood naked before him in just a lacy mint-green thong, I said, "You can finish the job."

He was on me in the blink of an eye, one hand possessively cupping the back of my neck and the other gripping my ass. He tugged me up until I was on the tips of my toes. He snarled against my neck and dropped his other hand to lift me, wrapping my legs around his waist. "You're gonna make me work for this, aren't you?" he asked before capturing my mouth. I made a non-committal noise, which turned into a moan as his tongue expertly stroked mine. *Fucking hell, he's good at that.*

My hands tangled in his auburn hair, my nails scraping against his scalp. At some point, he must have moved because the next thing I knew, I was deposited on the couch and Puck was on his knees before me.

He drank me in, his eyes leaving goosebumps in their wake. I was panting, my skin flushed. I needed him to fucking touch me, but instead, he just looked. "For fuck's sake—" I reached for him, but he pinned my arms to my sides.

"You're not in charge here, gorgeous," he said, and everything below my waist tightened. "We have all night, and I'm going to take my fucking time. Understood?"

I swallowed hard and nodded. My reward was a feather-light touch along the seam of my panties. "Fuck, Edina," he said when his finger drifted inward to the soaking wet fabric. "No wonder you're impatient."

"You could fix that," I deadpanned. His mouth closed around me, and I gasped as he sucked over my thong. I didn't even have time to enjoy the moment before he moved to my inner thighs, nibbling his way down, his hand mimicking his trajectory on my other leg.

When he returned to my core, he asked, "How attached are you to these?" He wrapped the string of my thong in his fist.

"Tear them off," I commanded, and he did, the fabric biting into me in a deliciously painful way before the scrap was discarded. I decided to push my luck. "Now put one finger inside me."

"What part of 'you're not in charge here' did you not understand?" he asked, circling my entrance.

"I've never been great with respecting authority." I surprised him by tangling my fingers in his hair and using my grip to bring him exactly where I wanted him.

The second he tasted me, he went feral. He pushed my thighs open wider and devoured me like he was starving. The contact, the intense stimulation of my clit, was just on the right side of painful. My legs straightened; my toes curled. He lavished every inch of my sex, but when he dipped his tongue in my entrance, I lost it. I rode his face as he worked me higher and higher.

"I want your hands," I said, and he obliged instantly, replacing his tongue with two fingers. His thrusts were deep and wild and connected with my G-spot. Every. Single. Fucking. Time. It was too good. I couldn't hold back anymore. The heat low in my belly traveled up my spine, and I almost completely lifted off the couch.

"That's right," Puck said, his voice hoarse with desire. "Let it go, gorgeous."

I exploded, a thousand pricks of light illuminating every inch of my body. I writhed against Puck's mouth as he sucked and licked me through the high of my orgasm. And when I came down, he pulled his fingers from inside me and licked them clean.

"I could live off this taste," he said, rising on his knees and kissing my stomach. I grabbed his chin tilting his head up, and then very slowly licked his bottom lip. He lost it.

In one fluid motion, he was on his feet and all of his clothes were discarded. I drank in his lean, chiseled muscles. There were smatterings of freckles everywhere, but Puck didn't give me much time to ogle him. Once again, I was lifted, and I would be a total liar if I said being manhandled like this wasn't a turn-on.

He deposited me by the door and spun me so my back was against his chest. With one large hand on the middle of my back, he pushed me down, and I braced my hands on the cool glass as his cock nudged my entrance. "This okay?" he asked, dragging it through my arousal, making himself slick.

"Fuck, yes." He slammed into me and instantly picked up a quick pace.

"If you need me to go slower—"

"Don't you fucking dare." *God, he feels perfect.* Just big enough to stretch me without hurting. Seriously, the perfect size. I must have said so out loud because Puck laughed.

"You feel perfect too, gorgeous," he preened, leaning down to kiss my spine. The tender gesture was immediately replaced by a fist tugging my hair. I cried out at the pain but matched his thrusts. "You like a little pain with your pleasure?"

"I think that's been established—" I inhaled as the hand holding my hair fell to my neck. Puck stilled, and my walls fluttered around him as I waited with bated breath for him to keep going. "Yes," I answered before he asked.

"Tap my hand if you need me to stop."

And then he squeezed.

It was the slightest pressure on each side of my neck, but enough to choke off my breath. I loved this feeling. I didn't tell many people about this particular kink; it was too dangerous to trust with a lot of one-night stands. But I got the feeling Puck had been around a while and knew what he was doing.

I trusted him.

Which was really weird considering I'd only met him a few hours ago and rarely trusted anyone.

His pace continued, hard and punishing, but drove me higher and higher. I reached between us and rubbed my clit as his hips slapped against mine. The sounds of our sex echoed against the glass, creating a soundtrack that had me building that much faster.

When the edges of my vision started to darken, Puck released me. Air rushed into my lungs, only to be expelled by my scream as I fell over the edge. My pussy clenched around him, and Puck swore as my orgasm dragged him into his own. He came with a long groan that was almost enough to have me coming again.

As we both came down, we stayed still, locked in this position until I could rise on my shaky legs. "I like the view."

Puck laughed heartily as he pulled out of me. I was about to ask where I could tidy up, but with one wave of his hand, all evidence of our orgasms was cleaned.

I turned back to face the Fae that just gave me the best sex of my life, suddenly unsure of what to do. Normally, I'd leave. Or kick the person out. But I was in a different realm.

"Don't even think about it," Puck said, handing me the wine.

"Think about what?" I downed the contents of the glass, and he swiped his thumb along my lower lip, sucking the small bead of wine that collected there.

"We're not done," he said with a positively evil grin. "On your back."

"Don't you need a minute?" Because his cock, while still glorious, was very much soft.

"I do. You don't." My mouth popped open, and since I didn't follow his command, Puck lifted me again and laid me on the floor. "I'm going to fuck you again, Edina," he said, kissing my collarbone. "But in the meantime, I didn't give these nearly enough attention."

His tongue flicked against one nipple as his hand dwarfed my other breast. He spent the next few minutes turning me on until he was ready for a second round.

We did this for the rest of the night. We had sex on every single surface in the treehouse, and after Puck finished, he worshiped my body.

Sometimes he went down on me, sometimes he just held me and kissed my lips. Once, he gave me enough of a break to drink a bottle of water and ask if he was actually the Puck from *A Midsummer Night's Dream*. "It's heavily embellished," he said impishly. "Shakespeare was too much of a diva to take any criticism that would have provided more accuracy."

Somewhere near dawn, we wound up in Puck's bedroom, located off the main space. It was sparse, almost as if he rarely came here, but the sheets were soft, and the mattress was just firm enough to bounce without sinking into it. Puck hovered over me, and my heels dug into his ass as he thrust inside me. We were slower this time, so slow that I could feel every inch, every ridge, and every vein of his cock against my walls as I squeezed him.

My eyes were closed, focusing on the friction of our bodies together in this position. "Edina," Puck whispered, kissing the corner of my mouth. "Look at me." I didn't. I couldn't. It was too intimate. "Gorgeous, open your eyes."

With a heavy sigh, I did. His forehead rested against mine, those emerald eyes staring straight into my soul, stripping me bare. And suddenly, it became hard to breathe.

"Puck," I murmured, as he rolled his hips and my lashes fluttered.

"I know," he responded, not breaking his gaze.

Something much more intense than an orgasm built in my chest. Something that fucking terrified me. I bit down on my trembling lip, unable to look away, but unable to keep this sweeping, intense emotion at bay. "I know," Puck repeated as a tear tracked down my cheek.

My orgasm came out of nowhere, and my chest cracked wide open with it. Puck came with me, a look of pure wonderment over his features.

We lay there until the sun fully rose, casting him in a golden light that made his hair look like fire.

He trailed a finger down my cheek and leaned forward to kiss me again.

"I have to go," I said when he was inches from me. Puck blinked. "Time works differently here, right? I don't know how long it's been in the mortal realm, but people will be looking for me. I'm supposed to go—"

"Edina," Puck cut me off, but I was already walling myself off. It was too much. I didn't know what this even was, but it was too much. And I needed to get out of here, back to my life. Back to reality.

"Please get off me," I asked, keeping my eyes shut against the hurt that must have been on his face. He sighed heavily but slid out of me and rolled over onto the mattress, cleaning me up as he went. I got up immediately, leaving the bedroom and hunting for my discarded dress and boots. I didn't even remember putting my boots down, but I found them by the door.

"Edina, please, just stop for a minute."

I found my little dress and shimmied it up. My wand was missing, it fell out when I took off the dress, but I didn't see where it landed, and I couldn't spend any more time here looking for it. I reached back for the zipper of my dress, when a warm hand landed on my hip, and drew it up. "I need you to just listen to me for a minute."

I ignored him. "Can you take me back to the portal?"

"I think you're Fae," Puck blurted. That got my attention, and I spun around to look at him. I laughed, because this had to be a joke, but his face was solemn and totally serious.

"I'm a witch," I asserted. "Not even a very good one."

"Fae emerge on their twenty-first human year," he continued. "Before that, we appear entirely human. We have rounded ears, we don't have wings or horns, and our magic is the level of a human witch." He grabbed my arms.

"My parents are witches."

"Or you're adopted."

I fought the urge to slap him. My parents told me about my birth, told me the exact date and time. And I looked exactly like my father.

"If this is some sort of ploy to kidnap me and keep me here—"

"It's not, Edina, I swear it." Puck looked serious, but wasn't this exactly what our teachers warned us about? Fae convinced humans to come to Faerie and then sold them into slavery. And because time was so different, they aged at an impossible rate and were dead in months.

"If I'm wrong," he said slowly, "then it's one day. You said your birthday is Christmas Eve, which is about twelve hours away in Faerie. If I'm wrong, I bring you home tonight, and you never need to hear from me again.

"But if I'm right..." he cupped my face in his hands. "You know the Kingdom of Magic's reaction to Fae. You'll be hunted. And I can't come with you, and I'm not sure when I'll be able to return to get you. Please stay."

He saw my answer in my eyes before I spoke and swiped his hand across his jaw. "If you're right," I started, "then I need to be with my best friend. I'm not just going to disappear to Faerie and never see her again."

"You would—"

"I don't trust you." He balked at the intensity of my words. "I trusted you with my body, but I can't trust you with this. I don't know you. I'm asking you to take me to the portal. If you won't, I'll figure it out. I grew up in Manhattan, I'll find my way."

Puck opened his mouth like he was about to plead with me one final time, but closed it again, and approached slowly, scooping me into his arms one final time. "Let's get you home."

Chapter Three
Edina

Present (Faerie)

I HATE THAT PUCK was right.

I hate that less than a week after our night together, wings sprouted from my back and my ears sharpened to points in the most painful experience of my life. I hate that despite my best friend moving heaven and earth to keep me safe in the mortal realm, I was forced to return to Faerie. And not just anywhere in Faerie...the fucking Winter Court, where it snows every single day, and instead of the pretty pastels of the Spring Court, the best I get is gray skies and snow. *So much snow.* I might have gone to school in New England, but nothing could have truly prepared me for living in a court that never gets warm. Even the beach, which is arguably my favorite part of this goddess-forsaken place, has an unforgiving, rocky coastline and the water is so dark it's more black than blue.

But most of all, I hated that I was not drunk enough to ward off that dream. *Can it be considered a dream if you're really reliving a memory?* Either way, I swear I drank enough to sleep dreamlessly. Since moving to Faerie, I've become an expert at just how much Faerie wine it takes to make me black out for the night. It's the only way I can sleep.

I must have severely miscalculated, because not only is the taste of the dream lingering on my tongue as I wake, but my brain thuds in my skull like a stampede of centaurs.

I blink into the pillow my face is shoved into and turn my head to the side, cracking my eye a sliver against the weak morning light streaming in through my bedroom windows. I usually remember to close the curtains around my four-poster bed, but apparently not last night. The limited amount of the room I can see is a wreck. Bottles are strewn around the white carpet, silver picture frames are askew, and clothes are tossed haphazardly over my vanity, the open wardrobe doors and the nightstand.

The male next to me is stacked with muscles on top of muscles, and he twitches in his sleep, his legs moving like he's running. I sniff and practically gag. He's definitely a werewolf, he smells like a dog.

A sharp pain lances the center of my back and I cry out. "Off my fucking wing," I growl, and a feminine squeak from my other side has me turning to the source. Her powder-blue hair is long and covers her bare breasts, which are a slightly paler shade of blue. She moves off my wing, but slides her hand into my hair, stroking the tangled blonde locks before she smooths them behind my pointed ears.

"Sorry, princess," she coos, her voice relaxing me instantly. She leans closer, tilting my head to meet her, and brushes a kiss against my lips. She tastes like brine and seaweed. *Right. A siren.*

Slowly, pieces of the night start filtering back to me. There was a tavern, a place that vaguely reminds me of *The Cracked Chalice* back home with its wood tones and magical customers. I remember many empty bottles before me, and sitting on the lap of...a brownie? No, that can't be right. Brownies are generally small in stature; I'm not sure I'd fit on their laps.

The siren takes my silence as approval and drifts her hands lower, toward my breasts. I get flashes of a very athletic threesome with the two beings in my bed, and it clicks. *That's* why the wine didn't last. I worked some of it off before I fell asleep.

I groan at my error. "You like that?" the siren asks, and I realize her hand is between my legs, tracing around my sex and not seeming to mind that I'm drier than a desert.

"I'm too sober for this," I grumble and swat her away. I roll on top of the wolf in search of my nightstand on his other side. My hand slaps the white wood until I find the bottle I'm looking for. I don't even fully sit up as I rip the cork out with my teeth and take a swig of the Faerie wine.

The wolf stirs, somehow taking me on top of him as an invitation to grope me. "Off," I bark. He literally whimpers, and I flop back into the center of my bed. "Both of you, out."

"You sure you don't want to play, princess?" the siren asks, trying to lace her words with magic that will make me submit. Jokes on her. I'm a Fae princess; there's no way her magic is stronger than mine.

Did you like how I slipped that in there? The fact that I'm actually the Princess of the Winter Court, heir to the throne, and only child of Queen Gwyneira is the worst part of emerging.

That's a lie. There are worse things.

But the royal title is toward the top of the list.

"Fuck off," I respond to the siren, officially in a bad mood. I tip the wine back like a baby with a bottle and let myself sink into the brooding I feel coming. The siren huffs, but she and the wolf grab their clothes from the floor and leave my suite.

"Should I leave too?" A brownie sits up from the floor. I scream and whack him on the head with the bottle hard enough that the glass shatters and what was left of the life-affirming liquid drips down his face. He shakes his head and reaches for the spot where I hit him, touching the blood that's coming from a cut from the glass.

Guess I didn't imagine the brownie.

"Fucking hell," I grumble, tossing the shattered bottle to the other side of the bed, and hearing an oomph when it lands. "Everyone out of my room." The two lying on my floor head to my door, and about six other Fae in my sitting room, follow.

Huh. I usually remember an orgy.

A lone figure moves upstream through the throng of people. He's tall and muscular, made more intimidating by giant black wings. His pointed ears are clearly visible, jutting out from his bald head, and he has a pinched look on his face that creases the rich brown skin around his mouth and eyes. He crosses his arms as he gets to the door that separates my bedroom from the rest of my suite.

"Hi, Daddy," I coo, grabbing my white fur blanket and wrapping it around my naked body. I step over the broken glass and spilled wine, rather than magicking it away because I know it'll drive him insane. As I anticipated, he makes a sound low in his throat before banishing the shards of glass while I busy myself digging around my wardrobe for the spare bottle that's buried behind my dresses.

"Just because I don't understand your sarcasm," the male at the door starts, "doesn't mean I don't know when you're taunting me."

My magic rises to my skin, and ice spreads from my fingertips to the bottle. When I'm convinced it's chilled, I take it out and down half the contents in one long, glorious pull. I probably need the whole bottle to deal with this today, but I'm pretty sure that any minute—

Yep, there it is. The bottle goes flying out of my hand in a torrent of cold water, smashing against the door to my bathroom. And if I'm judging the situation correctly—

"*Fuck!*" I scream as he turns the icy water on me. It's overdramatic since cold doesn't really affect me, and I was expecting it, but I don't appreciate him getting my fur comforter wet.

"Language," the male at the door says.

"Listen Four—"

"You know my name, Edina," he says, staring me down with his honey-colored eyes.

"There are too many of you," I shrug. I wasn't being glib when I called him Daddy. He's one of my fathers. My mother has seven husbands, and they all agreed not to do a paternity test and claim me as their own...until I became a changeling, which is just a fancy way of saying I was stolen and sold to humans in the mortal realm.

"You know, according to the novels my best friend makes me read," I say, turning to face him and all his anger head-on. "Four is the ideal number of men in a harem. Seven is just greedy."

"We're not a harem," he states, unaffected. He knows I'm trying to provoke him. Whenever I throw the *H* word around, my fathers all bristle. I know very well they have a loving polyamorous relationship, but I also enjoy getting a rise out of them. I figure I have to put them through their paces since they missed out on my rebellious teenage years.

"How can I help you, father number four?" I ask, trying to remember if I have any wine stashed in the sitting room. I know there's whiskey in the library, I might need to get that.

"She wants to see you," he says.

Fuck my immortal life.

Definitely need to hit the whiskey.

"Can I refuse?" I ask, my wings fluttering so much in my irritation I almost lift off the floor.

"No. You have five minutes." He leaves for my sitting room, closing the double doors behind him and leaving me alone.

I turn on my heel and storm into my bathroom, shutting the door behind me and sinking to the floor. I really wish one of the bottles of wine I had survived the morning. I could summon one out of thin air—that's one of the new abilities I gained when I emerged as Fae—but I don't trust wine or food I can procure from nothing. It has to come from somewhere, and when I asked where no one would or could give me an answer.

I make a split-second decision, flip on the shower, and squeeze my eyes closed imagining with all my wine-muddled concentration that I'm in the library. There's a cold, squeezing sensation, and when I open my eyes, I've teleported to the other room. It's adjacent to the sitting room, so I move very quietly so that Four doesn't hear me. I select the false book from amongst the real ones and pull out a flask before replacing the decoy on the shelves. Then I teleport back into the bathroom and down the contents of the flask before brushing my teeth to clear the evidence and banishing the flask into thin air.

Every morning I'm exceedingly grateful that the Fae managed to steal some human inventions...namely indoor plumbing. The rest I can live without, but my transition from the mortal realm to Faerie would have been exponentially worse if they'd not had running water.

I get in the shower and scrub my hair, washing away the scent of the partners I shared last night. There's no questioning why my mother wants to see me. I'm getting a talking to about the proper behavior for a princess. I've had the talk before, but there's never any punishment to go along with it.

I stay in the shower longer than five minutes, and when I get out, two fluttering pixies are waiting for me. They're what most humans expect when you say the term fairy. They're tiny—about the size of a dragonfly—with petite bodies, brightly colored hair, and wings that constantly flutter. They also have teeth so sharp they can tear through mer-hide, but that's a different story. My pixies, Althea and Brigid, are twins. Identical in every way, except for their hair, which is magenta and purple respectively.

"Morning, Highness," Althea says, her magenta hair matching the dress she's chosen for today. She motions for me to step into the dress Brigid holds. I don't fight them like I do my fathers. They're just doing their job, and I genuinely like the company as long as I'm not hungover.

I step into the velvet day dress, a simple sheath with a low-cut neckline that does nothing for my non-existent breasts, and long sleeves that cuff tightly against my wrists. Althea buzzes around doing my hair, while Brigid finishes buttoning me in before starting on my makeup. They work fast, chattering on about a ball tonight and how excited they are to see some of their friends from the Seelie courts.

I ignore the pit in my stomach that gets worse with every sentence. The Seelie Courts haven't been to our palace since I returned, so I've successfully avoided the one Fae I never want to see again.

A pang reverberates in my chest, only slightly dulled by the whiskey.

"Your Highness?" Brigid's voice is concerned, but I wave her off.

"I'm fine. Keep going."

When they're done pinning my hair into a ridiculous up-do and painting me to look like I didn't spend the last two mortal years drinking my weight in Faerie wine, I walk out to Four, who's sitting on the white couch, impatiently tapping his foot.

"I'm pretty sure a harpy, a vampyre, and a dragon had a threesome on that couch," I say, not waiting for him as I walk out of my room. Everything in the hallway is white, the marble floors, the walls, the décor. I'm sorry, the pictures are grayscale, but the frames are white wood.

"She's in the throne room," Four says before I can head for her private meeting room. I stop cold.

"Why?" I ask, trying to keep my voice light.

"She's entertaining a guest."

My breath grows shallow, and the whiskey threatens to make a reappearance. I clamp down on my bottom lip, the pain not enough to keep me in the present and not swimming through unwanted memories. They clog my throat and fill my stomach with lead.

"The General of the Summer Court Army," Four amends, and I release a breath, the lump in my throat going with it.

"And she needs me there?" I ask, my voice still wobbling.

"So she says."

I release a breath and straighten my spine. My legs wobble as I head toward the throne room. I'm vaguely aware of my other fathers falling in beside Four, but I ignore them. It's not that I don't like my fathers, some of them are a pain in the ass, but none are particularly bad. But every time I'm with them, I can feel their disappointment, sense their ruined expectations. Maybe I'm just projecting my own insecurities, but either way, it's not fun spending time with them.

I descend a flight of stairs and turn the corner to find dignitaries from the other courts who are staying in the palace for the ball. Seeing the different colors of the Seelie Courts—teal, white, green—makes me freeze. I scan the crowd frantically, my chest constricting painfully.

"Edina." Five is the kindest of my fathers, and his voice is gentle as he places a bronze hand on my elbow. I take a deep breath and turn to him once my calm mask is firmly in place. His blonde hair is tied in a low ponytail today, but his wings are tucked away to accommodate his blue suit jacket. It's formal for a day look.

At my urging, he guides me forward, and I walk with my head held high, not quite focusing on the other Fae as I make it to the throne room. The Winter Court soldiers stationed at the ornate double doors yank them open, and I steel my spine one final time as I enter to meet with my mother.

Chapter Four

Eldoris

Fuck me, it's cold.

I mentally curse the attendant who took my thick, winter coat when I entered the throne room. I know they were being polite, but I'm not accustomed to the bitter cold that seeps into my bones. Even my fire magic, which hovers just under my skin and makes me run hot, isn't enough to combat the chill of the empty throne room.

If this plan works, I'll have to get used to it.

I start pacing, hoping the movement will take some of my anxiety while simultaneously warming me up. Traversing the length of the dais, I focus on the silver throne carved with a pretty floral pattern that's so at odds with the court and its monarch. A stained-glass window behind the dais bathes the throne in a reflected rainbow. It's a stark contrast to the colorless decor but even the pretty colors can't obstruct the blizzard raging outside.

The rows and rows of empty chairs combined with the high-arched ceilings make the throne room seem daunting. I've never been in this room while it's empty. Even the few times when my mother had private audiences with the Winter Court Queen, there were countless advisors present, not to mention my sister and I. The emptiness seems to mock me, reminding me how alone I am today.

I should run.

I scrape my hand along my jaw, ruffling my coarse beard and then smoothing it back in place. My collar is tight around my throat, but my sister encouraged me to wear one that covers the tattoos that cover my entire torso and snake up the side of my neck. My horns, long and curved like an antelope's, jut out from my dark curls, their rich umber brown looking like an extension of my skin. I usually keep them retracted, but again my sister meddled in my appearance and insisted I need to appear *more Fae*. It's the same reason golden jewelry is affixed to my rounded ears, giving them the illusion of being pointed.

I plant my feet in front of the throne and roll my shoulders to stop my fidgeting. I'm here for a purpose, to propose an idea to the queen. It's a truly awful plan. The worst possible solution to the problem at hand, but that's of no concern to my mother or sister.

For as long as I've been alive, the Seelie Courts—Spring, Summer, and Day—have been at odds with the Unseelie Courts—Winter, Autumn, and Night. We've fought in bloody wars, and battles of wit and sub- terfuge. The times of peace between the Fae are few and far between. Recently, we were able to band together for the Witch War in the mortal realm, but everyone is waiting. Waiting for a fight to break out. Waiting for someone to try to establish dominance. Waiting for the other shoe to drop. While we wait, we play social games and establish dominance through outlandish parties. We try to seduce those not from our courts into a misstep through wine and Faerie Dust. We make alliances in the form of friendships or, more presently, marriages.

The back doors to the throne room open and I dip to my knee. The shuffling of skirts gets closer as the queen approaches, but I keep my eyes on the polished gray stone, thankful that there's not a layer of ice decorating the floor, as is customary in the Winter Court.

"You may rise, General."

General. Not *Your Highness.*

It doesn't matter to the royalty of the other courts that I'm the son of a queen. Ever since I emerged, and my twin sister was named the heir apparent, I've been General. Head of the Summer Court Army, until most recently when I was promoted to the General of the Seelie Armies. It's an honor disguised as an insult.

I stand and adjust my suit jacket before kissing her outstretched hand. Queen Gwyneira is a vision in white, her blonde curls piled in the center of a silver crown with sapphire gems. Her long neck is bare, leading to a modest corset that draws attention to her tiny waist before billowing out in about eight feet of tulle. Even though her dress is unadorned, it sparkles as she situates herself on her silver throne.

"Your Majesty," I say, putting on my most charming smile. Her eyes, such a light shade of blue that they're almost white, scan my body appreciatively.

"How are your mother and sister?"

"Well, thank you." This next bit is tricky to navigate. Gwyneira may appear young and beautiful, but she's been queen for millennia and hasn't kept her throne because of her kind temperament. "They send their regards."

An arch of a blonde eyebrow is my answer. She's unimpressed that the Queen of Summer Court isn't coming to her ball this evening, or the symphony tomorrow. It would be one thing if she sent my sister, Devorah; sending me alone is an insult.

"What matter is so urgent that it couldn't wait until the ball this evening?" Gwyneira asks. If possible, her voice is colder than before, and I know I'm about to lose her attention. I need to get through this quickly.

I swallow thickly. Every cell in my body is rebelling against the statement I'm about to make.

"I would like to propose an alliance between the Summer and Winter Courts." I'm surprised by how steady my voice comes out.

"Is there a war brewing that I'm unaware of?"

"No, Majesty," I respond, diverting my gaze from her piercing eyes.

"Then why would we need an alliance?"

I take a deep breath. "Children have been disappearing in the Summer Court." When I look up, Gwyneira has paled significantly. Her jaw ticks as she waits for me to continue. "The last time this happened—"

"I'm well aware, Eldoris." There's a bite in her words, but I know it's not directed at me. It's directed at the foe that we're facing.

Centuries ago, there was a queen. My mother's sister, my aunt, was obsessed with power. Although she was chosen to rule, she was afraid of the level of power my mother possessed and sought to increase her own magic. The means she used were nothing short of despicable. She stole magic from Fae children who had yet to emerge, killing the children. Children are sacred in Faerie, so as her power grew, it became tainted.

The Fae called it hellfire.

Gwyneira's magic was the only thing that stood a chance against the hellfire. She battled my aunt and killed her, but it appears the queen passed the means of obtaining this power along to a disciple. In the Witch War, we discovered there was not just one Fae with hellfire, there was an army of them, and despite our victory in the mortal realm, the Fae somehow escaped back to Faerie. I've been hunting them ever since, but they've been quiet until recently.

"I thought we eradicated them," Gwyneira says, her emotions still locked down. I don't respond, there's no real answer that would be satisfactory.

"So, this...*alliance*," she hisses the word, "is the Summer Court seeking aid to clean up their mess."

"And in turn, our armies will join," I finish. She appraises me, and all I can do is wait while her eyes scan over every inch of my body as if she's seeking lies on my skin.

"How do the other Seelie Courts feel about this?" she asks, toying with the wedding band on her finger. On most people, it would look like a nervous habit, but somehow Gwyneira makes it look like a power play, like she could somehow slip that ring around my neck and choke me with it.

"They understand." A bit of an exaggeration, but Spring Court has been pissing my mother off to no end, so she wasn't worried about their opinion. I'm not sure how the Day Court took the news that we'd be asking Winter Court for aid, Devorah handled that conversation.

Gwyneira clicks her tongue. "I assume you have a way to seal this alliance."

My brain and heart are screaming. *This is it. Just say the words.* My muscles shake, but I hold her stare. "With marriage." I'm not sure how I speak around the lump in my throat.

Queen Gwyneira's eyebrows shoot up to her hairline...and then she laughs. It's a harsh sound, cruel and jagged instead of warm and soft. "Marriage," she spits under her laughter. Then she goes silent. "Marriage."

I look up at the change of tone. Gone is the cruel delight, serious contemplation left in its wake. I'm not sure which I hate more. At least when she was laughing at me, I believed she wouldn't say yes. Despite my mother's urging to make this alliance, I want nothing more than to be rejected by the ice queen. She already has seven husbands for Goddess' sake.

"Marriage," she repeats, the hint of amusement turning up her lips. She snaps her fingers, and a blue-haired pixie appears over her shoulder. Gwyneira murmurs something to her, and the pixie disappears as suddenly as she appeared.

The room goes silent. No words are spoken for such a long time that I question if I've been dismissed. Gwyneira seems content to let me squirm, her eyes never leaving me even as we wait in silence. I glance to the windows on either side of the room. One leads to an orchard of white-barked trees that bear Faerie fruit, and the other overlooks the Atavi forest, a thick grove of evergreens. The snow comes down harder now and climbs up the bottom of the windows in thick drifts.

What feels like half an hour later, the pixie returns and mutters something. The queen gestures and the doors in the back of the hall fly open.

Edina, the princess who was raised as a changeling in the mortal realm, enters. Every time I see her, I marvel at how much she looks like her mother, all except her eyes, which are a rich, sapphire blue. Her hair is fashioned in a slightly less elaborate style than her mother's but has been curled and pinned up, calling attention to the day dress that is slipping off her shoulder.

She moves languidly down the sapphire runner, her limbs almost too relaxed. She gets halfway to the dais when she stumbles, but I'm not exactly sure what she stumbles on. I gasp and start to go to her, but another male is there first. One of the queen's husbands wraps an arm around her waist, minding her wings which are fluttering in uneven beats. She laughs jovially, but her smile doesn't reach her eyes.

"Goddess, help me," Gwyneira breathes, her usual impassive face has given way to anger.

Edina and her father saunter closer, Edina swaying precariously with every step. When they are level with me, Edina dips into a courtesy which is surprisingly graceful considering she walks like a baby centaur.

"Mother dearest," she coos. I sense the sarcasm in her tone, but I know the others don't. The Winter Court Fae are notoriously literal.

Gwyneira has her mask firmly back in place. "Edina, you remember General Eldoris of the Summer Court?"

Edina looks like she's noticing me for the first time. "Nice to meet you."

We've met. We fought side by side in a war. Then she avoided me at every party, ball, and other diplomatic function in the past human year. I'm not quite sure what I did to earn her disdain, but it's there.

"Eldoris has an interesting proposition for us," Gwyneira says. "He'd like our help in finding Fae who are converting their magic to hellfire."

Edina stiffens. Despite her years in the mortal realm, she knows what hellfire is, and how dangerous it is.

"I have agreed to his request," Gwyneira continues, which is news to me. "Our courts will solidify this arrangement in marriage."

Edina scoffs. "Don't you have enough husbands?"

I chortle but quickly cover the laugh with a cough. Edina's eyes light, amusement dancing across her features, but it's gone as quickly as it arrived.

"Edina—" Gwyneira's husband snaps at his daughter.

"Sorry." She holds up her hands in surrender. Her body is loose like her muscles are made of gelatin.

"Eldoris won't be marrying me," Gwyneira announces.

"What?" Edina and I ask in unison.

"Edina is correct. I have seven partners, and each one I married for love." Gwyneira and her husband share an almost undetectable look, but even that quick flash of affection warms the frigid room. "If you choose to secure the alliance, you'll marry Edina."

"Do I get a say in this?" Edina asks. I'd expect anger and outrage, especially from someone raised in the mortal realm, in a country that doesn't believe in arranged marriages. But Edina's voice is tired. Not accepting, but not overtly fighting either.

"Of course," Gwyneira says. "I would never take that choice for you. But I do believe—"

"Thanks, but I'm good." She salutes her mother and flies out of her father's hold, retreating to the entrance. I stare after her, mouth open as she saunters through the doors, flinging them open with magic and slamming them shut behind her. The clang from the doors echoes in the silence for far longer than usual.

"You found her this morning?" Gwyneira asks her husband. His eyes are the same shade as Edina's, which makes me believe this is her birth father. He runs a hand through his pitch-black hair and his dark wings twitch in agitation.

"Pacome did," he says, referring to another of the queen's husbands. He glances suspiciously in my direction before switching his intense gaze to his wife. They must have a Mental Channel established, a way to speak mind to mind. They've fallen out of fashion after a Night Court Fae figured out how to silently infiltrate those channels and started spreading secrets. But some still use them privately. I have one with my sister.

Gwyneira pinches the bridge of her nose, leaning her elbow on the armrest of her throne. I've never seen her show so much emotion, so much raw vulnerability. Concerned doesn't begin to cover the emotions radiating from her. She's at her wit's end.

"Eldoris," she says with pity in her eyes. "I would like nothing more than to enter into an alliance with Summer Court and help you stamp out the scum that plagues your court, but I'm afraid I can't help you if Edina won't agree."

The reason Fae seal their arrangements with marriage or something similar goes back millennia. As a whole, we're prone to tricks and deceit. Without a binding agent, there would be nothing stopping us from turning on each other. It's happened before, so I understand Gwyneira's concern.

"Let me talk to her," I say softly, turning the heads of both Fae.

"I'm afraid you don't know the extent of the situation," the male says.

"What is she on?" I ask, and they both wince. "Wine? Mushrooms? Faerie Dust?"

"It's wine and spirits," Gwyneira says. "But it's deeper than that. She hasn't been the same since—"

"I know," I assure her. "Let me try. I'm here for the next few days. If I can't get her to agree by then, I'll return to the Summer Court and tell my mother."

Gwyneira studies me, but the bitter edge in her eyes from earlier has disappeared. "You're a noble male," she smirks. "I'm afraid your time will be wasted, but if you wish to try, you may."

I nod my thanks and pause. "May I ask...Has anyone tried—"

"Everything," the male sighs. "We've tried everything to reach her. I'm afraid the Edina who came to us two mortal years ago is gone."

A GUARD LEADS ME to my guest room, turning down a non-descript hallway that I've never seen before. Fae have the ability to teleport, we have portals that take us between courts, and still, royalty is expected to host every dignitary, courtier, and advisor, not to mention the royals. As the Prince of the Summer Court, I've stayed in every palace in the realm, so the fact that I've never been in this hallway is peculiar.

The guard removes a key and opens the door, another oddity since guest suites are usually left open when they're unoccupied. He leads me into a simple guest room with clean white walls and a plush, navy-blue carpet, but there are hints of finery here that are atypical. The bed has thick velvet curtains that surround it, ready to block out the harsh winter sunlight after a night of reverie. The comforter is faux fur, and there are subtle accents of real silver in the mirror frame and decorating the large, white wardrobe.

"Your ensuite is through there." The guard gestures before opening the wardrobe and showing that my things have been deposited inside. "And through here," he points to another door beside the vanity, "are the rest of your rooms."

"Multiple?" I ask.

"Enjoy it, General." He salutes. "Not sure how long the hospitality will last if the princess rejects your offer."

That spread quickly. I thank the guard as he bows before scurrying off. So Gwyneira has me in some special accommodations, probably rooms reserved for the Unseelie Fae. *I should send a note to my friend from the Autumn Court and gloat about stealing his room.*

After discarding my tie, I sit at the vanity and wave my hand over the mirror, watching as it swirls silver. The wait is longer than usual, she's not expecting my call, and I undo a few of the buttons on my shirt before the mist fades and reveals the visage of my sister. To the casual observer, my twin would seem stoic and calm, but I can tell she's agitated. Her hair is just a touch out of place and is missing its usual luster, and her eyes look weary. She looks exactly like our mother when she puts on a face like that.

It always surprises people that we're twins; we look nothing alike. She's lithe and pale with sleek, chestnut brown hair, while I have our human father's umber brown skin tone and dark curls. If my eyes weren't the same ocean-blue shade as our mother's, people would talk. They still do, but not to question my parentage.

"I've only been gone a few hours," I quip, and she glares, swiping her hand down her face.

"It's a bad day." She doesn't need to tell me she's speaking of our mother, whose mind is slipping due to a rare illness. It's the reason she and Devorah didn't come to the Winter Court for this round of socialization. The bad days have started to outnumber the good.

It's another reason we need the alliance. Our court is in a precarious position. Not only is a foe with some of the most dangerous magic ever created roaming our streets, but our queen is fading and will soon be called home to the goddess. We need Gwyneira's protection if—when—Devorah needs to ascend the throne. Without it, we're vulnerable.

"Please tell me you have good news," Devorah implores.

"I have news, wouldn't call it good," I reply, and her eyes widen. "Gwyneira declined..."

She swears colorfully. "Then you're going to need to...fuck, I don't know," she whimpers. "We don't have another option. If we go to another court, they'll think something is up. They'll attack."

"We can handle an attack," I promise, but she just narrows her eyes at me. "The Seelie Army—"

"Please," Devorah scoffs. "Titania would be the one leading the charge. The combined Seelie Army is wonderful in theory, but the second their monarchs order something, they'll turn on us and you know it."

She's not wrong. The soldiers are bloodthirsty, most Fae are. They'd love the chance at another war.

"She wants me to marry Edina," I say. My sister falls silent for a long time, pursing her lips as she considers this curveball.

"She'll say no," she whispers.

"I'm going to talk to her again tonight, at the ball."

"Are you planning on seducing her?"

I balk. "You think I should?"

"She may be more amenable to an arranged marriage if she thinks it won't all be strategy and vanilla sex. You've heard the stories of her return."

I scrape my nails through my beard. Tales of Edina's exploits have been the talk of society since she returned to Faerie two mortal years ago. I dismissed the talk as gossip, but being here and seeing her makes me think the rumors that she is always drunk and taking some new Fae to her bed were on the mild side.

"I worry that the behavior is masking something."

"No shit," Devorah scoffs. "No one sleeps with Vlad unless it's a cry for help." Vlad was one of the first humans to be turned into a vampire—as opposed to *vampyres* in our realm which are born—and he's notorious even in Faerie. He comes every so often, tricks Fae into striking deals for favors, and then disappears back to his home, leaving you wondering when he's going to collect.

I find his antics hysterical.

"What was your excuse?" I mock and she glares.

"I had just found out my pampered life as the spare was over, asshole." Devorah never wanted the crown, we always assumed I would be the one who would take the position when our mother was ready to retire. But hearing her distaste for the role she was thrust into always makes my heart hurt. I wish I could take the burden from her.

"Edina hates me," I mutter and again Devorah purses her lips. "She's ignored me every time I've tried to speak to her since her introductory ball. Today she acted like we'd never met."

"Maybe it's not hate," she offers. "Maybe it's indifference."

"I'm not sure what's worse."

"Get her to say yes," Devorah says, her tone a touch more desperate than I've heard it. "Your court needs you. Do whatever it takes."

Chapter Five
Eldoris

Two Mortal Years Ago (Faerie)

I DON'T WANT TO be here.

Not just in the Winter Court, which was arguably the worst court in terms of weather and terrain, and not just in this drafty entryway with its non-descript gray stone and low lighting.

I didn't want to attend this ball.

Although this ball masqueraded as an official introduction of Princess Edina to the courts, it was a mating ritual. It happened anytime a royal Fae turned twenty-one. The entire realm lined up to meet the newly emerged male or female, hoping they would have found their true mate. It was pointless for me.

My sister clicked her tongue and moved out of the royal processional to fix my tie. "Come on, *General*," she teased. "I know you've been out of society for a bit, but that's no excuse for sloppiness."

Unlike me apparently, Devorah looked stunning. Her chestnut hair was in soft waves that framed her face but still showcased the sharp point of her ears, and her oceanic eyes were lined in thick, sweeping kohl. Her dress sparkled like the sun on the water, the teal gems a welcome color amidst the white of the Winter Court.

"Am I to pretend all night that I'm happy to be here?" I said, emphasizing my complete lack of enthusiasm. "Shall I do a jig to welcome the lost princess?" She scoffed and adjusted the golden jewelry on the top of my ears that Mother insisted I wear. The cage-like adornment gave the illusion I had the same points as my sister, even though everyone in Faerie knew I had *human ears*. Such a small feature that most wouldn't bother noticing, but it made my mother crazy.

"Anything would be better than that pissy expression on your face," my mother hissed from her spot in front of us. "You're the prince of the Summer Court, Eldoris. Just because you are allowed to command soldiers doesn't mean you can shirk the duties of your station." She turned forward without another word or room to dispute her.

Devorah resumed her place beside me but linked her pinkie with mine in silent support. *Think how fun it will be watching the girl squirm,* she sent to my mind in a conspiratorial tone. *She's been in the mortal realm her entire life, she's bound to make some glorious mistakes.*

Evil, I chided.

But it made you smile. She was right, I had a hint of a smirk on my face.

It would serve you right if she's your mate, I said, and Devorah's laugh echoed in the otherwise silent entryway. Our mother shot her an unimpressed look, and my sister instantly sobered, squaring her shoulders and becoming the perfect picture of a princess.

"How long are we to wait?" my mother fumed at the guards standing sentinel to the ballroom. They remained impassive. Devorah must have had the same thought I did, because we simultaneously took a step closer, in case she lost her cool and control of her fire. It happened frequently and was a problem we'd need to address sooner rather than later.

"Introducing The Royal Family and Society of the Summer Court." The doors flung open, and my mother stepped onto the sapphire blue carpet that led to the throne. The ballroom was beautiful, if not predictable of the Winter Court. White barked trees were interspersed between frosted windowpanes and enchanted snow fell from the high rafters, disintegrating before they reached the tallest of guests. Ice glittered over every surface, winking in the pale white faerie lights.

Devorah and I followed directly behind our mother, flanked by the rest of the Fae with power in our court. Wealthy merchants donned tailored suits not unlike my own, while dragon shifters wore glittering gowns dripping with gems. Once everyone of note was in the ballroom, the doors shut behind us with a clang.

Stop staring at the ground, Devorah said in my mind. Reluctantly, I looked up at the dais that held the Winter Court Queen and her lost princess.

I was shocked at how much the princess looked like her mother. She could have been a carbon copy if it weren't for her eyes. The soft velvet of her ballgown gently draped across her frame before widening at the waist. Her blonde hair was done in an elaborate design that was topped with a tiara made completely of ice. And although her expression was fixed in neutrality, she didn't hide the small sigh of relief when the doors closed.

Did you catch that? I asked my sister, who dipped her chin slightly in response. It seemed the princess was relieved her mate wasn't in our court.

Is she already prejudiced against the Seelie Courts? Devorah asked.

I'll find out.

We were introduced, and then the dancing began. Well, resumed for those who already arrived. The courts staggered our arrival in large balls so that each monarch got their moment of revelry. The Seelie Courts were always the last to enter an Unseelie event. If Spring and Winter didn't have such issues, I'm certain our group would have been last instead of second to last. I didn't have a problem with it. It meant less time I needed to spend in the company of these Fae.

A servant brought me a glass of spirits, and I downed the contents in one mouthful before signaling for a second. Devorah watched me with an unamused look. "It should be no hardship to entertain the princess for one dance."

She was right, Princess Edina was stunning. And she knew it. Not in an overt braggart way, but she had an air of confidence that stemmed from knowing she was the most beautiful woman in the room.

I spent the next half hour in monotonous conversation with elected officials and monarchs whom I'd known for centuries, but my eyes kept straying to the princess on the dance floor. She moved with assurance, masterfully following the lead even through the most difficult dances.

"Oh no," Devorah said, appearing behind me. She gestured to the dance floor. "Look who has the poor princess."

Ayelet was a personal advisor to the King of the Day Court and the worst type of Fae in existence. He crisped himself in the sun, so his skin appeared orange and his hair, which was once lush and blonde, was now brittle and straw-like. The last time he was invited to an event like this, he was punched by one of the Winter Queen's husbands for propositioning her. I was surprised he was even allowed in, let alone granted a dance with the princess.

"Go rescue her." Devorah smacked my arm and grabbed the glass from my hand. I was far too noble of a Fae to let her stand another minute in that male's presence and crossed the floor in three long strides.

"What do you say, Princess?" Ayelet asked the princess, and the scent of his arousal choked me even at a distance. She looked lost, unable to politely tell him to fuck off.

I cleared my throat. "May I cut in?" Ayelet turned and was about to deny me, but she screamed, "Yes!" a little too loudly. She shoved him away and jumped into my arms. I didn't waste a moment whirling her away, even as she watched the advisor approach one of the queen's husbands, most likely complaining about not getting his full dance.

At a distance, Princess Edina was beautiful. Up close...she was breathtaking. Some of her bravado cooled, and while it rubbed me the wrong way earlier, I found I strongly disliked the concern etched across her brow. She was unsettled, and I had the strong urge to bring a smile back to her face.

"I'm sorry to interrupt what appeared to be a love match," I joked and then remembered that Winter Court Fae rarely understand jokes.

"No, believe me—" Her lush pink lips parted, and she blinked those stunning sapphire eyes.

"That was sarcasm," she said in disbelief. "Oh, thank the goddess." I was startled by the laugh that erupted from my mouth, but she...fuck, she was charming.

"Winter Court Fae are notoriously literal."

"I was really afraid it was everyone." Her laugh was melodic and lilting and had me wondering if she was part siren the way it reeled me in. "Well, the ability to use sarcasm officially makes you my favorite Fae I've met so far."

I continued leading her across the floor as she blatantly checked me out. Her face was very expressive and hid none of her emotions. "You're thinking too hard, Your Highness," I said, and she rolled her eyes. *Rolled her eyes.* A royal, a princess no less, rolling her eyes at a ball.

And I knew for a fact that Faerie would never be the same once this creature was unleashed on our realm.

Thank fuck for that.

"I was trying to figure out how to address you," she said, her earlier confidence back in spades. "Is it 'Your Highness' or 'General'?"

I chuckled. "Since I'm your favorite Fae, you should call me Eldoris."

"Edina," she responded.

"How have you been enjoying Faerie, Edina?" Her eyes darted to my mouth when I said her name and her pupils flared the slightest amount.

I was immensely puzzled by her. She was relieved when her mate wasn't a part of our court, but looked thirty seconds away from taking me to her bed. I shifted my hand on her back and grazed the tiny piece of exposed skin beneath her iridescent wings. She leaned in closer.

Could it be that she just doesn't want a mate? It seemed so unnatural, but she was raised in the mortal realm. I could understand how the concept of a fated mate would seem daunting to someone who'd lived without that magic.

"It's a lot of snow," she replied with that same melodic laugh that was like a tether to my cock. *How is it she has this pull on me already?*

"You'll have to journey outside of the Winter Court soon."

"Is that your way of inviting me back to your place?" she teased.

"Diplomatically, of course." I winked.

"Oh, yeah." She bit her lower lip and I had to fight back a groan. "That's how I meant it."

The music cut off, and everyone politely applauded but I didn't release her. I was enjoying this, the easy flirting. I wasn't ready for it to end, and I could tell by the way she lingered in my hold that she wasn't either. I brushed my thumb along her lower back and a breath escaped those lush lips.

All at once, the impassive demeanor she exhibited on the dais was back, and she stepped away. "Thank you for the dance."

I should have let her go. She had countless others to dance with and another court arriving shortly, but I kept hold of her hand and reeled her back into my arms as the music started up again.

"Technically, it was only half a dance," I said, pulling her closer than before. "It would be perceived as an insult to my court if we didn't finish."

"Is that so?" She smirked. "So that's a common problem in your court?" Her eyes trailed down my body, only looking up through her long lashes after she viewed my growing bulge. "Failure to finish?"

I leaned in to whisper in her ear. "Not for my partners."

"Yes, please," she breathed, almost as if she didn't mean for me to hear that comment. A strangled moan escaped me as her scent permeated the air. She smelled like winter roses and sugar, and I wanted to coat myself with that scent in any way I could.

I turned slightly so my nose almost grazed the sensitive spot behind her ear, making her shiver and dig her nails into my shoulder. She was so responsive, I couldn't even imagine how she'd bloom under my hands, my tongue. Would that blush coating her cheeks spread to her entire body? What would her melodic voice sound like as she screamed my name?

The air between us crackled with electricity that had my cock seeking relief beneath my pants. When I returned upright again, her pupils were blown, and she was licking her bottom lip.

But before I could take this further, I needed her to know it was only for tonight. I couldn't promise her more than that.

I started to tell her just that when she asked, "Are you staying in the palace?" The music swelled, signaling the end of the song. I nodded and opened my mouth again to tell her I wasn't looking for anything serious, but she cut me off. "There's a music room down the hallway, first door on the left if you leave through the main doors. Meet me there after the ball?"

The music ended, and she looked up at me expectantly. But there was no hope in her eyes, no desire for romance. She was looking to blow off some steam.

Fuck it. I'll confirm her intentions later.

I kissed her cool cheek. "As long as you don't meet your mate."

"I'll see you later." She ran her nails down my chest and my eyes practically rolled to the back of my head. I had the strongest desire to toss her over my shoulder and take her to that music room right now. But I let her step away.

"Until then."

Edina sauntered away, and I was helpless not to watch as she bypassed the line of suitors and headed to two of the queen's husbands to grab a glass of water. She didn't look back.

I crossed the dance floor, returning to my sister, who looked like the cat who swallowed the canary. "Fun time?" she asked innocently.

"She's not prejudiced against the Seelie Courts." I snatched Devorah's drink and took a long pull of the wine.

"Mhmm, I can see that." Her expression turned serious. "I haven't seen you show that level of interest since Arella."

My stomach dropped and my palms started sweating. For a moment, while I was dancing with Edina, I forgot. The ache that lived in my chest was gone, and now it surged back with a vengeance.

"It's one night." My voice was full of gravel when I answered my sister. "She's not...it's one night."

"Okay," Devorah said, and the bells chimed, signaling the arrival of Spring Court. "Come on, let's go find Mother and watch the last processional."

I followed her as she tugged me through the crowd, but I was no longer present in the ballroom. I was miles away, holding a woman with lifeless eyes on the outskirts of a battlefield.

Chapter Six
Edina

Present (Faerie)

WHY DO THE RICH always serve liquor in such small glasses? My adoptive human parents used to do the same thing, serving expensive champagne in crystal flutes that barely held one sip. I expected more from a race that's known for its hijinks and overall debauchery but judging by this tiny-ass wine glass, the Fae are the same.

It's made so much worse by the fact that there's no bar at this ball. Drinks are served by slender, wraith-like Fae who hold tiny port glasses of Faerie wine on serving platters and only appear every thirty minutes. Thank the goddess I pre-gamed in my room and brought the flask holstered to my thigh.

Unfortunately for me, they went simple with the décor this evening. I mean, sure the ceiling is enchanted with falling snow. And sure, the entire dance floor is coated in a layer of ice that sparkles under the soft lighting and is spelled so that it's slip-resistant. But the usual flowers and evergreens have been removed, so there's nothing to hide behind, which means my carefully plotted exit will have to be timed perfectly to avoid my mother's notice.

I've been slowly working my way across the ballroom—which is about the length of a city block—for the past hour, narrowly avoiding the dignitaries and other royals who want to chat about things I know nothing about. I can't be too focused on the servants' hall, or they'll know where I'm going and try and intercept me, so I opt for a patch of wall that's unoccupied. No one stops me, and I retract my wings before sinking against the cool stone. If I'm unnoticed for a few minutes, then I can slip through the doorway and head to the tavern.

The music slows to a familiar tune, one that has a lump forming in my throat. I down the contents in my glass just as a server emerges with a fresh tray. I'm tempted to take the whole thing, but I settle on two glasses of wine, drinking the first one as fast as I can as the couples on the dance floor start to slow their movements, swaying closer together.

I can feel his eyes on me.

Eldoris is across the ballroom chatting with a few males I recognize but can't name, but his ocean-blue eyes are on me. He scans my body appreciatively, and I know he's remembering the time we danced to this song.

He wants me to *marry* him. If the pixies are to be believed—and they're always clued into the gossip of the realm—he hasn't given up yet. I can think of nothing worse.

It's not that he's *not* attractive. He's got the whole tall-dark-and-handsome thing going on. And goddess, those eyes. The unique color, their intensity...it's enough to make anyone swoon. Combine that with the tattoos I've only caught a glimpse of above his collar and he's solid fantasy material.

For a night. I can't do more than that.

"Princess," a voice purrs beside me, and I turn to find a male who's almost as broad as he is tall, his shoulders straining the material of his suit jacket.

"May I help you?" I ask, not quite turning on the charm yet in case my mother sent him over. But he has the look of someone who works with his hands, not some spoiled society member or advisor.

"You don't remember me?"

"Nope," I draw the word out and pop the 'p', bringing his attention to my lips before it drops right to my breasts. *Definitely not sent by my mother.* No, this male wants to fuck me and isn't hiding it at all.

He starts going on about how we met at something one time, but other than his size, the rest of his features are non-descript. His skin isn't too light or too dark, and it's not an interesting color like the pale blue of the siren I slept with last night. His hair is a sandy-brownish blonde, and his eyes are a muddled sort of brown. Even his horns are just little stumps that barely breach his hair. I laugh appropriately at something he says, and his smile is nice, but not show-stopping. Still, he's clearly interested, and I'm feeling lazy.

The hairs on the back of my neck raise. I know before I look that Eldoris is watching me again.

When I meet his gaze, I expect him to look away, but he just smirks and continues staring. It's not possessive, and it's not full of heat. *So, why?* Why does he keep watching me? He can't mean to talk about the arrangement here. If I rejected him in front of all of Fae society, that would be humiliating.

I renounce the ties that bind us.

My heart drops into my stomach as the words that destroyed my life echo in my mind so loudly that I swear I'm hearing them in real time. Pain bursts from the center of my chest out through my limbs, making my bones fragile and my nerves spark. My knees buckle, and I reach out and grasp the first thing I can find, which happens to be the Hulk's arm. "Princess?" he asks, but his voice is fuzzy and far away. The room spins as my breaths come in faster.

Fuck, fuck, fuck. Why can I feel the pain? I've been drinking since I woke, it should be dulled.

It's too much. My eyes are threatening to well. I won't cry in front of these vultures again.

So many eyes on me, unable or unwilling to move but not looking away.

I force myself to focus and my vision clears. No one is looking at me, not even my mother realizes I'm having a moment. This isn't a repeat of that day. I say that over and over in my mind, but my body isn't getting the memo. There's too much feeling rushing in, too much hurt. I need to get out of here.

A flash of movement catches my attention, and I see Eldoris coming toward me with concern etched on his face. *Nope.* I don't have it in me to deal with that. I can't be here anymore. I need wine and a distraction.

"Come with me," I order, grabbing onto the male's hand and tugging him out of the room and down the servants' hallway.

"Are you all right?" he asks, struggling to keep pace with me even though his legs are longer than mine. But he's not in flight mode, and I am.

"Peachy." I lead him down a series of twisting halls, stopping before a descending staircase. I take one step down, and my vision swims again. "Be a dear and grab whatever wine you can find, yeah?" I ask, pointing down at the wine cellar.

"Oh, I uh..." He looks uncomfortably at the stairs. "I brought a home-distilled whiskey if you'd rather. Aged five hundred mortal years in the same white bark as your orchard." He opens his jacket pocket, and hiding in there is a very large bottle of amber liquid.

"Done." I snatch the bottle and take three long gulps. It's foul tasting, but I can feel some kind of magic stirring in the liquid, the same as Faerie wine. This one is homemade, which means it's got a much stronger kick. Like moonshine, but magical.

It's perfect. I instantly feel looser, my earlier panic receding away, the pain melting as my limbs submit to the spirits. I tow the male down another hall until we reach the stairs that will take us to my chambers.

I take a step up, bottle in hand, and turn back to the male. "You coming?" He looks confused, and I roll my eyes. "If you don't want to fuck me, I'll have a servant take you back to the party," I drawl, and his eyes widen.

"Yes," he blurts. "I mean...goddess, yes."

"Let's hope you're better with your cock than you are with your words." I take his hands and lead him up the staircase to my bedroom.

HE IS, IN FACT, not better with his cock. Or his mouth...or any other appendage. Honestly, I got tired of trying to keep track.

"Fuck, that feels so good," he grunts behind me, and I make a non-comital *mmm* sound that spurs him on. I'm bent over the arm of the white fainting couch in my sitting room, my head propped up on my hand and the bottle wedged between the cushions. I wriggle it out and take another swig, still keenly aware that a male is pounding away inside me.

"You gonna come for me, princess?" he asks.

"Not a fucking chance," I mutter, and when he pauses to hear what I said, I moan breathily. "I said fuck yes." I just want this to be over.

His hands start pawing at the apex of my thighs. I don't mean my clit; I literally mean where my thigh connects to my hip. This male has been led astray, probably by some poor romance novelist who didn't want to use the actual term. I find it hard to feel bad for him. He's been alive longer than a human lifespan, which means he could have learned where the damn clitoris is.

My mind drifts to another time, another partner, one who made me come so many times I lost count. *No. Shit, I don't want to think about him.* I reach for the bottle, but the male is thrusting so hard that my whole body shakes and I can't get a good grip.

A door opens. My vision blurs as I look into emerald-green eyes and a tall lean frame.

"Oh, sorry." The voice doesn't match the image, and I blink rapidly until Eldoris is standing before me. Blue eyes, not green. Broad muscles, not lean ones. Dark hair, not red.

He spins back toward the guest room that attaches to my suite, then pauses, like he's not sure if he should intervene. Meanwhile, the male behind me hasn't stopped moving. "You wanna join?" he asks Eldoris, who turns back abruptly, fire in his eyes. He doesn't say anything, just stares the male down until he stops his thrusting but stays buried inside me. "What?" the male scoffs. "Everyone's heard she said no to your proposal. You don't own her."

Eldoris continues to stare until I can't take it anymore. "Get off me," I say, and when the male doesn't move, I push him back with a blast of icy water that leaves him sputtering. Eldoris averts his eyes like he wasn't just watching me get fucked and I use a cleansing spell before righting my dress and flopping down on the sofa.

"You can go," I call out, shutting my eyes.

"Umm," the male who was fucking me stammers. "What did you think about the liquor?" When I don't answer, "We spoke about stocking it in the palace? Down at the ball, right before—"

"Sure, sure." I wave him off. "I'll call you."

"What?" he whispers.

"It's a human thing," Eldoris says. "Means she'll be in touch."

There's a bit more muttering, and I think I hear something about blue balls before the door slams. "I meant you can leave too," I say when I'm sure Eldoris hasn't retreated to his room.

"Are you all right?" he asks, and I scoff.

"Perfect." I grope blindly for the bottle and take another swig. The burn of the liquor stings this time and I cough. "Goddess, that is truly awful."

"You could not drink it." I hear his smirk.

"What fun would that be?" When I pry my eyes open, Eldoris is still standing in the doorway to the guest room. "What are you doing in here anyway? Are you stalking me?"

"Your mother put me in here," he says, and I nod, before letting my head drop back to the couch. "I didn't know these were your rooms. And when I heard noises out here—"

"You came for a free show." I tease and stand, wobbling a little on my ascent. "Well, don't let me keep you from..." I gesture back to his room.

"Did you drink all of that?" he asks, pointing to the bottle, which is still very clearly half full.

"Not yet," I grin and saunter toward my room.

"Edina—"

"Unless you're planning on finishing what the Hulk out there started, I'm not interested."

I don't give him the time to form a response. I simply shut my double doors and use a spell to lock them.

I'M NOT SURE WHY it's so wet and cold.

I mean, it's the Winter Court. Obviously, I'm used to the cold. But waking up when it's wet is new. Even in my hungover state, I deduce that I'm not in my bed, but I cannot for the life of me remember leaving my room.

I crack open one eye and stare up at the gray sky with flurries of flakes falling, but never quite reaching me. I'm almost convinced I ended up in the ballroom with its enchanted snowfall, but I can see evergreens looming over me as well.

How the hell did I get outside?

I sit up and shake out my wings, but the snow that's gathered on them has turned to ice and sticks to the delicate flesh.

"Need help?"

My head snaps forward and I find my father, Three, sitting on a nearby rock, one leg crossed over the other. His purple eyes are hard, and he hasn't cast a shield, so snowflakes gather in his white hair.

I concentrate on harnessing the water around my wings, and it slowly bends to my will. It begins to melt and finally breaks off in a chunk that falls into the soft, powdery snow, leaving my wings free and unimpaired.

"Got it." Three doesn't look impressed. "How long have you been here?"

"I relieved Astor—" father number one, "—about an hour ago. We've been taking turns making sure you didn't die of exposure."

"Cold doesn't bother me," I say, caressing the snow on the floor of the forest. "You could have brought me inside if you were so concerned."

He summons an icicle to his hand and throws it at me. Before I can react, it hits a shield and falls uselessly to the ground a few feet in front of me. I beam, impressed at my magic for holding so well. "Your mother is the only one strong enough to break it, and we figured you wouldn't want her seeing you like this."

"Like this?" I feign innocence, and he misses the sarcasm dripping from my words. "I went for a late-night stroll and got lost."

His eyes drift down beside me, and I can see the neck of the bottle I was drinking last night poking up from the snow. I unearth it, and it's empty. *Damn.*

"Eldoris lingered in the sitting room in case you needed help after you went to bed. He said you were so drunk you were slurring your words."

"I was not—"

"Then you came out of the room to get more wine, saw him, and decided it would be faster to get to the wine cellar if you dove out your window."

"That doesn't sound—"

"Eldoris doesn't have wings, but he got your lady's maids and had them follow you and report your location. He was prepared to sit here with you to make sure you didn't aspirate on your vomit, but we took over for him once we were apprised of the situation."

"How would you have saved me if I was shielded?" I snark, the ever-present ache in my chest already twinging. Soon the nausea will start, and then the body aches. I need to head this off. I need a fucking drink.

Three pinches the bridge of his long nose and ignores my question. "You are to go to the mortal realm today," he announces.

Something close to elation replaces the hurt in my chest. "But Mother said I had to wait until after the parties she has scheduled—"

"That was before there was news to share." He extracts something from his jacket and extends a packet of papers.

When I agreed to move to Faerie to assume my role as the Winter Court Princess, I negotiated a way to return to the mortal realm as often as I could. My official title is *The Ambassador Between the Unseelie Courts and the Kingdom of Magic*—the hidden government that is comprised of witches and Magical Creatures. For the first time ever, the Unseelie Fae have a better relationship with humans than the Seelie Fae, and that's all because of me.

"You have to be back in time for the symphony tonight," Three continues.

"That's only a week there," I argue. It might be less, depending on the time difference. "I'm allowed two weeks per mortal year."

"You can take an extra week *next* mortal year," he says with a dismissive wave of his hand. "Go. Deliver the news to the Queen of the Kingdom of Magic and visit your friends. Maybe they can knock some sense into you."

If I had the kind of relationship with Three where I would hug him, I would. Instead, I dispel my shield, grab the papers, and take to the sky, heading directly for the portal that will lead me to the mortal realm.

I'm going home.

Chapter Seven
Edina

Two Mortal Years Ago (Mortal Realm)

IT WAS MY TWENTY-FIRST birthday, and I spent the entire day with intense dread coiling around my body. My head throbbed, my stomach churned, and I couldn't even blame the hangover. Katie, my best friend in the entire world, threw me a hell of a birthday party, but even a night of drinking and dancing—and eventual sex with a random guy—couldn't erase Puck's warning.

I think you're Fae. Fae emerge on their twenty-first human year. Before that, we appear entirely human.

No, this wasn't a hangover. This bordered on a panic attack. And it was incredibly ill-timed because Katie was going through her own panic attack, which was why we were fighting as we walked back to her stepfather's house from our coffee run. I wasn't even sure what the fight was about because all I could focus on was the throbbing in my back and the pounding in my head.

The closer it got to four o'clock—the time I was born—the worse things got. Each tick of the clock was a death knell bringing me closer and closer to my biggest fear.

No. Puck was wrong. I wasn't Fae; I was just a witch like my parents and all my friends. There was nothing special about me magically.

I wasn't going to emerge.

I repeated the affirmations in my mind while snow began to fall, making the idyllic village in the English countryside look like something out of a Christmas movie. For a moment, the light precipitation on my skin made me feel better, the cold becoming a soothing balm to my feverish skin. I suppressed the urge to press my frozen drink to my face to soak in the cold.

Katie and I continued bickering until we reached the picket fence that surrounded the cottage. A frost-coated trellis covered the misshapen stone walls, and the open lawn before the house seemed to shudder as snowflakes landed on the dead blades of grass. The light slanted as it sunk toward the horizon made all the weaker by thick gray clouds.

Katie dealt a low blow in our argument. I returned the favor.

We rarely fought—I could count the number of fights we'd had on one hand—but when we did it was always awful. That was the problem with knowing someone better than they knew themselves. You knew exactly which button to press for maximum impact.

We stared at each other. I could see the apology on her lips just as I opened my mouth to give her one of my own.

Then everything erupted.

Pain sharp enough to have me doubling over pierced my shoulders. A wave of dizziness overtook me as if someone clapped me over the ears. My cup slipped from my fingers, the Christmas red of the frozen drink splattering on the cobblestone path like a bloodstain.

No. This can't be happening.

"I'm gonna be sick," I groaned and ran up the uneven stone walkway, throwing open the large oak door and sprinting up the stairs.

I crashed into my guest room, aiming for the bathroom. My stomach revolted, the pain making me feel like I was going to puke, but I only made it a few steps before it felt like someone stabbed me in the back. A gasp escaped my lips as I was blinded by pain. I braced myself on the edge of the bed and curled in on myself, hoping for any kind of relief.

Fabric ripped and my sweater sagged down my outstretched arms. My shoulder blades split down the center. The cartilage in my ears stretched and popped. Stars burst behind my closed eyes and a scream bubbled up in my throat. I'd never felt this level of agony.

And then it was over.

I blinked my eyes open, staring at the comforter beneath my hands as I tried to process everything that just happened. A clock ticked loudly and I immediately sought it out. Two minutes after four.

I knew what it meant. I knew what happened, but I couldn't bring myself to face the facts. Couldn't bring myself to look in the full-length mirror opposite my bed.

A tear slid down my cheek and I gasped when it froze as it dripped off my chin, a perfect little ball of ice landing on the comforter beneath me.

I have to look. I have to know for sure.

I released a breath that came out in a puff of cold air and rounded the bed to meet my reflection in the mirror.

My blonde waves were tucked behind pointed ears, and I immediately shook the locks loose to cover them up. I couldn't do the same for the wings that extended through the ripped shards of my sweater. They were iridescent, the winter light that leaked through the window making them shimmer, and swirling snowflake patterns danced between the soft, rounded edges. They twitched as I turned to examine them like they were begging me to fly, but I stayed firmly on the ground.

The largest change was my eyes. The sapphire blue of my irises glowed electric, just like Puck's did when he removed his glamour for the first time. I looked menacing and powerful. I felt like pain could never touch me again. And for the first time in my life, I was exactly who I was supposed to be.

You know the Kingdom of Magic's reaction to Fae. You'll be hunted.

Puck's words shattered my brief moment of euphoria, replacing it with terror. I was in a house with three high-ranking members of the magical military. They would turn me in, they'd have no other choice.

Steps ascending the staircase turned my breathing shallow as I scrambled backward onto the mattress. More tears flowed down my cheeks, freezing as they went. It wasn't until I heard them clink against something that I looked down and realized ice was spreading out from my fingers. In the blink of an eye, the ice had encased most of the room. It blasted out, slicking the floor, the floral wallpaper, and the bed frame. Menacing icicles jutted from the ceiling, melting and reforming as I tried to calm my racing heart.

"Oh fuck."

Katie's voice pierced through the panic, and my eyes cleared for a moment as I watched her take in the scene. She ran a hand through her chestnut hair, her unique auburn eyes flitting around the ice-coated room in confusion. I hugged my knees to my chest.

I was so fucking scared.

Katie was my best friend, but at the end of the day, she was a soldier, and so enmeshed in court life that I didn't know what she would do. I needed her. I was terrified of her.

"Katie," I plead. Frozen tears streamed down my face and I pushed my hair back to keep them from freezing the strands. She gasped when she saw my ears, and then my wings. More ice blasted from me, coating the mirror this time.

"Holy fuck," she repeated. "How—"

"He said I was, but I didn't believe him." I knew she didn't know what I meant, but my breaths were coming in jagged now, and my thoughts were scattered.

She skated across the ice floor and landed on the bed beside me, wrapping me in her arms. She took great care not to touch my wings as she squeezed me tight, unbothered by the ice thickening around us. I melted into her embrace, my need for a safe place overriding my fear of her job.

"Who said what, E?" she whispered, rubbing circles into the non-winged part of my back.

"The Fae I met, Puck. He told me—" a hiccupped sob cut off my words, "I was Fae, but I didn't believe him. He told me my powers would manifest on my twenty-first birthday."

She stroked my hair and her fingers brushing against my ears actually felt...nice. The fact that she wasn't shrinking away from my new form helped calm me. My breathing slowed and the ice around us thawed.

"But you were fine this morning," she murmured, more to herself than to me.

"I officially turned twenty-one at four o'clock."

Her brow furrowed as she took in my words. "He came for you." It wasn't a question, but I nodded anyway. It was a thought that plagued me since I left Faerie. I couldn't pretend it was a coincidence that Puck found me in that bar. I didn't know why he came for me specifically, but there was no doubt in my mind he was looking for me.

"He was mad I was leaving," I admitted, not meeting her eyes. "But I told him I couldn't miss Christmas with you. Not if—"

"Not if what?"

I sighed. "Katie, they'll want me to go to Faerie." Puck didn't say it explicitly, but I knew in my bones I'd have to go back. I didn't know much about changelings—Fae who were brought to the mortal realm—but I knew I had a family in Faerie.

And Puck. I wasn't even sure why but I was desperate to see him again. It was an instinctual feeling deep in my gut that urged me to find him.

"No," she insisted, ignoring all the potential issues that would arise if I stayed. "Absolutely not. You're not leaving. We'll figure out a way for you to stay."

"How?" I asked, pulling away from her. "If I stay here, I'll be killed. I can't even leave this room. And this power..." On cue, icicles exploded from my body. Katie ducked to avoid being impaled as they soared across the room and embedded themselves in the wall.

"Katie, I'm scared." My voice trembled. She pulled me back into her and I sank into her warmth. I felt so cold, and while the snow and ice around us didn't bother me, the lack of warmth under my skin felt foreign.

"I'll help you figure out the magic, how to hold it back," she said, moving firmly into problem-solving mode. She always was able to do that, switch into her military calm, and get us out of sticky situations. "But I'm not letting you banish yourself to another realm where you don't know anyone. You've heard the stories, E. The Fae are—"

"Don't you dare finish that sentence," I said through my teeth, a primal urge rising in me and turning my voice into a dagger sharper than the icicles hanging from the ceiling. "Look at me, Katie. *I* am Fae."

Her teeth chattered and she dipped her head in apology. I knew it would take her longer than a few minutes to get over everything we'd been taught about the Fae, but I hated that was her first reaction. As if I was in more danger from my own kind than here.

My own kind.

Fucking hell.

"Are you going to turn me in?" I asked. I almost didn't recognize the cold edge in my voice. It was calm even though my emotions were a tempest of confusion and fear. I needed to know if the comfort my best friend offered extended past this room.

"What?" she reared back as if I slapped her. "Edina, you're—" I couldn't help the involuntary flinch when she reached for me. I needed the words, not physical comfort.

"You're my sister. I'm on your side, *always*," she said, and my chest caved in at the admission. I wasn't sure what I would have done if she chose the Kingdom over me.

"What do we do?" I breathed, sinking back onto the frozen mattress and staring up at the ceiling. I was momentarily surprised the motion didn't hurt my wings, but it felt the same as lying down with my hair over a pillow. Katie flopped beside me and shook her head in dismay. "If I can get to a portal—"

"How are we going to get you to the portal?" she asked. "Going to the palace would be suicide. And then what? You're just going to walk into Faerie and say, 'Hey, who wants to adopt a changeling?'"

"No. I'd fly obviously."

A smile ticked up the corner of my mouth and Katie chuckled. The moment was so normal I almost forgot the fucked up situation I was in.

"We will figure this out," Katie vowed once our laughter died down. She grabbed my hand. "E, I love you more than anyone else in this world," her voice grew thick with emotion. "I will figure something out, I swear."

Chapter Eight
Edina

Present (Mortal Realm)

I FIRE OFF A text to Katie letting her know I'm in *The Cracked Chalice* and place my phone on the bar top, knowing she'll be along soon. It's earlier than I typically spend in a bar, but I had a bad dream—the same dream that's plagued me every night I've been in the mortal realm—and I needed an escape. Joe isn't in yet, so I round the bar and hunt down the bottle I'm looking for.

Today is the day I need to return to Faerie and I'm dreading it. The week passed too quickly in a blur of stupid meetings and other royal obligations. Unfortunately, my mother's letters about the affairs in Faerie were cryptic as hell, meaning I had to decide what to tell the humans about the 'hellfire' situation she alluded to. Ultimately, I told my vampire friend Vlad everything and let him decide what to pass on. He's one of the advisors to the queen and has spies everywhere, so he knew most of the information already.

Normally, when I'm here for two mortal weeks, I spend the first week doing my duty, then Katie and I spend the second in her beach house in Santorini. This week I've had no time for fun unless you count binge-watching the reality TV shows I missed all year.

Bottle and glasses in hand, I return to the stools and pour sickly-sweet green liquid into four shot glasses, sloshing some onto the already sticky bar top. The liquor here isn't strong enough to ward off my nightmares, but it still helps with the pain.

The bell on the door tinkles and the scent of vanilla and lavender mixed with rain eclipses the smell of stale beer. There's the click of boots on the worn, wooden floorboards, and I slide a shot glass across the bar as the stool beside me is pulled out. Katie hoists herself up onto the stool, swearing as her short legs work overtime. She's dressed down today, in a sweater and leggings, and her chestnut hair falls in loose waves. Her auburn irises almost look red in the early morning light.

"Where's your hubby?"

"He has plans with his sister and the kids," Katie says, referring to her nieces and nephews. "He said something about a run."

"Exercise," I scoff and take the shot I designated for him, followed immediately by the one I poured for his sister. "Totally overrated."

She laughs, raspy and deep, and takes the shot of absinthe I left on the counter for her. "God, how do you drink that shit?" She shudders violently in the aftermath of the liquor and searches for a chaser.

"It's the closest thing you have to Faerie wine." I take my third shot and fill all four glasses again. "The 'green fairy' is actually a pixie who brought the absinthe recipe here and would only show herself to people after they drank enough. My lady's maids told me pixies still cross realms sometimes to play that joke on unsuspecting humans."

"Why do I kind of love that?" she laughs.

"Because you're evil."

"I'm an angel," she quips and then frowns. "I bet angels are real and in some other realm that Vlad just hasn't told us about yet."

"Wouldn't surprise me."

Joe, the bartender, comes out a side door that leads to his upstairs apartment and pauses when he sees us. The little hair he has is damp, and he's in a plain t-shirt and jeans. "How in the hell did you get in here?" he asks, but there's no malice in his tone and his face breaks out in a ridiculously goofy grin.

"Oh please," I bark a laugh. Katie stands on the edge of her stool, leaning over the bar to embrace the bartender who sketches a bow before hugging her. "We're two of the most powerful beings in this realm."

"E had me modify your shields when I strengthened them last year, so they recognize us without tripping any alarms," Katie adds, sitting back down.

"It makes us look more badass if he thinks we broke in." I sigh dramatically, causing them both to laugh. Joe eyes the half-empty bottle of absinthe. "It's not stealing, my card is on the register. You're the only reason I still have a human bank account...you should be honored."

Joe, unlike most of the witches who knew me before I emerged, never batted an eye at the fact that I'm Fae. Other than Katie, my old friends didn't know how to react to me after everything. I found myself keeping my wings retracted and my ears camouflaged whenever I was around people from my human past. Not Joe. The one time I tried to retract my wings because it was a crowded night in the bar, he lectured me about not hiding how amazing I am.

"I'm always honored you two drag your important asses into my shithole," he chuckles. "How about some food to wash that down?"

I shake my head but Katie nods enthusiastically. "And coffee please," she says. Joe salutes and disappears into the kitchen to whip us up something.

Katie and I fall into an unnatural silence as I refill the three shot glasses again. "How bad does it hurt?" she asks, placing her left hand on my knee, her canary diamond ring stark against my dark denim. "Scale of one to ten?"

"I'm fine, babes." I take the shots. The absinthe isn't doing it today. Maybe because I know I'm leaving in a few hours.

"You're fine," Katie scoffs, pulling my attention to her concern-tightened features. "I just got a text at seven a.m. that asked me to meet you in a bar that isn't even open yet, only to find you've already drank half a bottle of nasty-ass liquor that I know for a fact you hate. You're fine."

"I don't need a lecture," I slam back another shot. "I have ten parental figures. I'm good without an eleventh."

"You're self-medicating."

"No shit."

"Is it helping?" She pries my fingers away from the glass in my hand. "I'm not sending you back to Faerie like this."

"Like what?" I demand, finally meeting her eyes. My chest is tight, like bands of muscle have wrapped around my heart and are squeezing.

"On the verge of collapse."

That's the problem with old friends, they know when you're lying. She can see through my façade too perfectly. I've been slowly breaking, shattering piece by piece for almost two mortal years now and I'm one tiny crack away from turning to dust. But nothing I do stops it.

"What can I do?" I ask, my voice soft. "I've seen every healer here and in the Unseelie Courts. I even saw a *doctor* for fuck's sake. Nothing helps." I rub at my chest. Even though the alcohol has numbed the sharp pain, there's a dull, radiating feeling in the center of my chest. It's always there, even when I'm passed out.

"You can stay," Katie offers. "Don't go back."

"My mom—"

"Said it's okay," she says, and my eyebrows shoot into my hairline. "All the letters sent were addressed to the queen, but one was addressed to Kathryn. Vlad just gave it to me last night."

"Why?"

"He read it, of course." She rolls her eyes. "Said he wanted to see if what your mom claimed had merit." She pulls a piece of paper from her bra and places it on the bar in front of me. I don't open it; I don't want to know what my mom said. "She's worried about you. She said she'd do anything to help, including letting you stay in the mortal realm."

"I'm good," I insist.

"You're not." She's using her soldier's voice on me, the one that says she won't listen to my excuses and that I need to follow her orders. "You're not eating—"

"I eat."

"You got dressed in front of me. I could count each one of your ribs, E."

I feign a gasp. "Babes, you can't be checking me out. You're a married lady."

She ignores my joke. "I haven't seen you sober since you got here."

"Like you said, I'm self-medicating."

"And what happens when that doesn't work?" she retorts, forcing me to stare into her auburn eyes. "What's next when Faerie wine and absinthe stop helping? The Fae equivalent of heroine?"

"Faerie dust," I correct.

"The fact that you know that scares the shit out of me," Katie breathes. "You told me the other day you knew almost nothing about Fae life, and yet you know exactly what drug to try next."

I swallow, turning my attention to the bar top and the rough grooves that have broken through the varnish, leaving jagged shards of wood for me to run my finger over. "It's not like I didn't try," I say. "No one can help me. Not even you."

I hear Katie release her breath in a frustrated sigh. "I could kill him?" she offers, and that pulls a smirk out of me.

"Still not sure that would solve everything." I sigh and drop my head into my hands, pressing the heels of my hands into my eye sockets. "She really said I could stay here?"

"She's terrified." I feel Katie's head land on my shoulder. "I am too. I don't know what I'd do without you. You're supposed to outlive me."

I tilt my head to lie against hers. A tear slips down my cheek and lands in her hair.

Katie is my best friend, my family really. I'd do anything to protect her. And the fact that I might be the one hurting her, the one causing her concern...I can't do it.

"Fucking hell," I grumble. "Okay. I'll stop drinking. It's not like it helps."

"E—"

"I promise I'll sober up. I'll figure out some other way to deal with the pain."

"Love you," she says, as Joe places two greasy grilled cheeses and two cups of coffee in front of us.

"Love you most." I kiss the top of her head, and she sits up to eat her food.

"I'm sending Vlad back with you," she says, before taking a bite.

"I don't need a babysitter."

"I'm not saying you do. But do you have anyone you can talk to in Faerie?" I pick at the crust of my sandwich, flaking it off onto the plate, not giving words to the answer she already knows.

"No," I reply. "His life is here. He's got responsibilities, a baby vampire—"

"Just for a bit," Katie insists. "Unless you feel comfortable confiding in someone else. You're going to need people around you, and since it can't be me—"

I don't know why I think of Eldoris at that moment. It's probably just because he's staying in my room.

"I'll call you every day," I promise. "I'll use the mirror and call you at some point to check in every Fae day, so roughly every two weeks here." I take a giant bite of the grilled cheese to make my point, the food turning to ash in my mouth as my stomach roils.

Katie sighs. "If I don't hear from you, I'm sending the vampire."

"Deal."

Between the coffee and the food Katie made me choke down, the absinthe has been effectively quelled and I'm so sober I can't stand it. I'm not sure what it is about Faerie, but the pain is always exponentially worse here than in the mortal realm. The last time I came back, it felt like someone punched a hole in my chest the second I walked through the portal doors into the tavern. I spent the rest of the night drinking myself under the table.

I took the other portal this time, the one that leads into frozen waste-lands.

I leap from the portal entrance into the ramshackle building and grunt in pain. It feels like a thousand knives are bursting from the center of my chest and nicking every inch of my body on the way out. I breathe in through my nose and out through my mouth, focusing on the breath and not the pain.

I can do this. I do not need a drink to get through this.

My bones feel brittle as I step over worn white-wood floorboards to the door that's hanging on its hinges. I take another breath, and the wind takes my moment of hesitation to blow the door open, sending a gust of slanting snowflakes right into my face.

The cold actually makes me feel better, and I step into the knee-deep snow and let it gather around me. This is why I slept in the snow the other night. The realization is hazy, but I remember the winter air felt so good that I decided to stay.

Maybe I'll move out here and use my magic to make an igloo. Or an ice palace. Yeah, that sounds better.

"Princess?"

I sigh. *They always interrupt my best ideas.*

I let go of the dream of ice towers, bridges, and turrets and find Bylur, the captain of the guard for the palace, standing at attention. The silver insignia of the Winter Court stands out sharply on his dark blue tunic, and he regards me curiously. "May I escort you back to the palace?"

I nod, and my chest twinges. Again, I remember that it only worked for a few minutes the other night, which was why I downed the bottle of whiskey. Bylur's hand takes mine and the familiar sensation of squeezing that comes with teleportation envelops me. My stomach lurches, and I'm certain I'll be sick when we land just outside the gates of the palace.

My wings snap out and with a quick word of thanks to the guard, I fly inside and through the halls to my rooms. I'm about to be sick, and I don't need any witnesses using this incident as fodder for the gossip mill.

I crash through the front door of my suite. "Oh," a surprised voice says, and my eyes flit to the couch, where Eldoris sits, one leg propped on the other with a book in his hand. He stares at me, sitting unnaturally still as he watches me across the empty sitting room. He's in a simple pair of navy sweats, and a white t-shirt that does nothing to hide black ink covering every inch of his torso. I've only ever seen hints of those tattoos before, and somehow that, coupled with the fact that he's barefoot, makes me feel increasingly awkward in my own rooms.

His muscled arm lifts, brushing through his dark curls while avoiding long, curved horns in the process. He had them retracted the other day and it was almost enough to let me forget he's Fae.

"I didn't expect you back—" he starts thickly, and then clears his throat. "I can go to my room. Or ask for another if I make you uncomfortable."

I realize I've been standing frozen in the doorway staring at him this entire time. I attempt a smile, but it feels lackluster. "You're going to ask my mother, the Ice Queen herself, to rearrange your accommodations?" His eyes, that odd mix of blue and green that remind me of the ocean in the Mediterranean, flick down and that's the only confirmation I need. I point to the door to the right "You can have free reign of the suite for your time here, just stay out of my room. You leave when?"

"I'll be here for three days," he says. "But I was hoping we could discuss the events of the throne room yesterday. I know that's not what either of us expected—"

"We can talk on the way to the symphony," I say dismissively, and walk toward my door.

Eldoris' mouth forms a tight line, but he agrees. "I'll meet you out here at quarter-to-seven."

I mock salute him and slip inside my room, sliding the heavy wooden door shut behind me.

As soon as it's closed, I'm running to the bathroom, crashing to the floor. The pain that was suppressed in the cold comes back tenfold, sucking the air from my lungs and squeezing all my vital organs. I cry out as a vice-like grip wraps around my heart and squeezes. It flutters like mad, my pulse skyrocketing and my breaths turning so shallow I'm convinced I'll be blue before the pain is over. I heave and double over the toilet, throwing up the remainder of any food or alcohol I consumed in the mortal realm.

A floral scent from my memory assaults me. When it hurts the most, the universe likes to remind me that this scent should be comforting. Instead, it makes me puke all over again. It's too sweet, too floral, but since it doesn't actually exist, there's nothing I can do to banish it.

"Your Highness?" Brigid's tiny voice calls from the doorway of the bathroom. "Should I call for the healer?"

"No," I insist. Her small body lands on the tank of the toilet and she hands me a cup of water. I thank her and she settles in to look over me.

The nausea fades, leaving me with the feeling of being wrung dry. My chest still aches but I think I can manage. *At least I didn't cry this time.* When the crying starts, it's almost impossible to stop.

"We should get you ready, Your Highness," Brigid says, her little hands clasped together the way they do when she's nervous. "Your mother made it very clear that you are to attend—"

"Are you sure you don't want the healer?" I turn and find Althea, her pink hair mussed from her fingers.

"He's done all he can." That's what happens when you're the first Fae to experience something. No one knows what to do to fix it.

I sit back on my heels and Brigid flushes away the evidence of my puking. When I stand to rinse my mouth out, I catch sight of my appearance. Goddess, no wonder Katie was worried. The bags under my eyes are so dark they look permanent, and I'm so pale...I seriously could double as the scream mask. Even my hair looks like it has less life in it than it did this morning.

I don't look too long; I can't make myself.

I drag my body to my vanity and plop in the chair.

"We'll get you sorted," Althea says gently. I nod listlessly, begging my mind to quiet and my body to go numb, but it doesn't. It's been numb for too long, and now it's intent on feeling everything.

The scent of wildflowers rolls over me as a tightening happens in my chest again and the pixies set about making me presentable.

Chapter Nine
Eldoris

WE'LL TALK ON THE *way to the symphony.*

I don't know why such a simple sentence makes me so nervous. Probably because the fate of my court is in the hands of a twenty-three-year-old who grew up in the mortal realm. Edina seemed more amenable today when she arrived back from her trip, even if she did get away from me as fast as possible.

She doesn't need to like me. She just needs to understand the importance of this match, and how much it would benefit both our courts.

I shower and dress for the symphony, donning my navy tux with black lapels and affixing golden cuffs to my ears. As an afterthought, I tuck a turquoise handkerchief into my breast pocket in honor of my mother.

When I step into the sitting room at a quarter-to-seven, Edina's door is still closed. Even though I've been given free rein in the common spaces, I feel like I'm intruding. I sit on the fainting couch, then stand again, then prop myself up on the arm. Five minutes pass, then another three, and still the door remains closed.

Tentatively, I knock on Edina's door. "Your Highness?" I call. No answer. "We'll be late if we don't leave soon." The wards prevent teleporting within the halls, at least for me, and the concert hall is far enough away that, even at a run, we'll be cutting it close.

"I'm rather fond of my appendages, and I fear what your mother will do to me if the curtain rises and we're not—"

The door swings open and a pixie with bright magenta hair floats at my eye level. She flashes her pointed teeth in a truly wicked smirk. "Princess Edina left twenty minutes ago," she says innocently. "Good luck with that one, General."

She laughs tauntingly, but I'm already barreling out of the room and down the winding hallways, swearing under my breath. The amphitheater is attached to the palace but at the opposite end of Edina's rooms. Another reason I was hoping to walk with her is that I'm not entirely certain how to get there from here, so I take the extra time and head to the throne room, navigating myself to the theater from there.

I genuinely don't know if it's better if she left without me on purpose, or if she forgot. I can work with hatred; apathy is a whole other ballgame. It's hard to get someone to help you if they're unconcerned with your existence.

I skid into the entryway of the amphitheater, which has a few Fae stragglers obtaining glasses of wine and making their way into the general population seats. Swinging around the bar, I make a break for the sweeping staircase, cursing my luck that I was born without wings, and charging up three flights to the private boxes. I make it just as the lights dim, sliding behind a thick velvet curtain into a private balcony with four chairs.

Three heads swivel to me. Larisa, the princess of the Day Court fluffs her honey-colored hair in a derisive motion and promptly looks back at the stage where the opening act, a trio of pixies, has begun to sing. Seated beside her is Behar, one of my commanders in the Seelie army whom

I haven't seen since he was sent to Day Court. Seeing him beside the princess is a shock. He dips his chin, and I pat his shoulder as I move past him and slide into my seat beside Edina.

"Did Brigid give you my message?" Edina whispers, leaning into me the slightest amount. She looks stunning tonight. Her hair has been piled atop her head in a mountain of curls that I imagine makes it hard for Larisa to see anything. Her dress is off her slender shoulders, accentuating her prominent collar bones. But her eyes aren't completely focused, and there's an air of melancholy that hangs over her.

"That you left without me?" I tease, trying to keep my tone light. Her mouth opens in a perfect O.

"Mother called me down early to meet with some of the dignitaries that arrived today," she says. "I asked one of my lady's maids to tell you."

"Pink hair?"

"Purple." She swears. "I'm so sorry, I knew I should have left a note."

"It's okay, I made it."

I turn my attention out of the box and to the stage. Polished wood gleams under the bright lights. Thick red curtains block off the bulk of the stage, leaving only the lip exposed, and the trio is hovering over a microphone, clustered in a group and crooning a song in tight three-part harmony. They sway and bop to the melody, their little wings fluttering in time to the beat.

The patrons bob politely to the tune, which sounds more like it belongs in a USO tour in the mortal realm, but no one seems to mind. Everyone is too excited for the main event.

Edina checks a slender silver watch on her wrist before tucking her hand back under the folds of her dress. I arch an eyebrow when she catches me looking and she gives me a weak smile. "I never understood the appeal," she says, and we applaud as the song comes to an end. "The Siren Symphony is my least favorite event."

"Are you serious?" Larisa asks, completely aghast. She clutches a string of pearls around her neck and everything.

Edina shrugs. "Yep. I don't get it. I'd much rather be in a bubble bath right now."

"With a bottle of wine, no doubt," Larisa scoffs loud enough for us to hear, but low enough that she can feign innocence. Beside her, Behar grips her arm in his large hand, a silent command to stop. She shoots him an icy glare.

Edina completely ignores her and turns to me instead. "What am I missing? I've only seen the sirens sing once, and it was beautiful, but I don't understand this reaction." She gestures to everyone who is waiting with bated breath as the pixies take their final bow and flit off stage.

In the orchestra pit, a line of trained soldiers forms, placing themselves between the audience and the stage. The theater goes silent as everyone prepares for what's coming.

"When you watched last time, did you lower your mental shields?" I ask, and Edina's eyes widen.

"Of course not."

"That's why. Siren magic allows them to manipulate your emotions, your desires, your entire outlook. They don't just tell a story with the music; they make you feel it. It's..." Intense? Terrifying? "...liberating. Especially for those who have been alive for thousands of years and their emotions have hardened with time."

Her brow crinkles in thought and I have the strangest urge to reach over and smooth it out. "Will you do it?" she asks. "Lower your shields?"

I give that some thought. It's been a long time since I've allowed myself to be swept away by the emotional tide the sirens provide with their music. But I get the feeling that Edina is looking for something. A partner in crime, maybe? Confirmation that she won't be the only one who looks foolish?

"I will if you will," I say with a smirk that turns the corner of her lips the slightest amount.

"Let's do it."

The amphitheater is plunged into darkness, the creak of the curtains opening the only sound that fills the space. I relax my mental shields, dropping away every defense I have inside my brain so that the sirens will easily be able to sway me. Beside me, Edina stiffens, grasping the armrests of her chair with a white-knuckle grip.

"If you need to leave, and can't get your shields back up," I whisper, "just tap my arm, and I'll get us out of here." That's also why we have guards in front of the stage who remain shielded. The theater hosts the most influential people in Faerie and they're willingly submitting to a group of twenty.

"You underestimate my mental magic," she chides, but her tone is jovial. "I've studied under the best."

"I didn't know they made that a priority in the mortal realm, my apologies," I murmur. "Though, I'm not sure I'd call Katie the best."

"I forgot you know her," she chuckles. "Would you say that to her face?"

"Never. She fucking terrifies me."

The laugh Edina lets out is...fuck, it's beautiful. Melodic and rich, it wraps around me, promising joy and happiness. I'm about to say something else, just to hear her laugh again when the lights come on, illuminating a choir standing on the stage.

Sirens have three forms; an underwater sea monster with gills and barbed fingers, a half-humanoid form where the top half is human and the bottom half has a beautifully scaled tail, and finally the form they're in now, completely humanoid. They stand on two legs but remain completely naked. Skin tones range from the palest pink to deep sage green, with hair that grows long and untamed.

A female siren with pale blue skin and cobalt hair that drapes long enough to cover her breasts steps forward. She inhales deeply, an action that's echoed by the chorus behind her, and sighs. I feel the sigh in my whole body. It makes my jaw unclench, my neck relax, and my shoulders come down from my ears. They sigh again, and I relax further, melting like a pad of butter into my seat. One quick look at Edina tells me she's experiencing the same sense of relaxation. After the final exhale, my eyes drift closed as I'm completely held at the sirens' mercy.

They begin to sing a light melody, and I'm transported to a sandy beach. Laughter echoes over the wind, harmonizing with the crash of the waves against the shore. I run toward it, laughing as my feet send sand scattering in short bursts. The laughter increases, and I catch sight of dark braids disappearing around a cliff. I chase after them and the female they belong to, stumbling when the sand gets softer the farther away I drift from the water's edge.

The terrain changes, to the green jungle of the Summer Court. *Home.* The air is thick and sweet with the scent of jasmine, and soon sweat is pouring down my chest. It's so hot that I tear my shirt off, flinging it on the path behind me as I keep chasing the female with the braids. I'm getting closer, her laughter grows louder, but still not as loud as the large insects that buzz from the nearby plants.

The female shrieks as the music comes to a pinnacle, and she staggers on the path, tripping over a vine and falling gracelessly. I run faster, the music making my blood pump in my veins. When I reach her, she's rolled over, lying completely naked on the floor of the jungle, nothing but a few grains of dirt dusting her dark breasts.

Her warm brown eyes meet mine and her ebony skin, dewy with sweat, seems to glow under the fading light. A pink tongue swipes across her lower lip, and the music changes again, urging me forward. I drop to my knees, seating myself between her thighs, and she opens for me, revealing a cluster of dark curls. She slides her hand down her body, her breaths shallow as she uses her fingers to bare herself to me, showing me the perfect pinkness of her pussy.

Beside me, I hear a gasp and a moan of pleasure. But I can't focus on anything but the Fae before me, waiting for me to claim her.

I lean forward to brace my forearms by her head, careful not to pull her hair. Somehow my pants have disappeared, and my cock is seated at her weeping entrance. I can't hear her, but her mouth forms my name, and I lean forward to kiss her at the same moment I slide inside. I swear as she wraps around me, her legs clinging to my waist.

Suddenly we're upright, in a shower, and I'm pounding into her as her mouth opens in a silent scream. "I love you," I groan, the sound of our skin slapping together suddenly audible. Her mouth moves again, but I still can't hear her. She tightens around me as she comes, and a rush of pleasure zings down my spine, from my head to my toes, igniting every nerve as I come with her.

The music stops, the vision fading as I pant in the aftermath of the carnality I just felt.

Before it releases us completely, the magic begins again. This time the song is soft and romantic, but sad.

The vision begins again, the braided female dancing with me, wrapped in my arms. It switches again to the two of us tangled in bed sheets, to sneaking kisses in tents filled with soldiers. She stands beside me as we stare out at an army with black tunics, dark magic coiled in their hands.

The music turns melancholy. Notes that should be sweet and pretty are tinged with sadness like someone wrapped the entire melody in a wet blanket. I know what's coming. I should snap up my mental shields, but I must be a masochist because I don't.

The female with the braids is struck by a spell and falls at my feet. I scream, fire exploding from me in a blast that takes out rows and rows of opposing soldiers. I scoop her into my arms and run to the back lines. Several officers with wings offer to take her, but I can't let her out of my arms.

By the time I get her to a healer, the female with the braids is gone. The laughter in her eyes has quieted, and her glowing skin has dulled. I set her down on the bed we share, and I cry.

Hot tears flow down my cheeks as the music quiets again, ready for the final movement. But I'm not ready to move on. I keep my eyes firmly closed, holding onto the past, trying to find the way her face looked beneath me from the previous movement or the way she looked when we were dancing. All I can see are her lifeless eyes staring up at me.

The music begins again, and this time I see myself. I move listlessly as time flies by at a whir. Years pass in much of the same. An entire symphony of grief.

And then the scene shifts. It doesn't show specifics anymore, but the melody lightens. Colors explode around me, shades of blue that I would normally view as depressing now signify peace. Bright yellows explode over the canvas and my chest begins to feel lighter. It feels dangerously like hope.

A crescendo of voices swells, promising me that things are looking up.

The colors dance like they're trying to solidify, the yellows forming the long, curling tendrils of hair, the blues settling into the bodice of a dress. The head of the creature before me turns.

The music stops, and the vision is gone.

The entire theater erupts into applause, but I keep my eyes clamped shut, desperately trying to see who the vision was about to show me. When it's clearly gone, I reestablish my shields and open my eyes to turn to ask Edina what she thinks.

The seat beside me is empty.

"Where is she?" I turn and balk when I see Behar. The ebony skin, the warm brown eyes, he looks so much like his sister. He swipes away a stray tear and shakes his head in confusion.

"How would we know?" Larisa huffs. She runs her fingers through her honey-colored hair, pushing it back to reveal the intricate butterfly tattoo that rests on her temple, the golden color stark against her sienna skin. She grits her jaw, and the insect's wings seem to pulsate. "We were enjoying the performance."

I push past the two of them, Larisa's shrill voice calling after me as I exit the box and run the short way to the stairs, where a Fae guard is standing at attention.

"General," she bows. "There's another performance starting—"

"Have you seen Princess Edina?" I cut her off, and her eyes widen.

"Yes, she said she was retiring for the evening."

"When did she leave?" I demand.

The guard looks side to side, like telling me will somehow get her in trouble. "After—after the melancholy movement. She was crying."

I swear under my breath and take off at a run down the stone steps. For the second time tonight, I wish I could teleport in this palace.

It takes far longer than I remember to get back to Edina's suite. I throw the door open, only to be greeted by an empty sitting room, and the door to her bedroom closed up tight. There's a strangled sob beyond the doors and I'm there before my brain registers that I'm moving.

"Edina?" I call, knocking on the door. I try the handle, but it's locked. "Edina, are you all right?"

"Good," she hiccups. The pain in her voice is so raw it cuts through me.

"May I come in?" I ask, lowering my voice and leaning closer to the white wood that's decorated with swirling silver whorls. There's no answer for a very long time, and when she does speak, it's clear she's grappling for control.

"No," she says. "Just leave me alone, please."

I can't leave her like this. I know what I felt after that movement from the sirens, and my pain is more removed. Hers is still fresh.

"You're supposed to stay for the whole symphony," I say. I'm met with silence, so I continue. "It's always the saddest in the middle, but it gets better. The sirens like their stories to have happy endings. The final movement is always one that speaks of hope."

Silence.

I lean my back against the door, tilting my head to the side so she can still hear me. "I know a lot of people say this, but I understand what you're going through." She scoffs, which I take as a good sign, and keep going. "Not exactly, I suppose."

I take a fortifying breath. I don't talk about this with anyone, but I think Edina needs to hear it. "My mate's name was Arella." Her beautiful face, framed by her signature braids, comes unbidden to my mind. "She grew up in the Summer Court Palace with her brother, Behar. He was the Fae who sat behind us tonight."

I sink to the floor. "Her parents were cooks, so we grew up playing together on the palace grounds. There were four of us, all close in age, though Behar was a bit younger. She was my first kiss when we were just children. Even before we emerged and were certain, I knew Arella was mine.

"She emerged first—she was the oldest—and I spent two whole weeks holding my breath, waiting for some mate to show up to claim her. Then I emerged, and we had a ball, much like the one..." I trail off, knowing she won't want to think about the ball that marked her entrance into Fae society.

"And she was my mate," I say simply. "My mother was furious a commoner was my mate, but she had already decided to pass the throne to my sister, so eventually she accepted it. Arella and I were happy. She joined the army with me so we wouldn't have to be apart. I used to joke that she loved being a soldier more than she loved me."

I swallow hard. "There was a battle. A skirmish between us and Night Court. And she—" I clear my throat. "She died in my arms."

The other side of the door is silent, and I'm not sure if that means Edina is listening carefully or if she's cast a soundproofing shield between us. I let my revelation sit for a moment, not wanting my voice to break as I continue. "So, you see, it's not the same pain—" a tear falls down my cheek, "—but I do understand yours. It's also why I can't leave you alone right now."

More silence. I sigh heavily. "After Arella died, I wanted to be left alone too. I'd like to tell you it was to process or to grieve in private. But honestly, some days I wanted to be alone because I wanted my mate back. I wanted to die so I could see her again.

"My sister sat outside my door every day making sure I knew someone was there. So, you don't have to let me in, but I'll be right here tonight if you need someone."

I don't expect her to respond, and she doesn't, so I lean my head back against the cool wood and close my eyes, willing away the sight of Arella's lifeless eyes.

When I finally fall asleep, it's not Arella I see. It's the swirling shades of blue and yellow shown to me by the sirens.

Chapter Ten
Edina

WHEN THE FAINT SLIVER of dawn light peeks through my curtains, I lift my head from the pillow. It throbs from a night of crying. I scrub at my eyes to clear the crusted-on tears and peel myself out from under my thick fur comforter, wrapping the heavy thing around my shoulders as I pad to the double doors of my room.

The Siren Symphony showed me memories I didn't want to relive, memories that triggered the tears I'd been successfully holding back. They were so clear, so real. More real than any dream I've had of the same event. I didn't want anyone to see me breaking, so I ran.

I didn't expect Eldoris to follow me. He doesn't owe me anything, especially not his story. The pain he described and the sense of hopelessness I heard in his voice struck a chord. For the first time since I moved to this cursed realm, I didn't feel so alone.

I crack open one of the doors and peek out. Eldoris is still wearing his dark tux from last night, though his tie has been discarded and he's wearing the jacket like a blanket. He shifts at the creak, his turquoise eyes framed by dark lashes slowly blinking open. I slide out and shut the door behind me as he straightens, regarding me curiously.

Sitting beside him, I shift the blanket so it lies over the both of us and fold my knees into my chest. I stare out at the clinically pristine sitting room, aware of Eldoris' gaze the entire time.

"Have you been trying to tell me that story since my welcome ball?" I ask, turning to look at him. He scrapes a hand down his beard.

"Not that night," he says carefully. "But after. In the mortal realm." When Eldoris came to aid in the Witch War, he was constantly seeking me out, and I not-so-subtly evaded every attempt at conversation. We fought side by side, and I still managed not to speak to him.

"I thought..." I bury my hands in my face. "I thought you were going to confess your love for me or something. That's why I avoided you."

I peek out from behind my hands, and Eldoris is staring at me, shocked. "Edina—" he starts then bites down on his lips, clearly trying not to laugh. "We danced together once."

"You're attracted to me," I point out. "We were going to sleep together."

"Yes, but..." he looks torn between speaking honestly and trying to spare my feelings. "No, I didn't fall in love with you from one conversation."

"I get that now," I say, and Eldoris' laugh is finally let loose. It's rich and deep and it rumbles through me in the same way it did the night we met. I try to purse my lips, but it doesn't last long until I'm smiling with him.

When his laughter dies down, we sit for a moment, watching as the sun illuminates the sitting room, getting stronger and stronger by the second. "I thought you hated me," Eldoris says.

"I don't hate you," I say with a sigh. "I just associate you with the worst day of my life."

"I think that's worse."

Now it's my turn to laugh. I have the strongest urge to rest my head on his shoulder, but I ignore it and lean back against the door instead. "I'm sorry about your mate," I say softly.

"I'm sorry about yours."

"He's not dead." On cue, my chest twinges, the familiar ache spreading. I stand, leaving the comforter on the floor. "We should get ready."

"For?" Eldoris asks, standing as well, stretching his arms overhead. His shirt, untucked from spending a night on the floor, rides up and exposes a patch of inked muscle.

"Breakfast with my parents," I tell him, dragging my eyes back to his face, which is set in a smirk. "I informed them we needed a meeting. We have things to plan."

His mouth pops open. "What things?" he asks, and then his lips part. "You're...you're saying yes?"

"I'm not an idiot, Eldoris. I know what this kind of alliance will mean for our courts. I was always going to say yes."

"You were just making me sweat first?"

I bite the inside of my cheek. "Maybe I was trying to figure out how to let you down gently."

"Since I'm madly in love with you."

"Obviously." I expect laughter, but Eldoris gets very serious.

"If you're looking for love, Edina, I'm not the male to give that to you," his tone is solemn, his eyes haunted. "I don't think it's possible for me."

I reach out and hold his hand before tossing him a wink. "Promises, promises," I tease, wrapping the blanket back around my body. "Ten minutes, and I'll meet you back out here to head to the solarium for breakfast."

"I've heard that before," he snarks, but goes to his room, leaving me in my doorway.

I'm engaged.

Huh.

WHEN ELDORIS AND I arrive in the solarium, my mom and seven fathers are all waiting at a large circular table. The room reminds me of an igloo. Its rounded ceiling and walls are made up of squares of glass framed in silver that shimmer in the rising sunlight. The Atavi forest surrounds us, fresh falling snow collecting on the evergreens and making it feel like we're in a snow globe.

The men all stand and bow. Though I'm their daughter, I still outrank them, and my mother is a stickler for court dynamics, even if we are alone.

"Morning," I greet everyone, and the men return to their seats as Eldoris and I bow to my mother.

"Good morning, Edina. Eldoris," she says from her place at the head of the table. It's impressive that she's at the head of a round table, but her energy commands it. You know from the minute you walk in the room who is in charge, even amongst the other monarchs.

My mother is widely agreed to be the most powerful Fae in existence. Her magic single-handedly ended countless wars and her reign has been bountiful for the Fae of Winter Court. She's cold as ice and sharp as a knife, and her brain always working, always strategizing, but she's good to her people.

To me, that sounds exhausting.

Eldoris wears a tan sports coat that looks better suited to the beach than the tundra we live in. His aqua shirt brings out the color in his eyes, and he's gone without a tie, showing off the hint of tribal-style ink that snakes up his neck. He pulls out my chair, and I slide into it, carefully arranging the thick skirt of the day dress I'm wearing. It's a simple garment but heavy and lined with fur to combat the cold. Although the ice in my veins means I rarely feel cold, it's the style in Winter Court and as the princess, I must adhere to what's in fashion.

"Did you enjoy the symphony last night?" Father Five, who is seated beside me asks as Eldoris takes his position on my other side.

"It was something," I say with a grimace. My fathers don't perceive sarcasm, so Five goes about his business, picking up a carafe of coffee, pouring me a cup.

Everyone makes pleasant conversation about the movements in the symphony while we raid the breakfast in the center of the table. Plates heaped with pastries, fruit crystallized with sugar, and something that looks like a bread dish are passed. My mother doesn't move while Six beside her fills her plate. I'm about to reach for a croissant when Eldoris beats me to it, placing the pastry I was eyeing on the plate for me. I huff but nod in thanks. Another stupid tradition. A princess should never serve herself.

I use my magic as a workaround and summon a helping of the sugary fruit as well as milk, sugar, and whipped cream to add to my coffee. Eldoris watches me with intrigue. "I have a sweet tooth," I say, popping a piece of the fruit in my mouth and groaning at how delicious it is. I had this the other day; I don't remember it tasting so good.

"Would you like to try this?" he asks, holding a piece of the bread thing. "It's a sweet bread, a delicacy in Summer Court." He turns to my mother. "It's very kind of you to serve it."

"Of course," she says. "We want you to feel at home." Eldoris places a piece on my plate before serving himself.

"Now that we all have breakfast," my mother says, her pale blue eyes trained on me. "May I ask why it was so important to call this meeting with such haste? The pixies informed us of your request around three in the morning."

All eyes turn to me, including Eldoris' as he waits for me to take the lead on this like we discussed in our trek down here. I place my hand on his, not really sure why, I just feel like I should. He squeezes my fingertips in solidarity, and I release a small puff of air.

"I have accepted Eldoris' proposal," I say, cutting straight to the point. "We'd like to announce the engagement—"

"Betrothal," my mother interjects.

"Is there a difference?"

"Yes, there is," Father Three says, his purple eyes large and dark against his pale skin. When I was sober enough to take classes, he was my etiquette teacher, so I'm sure I'm about to get a tongue-lashing for my lack of knowledge between the words.

"In Faerie," Seven says, running a hand through his blue-black hair, "a betrothal is a period in which the couple essentially tests out marriage. They do everything a married couple would do, live together, dine together..." he drifts off, letting the other implications hang in the air.

"After the betrothal period," Two continues for him, "the couple makes a final decision on their match, and then a wedding is planned."

"Eldoris and I are both in agreement," I say. "This is a marriage of alliance, not love. Can't we just announce that we're getting married and plan the damn wedding?"

"No," my mother says sternly. "That's not how things are done."

"Fine," I say on a heavy exhale. "Then we'd like to announce our *betrothal* at the ball this evening."

"No," my mother says again, and I fight the urge to growl at her. As it is, my hand tightens around Eldoris'.

"Why. Not?"

"The Summer Court Queen needs to sign off on this as well," my mother says.

"She was in favor of the match—" Eldoris starts but is silenced by a glare.

"Unless she can be here by tonight, then we will wait to announce the happy news. It will go a long way to have both families present when the announcement is made."

Eldoris' jaw is ticking, but he nods and his eyes go unfocused. Everyone waits, silent, watching him, and I realize he's having a mental conversation.

After a long moment, he announces, "My mother and sister will be here in a few hours."

"Wonderful," my mother says. "Then we will announce your union at the ball tonight."

I smile so hard I'm sure my face will crack in half. It's literally what I just asked for. She just had to make sure it was done her way.

"And then," my mother continues, "we will host your betrothal ball tomorrow."

"Another ball?" I exchange a glance with Eldoris but before I can ask, Four says, "It's customary to host an all-day affair for the newly betrothed couple. Much like your welcome ball, Edina, all Fae will be encouraged to attend, if only for a bit."

"And since they will need time to arrange travel and the courts will need to set up a portal schedule, we will give them twenty-four hours."

My mother's tone has a hint of finality to it, so I stay silent. "I'll send the seamstress to your room after breakfast to discuss the gowns you'll wear for all the events."

"Anything else?" I ask, my head is suddenly pounding, and I could really use a nap.

"There is much to go over," Seven says. He's been in charge of teaching me about the customs and history of Faerie, though I'll admit, I've missed my fair share of lessons. Okay, all the lessons since I arrived two mortal years ago, but I went to the ones during my first trip here. "Let's set up a time today, and I'll go over what you should expect."

"I'll attend with you if that's all right," Eldoris offers. "I'm curious if the protocols differ between courts."

"Very well," Seven says.

"One final thing," Eldoris says, making everyone sit at attention. "After the ball tomorrow, I am due to continue the search for the Fae with hellfire before they drain any more children of their magic. I know we will need to discuss the merging of armies, but until that is sorted, I would like Edina to join me."

"Absolutely not," my mother says at the same time I say,

"Hell yeah."

"Edina is needed here. We've lost two mortal years in training her to become queen—"

"It's like two months here, it's not that big of a deal," I mutter.

"—and she is woefully behind. Sending her to the front line isn't plausible."

"Your Majesty," Eldoris says, still calm but with a bit of an edge to his voice, "If we don't stop this rogue group of Fae, we will be facing an army of hellfire. Again."

"Again-again if you count the Witch War," I mutter. My mother shoots me daggers. "I'm useless here, but I can fight. I have centuries to learn how to govern. If we let this problem get out of hand, I may never have the chance."

My mother sucks on her teeth. "Besides, I should stay with my betrothed," I say, and she narrows her eyes.

"Yes, fine," she says with a dismissive wave of a hand. "But you'll need to find a replacement, Eldoris. Edina will need to return to court at some point and, as her husband, you will too."

"I understand."

"Then," my mother stands, and all her husbands follow suit. "I shall see you at the ball this evening."

She turns and strides from the solarium, followed by my fathers who look like a row of ducklings. Seven turns back as he reaches the door. "I'll meet you in the library around midday. If anything changes, I'll send word with Althea."

And with that, Eldoris and I are left amongst the half-eaten pastries and drained carafes of coffee. "That could have gone worse," Eldoris says, picking at his sweet bread. I snatch the loaf and rip off a hunk, cramming it into my mouth.

Chapter Eleven
Eldoris

WE GET BACK TO the suite and Edina pales. Her hand flutters to her chest and she opens her mouth to say something, but then immediately snaps it closed and runs for her bedroom, leaving the door open in her haste.

"Edina?" I ask, following slowly into the undisturbed room. The curtains around her four-poster bed are drawn back, and the fur blanket she draped on me this morning is back on her made bed. Sunlight illuminates the white room, made even brighter by all the snow outside reflecting its rays.

"I'm fine," she says, but it's garbled, overtaken by the sound of retching. I move faster, getting to the open doorway of her bathroom just as she sits back from the toilet and flushes away the evidence. Wiping her mouth with the sleeve of her dress she shudders. "It happens, don't worry—"

She swallows heavily, closing her eyes and breathing in deep, her nostrils flaring. Her bottom lip quivers and she swears before turning back to the toilet and vomiting again.

I cross the bathroom and kneel beside her. Scooping back her hair with one hand and rubbing soothing lines up and down her back with the other, I sit with her and wait for the episode to subside.

"Fucking hell," she grumbles, flushing again. She sinks back on her heels, her shoulder resting against mine. "Sorry you had to see that, it's gross."

I don't know what to say, so I brush aside the damp strands of hair sticking to her face. She hums in contentment as I play with her hair, relaxing into me further. "Can I get a healer?" I ask. "Maybe he'll have a tonic—"

"Nah," she says, brushing me off with a smile I'm beginning to realize is disingenuous. "Nothing works for this." She closes her eyes again, her hand massaging the space right above her heart.

"This is related to the mate bond?"

"Gold star for you," she monotones and stands with a wince like the movement makes her bones hurt. I go with her, keeping one hand on her elbow as she staggers. "Did you feel like this?" she pants with exertion even though we're barely moving. "I think I could live with the emotional trauma, but the physical pain…"

A tear tracks down her cheek and irrational rage flushes through me. She's been in physical pain, so much that it makes her vomit every day, and no one has done anything. We're Fae for Goddess-sake. We have magic for everything. There's an entire city of healers in the Day Court. There's no way that none of them were able to help.

No wonder she's been drunk for the past two mortal years. I can't imagine being in that kind of chronic pain day in and day out without hope of relief.

"Eldoris?" Edina asks, and I realize I've been staring at her with who-knows-what emotions plastered on my face.

"Sorry, I—" I run my free hand through my hair and guide her to bed, pushing back the comforter. "No, I didn't feel like this. There was a burst of physical pain right when Arella died, that felt like the mating bond exploded. And then, for a long time, it felt like a phantom limb. I would swear I'd feel the bond, that I could sense Arella's emotions, but it wasn't there."

Edina hums and I tuck the blankets around her. "Mine didn't explode. It shattered."

"You still feel it?"

"Every day."

I hate how resigned she sounds. She's given up, prepared to live a painful existence.

How can I stand by, be her husband, and let her live like this?

Edina nestles into her pillows with a large yawn. "I'm gonna try and nap. Don't be alarmed if you hear more crying, it usually comes after the vomit, and I don't have the energy for a silencing spell."

"Then I'll be just outside," I say. She opens her mouth to protest, but I slide through the door, murmuring, "Sleep well," as it closes with a resounding click.

I slump into the same position I held the night before, propped against her door, and reach out to my sister.

Dev? Who would you say is the best healer in the realm?

THE LIBRARY ATTACHED TO Edina's rooms is cozy and what it lacks in size, it makes up for in the sheer volume of books. They're everywhere, crammed into the built-in bookshelves, stacked in piles in the corners, littering every flat surface in the blue-carpeted room. Faerie lights offer just enough illumination that I can see a few titles and I'm surprised how many are from the mortal realm. I wonder if Edina brought them or if her parents did to make her feel more at home.

Edina's father Ciaran, or Seven as she calls him, sits across a small wooden table, his sapphire eyes which are unnervingly like his daughter's fixed on me. I can tell he doesn't like our arrangement, many people won't. The Unseelie and Seelie Fae have been at odds for so much of our history that an alliance will be vexing to most of the population, especially those who have been around for a while. But my court needs this, so I'll ignore their qualms and keep pushing forward.

Edina strolls into the library looking a little green. Her father and I pop up to help her into her chair, and then end up staring at each other, both of us unsure who's supposed to help in this situation. She doesn't miss a beat and pulls out her own chair, flopping into it.

"Let's hear it," she says, putting her feet on the seat of the chair and hugging her knees to her chest. She's wearing an oversized white sweater, leggings, and a pair of fuzzy socks. With her wings banished, she's never looked more human.

Ciaran rolls his eyes in another move I've seen from his daughter, and we both take our seats. "What do you know of marriage within Faerie?"

"Assume I know nothing," she says. Her tone is flippant, but I can see the worry creasing her brow. Her father must notice it too because he reaches across and holds her hand.

"Right, from the beginning then," he says gently. "Marriage between Fae is a magically binding contract. Some have broken it in the past, but it comes with severe consequences, which is why the couple or group seeking marriage must go through a betrothal period to ensure they're ready to commit for eternity."

Edina pales further. "So, no divorce in the Fae realm?"

"No, that's a human concept." Her father looks between the two of us. "If you're not certain—"

"How does it work for other political marriages?" she asks, leaning forward. The sleeve of her soft white sweater slides up her arm.

Ciaran and I exchange a glance. "There aren't many," I say slowly. "The most successful in history is—"

"Mine and your mother's," Ciaran replies.

"But you're mates," Edina says.

"Yes. But the marriage is what bound Night and Winter Courts together, not the mating. If we had chosen not to marry, the Unseelie army as you know it would not exist."

"Are there others?"

"Yes. But none that are current."

"Queen Titania had a political marriage," I tell her. Upon hearing the Spring Queen's name, Edina flinches. "Her husband, King Oberon, died under mysterious circumstances roughly four hundred mortal years ago, but they were married for so long, the Day Court and Spring Court remained in good standing."

Edina rests her head on her knees. "And would our marriage be..." she swallows, searching for the words. "I mean, I assume we'd be married in name only. How does that work with the magical contract? Do we build in a clause that says we can screw other people?"

"Goddess," I breathe, glancing at her father for help. He remains silent.

"What?" Edina smirks, clearly loving that she's got me flustered. "We're going to be shackled together forever for the sake of our courts. You mean to tell me we're expected to only fuck each other for infinite centuries?"

"Typically, the couple agrees to be faithful," Ciaran says, finally. "Though everyone's opinion of that is different. In my relationship, it's only the eight of us. Some have open relationships. Some agree to be monogamous except if there are fertility issues. The magic around fidelity can be fluid, and you can decide that before your wedding."

Edina is still looking at me expectantly. "I think..." I start slowly. "We would need to discuss that over our betrothal period and find what works for us. Ideally not while your father is present."

"However," Ciaran says. "You will be expected to have children." Edina goes white as a sheet. "You are the future queen. If you don't have children, who will the throne go to after you?"

"Mother has reigned for millennia." Edina grips the edge of the table and the temperature of the room dips. "As it is, I'll never have to be on the throne, never mind these hypothetical offspring."

I place a hand atop hers, and ice spreads from her skin toward mine. "It doesn't need to be tomorrow," I say, my breath visible under the brief loss of her control. "It can be in fifty mortal years. Or one hundred mortal years. Even longer."

She huffs, puffing out air from her nose, giving the impression I'm squaring off against a charging bull. "And we'd have nannies," I add, trying to lighten the mood. It has the opposite effect. Edina's eyes go so dark they're almost navy and her whole chest caves in on itself. I think she's about to yell at me, or at least tell me why that comment elicited such a reaction, but she pulls her hand from my grasp.

"I need a minute." She stands and turns to go but is stopped by Quintin, the father Edina calls Five, as he appears in the doorway. His long blonde hair is mussed, and the expression on his face is haunted. A rock settles in my stomach. I've seen that look before.

"You're needed in the throne room," he says, his voice shaking. "Both of you. Fast as you can." He tosses Edina a pair of boots, which she slips on without further question.

"You can't teleport here, right?" Edina asks, and I shake my head. She wraps her arms around my waist, and her rosewater and sugar scent envelops my senses. Cold magic squeezes as it wraps around us and takes us from the library into chaos.

The hallway outside the throne room is filled with soldiers running past us toward the front doors. Noble Fae are screaming and crying as brownies and pixies encourage them to return to their rooms. The upheaval swirls around us as we stand still, taking it all in for a moment before we both snap back into reality.

Edina throws open the doors and charges down the sapphire blue runner with me close on her heels. Gwyneira isn't on her throne but standing in a cluster of the other monarchs, speaking in hushed tones. There are two circles, the inner circle with the monarchs of the courts, and the outer ring with their children. Only one monarch is missing, Queen Titania of the Spring Court.

When Devorah sees me, she releases a breath. "Mother, they're here," she says. My mother looks ever an imposing figure, but her eyes are cloudy, and even without Devorah using our mental connection, I can tell that today has been a bad day for her.

I approach the circle and kiss her on the cheek. "My son," she croons. "I hear congratulations are in order. Arella is a wonderful girl."

Larisa sucks in a dramatic breath. "Edina, mother," I say gently.

"Of course," she says, brushing me off, but I can see her confusion. "That's what I meant."

"What's happening?" Edina asks.

"There's been an incident," Gwyneira responds. Her voice is devoid of emotion, a complete ice queen. "A child was found dead a few miles from here. Drained of their magic. General, you're needed at the scene."

That's what I was expecting, but hearing those words never gets easier. It's made worse that they were right under my nose this time. For too long these Fae have eluded me, taking the thing most precious in our realm. They need to be stopped, but I'm out of ideas.

I shove down the feeling of inadequacy, and start heading toward the door when Edina says, "I'm going too."

"You're needed here," Gwyneira commands, a pinched look on her face.

"I'm a fresh set of eyes. I'd be more useful at the scene, not stuck in a room debating what to do when we all know you're not going to actually do anything."

Larisa's mouth pops open. Devorah stifles a laugh.

Edina doesn't wait for their reactions, just strides past me through the doors.

"I'll uhh—" I stammer in her wake. "Report back when we're done."

The entire room is frozen as I follow Edina into the hall.

Chapter Twelve
Edina

ONCE WE BREACH THE palace gates, Bylur, the head guard, teleports us to the village that reported the attack. It's close enough that I can still see the glittering spires of our castle, but far enough that it appears to rise directly from the forest of evergreens. Snowflakes trickle down from the sky, swirling and dancing before they join the ever-present dusting on the ground.

The village is surrounded by a thick, wooden wall and the gates are already open in preparation for our arrival. Eldoris and I lead the way, my boots clicking on the recently shoveled cobblestone path as we cross the threshold into the village. It's a quaint little town comprised of cabin-style homes made from a mix of brown and white-barked wood making it look like a chessboard.

While the entrance was quiet, the town center is in upheaval. Females are sobbing, one draped dramatically on a bench as her family tries to pull her up. Males stand in the dead center with crossbows and swords, ready to attack at a moment's notice. A brownie hands out cups of steaming hot liquid to mourners, patting their heads with her worn hands. She looks up and catches my eyes, offering only the slightest dip of her silver-locked head in acknowledgment. It's enough to draw the attention of the others, who bow upon seeing me.

I will never get used to that.

Eldoris places a hand on my lower back and walks with purpose toward a male standing so rigidly that I could mistake him for a statue. His skin is sickly pale and his eyes have a vacant quality that only comes from experiencing immense grief.

"General. Princess." He bows as we approach. "I'm Reynolds. Thank you for coming so quickly. I'm sure you're busy." There's no bite to his words, just sincerity, and I struggle with what to say in return.

I defer to Eldoris, who gives him a soft, understanding smile. "This is your home?" he asks, gesturing to the white-barked house behind us, and the male nods.

"My daughter...her body." he breaks off, clearing his throat and Eldoris places a hand on his forearm. The man grabs onto Eldoris like he's his lifeline, his knees buckling. "She was just outside the wall. We bought a dog for her birthday, and she took him for a walk. My wife was two seconds behind her—"

"This isn't your fault," Eldoris says. The male's eyes well with tears and he breathes deeply to keep from crying. "We'll need to go to the site where your wife found her, but may we see your daughter first?"

"Sadie," he says, and at the sound of her name the male breaks. He begins openly weeping, large shuddering sobs that shake his whole body. Eldoris shifts his hold, his arms beneath the male's armpits to keep him upright, while still offering consoling words. I swallow thickly, tears prickling in my own eyes.

I've been in a war; I know what grief looks like. But it's not something I prepared myself to encounter today. I was so focused on gathering clues to the Fae responsible and steeling myself to see the child that I forgot she left behind grieving parents.

When the worst of the male's tears have subsided, Bylur takes Eldoris' spot. Eldoris once again guides me forward through a white-picket gate and up a path to a deep blue door. We click it open and are met with a keening wail.

"If you want to wait outside…" Eldoris starts, but I shake my head. I'm here, these people have seen me. I won't have them calling me a coward behind my back because I couldn't face a sobbing mother.

We walk into the kitchen where the crying is the loudest and find a ring of Fae surrounding the table. When one sees us, they usher the others aside, so we have access. Stretched out on the table is a small corpse. I've never seen a Fae child before, they're incredibly rare, but she looks human.

Except the life has literally been sucked from her body.

Her skin is mottled in different shades of gray, the darkest around her chest where her tunic has been torn. Her little mouth is open in a silent scream, but someone closed her eyes. The combination is somehow worse.

"Princess." Across the table is a woman with the same pale blonde hair as the little girl. She's slumped over, as if lifting her head off the table was all the strength she could muster, and her hand is locked with her daughter's. "I humbly—welcome you—to our home," she hiccups.

I don't know what to say, but I clear my throat. "I am so sorry for your loss."

The woman nods and then begins that keening wail again as she slumps back on the table. I swipe a tear away and Eldoris' hand, which is still on the small of my back, twitches like he wants to hug me, but doesn't move.

"Her magic was drained," he says to me more than the rest of the Fae, although some nod in agreement. "See that mark?" He points to her heart, right where the skin is the darkest. "That's where magic resides. We are still unsure of the spell, but it acts quickly, attacking the magic at the source and convincing it to dislodge from the body. It can only happen in those who have yet to emerge."

"And this morphs the caster's magic?" I ask.

"It's an evil process," he says, and again the women murmur in assent. "The strength given from the spell comes with a price. It taints the magic you're born with."

"It turns it to hellfire," I say in understanding.

Eldoris takes a step closer to the table. "A necromancer who works with my army will be arriving shortly if you'll allow him to take a look at your daughter's body. If she saw anything in her final moments, who attacked her, which way they fled, it may help us find them."

The mother lifts her head again, with a look of unbridled anger and desire for retribution. "I'll be in the front row of their execution," she seethes.

Fae will never cease to surprise me with their savagery.

Softly, as not to disturb the owners, Eldoris explains a quick spell that can help us track the magical signature of the Fae obtaining hellfire. "Every Fae's magic is different and leaves behind traces," he says. "The signature will give us an impression of the caster. If they've performed magic anywhere else, we may be able to sense it."

He casts the spell on the girl's hand as a demonstration and then encourages me to try over her heart. My magic responds to my bidding with the slightest thought, hovering over the magic infecting the little girl and sending it to me. The magical signature feels like an arid, dry heat that reminds me of summer in the desert. "Is it what you expected?"

I ask after I describe it to Eldoris. The heat lingers with me a moment longer, tickling my nose with the scent of sweat and something vaguely plant-like.

Eldoris shakes his head and performs the spell himself to confirm my findings. "Most Fae with fire magic live in the Summer Court, though some have migrated to other areas and have reproduced there." He swallows as he ponders. "The scent reminds me of the desert stretching between Day and Night Courts."

"The floral?" I ask.

"A cactus bloom, I think." I can tell he's thinking more, but he shakes his head as he realizes the mother is hanging on every word of our conversation. "The necromancer will be able to tell us more."

We give our condolences again before one of the townsmen leads us back out of the house and through the gates, pointing in the direction of the attack. "Can other forms of magic be enhanced?" I ask once we're alone.

"Not that we've seen," Eldoris says, but the worry line across his forehead is still prominent.

"You think it might be possible," I surmise. "That's why you're worried. If the Fae was from another court, with different magic, then that would increase your search to everyone in the realm."

The crunch of snow beneath our boots and the ticking of Eldoris' jaw is my answer.

"We're not there yet," he says after a moment. "I'll have my team investigate any fire Fae who moved to Day or Night Court. And..." I turn to him fully as he swipes a hand over his face. "I can check in with an informant in the Underground."

"The Underground?"

Before he has the chance to answer, an uneasy feeling creeps over my skin. We round the edge of the wall and I'm instantly hit with the sense of wrongness.

"Just there," Eldoris says, pointing to a brown splotch amidst the white. Even the snow is wary of this place, of this magic, refusing to fall on the spot. The dark, cloying feeling that makes me want to vomit intensifies. It feels like the air has been tainted, destroyed.

I try the spell he taught me inside, but the magic evades me. It dances around the evil and then sinks back into my skin before giving any answers. "Why don't I feel the same signature?" I ask.

"We believe there are other Fae alongside the caster performing other spells to confuse our tracking methods. The reading we got back in the house is the clearest I've seen thus far."

I try again, this time zeroing in on the bare grass. But I still come up empty

"Can hellfire be transferred?" I ask, an idea taking shape.

"Only to humans," Eldoris replies.

"We should move the children to secure locations," I say. "It's my understanding that there aren't many."

"A handful in each court."

"We have so many rooms in the palace, I bet the other courts do too. We should move all families with children who haven't emerged into the palaces until we handle this problem."

He sputters for a moment but then flashes me a dazzling smile. "That's brilliant, Edina."

"Seems like common sense to me, but sure," I brush him off, but he grabs me by the shoulders, forcing me to look up at him. The warmth of his hands seeps through my sweater, and his oceanic eyes shine down on me.

"No," he asserts. "Don't sell yourself short. That's a fantastic idea that will save lives and stop them from expanding their army."

"You think?" I ask, his praise warming my insides the way his hands do my skin.

"We'll bring it up to the monarchs when we get back."

I smile. Not the practiced smile I've perfected, but a real, genuine smile. Eldoris rubs my arms up and down, his eyes locked with mine. The air between us shifts as I remain ensnared in his gaze. I lick my bottom lip and watch as he tracks the movement, his hands tightening around my arms just the slightest amount.

Something in my chest twinges, it's not enough pain to hurt, but it's enough to bring me back to myself and shatter the daze we've slipped into.

"We should head back," I say. "We have an engagement to announce."

He extends his arm to me, and we teleport away from the tainted magic and back to the front of the palace.

Chapter Thirteen
Edina

BEFORE WE GET TO the ball, there is a small banquet for the monarchs, their spouses, children, and advisors. Just a simple affair of the fifty most influential Fae in the realm. The throne room has been cleared of chairs for the event, and in place of the runner is a long table that seats everyone, making it impossible to speak to anyone who isn't in your immediate vicinity. The center of the table is covered in boughs of evergreen that sparkle with magical ice, and each silver setting gleams under soft candlelight.

Once everyone is seated, a pixie snaps her fingers, and bowls of creamy, orange soup appear in front of each place setting. My mother daintily dips her spoon in the concoction, tastes it, and then gestures for us all to begin. It's an odd tradition that the hosting monarch tastes the food before their guests, but it's supposed to assure people the food hasn't been poisoned. I pointed out that everyone else's food could be poisoned, but I guess it's the gesture that counts.

I take a spoonful and my tastebuds are flooded with warm, rich spices. I expected it to taste sweet, like pumpkin or butternut squash, but the soup is savory with quite the kick of spice. The closest comparison I can make is a curry, but I've never tasted anything like this.

"It's a squash," Devorah, Eldoris' twin sister, who sits beside me supplies. She looks nothing like her brother, except for the eyes. Her hair is straight and the combination of her dark hair, porcelain skin, and her light eyes is striking.

"I'm surprised you've never had it," she continues, lifting the soup to her lips. "It's a traditional dish in Winter Court."

I nod, taking another spoonful. It's odd being schooled on my own customs by someone not even from my court. I know she didn't mean it maliciously, but over and over today I've realized how little I know of Faerie. I was ravenous to learn all I could when I arrived for a short trip two mortal years ago. *But when I returned for good...*

I ignore the full glass of wine and sip my water. "Though, I suppose you haven't been here very long," Devorah says like she's been reading my thoughts.

"Two years."

"Mortal years, which isn't very long at all," she amends. "You'll learn to let go of time. In the meantime, you should give yourself some grace."

"For?" I ask, feigning innocence. I'm starting to trust Eldoris because we have an agreement, but I don't know Devorah. I'm certainly not going to admit to my shortcomings. Fae, even the nice ones, can be ruthless and cunning.

"Grieving," she says simply, making me drop my spoon so little orange droplets spread all over the pristine white tablecloth. I get a look from my mother, but Devorah just smirks. "That's what it was, right? The drinking, the males...and females from what I've heard, you don't discriminate."

"Dev, leave her alone," Eldoris snaps from across the table and three seats down. She laughs brightly and strategically tucks a lock of hair behind her pointed ear.

"Am I to ignore her past?" she asks her brother. "Am I not allowed to be curious? To make sure she won't hurt you."

Eldoris' knuckles are white, and his cutlery starts to melt in his grip. I flick a blast of icy water at his hand, and he drops the molten spoon in surprise. A servant is there to clear it and replace it with a new one in seconds.

I set my spoon aside, not in the mood for soup anymore, and the meal magically vanishes. "Anyway," Devorah continues, dabbing her mouth with a napkin. "I bring it up because Eldoris is a good male."

"I know that," I respond, meeting her eyes.

"And he's been through a lot. Almost as much as you, if not more."

A plate of something red that looks like beets appears before me. "I know that too." She arches an eyebrow. "He's the first person in this realm who didn't make me feel judged for my trauma response."

"Trauma?" she scoffs.

"I emerged as Fae in a realm where I would be killed for what I am," I say. "Then I came here and was rejected by my fated mate before being returned to my realm to fight in a war. Not to mention the fact that the mating bond *hurts*, which healers don't understand. It feels like my bones are shattering every second of every day, and my organs burst only to be put back together again. So yeah, I'd say I've had some trauma."

I sip my water. "But your brother didn't judge me for that, at least not to my face, and has done nothing but try to help me and help our courts in the process. So, you don't need to lecture me, threaten me, or whatever you were planning on doing."

I stab my salad and bring the beet thing to my mouth and find it tastes just like beets. It's disgusting, but I chew and swallow the bite I have without taking my eyes off Devorah.

Her entire face breaks into a smile. "Oh, I like you," she says, loosing a light laugh. "We're going to be friends."

I eye her skeptically, but in my peripheral, Eldoris relaxes slightly, even though he hasn't stopped his conversation with the prince of the Night Court.

Devorah moves to more casual conversation, style in the different courts, and vacation spots throughout the realm, and when she realizes how little I know about Faerie, she asks me a million questions about what it was like growing up in the mortal realm.

When the conversation finally lulls, after the main course has been cleared, I ask, "Why isn't Spring Court here?"

She regards me knowingly. "I'm not sure," she replies. "I know Queen Gwyneira invited Queen Titania. I'm sure they'll be here for the ball. Knowing Titania, she'll want to make an entrance."

I chew on the inside of my lip. "Do you want me to keep them out?" Devorah asks, and now it's my turn to arch an eyebrow. "Okay, fine, I'd have my guards do it, but if you don't want them here—"

"It's okay," I say, and she purses her lips.

"Offer stands," she says after a minute with a shrug. "If you ever want them out, just say the word and I'll take care of it. Our courts are aligned, she'll have a harder time picking a fight with me than with you."

I appraise her, the sincerity in her tone showing on her face and the way she stabs a piece of fruit on her plate. "I like you too," I say, and she laughs loud enough to have several of the others looking in our direction.

AFTER DESSERT, MY LADY'S maids retrieve me to change into my gown for the ball. Eldoris and I will be making our entrance together after our mothers announce our betrothal, and apparently, the entrance requires a costume change.

"All done, Your Highness," Althea says, prodding my shoulder so I turn on the pedestal they have me standing on.

I'm not a fan of ballgowns, typically I hate them. But I have to admit, they nailed the princess bride look with this one, and I do feel pretty. The straps are sheer organza that forms a deep-v neckline. Silver appliques glitter over the material to my hips, where it gathers and abruptly poofs out in a sea of tulle. Althea clicks her tongue as she adds a diamond pendant that hangs down on my chest between my nonexistent breasts, but somehow the gem highlights them in a way that makes it look like I have cleavage.

My hair is left down, on my request, and lays in simple curls spelled to fall perfectly. A delicate silver tiara inlaid with pearls sits atop my head.

"It's great," I say, smiling as wide as I can. My stomach is a flutter with butterflies, and I'm convinced I'm going to lose my dinner, when a warm voice says, "Wow."

I turn and find Eldoris in a charcoal tuxedo that compliments my dress perfectly. His mouth is parted as he looks me over, his eyes a mixture of emotions I can't—and am not sure if I want to—read. His hands are clasped behind his back, which somehow accentuates the muscles in his broad shoulders, and his horns have been banished, leaving his curly hair unimpeded.

"You look..." He swallows, and I give him a flirty smile.

"I hope the end of that sentence is good," I tease, and he laughs, but never actually comes up with a word.

"May we have a moment?" Eldoris asks my lady's maids, who bow and fly out of the room. I wait until I hear them a bit away and then cast a spell around my rooms, so they won't be able to listen in. Pixies are terrible gossips.

Eldoris' eyes brighten and he extends a teacup full of steaming liquid. I take the cup, inhaling the aroma of mint and some kind of fruit, but the color is so dark I can't tell if it's black, blue, or purple.

"I'm not sure," he starts, "but I think I found something that will lessen your pain."

I stare down into the cup, and then back at Eldoris. His ocean eyes are so bright, so hopeful. "How—"

"Larisa, the princess of Day Court," he says.

"She hates me."

"She doesn't hate you, that's just her face," he hurries on. "She's brilliant when it comes to the healing arts."

"Go figure," I murmur, looking into the concoction again, part of me now worried it's poisoned.

"I didn't tell her it was for you," he continues. "I just asked her what she would do for someone who is in chronic pain that magic, tonics, or potions can't touch. She threw a book at me and told me a page number, and then said if I was really asking for erectile dysfunction remedies, to look in the index of the same book."

I laugh despite myself. "The book said to try Elderberries. I brought it to your healer, and they combined it with mint for your stomach and some kind of magic that made the mixture glow before it started steaming."

He looks at me expectantly, but I'm frozen. I've spoken to healers before looking for a solution for my pain, and nothing ever worked. "You're probably skeptical," Eldoris says, "but Larisa said natural remedies in Faerie almost always work. Something about the way the plants grow here because there's magic in the soil. Most healers have gotten lazy and rely on magic, but basics are always reliable."

"This is..." I'm not someone who is easily rendered speechless, but I am right now. Eldoris went out of his way to speak to a person who, quite frankly, is taxing on a good day, all so he could help me. I know my family has been concerned, but no one in my life has gone this far to do something so nice.

I clear my throat. "Thank you." I sip the tea, the mint, and the fruit overwhelming my taste buds in an amazing way. "It's sweet," I remark, and Eldoris' cheeks turn pink.

"I asked them to add sugar," he says. "I saw how you drink your coffee."

My heart does this weird fluttering thing that I've never experienced, so I take another long sip. The warm liquid seeps into my chest, warming me from the inside out. A third sip and the pain plaguing my bones lessens. I inhale sharply before downing the contents of the cup.

My stomach is settled, not at all churning, and everything else is...*okay*. And I'll take okay. Okay is a major improvement from excruciating pain. I can still feel the splintered mating bond, but the throbbing is dulled to a mere twinge.

"By the goddess," I breathe and set the cup down on the coffee table in the sitting room.

"Did it work?" I cut Eldoris off by throwing my arms around his neck. His arms encircle my waist, beneath my wings, which are out tonight. I bury my head in his neck, and he smells like sandalwood and salt, the embodiment of the ocean. His arms are warm around me, and I lean into the warmth a little bit longer than I mean to.

"Thank you," I murmur, letting go and straightening back up.

"Of course," he says, tucking an errant strand of my hair behind my ear. "I take care of what's mine."

I cannot explain the little flip my stomach does, or why I need to swallow before I speak. But I school my expression quickly and loop my arm through Eldoris'. "Come on, fiancé."

"That's a human term," he says.

"Yeah, well, that's what you get when you're *betrothed*—" I roll my eyes emphatically, "—to someone who was raised human."

His smile is megawatt. "I'll learn to deal with it."

We walk arm in arm to the back entrance of the ballroom, where we'll be making our grand entrance. Our mothers will announce our betrothal to the guests from the dais with my mother's throne, and then the doors will dramatically open, revealing us to everyone.

We reach the doors, and a wave of nerves overwhelms me. The last time I was at these doors was my first entrance into Fae society and the worst night of my life. I've avoided the big parties since then, and I certainly have refused an entrance, even if I was forced to go to the event.

The guards at the doors grip the handles. "Ready?" Eldoris asks, and I nod, unable to speak. "Remember, after we're announced, we'll descend the stairs, and a receiving line will start. Once everyone has wished us well, we'll dance, and then our obligations are done, and we can do whatever we want."

"Okay."

I can't hear the announcement, but the cheers that erupt from the crowd are deafening. "Here we go," Eldoris says with a squeeze of my hand.

The doors are thrown open, and we step out onto the balcony that overlooks the vast ballroom. It's simple tonight, letting the majesty of the room speak for itself. The swirling snowflake patterns in the walls are highlighted with real snow, the giant chandeliers drip with icicles, and the marble tiles are coated in glittering rime.

We step to the railing, and although the room is filled with Fae, my eyes are magnetized to one who is standing beside Devorah. Emerald green eyes, slightly narrowed, lock with mine, and my breath hitches. He's wearing a black suit, making him look paler than usual, and that makes his reddish-brown hair stick out like a neon sign.

Puck.

My mate.

The male who rejected me.

Chapter Fourteen
Edina

Two Mortal Years Ago (Faerie)

STILL HIGH ON THE dance and flirtation with Eldoris, I pranced over to the dais with a smile on my lips. My fathers informed me that Spring Court would arrive any minute, which meant I only had one more round of courtiers to speak with before I could sneak away.

The ballroom sparkled as I maneuvered through the couples whirling on the ice dance floor, ignoring the few who tried to get me to dance with them. The orange male Eldoris saved me from earlier was eyeing me with hunger, but I could ignore one pervy Fae. This night, which started as a tedious affair, was looking up.

Maybe because it was almost over.

"You're in a good mood," my mother commented when I arrived and took my place beside her throne.

"I am." I was getting laid tonight and going back to the mortal realm in the morning. Things were looking pretty rosy.

A throbbing sensation built in my stomach, and I winced in pain. I took a few deep breaths, fighting the urge to run off the dais and find somewhere to throw up. It happened again, this time more persistently and I doubled over, inhaling sharply.

"Edina?" my mother asked from beside me, her usual cold exterior fracturing slightly.

"I'm okay—" I managed as the nausea rolled again. It felt like something was behind my belly button and pulling.

"Introducing, Her Majesty, Queen Titania and the society of Spring Court."

The doors opened and I looked up, and the entire room fell away as I found a pair of emerald eyes.

My feet moved on their own accord as I descended the steps of the dais, drifting down the sapphire runner toward the incoming group. The pulling in my stomach urged me to go faster, but my feet were like lead. His red hair was darker than I remembered, the color almost brown in richness. There was a smattering of freckles across the ridge of his nose that contrasted sharply with his pale complexion. His strong jaw was hanging open as he looked at me, and his throat bobbed as the tugging around my middle grew.

"Puck," I gasped, and the crooked smile that was charming enough to make me follow him into another realm graced his face.

"Edina," he said. The woman at his side cleared her throat, dragging my attention away from the only male who ever made me regret leaving after a one-night stand.

The female was in a green gown as wide as she was tall. Her wings fluttered in irritation at my interruption of their ascent to see my mother, her pale features pinched in agitation.

"I suggest you learn your place, girl," she scoffed. "You're in the presence of a queen."

Oh shit. I forgot Puck worked for the Spring Court Queen. I dipped into a curtsey. "My apologies, Majesty," I said in my clearest voice. "I was just..."

I looked up and Puck broke away from his queen and stood in front of me. He extended a hand to me, and if the noises she made were anything to go by, Titania was unhappy about this turn of events.

"You're—" I started, and he drew me in close, resting his forehead against mine.

"I suspected the night we met," he murmured. "I wasn't sure since you hadn't emerged. And then you left..."

I'd never been one for romantic gestures, for romance of any kind. The whole thing usually turned my stomach. *So why was this moment everything?* Why was it that the world narrowed to just the two of us like we were encased in our own special kind of magic? Why was it that all I wanted was for him to sweep me off my feet and kiss me in front of an entire room of people?

"She's your mate?" Titania screeched, and Puck nodded, not turning around, clearly as captured by me as I was by him. His fingers interlocked with mine and the pulling in my stomach that made me nauseated moments ago was replaced with warmth and a rush of emotions. Even the scent of the room changed, filling up with a floral fragrance that invaded my senses.

"No." The word was like ice being poured over our bubble, and Puck broke away from me to turn and look at his queen. The entire guard behind her had magic shimmering in their hands. Vines sprung up between the cracks in the marble and ice.

"Titania, enough," my mother said, and her guards called ice magic to their hands from where they lined the aisle.

Titania chuckled and fell into step beside Puck, who looked between us both. "I believe you're mistaken, my dear."

"I'm not." I'd never been surer of anything in my life that the male across from me was my mate. Even if I knew nothing about mates, I would have known we were destined for each other.

"But you are." She gave me an evil grin before turning her poisonous glare at Puck. "Puck has been my right hand for centuries. He *belongs* to me." She leaned heavily into the word belongs, and Puck visibly flinched and took a step away from me. I chased him a step but stopped when vines snaked around my wrists.

"Titania, enough of this," my mother hissed from her throne. "You cannot deny a mating bond."

"You're right, Gwyn," she said, her smile colder than the ice storm outside. "But Puck can."

There was a collective inhale from all the Fae who stopped to watch us. "Puck..." I started, but he held up a hand and I saw it. Defeat, resignation, and something cruel in his eyes.

"I'm sorry," he said, his back completely rigid as he squared his shoulders. "I renounce our mating bond."

It felt like someone just reached into my chest, grabbed my heart, and squeezed until it popped. I inhaled sharply as the words rang out in the now-silent ballroom. "No."

"What?" my mother demanded, suddenly directly behind me, no longer on her perch on the dais. I could feel my fathers forming a half circle around the two of us, like silent sentinels.

"I renounce the ties that bind us," Puck said. "You are not my mate, Edina of Winter Court."

The queen at his side gave him a proud smile which turned into a sneer when her eyes settled on me. Puck's features twisted in pain as the bond between us pulled taut and then shattered into a thousand pieces. It was like someone stabbed me with a hot poker and twisted before dragging it through my entire torso. The pain radiated in every muscle, every bone, every strand of my hair. It hurt to breathe; it hurt when I held my breath.

My dress ballooned around me like a gigantic cupcake as I sank to my knees. I clutched my chest as my somehow still-existent heart crashed wildly against my ribcage. Folding in on myself, I buried my face in the mountain of velvet, trying to hide from the thousands of Fae staring silently at this display.

"Get out," my mother said, taking a step towards the Spring Court Queen. My fathers completed the circle that surrounded us, and Five dropped to the floor, practically pulling me into his lap. Another one of my fathers held me from behind, the two hugging tight enough to break me, while a third stroked my hair.

I focused on the only thing I could, controlling the magic that wanted to surge from me in a blast of icicles and snow. I held onto it, willing it to stay within my skin as I shook. Frozen teardrops slid down my cheeks and plunked on the floor.

I heard Titania's cruel laughter as the temperature in the ballroom dropped to arctic temperatures.

"Edina," Puck's voice was strained. I didn't look up. I couldn't.

"You have thirty minutes to get to the border, or I will slaughter each and every one of you," my mother said, her voice deadly quiet. The sound of footsteps picked up around me, and I dared to lift my head. Between the gaps in my fathers' legs, I saw Puck disappear through the door. He didn't bother turning around.

The rest of the ballroom was frozen, unable or unwilling to move but not looking away.

"I need to get out of here," I said, standing, and taking Five and Four—the one who was at my back—up with me. I would not fall apart over a male, and I certainly would not fall apart in front of thousands of Fae. My ice seeped through my veins, strengthening my spine and walling off the crater Puck left in my chest. My mother broke through the circle to stand before me.

"We'll go back to your room," Seven said, reaching for my arm, but I shook my head and pulled away from his grasp.

"No, I need to go home. I need to get out of this realm." Tears threatened to fall again but I held them back.

"Edina," Five said softly. I turned, my magic rising around me, winter wind pulling sections of my hair from its fancy updo.

"I'm not asking." Ice crept up my arms.

"You can go," my mother's voice rang out, silencing my magic and the mad thoughts raging in my head. "Astor will accompany you and continue your training, but you may leave."

Astor stepped forward and took my arm. "We'll leave immediately," he said, and his hand squeezed reassuringly. The tenderness had tears threatening to fall again.

"Edina," my mother called, and I turned back towards her. Her face softened, almost appearing gentle as tears brimmed in her eyes. "I'm so sorry, my darling. You didn't deserve that."

"I'm fine," I said. "I'm not about to get worked up over a mediocre fuck."

The ghost of a smile crossed her lips, but it was gone before I could register it. "You'll return here as soon as things are settled after the witches' war."

"That's what I promised."

She turned on her heel without another word. My fathers disbanded, revealing the ballroom again. The music started up and people continued mingling. Everyone avoided looking at me, heads conveniently turned or looking down into wine glasses. Except for one. A pair of ocean-blue eyes found mine through the crowd.

"Astor," I said, turning away from the concerned look on Eldoris' face. My father offered me a small smile. "Let's go home."

He took my arm, teleporting us to the portal that would take me to the mortal realm.

I'd be fine. I never wanted forever with someone. I didn't need a mate.

Chapter Fifteen

Eldoris

Present (Faerie)

EDINA GOES COMPLETELY RIGID, and it doesn't take a genius to figure out why. I glance at her in my peripheral, and the color has leeched from her face, her once smiling expression, now stony and cold.

Fucking Puck.

I release her arm and place my hand on her lower back, which breaks the spell she's under and pulls her attention to me. Her eyes are wild, like a spooked animal. Maybe she hoped he and Titania wouldn't show up, maybe for a rare moment, she forgot about him. Whatever it was, Puck's presence beside the elite group near the dais rocked her.

"What can I do?" I whisper as we begin to descend the sweeping staircase. Fae nobles and other higher members of the different courts are already lining up to wish us well, and they'll tear her apart like this. Any sign of weakness, and they'll seek to exploit it.

Edina releases a shuddering breath, and then a plastic smile that doesn't reach her eyes is fixed on her face. "I'm alright," she says. "It was just a shock."

Her white-knuckle grip on the railing says otherwise.

We reach the bottom of the stairs and are greeted by the first in line, an advisor for the Day Court, the same one I rescued Edina from during her first trip to Faerie.

"Best wishes, you two," he says, his leathery skin an even darker shade of orange than the last time I saw him. "May your courts prosper under your new alliance."

Edina thanks him warmly, missing the dig. Day Court isn't pleased with the fact that a Seelie Court made an alliance with an Unseelie Court. The next to greet us is an advisor from Spring Court, which goes much the same way.

"Fuck," I mumble when the female breezes away from us in a cloud of faux-floral scented air.

"What?" Edina asks out of the corner of her mouth as the next couple, Winter Court Fae whose names escape me, give us their congratulations.

"Political bullshit," I respond through gritted teeth as they leave and Izar, the Prince of the Night Court, arrives.

"You should have told us!" he booms, shaking my hand and kissing Edina on the cheek. Even though we've been on opposing sides, Izar and I have always had a good relationship. He's the second in line for the throne and refers to us both as 'the spares.'

"We wanted it to be a surprise," Edina says, but her attention is elsewhere.

Titania, the Queen of Spring Court, pushes past the receiving line, towing Puck along with her. Titania is a small female, so short there were rumors that she was part pixie, but she makes up for it by piling her red hair on top of her head in a hair-do so high and elaborate that her curls reach my shoulder. She's wearing an emerald-green ballgown that is comprised of vines that snake up her arms and torso, reaching for her pale, pinched face.

"It certainly was a surprise," she coos, her smile warm but her eyes like ice. She links her arm through Puck's pulling him close in a move that has Edina stiffening. "We're so happy for you, aren't we, Puck?"

"Yes," he clears his throat, completely ignoring everyone but Edina. "Congratulations."

Titania's cheeks redden. "It makes sense," she continues. "Since neither of you has a mate. It's good you've decided to use that heartbreak for the greater good of your courts."

Edina makes a sound in the back of her throat that's feral, and I slip my arm low around her waist and squeeze her in close. "Always a pleasure, Your Majesty," I say in dismissal.

She harrumphs but leaves the line with Puck backing away after her, keeping his eyes on Edina. Izar, who has been watching the whole exchange with rapt attention whistles low. I turn to Edina, who has completely curled in on herself, her chest concaved, her hands trembling.

"I need a minute," she says, a frozen teardrop beading on the corner of her lashes. I fight the urge to wipe it away.

"I'll come with you—" I start, but she shakes her head.

"I need a minute alone." She breaks away from me before I can respond, and I watch her go, her wings fluttering as she walks and the tulle of her dress swishing around her ankles.

"That was brutal," Izar says, dragging a hand across his stubbled jaw, the dark blue-black color contrasting with his warm, beige skin. His gray eyes are alight with mischief, and I know he's loving the spectacle. "You sure you want that trouble?"

I glare at him. "Edina isn't trouble."

"I meant Puck." He gestures to the door Edina disappeared through. Sure enough, a shifty-eyed Puck is following her, slipping through the doorway as Titania is distracted in conversation with Gwyneira.

"Fuck. Stay here, deal with this line." Izar opens his mouth in protest but I'm already on the move, my long legs carrying me across the empty dance floor. I nod to a few who have left the line to try and greet me directly, quickly shaking a hand or two before brushing them off and making it to the door.

This door leads to a long, cold hallway. It's not decorated like the others, which tells me it leads to servant quarters or the kitchens. A few pixies yelp when they see me, and a vampyre practically bowls me over, but otherwise, the workers ignore me as I walk farther and farther away from the party.

"Puck." Edina's voice makes my stomach drop. It's breathy and pleading and... this is a bad idea. Why did I follow them? She and I haven't set up any ground rules. If she wants to sneak off and screw the mate who rejected her—

"Leave me alone."

The words spur me to run, rounding the corner until I find them. Edina is backed into a small alcove, an indent in the stonework that is big enough for just her body. Puck is caging her in, his arms bracketed by her face as he leans into her space. She has a hand on his chest, gripping the lapel of his jacket like she's unsure if she's trying to push him away or pull him in closer.

"Edina," Puck pleads. "Just listen to me."

He reaches for her, and she cringes.

Something inside me snaps. This male is the reason she cries herself to sleep every night, the reason she's been sick, the reason she's been drinking herself into a coma since she returned to Faerie. And now he has the audacity to try and touch her when she's said no?

I cross the distance in two huge steps, wrap my hand around the collar of his shirt, and yank him away from her. His brown and leathery wings snap out, shredding his jacket as he steadies himself. I place myself between him and Edina, blocking her shrinking form with my body.

"Back the fuck up," I growl.

"This doesn't concern you, Eldoris," Puck responds, trying to move around me. I block him.

"Edina is my betrothed. It absolutely concerns me."

"She's my mate!"

"You lost the right to call her that."

Vines snap out from Puck's hands just as fire erupts from mine. We stare at each other, chests heaving, magic ready to be thrown.

"Edina?" Puck calls like he can get her to go to him. Edina leans her forehead in the center of my back, between my shoulder blades, and doesn't say a word. I can feel her still shaking.

When he realizes she won't answer, Puck's face drops. I see that he's in pain too, but it's not enough to make me feel bad. He got them into this mess. "I'm sorry," he says, dropping his magic. Edina's hand fists in my jacket, but she's silent. Puck sighs and walks back in the direction of the party.

I wait until I hear the door swing open, emitting the sounds of revelry in one jarring blast before turning back to Edina and scanning her body for signs of distress. Her dress is undisturbed, there are no marks on her skin. The only sign that anything is amiss at all is the small pile of frozen teardrops at her feet.

"Did he hurt you?" Her eyes are unfocused, but she shakes her head. "I need to hear you say it, Edina. Are you hurt?"

"No," her voice quivers. "I can't go back in there."

"Of course." I take a step back and hold out my hand in an offering. As much as I want to comfort her, I won't touch her right now unless she specifically allows me to. "I'll take you back to your room."

She eyes my hand for a moment before slowly placing hers in it. I interlock our fingers, moving with trepidation so that she can stop the contact if she needs it. I want to pull her into my arms and hug her so tightly it erases this last hour from her mind, but I won't overstep her boundaries.

We walk through the servants' corridors back to her suite. Edina is quiet the entire way, but she keeps giving me a look I can't decipher. I think she's still in shock, but there's an air of confusion and awe in her gaze. She looks like she's trying to mentally solve a complex math problem.

I open the door for her, illuminating the sitting room with a ball of magical light and waiting to take my cues from Edina. My blood is still thrumming, this intense desire to find Puck and lay him out for thinking he could corner her. If I didn't think she needed me, I'd do just that. As it is, she's staring at me like I'm the one thing that's real in this world.

I'm not going to examine why that makes me swell with pride. I'm a protector, that's all. It has nothing to do with Edina specifically.

After a few moments, and opening and closing her mouth a few times, she gives me her back. "Can you unzip me?"

I hesitate, causing her to turn and look over her shoulder. Her slender neck somehow looks longer in profile, and her lashes brush her flushed cheeks as she blinks up at me. I step to her and brush her hair aside, my fingers lingering on the exposed skin of her shoulder, making her gasp. I feel the sound everywhere, heat rushing through my blood as I imagine her making that sound beneath me.

Shit. I shouldn't think like that. Not when she's hurting and vulnerable.

But a traitorous part of my mind reminds me that she could have used magic to undo her zipper.

Releasing a breath, and trying my hardest to banish that thought, I slide her zipper down, the sheer material almost as soft as her skin. As soon as it's lowered, she thanks me without turning around and slips into her room, closing the doors behind her.

I swear under my breath, and storm to my room. I shut the door and lean against it, my adrenaline still raging. My brain is scrambled, warring between the desire I felt in that moment with Edina and the need to protect her. I shed my jacket, yank off my tie, and start undoing the cufflinks on my shirt.

What's happening? Devorah's voice rings out in my head and makes me wince. I'm not in the mood to deal with her. *Where are you? Gwyneira's head is about to pop off and Puck looks like he went two rounds with a dragon.*

I swear again and pull my shirt over my head, not bothering with the buttons. My skin feels too hot, too tight. Bending over the mattress and breathing deeply, I attempt to slow the thudding of my heart against my ribcage. If Devorah senses my agitation, she'll come up here and start demanding answers.

We're retiring for the evening, I tell Devorah when I get myself under control. *Please apologize to Gwyneira, but it's necessary. Goodnight, Dev.*

But—

For the second time in our lives, I close off the mental connection to my twin, sealing off her means of communication. I'll pay for that later, but I can barely handle my own thoughts right now, let alone my meddlesome sister's.

I finish changing for bed, and gather the comforter and a pillow, ready to spend another night on the floor when there's a soft knock at my door. Edina is there in nothing but a silk tank top and a pair of shorts so short they barely cover anything. The soft pink warms her skin tone, making it look like she's wearing nothing but a blush. We stand there, staring at each other for a moment before Edina wraps her arms around my waist.

"Thank you," she says, as I envelop her in my embrace, hugging her the way I've wanted to all night. When she pulls away, she looks at my ready-to-go blanket and pillow and makes a face. "You're not sleeping on my floor."

"I am, actually." She still has a shell-shocked look about her, but that gets a small smile.

"If you insist on being closer than your room, which I'll point out is literally steps from mine—"

"I do. But go on."

She takes my hand and crosses the sitting room into her room. "Look," she says, pointing to her bed. "I realize sleeping on that side—" she points to one side of her truly giant mattress "—may actually be farther than sleeping outside the door, but it has the added benefit of being, you know, a bed."

"I don't need a bed."

She looks down and starts toying with the hem of her tank, which has ridden up and is exposing her stomach. "I know," she says, her voice so small. "But I don't like sleeping alone." She lifts her sapphire eyes and I'm a goner. How am I supposed to say no to that?

"No funny business, I swear," she adds, lifting her hands in faux surrender. "You can stay on your side; you don't even have to cuddle with me."

"Oh, then no deal," I smirk, and Edina chuckles, wrapping her arms around herself. I jerk my head towards the bed. "Get in then."

She walks over to her side and slides under the massive white fur blanket, and I mimic her on the other side. She curls up on her stomach, so her wings are in the air, and I do the same, so my horns hang over the pillow. "Don't puncture my pillow," she quips and then flicks her fingers to extinguish the lights.

Chapter Sixteen
Edina

I STORM FROM THE ballroom into the servants' hall, gulping down large breaths and trying to get myself together.

"Edina." At the sound of Puck's voice, I start moving, scurrying further down the hall, but he pursues me. Again, he calls my name, and this time the bond between us gives a sharp tug.

"Why are you following me?" I turn in a huff, but every bit of bravado I summoned to ask that question evaporates. Up close, I can see the bags under his eyes, the sharpness of his jaw that wasn't there when I saw him last.

"Just let me explain," he pleads taking a step closer. I back up, but he takes another step. Again, I retreat until my back hits the stone wall. I'm in an alcove, just large enough to fit one person. Puck leans in, bracketing his arms on the wall beside me.

"Puck," I breathe and place my hand on his chest to stop him from advancing further. His heart is hammering. "Leave me alone."

"Edina, please, just let me explain."

Explain.

My throat hitches as my mind narrows in on that one little word.

I'd like to be strong enough not to care why he rejected me, but the truth is, it's been plaguing my every thought. All I've wanted to know is why he said no, what about me made him shatter a bond that's built into the very fabric of our beings. How could he ignore that?

He reaches for me, and I flinch because I know somewhere deep in my soul that if he touches me if I hear his reasoning, I'll forgive him.

I hate that he's made me that weak. That he's turned me into the girl who would willingly overlook the way a man hurt her and run back to him.

But I would.

His palm is so close I can feel the heat radiating off his skin onto my cheek. And then, he's gone, and Eldoris is in his place, his horns extended so he looks like some kind of mythical warrior god. He doesn't even look at me, just body blocks me from Puck, whom he's thrown across the hallway.

And I relax, because I'm safe from making a terrible mistake.

I SIT UP IN bed, hugging my knees to my chest as my brain whirs at a million miles a minute. Last night keeps replaying in my mind. Over and over again I see the desperation in Puck's eyes, the fury shaking Eldoris' limbs. And every time I replay the scene, the idea takes shape. A crazy, stupid idea that would never work.

Except what if it does?

I sip the steaming elderberry tea, which Althea brought the second she saw that I was awake. When I woke, it was from the same dream that always plagues me, but then I drank the tea, and it took the edge off the pain, even if I couldn't get back to sleep.

When the sun finally starts trickling in through the open drapes, Eldoris stirs beside me. I rest my head on my knees and wait. "I can feel you thinking," he says, blinking open those ocean-blue eyes. "Did you sleep at all?"

"A little," I answer honestly. "Better than last night. Not as good as when I was passed out drunk." I smirk to let him know I'm teasing, but his lips purse.

"What's on your mind?" he asks as he rises to a sitting position and retracts his horns.

"I have an idea." He waits for me to continue, but suddenly I can't sit. I get out of bed and start pacing the length of the mattress. "It stands to reason people will have heard about last night."

"They already have. My sister asked if we were okay. She didn't know the details, but everyone knew something was wrong when Puck returned with his jacket shredded."

I nod enthusiastically. That was part of the plan that I needed. "Then...what if we told everyone you reacted that way because...we're actually in love." Eldoris' brows knit. "We never outright said it was a political marriage, it could very easily be a love match. It wouldn't be hard to fool them."

His face softens, and the corners of his lips turn down. "It wouldn't work," he whispers.

"Why not?" I ask, hating how small my voice sounds.

"Because no one has seen us together." He swipes his hand down his face.

"We can say we were keeping it quiet. Seeing each other in secret because our courts have been at odds, and we weren't sure—"

"Edina," Eldoris is suddenly standing before me, and he grabs hold of my hands, which I didn't realize were shaking. "We'd be found out.

Someone you spent the night with, or someone I was on a mission with would debunk our story. There are too many pitfalls."

I release a breath, my shoulders sinking. "You're right," I extract myself from his hold. "You're right, it was a stupid idea. I shouldn't have mentioned it."

Eldoris gently grabs my chin and tilts my face up so I'm looking him in the eye. He studies me, his eyes leaving no feature of my face unexplored, and I can't help the wobble of my lower lip.

"You want to make Puck jealous?" he asks, and I shake my head as much as I can in his hold.

"I want to make him hurt," I reply, my voice dark and rough around the edges. "I want him to hurt more than I've ever wanted anyone to hurt. And I'm not a docile person. I've wanted to kill before, but I want worse for him. I want him to know one fraction of the pain he's caused me."

I expect Eldoris to back away or react horrified. He's always been kind to me, almost gentle.

The smile he gives me is not gentle. It's one of a warrior who's set his sights on the enemy.

"They won't believe we're in love," he says slowly. "But they might believe we're falling in love."

I blink, unsure if I heard him right. "You want to...fake fall in love?"

He shrugs. "I think it could work. And if it doesn't, we'll let it fizzle."

I think this idea is crazier than mine. I've seen people fall in love, both in person and on television, but can we replicate it enough that people believe it? And could we pull this off without one of us getting hurt?

Okay, can we pull this off without me hurting Eldoris? My heart is too battered to get hurt, and I like Eldoris enough that I wouldn't want to break him.

"To be clear," I press, "we wouldn't actually fall in love. We would just go through the motions." He nods and releases my jaw but takes my hands in his again. "We'd have to make it believable."

"Yes."

"Which means at some point, we'd need to be physical."

"Such a tragedy," he smirks, and I bite my lip.

"If you're doing this as a way to have sex with me, you could have just asked." His laugh is loud and full and is impossible not to join in.

"Good to know," he says, eyes twinkling. I'm brought back to the moment we met when our chemistry was undeniable. One dance and I was ready to go off with him, and I know he felt the same. There is no doubt people would believe we were attracted to each other, or even making the best of our situation, but for this to work, they need to believe we're in love.

"We'd need to take it slow," I say. "The slow burn to end all slow burns. The kind where main characters don't get together until the final season."

"I have no idea what that means."

"It's a television reference. It means we need to have steps. Super subtle, increasingly more adorable steps."

"I can do that."

"And we'd have to be completely committed, even when we're alone."

"The pixies find out everything," he agrees. "So, our steps should include private moments when we know they're listening."

Eldoris smiles. "This is crazy," I say.

"Possibly." His hands are still holding mine, his thumb brushing over my knuckles in a soothing motion.

"Why would you agree to this?"

He takes back his hand and runs it through his curls. "You're agreeing to marry me for eternity for the sake of our courts," he says with a sigh. "You get almost nothing from our arrangement."

"And you do?"

"More than you know." He steps back and holds his hands out. "So, if you want to hurt him, then I'm your weapon."

"Fuck, that's hot," I breathe, and again Eldoris laughs, but I wasn't kidding. That statement made every inch of my body feel alive with electricity, little shocks seeming to gather in my core. "Promise you won't hate me when I don't fall for you."

"Edina, all I expect from this marriage is a partnership. All I hope from this marriage is friendship...with maybe some benefits." I chuckle. "I won't fall in love with you."

"I won't fall in love with you," I challenge, and stick out my hand to shake his. "This is the way humans seal a deal."

"I'm aware. You know I've spent some time with humans." He takes my hand.

"And yet you didn't understand the television reference."

"Forgive me. When I'm in the mortal realm, I don't waste time watching entire catalogs of television shows."

"That was literally my favorite hobby." We're still holding hands. I release it and step back. "So, breakfast this morning..."

"Should be step one," he says. "We have an entire calendar full of events coming up, and those should be where we make the biggest steps forward in our plan. If we take these steps in front of the soldiers, the gossip won't reach as far as if we do it in court."

"And those steps are?"

There's a knock at the door, and we both jump. "Step one," Eldoris says hurriedly, "is intrigue. That's all you have to do, act like you're confused and intrigued by my reaction last night."

"Not even a lie," I admit. "I'm deferring to you on this, by the way. I only know the steps second-hand."

"You've never fallen in love?" he asks as I cross the room.

"Once, and look how that turned out for me," I gesture wide, and Eldoris frowns. I don't give him a moment to answer when I throw the door open, drop my silencing spell, and regard my lady's maids.

"Good morning, Princess," Brigid says icily. She assesses me with sharp scrutiny, and when nothing seems amiss, she flashes a smile full of sharp teeth. "You appear well."

"Much better, thank you."

Both sets of eyes leave me and look at the bed, where Eldoris, who was on his feet moments ago, is now lying under the covers...shirtless. "Morning ladies," he croons and gets out of bed. He's kept his pants on, but every inch of chiseled, inked perfection is on display. I'm pretty sure drool comes out of my open, gaping mouth, but my eyes are questioning, because we just agreed to take things slow.

"You...stayed in here, General?" Brigid asks, and then very noticeably sniffs, like she's trying to smell if we had sex.

"Yes," he says simply. "Edina asked me to stay after the events last night." He fetches his shirt and throws it over his shoulder as he walks over. "I'll let you get ready. We'll walk down together?"

I nod, completely mute, and Eldoris flashes me a smile before crossing the sitting room to his bedroom. All three of us watch him go.

"Fake fall in love?"

I stare into the handheld mirror that holds the image of my best friend. Her chestnut hair is piled on top of her head, and her skin is dewy and red. Judging by the strap that looks like a sports bra, I caught her in the middle of a training session. Katie is the strongest witch in the entire realm, and she still trains like she's got something to prove. It's one of the reasons the soldiers she commands respect her so much.

"That's about the size of it." I'm hiding in the bathroom with about a hundred wards surrounding it so that no one will hear our conversation during my mandated check-in call. Not that I mind it, I'd use every excuse I have to talk to my best friend.

"How do you fake fall in love?" she asks, her auburn eyes narrowing the way they do when she's devising a strategy.

"I was hoping you'd have some ideas," I say. "I wanted to pretend we were in love this whole time—"

"But people wouldn't believe that." The hand not holding the mirror comes to rest on the junction of her neck and shoulder, giving me a glimpse of her tattooed ring finger. "Well...what kind of romance are you pretending to have?"

I look at her like she's crazy, so she keeps going. "Are we talking intense, passionate love? You know...screaming, crying, and kissing in the rain kind of love."

"That sounds like a lot of work."

"It is," she says and shudders. "The most believable for you both would probably be a friends-to-lovers situation."

"You read too much."

"My obsession with romance novels is going to help you here," she laughs. "But fair warning, every fake dating book I've ever read ends with the fakers in love for real."

"Not gonna happen," I say. "His mate died. Mine is annoyingly alive. This is just about revenge."

"Mhm," she intones.

"Oh," I start, pivoting the conversation away from that minefield. "Eldoris found this tea that's been helping with the pain. It's only like a *six* today, and I'm sober."

"Holy shit, E. That's amazing." Katie's face splits into a smile, and then she says, "So, he just *found* this remedy?"

"He asked the Princess of the Day Court, who apparently studies healing compulsively even though she's the biggest bitch I've ever met—and why are you looking at me like that?" I ask because her expression has morphed into that of a cat who's got the cream.

"I'm not looking at you in any way." I arch an eyebrow. "That was just really nice of him. Shows he was thinking of you."

"Not all Fae are self-centered assholes," I retort, knowing exactly where she's going with this and wanting to put a kibosh to it right away.

"When I saw you last you didn't think that." She smirks. "No, but seriously, I'm glad he's taking care of you. And I know it's only been a few days there, but you already look better."

"As opposed to the steaming pile of trash I was when I visited? Thanks," I deadpan, but I know she means well. It comes from a place of love.

Katie looks off to the side, and I recognize her partner's deep baritone voice saying something before her expression turns heated. "Ew!" I call, pulling her attention to me.

"You didn't hear him."

"I'm assuming." We both laugh. "Go get some sex, I can call you again tomorrow."

"He can wait, this is your time."

"I don't have any more gossip for you, but I can tell you about the hellfire bullshit we're facing." Her face pales, but she nods, and I tell her of my trip to the village. "We'll head out and meet up with some soldiers soon to try and track down the Fae who are draining the children."

"It's a smart idea, moving them all into the palaces," she praises. "Very strategic, but also will gain you a lot of clout with the people. Very princess-ly."

"I learned from the best," I say, and she rolls her eyes at me. "I should go, I have an engagement brunch thing." I wrinkle my nose.

"Love you," she says.

"Love you most." And then, to her partner, who I know is lingering nearby but out of the picture, I call, "Love you a moderate amount."

"Feeling's mutual, E," he laughs.

"Take care of our girl," I say, and wave my hand over the mirror. The picture of the two of them kissing crystalizes and then turns back into my reflection.

Chapter Seventeen
Edina

THE ENGAGEMENT—BETROTHAL, WHATEVER—BRUNCH WAS more
of the same, but this time, instead of standing at the stairs for our receiving line, we stood in front of my mother's dais where she could *keep an
eye on us*. At least it made the process go faster. My mother is incredibly
impatient and shooed people along after a few seconds.

Pretending to be on the cusp of a budding friendship with Eldoris
wasn't difficult. He's easy to get along with, and I found myself having
fun with him. Before each new well-wisher, he'd lean in and whisper little
comments about them, telling me hysterical anecdotes from parties of
years past. More than once I had to stifle laughter before speaking.

When the receiving line is finally gone, I grab his arm and tow him
toward the food. "I need sugar if I'm gonna deal with this any longer," I
laugh as I beeline toward a platter of sugar-crusted scones.

"Might want to lower your voice," he chuckles, clearly not bothered
that I've just offended any Fae in the area. Not that any of them would
say anything to a princess, though one female in a gaudy floral dress does
look mildly affronted.

"I'm sure I've said worse."

"Can you really not remember anything from when you were drinking?" he asks, ignoring my self-deprecating humor and going straight to concern. I've noticed he does that a lot. He'll enjoy and even match my sarcasm, but anytime I make a joke at my own expense, he gets very serious. It would be admirable if the humor wasn't my self-defense mechanism.

"Pieces," I say, stuffing a scone into my mouth, hoping he'll let it go with that. Of course, he doesn't and just waits for me to finish chewing. "I perfected the art of blacking out. So, I have flashes of parties, bars, sex... but no specifics."

The admission sits between us for a moment before he says, "Taverns. Bar is a human term."

"That was your takeaway?"

"Edina, I lost years after my mate died," he says, leaning in close. "Just because I lived like a hermit during that time doesn't mean I remember it. I'm not going to fault you for doing what you needed to survive, but I'm glad you're moving on from that period and into—hopefully—better times."

I stare at him, momentarily stunned. Mentally, I know Eldoris is accepting and supportive, but I keep forgetting what it's like to talk to someone who's been there. It's refreshing and makes the weight on my shoulders a little bit lighter.

"Are you ready for our trip?" Eldoris asks after I spend a few moments gawking at him, and again I'm left stunned that he knows exactly when to change the subject.

Tomorrow, we're leaving to meet up with one of Eldoris' informants in the Spring Court, but other than that he's been cagey about the details.

"My lady's maids will be joining us," I say. Brigid and Althea were less than thrilled to be coming on the road with us, but my mother insisted. "So that's happening."

"That's good, an extra layer of protection," he says, and I arch an eyebrow. "Don't underestimate pixies. They're little, but their teeth are sharp and they're vicious."

"Oh, I know," I muse, grabbing another scone before we start ambling back to the dais. I've seen my lady's maids fight each other, and as a bystander, I was terrified. "But it will make it hard to do anything secretively."

"Don't worry," he smirks, and places a hand on my lower back, steering us over to a small group that's close to the dais, but not on it. "Have you met everyone?" he asks in my ear.

I recognize Larisa and her boyfriend—whose name I don't know—in matching outfits of gold. *Swear to the goddess he's in a gold suit.* Devorah is resplendent in a silver gown that looks molten against her skin, and I vaguely recognize the male with blue hair so dark it's almost black who greeted us last night before Puck arrived, but I don't know his name.

"This is Izar," Eldoris says, and the blue-haired male dips his head in acknowledgment. "Prince of the Night Court. His brother is King Zahir." He gestures to the dais. King Zahir and Izar have the same broad build and beige skin, but Zahir has long, flowing white hair, and curled horns that remind me of a ram protruding from the top of his head.

"Where's your sister?" Eldoris asks Izar in greeting, and the male just shrugs.

"Hiding, I'm sure," he says, his voice melodic and sweet, and reminds me of a siren.

"You know Larisa," Eldoris points to the honey-blonde, "and her lover Behar." *Ah, that's his name.* "And you remember Devorah. And this," he points to a burly male with warm chestnut hair that sticks out in all directions and a bushy beard that matches, "is Radley, Prince of the Autumn Court."

"It's nice to finally meet you, Edina," he says. "We met the night of your party, but only briefly."

"We danced." I remember feeling small in his arms even though he's an inch or so shorter than me. The best way I can describe it was feeling like I was wrapped in a warm hug while we danced.

"That's right," he says, a full smile breaking out on his face. His smile is the kind that promises fun and makes you want to smile too. "Though you weren't nearly as taken with me as you were with this one." He jabs Eldoris in the side, and we exchange a glance. Taking the opportunity to play up the ruse, I look away shyly, or what I hope appears shy. I haven't acted demure a day in my freaking life.

"It's nice to meet all of you...again," I say and that earns me a few nods of approval.

"Of course, darling," Devorah says, snagging me around the waist and tugging me away from her brother. "You complete our little group. We have a full set now...if you count Puck." I try not to bristle at the name. He hasn't arrived at the brunch today, but Titania is here so I assume he's still on the palace grounds. "But who does?"

"Sorry, what group?" I ask.

"We're the second generation," Devorah explains. "The monarch's children."

"Zahir was too, but he graduated to monarch, so we don't include him," Izar quips.

"Wait. Puck is Titania's child?" I screech, and everyone laughs.

"No, which is why he really doesn't count," Devorah continues. "But he was born around the same time as the rest of us, so we invite him to the occasional group event."

So I'll be seeing him more. Perfect.

"We can ditch him if you'd like," Radley offers. "He's been a bore since he started fucking—" Izar smacks him in the gut, causing him to double over with an *oomph.*

"Not necessary," I shrug, glad I didn't have to hear the end of that sentence. I meet Eldoris' gaze and it's clear he wants to tug me out of his sister's grip, but I get the feeling one doesn't toy with Devorah when she's taken it upon herself to befriend someone.

"So, are you planning a long betrothal?" Larisa asks, her voice dripping in disdain and her features pinched in a way that makes her look like she's smelling bad cheese. I really don't know what the hell I did to her to make her hate me.

"We're not in a rush," Eldoris supplies.

"Makes sense. Draw it out, get the most out of the alliance before either of you is forcibly bound with magic." She turns to me with a placating look. "Did you even know that's what a Fae marriage entails?"

"Larisa," Eldoris barks.

"What? It's not a secret she was raised in the mortal realm and hasn't done much since arriving. Unless you count the entire lesser Fae population."

There's a collective gasp amongst the group. I get the impression their shock isn't about my virtue, but the insult she just used.

"Enough," Eldoris says, but Larisa is undeterred.

"Has she even left Winter Court? I know she didn't attend the party I threw celebrating our success in the Witch War, even though she was the one who insisted we fight." She flips her honey-colored hair.

"Leave her be," Behar says softly, but loud enough for everyone in our circle to hear. The look she gives him is murderous.

Larisa opens her mouth to speak, but then a male voice behind me says, "Hi."

Everyone turns, but I don't need to. The hair on the back of my neck is sticking up, my entire body erupted in goosebumps just from the sound of one word. Devorah tightens her grip on me, and Eldoris not-so-subtly takes a step closer.

"I just wanted to say goodbye, and I'll see you all for the joust," Puck says. I give him my profile. I did tell this little group that I didn't want them to kick Puck out because of me, the least I can be is civil.

The skin under his eyes looks bruised, but that's not what's disconcerting. His eyes are dull like the mischief that drew me to him has been leeched from his soul.

"Puck," Titania's voice is like a whip cracking, it makes everyone in our circle flinch. "I thought you were heading back to the palace to attend to the festival details."

"Yes, Your Majesty," he says. He looks like he's trying to summon some of that zest for life he has, but it falls flat. Titania notices. "I was just making sure everyone had our invitation to the joust."

"Of course, they do," she waves a dismissive hand. "Off you go." He walks out the doors without a backward glance.

Titania, wearing a pastel pink dress that does nothing to flatter her coloring, gives us a fake smile. "As future heirs to the thrones...well, most of you," she shoots at Eldoris and Izar, "I would expect you to mingle with some of the dignitaries at this event. Not huddle in the corner of the ballroom like sullen teenagers."

She turns on her heel and retreats to the dais, where the other monarchs are watching us with disapproving looks.

"Bitch," Radley breathes. His father, the King of Autumn Court, scowls in his son's direction. They look a lot alike, same chestnut hair, broad muscles, and unruly beard, but the king is a brownie, so he's far shorter.

"Let's dance," Eldoris says to me and offers his hand. I gratefully take it, happy not to socialize with *dignitaries*, and let him lead me to the center of the dance floor.

Because it's the afternoon, the orchestra is playing background music, and no one is dancing. I'm about to point this out to Eldoris when he motions to the conductor and they start playing a lively dance I recognize from my lessons with my fathers when I first arrived in Faerie. "Do you know these steps?" he asks.

"Maybe."

"Follow my lead." And then we're off, whirling around the floor in a flash of movement that's so quick it steals my breath and makes me laugh. I follow him, my feet remembering the steps even when my brain can't keep up. I'm vaguely aware of a few couples joining us on the floor, but I do my best to focus on Eldoris and act enamored by him.

The next song is slower, and Eldoris pulls me closer and minimizes our movements. It reminds me of a box step in a waltz, but more contained and without the turning. "Everyone is watching," he says, gazing at me with a myriad of emotions.

"Is there something I should be doing?" I ask, and he shakes his head.

"We're keeping it simple, remember? Intrigue."

"Right." I lean in a little closer. "You know, when I told my friend of our plan, she said people may believe us more if we pretend to be, and I quote, 'friends to lovers.'"

"Makes sense."

"You know what that is?"

"It's pretty self-explanatory, Edina. We become friends, and then bait people with the idea that we're falling in love."

"That's pretty much the gist." I sigh, looking away from him and catching Radley and Izar laughing with a group of females.

"What is it?" Eldoris asks, following my gaze.

"I just...I could use some friends here. *Real* friends. All my friends are in the mortal realm."

"You have me," Eldoris says like it's the most obvious thing in the world. Like we didn't just start talking two days ago. "And Devorah. She's insistent that you'll be the best of friends. And the rest of the second generation likes you."

"Larisa excluded."

"She's a pain in the ass," he says, and I can't help but laugh. "And she's always been close to Puck, or was before..." I let him trail off, knowing he's alluding to how he was before he was with Titania. I might not know the details, but from what I've gathered, Puck has changed a lot since his involvement with the queen.

"Give her time," Eldoris continues. "She'll come around."

"I don't need her approval," I say, replaying her accusations in my mind. "Who are lesser Fae?" I ask, and Eldoris stiffens beneath my fingers.

"Larisa said—"

"She shouldn't have," he snaps, making me balk. "It's not a term that's used anymore, but it used to mean those who didn't have elemental magic."

"Like necromancers?" I ask.

"As well as those who can shift forms, like sirens and werewolves. Their magic was distrusted because the 'Noble Fae' didn't understand it, but it hasn't been that way since before I was born. Now, the only people who cling to those notions are ostracized. Larisa will be punished for her comment, I'll make sure of it."

"You take this personally," I murmur.

"I'm half-human," he says, his hands on my back gripping me a little tighter. "I wouldn't exist if people clung to the old ways."

The music changes again, and he gives me a small smile. "This is too serious a conversation to have when we're supposed to be flirting. Pretend I said something funny." I laugh way too loudly, so much so that everyone in the vicinity turns to look at us. "We're in trouble if that's the extent of your acting skills," he teases. The challenge sinks into my skin, my competitive nature flaring to life.

I take a step closer and look up at him through my lashes. "Maybe I just need more warning." My hand trails from his shoulder to the lapels of his jacket where I toy with the material. I use my grip to pull him down as I press up on my toes to whisper in his ear. "Better?" I ask. When I pull back, I go close enough that his beard brushes against my cheek.

"Better," he murmurs and flashes me a roguish grin before he starts spinning me around the dance floor.

This time, my laughter is genuine.

THE BRUNCH ENDS AND everyone retires to their rooms for the late afternoon until the next ball starts tonight. I don't know how they do it. Being around people for that much time is exhausting when you need to put on a persona. Everyone expects me to be the powerhouse future queen, to be as cold as my mother.

That's not me. Not even remotely.

Don't get me wrong, I use sarcasm as a defense mechanism the same as any other born-and-bred New Yorker, but I'm outgoing. I like talking to people, making new friends, and telling a joke once in a while. But if I'm not glaring daggers in their direction, I get uneasy looks. They don't know how to handle me being my own person.

Everyone except Eldoris. And occasionally Devorah, although I did catch her looking at me with quiet surprise on multiple occasions.

I'm using the time before Althea and Brigid arrive to pack a bag for my trip on the road with Eldoris. A knock on my suite door pulls me from staring at the closet in total dismay, unsure of what the hell I'm supposed to pack. Everything I have is suited to court life, except for my one pair of leggings, which are the thick, fuzzy kind that will make me sweat bullets in Spring Court.

"Come in," I call, flinging magic at the door to open it. Eldoris walks in with a giant rolled-up map in his hands.

"I wanted to show you our itinerary for the foreseeable future," he says, gesturing to the map in his hands. Each court rotates hosting elaborate events, and as royalty, we're expected to attend. The Spring Court is just the first stop on a realm-wide tour that I'm actually excited about.

"Want to join me in the—" he breaks off when I pull out my favorite sweater, judge it, and then toss it on the bed to pack. "What are you doing?"

"Purging," I deadpan. "I've decided anything that doesn't bring me joy is going to be dropped into the sea for the water sprites."

"As long as you have a plan," Eldoris smirks. "However, if you were packing, I would tell you it's not necessary. Clothes in the fashion of the courts will be sent ahead of us, and for the camping trip, we can summon anything we might need."

That makes so much sense I want to punch someone in the face. Eldoris chuckles at my expression and heads back into the sitting room. "Come on," he calls over his shoulder and goes toward the back of the room and into the small dining room attached to my suite.

The desire to keep everything white or gray in the palace didn't extend to the dining room, which is done in creams and browns. I'm not sure what inspired the deviation, but it feels like walking into a sepia-toned picture. *Little victories.*

Eldoris shoots a ball of orange fire into the fireplace, which erupts with warmth in the otherwise drafty space. Above the brick fireplace is a painting rendered from my entrance to my welcome ball. I'm on the balcony in the ballroom, flanked by two of my fathers who look at me with pride, while I gaze out over the crowd gathered with wonder in my expression.

When I arrived in Faerie, I was terrified, but that terror soon faded into a thirst for knowledge. I wanted so badly to understand this place, these people. That's what I remember thinking when I looked at everyone. That I had finally found a place where I belonged.

Puck rejected me a few hours later. Not much else mattered after that.

"You were beautiful that night," Eldoris murmurs. His back is to the painting, instead, he looks directly at me, his ocean eyes seeing straight through to my soul. "So full of life."

"You just wanted to bang me," I joke, brushing aside the uncomfortable feelings that seeing that picture brought up. Eldoris doesn't laugh, he just waits, giving me the space to come up with what I want to say next. "Will you teach me? About Faerie and Fae and...everything I'm missing?"

A small smile stretches across his lips. "I can do that."

I walk over sliding up beside him and look down at the maps he has laid out. "Larisa was right before," I say, taking in the vast expanse of the realm. "I've never left this court."

"Well, this tour will show you everything. From the palaces to the taverns, from the ocean to the mountains. I hope you're ready."

And I am. I'm really ready. I want to meet people who don't belong to the courts, I want to see each celebration and learn why it's celebrated. I want to soak it all up like a sponge.

"Can we go to the ocean first?" I ask. I've been to the coast in the Winter Court, but it's not the same. There's a cliffside that leads to a shore of obsidian rocks, and a sea so cold even my tolerance was tested after a few minutes. I would kill to be on a beach that's warm.

Eldoris ponders. "We're needed in Spring Court," he says, and I fight hard to not show him how disappointed I am.

"That's okay. We'll get there eventually."

He frowns but draws my attention to the map that's unfurled on the table. It's a map of the entire realm, depicted with forests, meadows, and mountain ranges.

"Wait. Did you say camping?" I ask. He points to a forest in the Spring Court that borders a large meadow. But that's not what draws my attention. In the center of the meadow is a large black spot and leading from it, a very faint brown line that branches off into every court in the realm.

Eldoris surrounds us in a magical shield, keeping our words private. "This is where we'll meet my contact," he says, and then he explains the plan.

Chapter Eighteen
Eldoris

"TELL ME WHY WE'RE not teleporting directly to Spring Court," I ask as Edina and I exit the palace and walk down the cobblestone pathway through the grove of white-barked trees. Their limbs are ripe with bright red faerie apples that pixies are collecting to export to the other courts. When I link her arm in mine, the pixies pause their work and start chattering amongst themselves. In a few hours, the entire realm will hear about this small action, which would normally drive me crazy but works to our benefit now. "Why do we need to use the portal?"

Edina glares at me from over her coffee cup that's piled so high with whipped cream that the lid doesn't fit. She's wearing a short-sleeved tunic this morning in Seelie Army brown, which floored me when she first emerged from her room this morning. I'm just not used to it; I've only ever seen her in cooler tones. At least that's what I'm telling myself. It has nothing to do with the fact that she's in my army's colors. Nothing at all.

"Because each court is paranoid and has wards surrounding their territories," she drones. "Each ward is different, but they all prohibit teleportation from the outside in."

"Correct. And why are you teleporting us to the portal?"

"Remember all the good times we had before I asked you to be my tutor?" she deadpans. Snow falls lazily around us, sticking to our hair and clothes, and while I'm freezing, Edina is unbothered. "Winter Court's wards are notoriously strict. They make it so no one can teleport unless they are from Winter Court. Because my mother is insane."

"But safe," I reply, happy with her progress. We spent several hours before the ball going over all the details she would need to know for this mission, and then some more in the dark from opposite sides of her bed. She may gripe about it now, but her desire to learn is palpable. "No one has successfully breached the Winter Court's defenses in a long time."

Edina scoffs. "I hate how vague you all are with time. A *long time* could be three hundred or three thousand mortal years ago."

I shrug. "We're immortal. Time is limitless. Fae only started keeping track of the passage of time since we discovered the mortal realm, and that's only because we left for a bit and when we returned, all the humans we dealt with were dead." She rolls her eyes. "You'll see, it'll happen for you too."

"Still fucking weird. If I asked you how old you are...do you even know?" I have a ballpark, but something in my gut tells me Edina would panic if she learned I was over five hundred mortal years old. She takes my silence as confirmation. "You must think I'm a child."

"You've emerged," I respond. "Age stops mattering after a Fae emerges."

We reach the end of the walkway and Edina prances ahead, waving to the guards at the wall as they open the gates for us. They salute and I watch as their cold faces soften. I don't think she even realizes the effect she has on people, on how much they love her even after such a short time.

"Come on, teach," Edina calls over her shoulder. "We've got criminals to hunt down."

I jog until I'm by her side, and she very calmly laces our fingers together. Her eyes meet mine as snow begins to swirl around us and her magic begins to press in, squeezing us until the palace fades and we're teleported to the middle of a tundra.

"You took me to the bad portal," I joke as the wind whips around us, tugging at my tunic. Edina's hair floats around her face like a halo and she points to a small cabin that blends into the white backdrop.

"How do you even know there's another portal?" Edina asks with a teasing smile.

"Everyone knows there's a Seelie and an Unseelie portal."

Edina manipulates the snow around her, creating a bubble that's impervious to the wetness and she beckons me into it. When I'm out of the elements, I call my fire to the edge of my skin, just enough to give us a little warmth as we trudge through the snow toward the cabin.

"The other portal is in a tavern," Edina says. "And the last time I was there, I slept with the owner. I figured parading my betrothed inside would be in poor taste."

"That's fair." I reach for the cabin door and yank. It almost flies off the handle, but I keep hold of it and usher Edina inside, following before I magic the door back in place.

The cabin is made of the same white-barked wood that was in the grove, and poorly constructed enough that the wind trickles through gaps in the walls. There's no furniture, no decorations, just a colorless room with two doorways, the one we came through and the other that emits a blueish-purple mist.

"Spring Court, here we come," she says, crossing the worn floorboards to the portal entrance.

"What is a portal?" I ask, and Edina whines as we step into the mist, closing the door behind us, and hurtling through space.

"An entrance to a ley line," she says. "And before you ask, a ley line is a natural stream of magic that can be traveled along. There are more in Faerie than in the mortal realm, but they exist there too. Fae can open entrances to the ley lines wherever they please, though most entrances have been around for millennia."

"Brilliant," I say, and though she pretends to hate it, she preens under the praise. In seconds, we approach an ornate wooden door covered in vines with thorns sharp enough to skewer a smaller Fae that will lead us to the Varesen Forest in the Spring Court. It's the closest portal entrance to where we're going.

I let it pass. Edina looks at me curiously, but we keep hurtling forward until we reach another doorway. This one is so non-descript that it's almost undetectable save for the heat emanating from the mist. "Here," I say, bending my knees. Edina follows suit, and we both dive off the ley line into the doorway.

We emerge in the dark of a cave. "Where—" Edina starts, but I grab onto her hand and teleport us away before she can register the heat or see beyond the dark rock walls. My magic wraps us in a warm embrace, squeezing and depositing us on a pink sand beach that's surrounded on three sides by jungle vegetation.

A soft breeze blows, dissipating the humidity and making the sun overhead feel less unrelenting. The crash of the surf and the squawking of gulls are the only noises that filter to us in this private oasis. The cove is close to my palace, but far enough away that we won't be bothered by over-ambitious servants or courtiers. It's tucked away, shielded by the thick trees.

It's my own little paradise. A place only a few know of.

Edina gasps, her hand flying to her mouth as she takes in the scenery. The water is a swirling mix of aquamarine and azure that glitters under the golden sunlight. Pearlescent shells dot the shoreline like hidden diamonds in the rose-gold sand. In the distance, flashes of crimson and violet tails splash, frothing the surface white as water sprites enjoy their vacation from the cold temperature of their home in the Winter Court.

"You wanted the ocean," I murmur.

"I thought we didn't have time—" Edina is drawn to the water, her body swaying toward it unconsciously as she stares out at the horizon.

"I made some adjustments."

Her eyes fill with tears, little frozen droplets sticking to her lashes before she launches herself into my arms. No sooner than I return her embrace does she break away and run toward the ocean with laughter that carries on the sea breeze. She dives straight into the water, staying beneath the surface for such a long time I'm almost concerned for her safety. When she emerges, she's laughing in pure, unadulterated glee.

"You coming in?" she calls, her tunic clinging to her body as she bobs along with the waves.

"If I come in, will you ever get out?" I ask, and she laughs again, and the sound makes me feel lighter, like I'm floating beside her even with my feet firmly on the ground.

I take a seat on the sand, digging my hands beneath the sunbaked surface to the cooler grains and letting them sift beneath my fingers as I watch Edina alternate between floating along with the waves and diving beneath their depths. I've seen her thrive in the snow and ice, but this...she was made for the ocean. For *my* ocean.

I'm transfixed by her.

Finally, she emerges from the sea, looking like a siren as she wrings out her hair naturally before using her magic to dry herself off. Her smile is infectious as she comes over and hugs me again. "I'm not sure what I did to deserve you as a friend," she murmurs, and my throat tightens. I don't answer, I'm not sure I could if I wanted to, but I hold her tighter.

"Thank you," she says, breaking away and flashing me another grin. "Now, let's get to work. We don't have time to dawdle." Her musical laughter wraps around us tighter than my magic as I teleport us back to the portal entrance.

"It was worth it," I whisper, low enough that she doesn't hear it as we step back into the mist and head toward the Spring Court.

THE PORTAL SPITS US out into an old oak tree with an archway carved into the bark. I swing the door closed behind us and Edina regards the knot that serves as a doorknob. "Curiouser and curiouser."

I chuckle and she spins back to me, amusement lighting up her features. "You recognize that quote?" she asks.

"I spent about fifty years in the mortal realm," I tell her. "I came across *Alice in Wonderland.*"

"You're maddeningly inconsistent with your pop culture references."

"Apologies. I'll do better."

I gesture ahead before taking a few steps into the enchanted forest. The trees all seem to lean closer, their thick branches bending and swaying as if to get a better look at us. One gets so close to Edina that it drops a hunter-green leaf in her hair, but when she brushes it away and turns to look, they snap back to attention. The wind rustles through the leaves, bringing their laughter as they welcome us into the court.

The light that filters through the canopy catches on dew drops and makes the entire place seem to glow. Patches of neon pink and yellow wildflowers emit a sweet scent that mixes with the earth and wraps around us. The flutter of wings is soft along the breeze, and for once, the chatter of the smaller Fae that live in these woods can't be heard. It's as though they're trying to make a good impression on the princess.

Edina studies a bright red and white toadstool that grows around a tree so large three males couldn't wrap their arms around its trunk. She places her hand on the rough bark and hums. "I forgot..." she swallows. Her gaze bounces between the different trees, taking in the array of green and brown that ranges from lime to shamrock, from taupe to coffee. She watches an iridescent worm as it inches its way up a tree before disappearing into a microscopic hole.

"I guess it's easy to forget how much color is in Faerie when you're stuck in the Winter Court." Birds chirp and Edina tilts her head to the sky. "I was here once."

"Not here," I assure her. "Puck's treehouse is on the other edge of the meadow, close to another portal entrance. You wouldn't have been this deep into the court."

Edina's shoulders deflate, and a breath leaves her lungs. I'm not sure if it's relief or disappointment, but I don't press. We walk a few more steps when I realize the forest around us has gone quiet. I hold up a finger, and Edina uses her magic to form an icicle so sharp it's practically a spear.

A pop sounds, and then a shrill voice screams "Your Highness!"

"Shit," Edina grumbles but drops her weapon into the grass as Althea and Brigid swarm around her, fussing over her ocean-formed waves.

"You left without us," Brigid scowls, wagging her finger in front of Edina as if she were a small child.

"We searched the entire court!" Althea swipes at her forehead. She isn't sweating.

"Well, you found us, so yay..." Edina trails off, letting the sarcasm drip from her words. The lady's maids don't notice.

"We are your personal guides. It is our job to ensure your safety and—"

"I'm perfectly capable of taking care of myself—" Edina interjects, but they ignore her and keep prattling on about how she needs protection.

"Ladies, you're just in time," I drawl, pulling both their focus. "We need to scout the area for a campground where we won't be seen. Have you seen anything that fits the bill while you were searching the entire court?"

Brigid scowls. Althea beams.

"There's a perfect spot, just on the edge of the Varesen Forest," Althea says. "Assuming it will be just us four. If we're meeting an army—"

"No army."

Edina looks at me with a question in her eyes, but I shake my head the slightest amount. Althea and Brigid think we're scouring the area in search of the hellfire Fae, and while that's true, they don't know our true destination.

Our true destination lies in the Etherealia Meadow. Or rather, beneath it. In the Underground.

The Underground is a series of tunnels that span the length of Faerie. They're notorious for housing most of the criminal activity in the realm. It serves as the main highway for faerie dust, certain types of highly illegal and addictive mushrooms, and weapons forged with iron. There are also enough open caverns that people can stay down there if they're being hunted for months without having to resurface.

Most of the Underground is run by the Princess of the Night Court, who has aptly been nicknamed Hades. However, one section remains out of her control, the section under the Spring Court. With Hades' permission, I've searched every inch of the Underground for the hellfire Fae but have come up empty.

This is the last place they could be hiding.

Brigid and Althea fly ahead of us and I slow my steps. Edina follows suit and as soon as the pixies are far enough away, she whispers, "What are we going to do? They won't let me go into the Underground."

I smirk. "What must travelers be careful of when passing through the Etherealia Meadow?"

Her eyes widen. "Poppies. Like in *The Wizard of Oz*."

"Correct," I say. "These poppies may be just a drug for normal-sized Fae, but for pixies, it'll knock them out for hours. Days if we're not careful of the dosage."

"You want to drug my lady's maids?" Edina feigns shock and approvingly scans my body. "I didn't think you had it in you, General."

"You have no idea," I wink.

Chapter Nineteen
Edina

AFTER THE PIXIES SHOW us a place to camp, we scout the Etherealia Meadow and surrounding hills loud enough to draw attention. We want Titania's spies to believe we're searching above ground for the hellfire Fae so that when we approach the tunnels in our disguises later, they won't be suspicious.

Our detour to the Summer Court and the day spent under the spring sun have me feeling more relaxed than I have in years. This quest has not only given me purpose, but I just now realize how desperately I needed the sunshine. I miss the *warmth*. I miss the sun soaking into my skin. I miss the way the breeze doesn't hurt my face but instead brings the scent of flowers.

When the sun sets, we—and by we, I mean Eldoris—set up three tents at the edge of the Varesen Forest. The hum of insects and chatter in a Fae language I don't recognize fills the cooling air. The canopy of trees is just thin enough that I can see stars twinkling in the cobalt sky.

"Are we safe?" I ask Eldoris, who has finished the tents and is manipulating the fire with his magic, so it grows stronger. "The last time I was here, Puck said something about not lingering in the forest at night—"

"Was he trying to get you in bed?" Eldoris asks, handing me a piece of something that looks like jerky.

"Maybe."

He gives me a knowing look. "The creatures who live in this forest are docile...Or they'll be too afraid of us to try anything."

"What's in this tea?" Althea asks. For the first time since I've known them, Brigid and Althea are sitting, rather than hovering in the air. They've claimed a nearby log, perching on the remnants of a branch to give them extra height.

"Do you not like it?" Eldoris asks.

"It makes my mouth taste funny."

Althea's head dips forward and jerks back up as she fights the effects of the poppies.

"Did you—" Brigid slurs. "Did you drug us?"

"What makes you think that?" Eldoris asks with a cheeky smile. Brigid gives him one withering stare before her little frame collapses in a heap right onto Althea. The momentum sends them both tumbling into the brush.

"Oh shit," I gasp, standing and crossing to the spot where they fell. In a heap of wings and limbs, my pixies snoring loud enough to wake the entire forest.

I lift and gently carry them into the tent Eldoris points to, depositing them on miniature mattresses and covering them with miniature blankets. They hum in contentment in their sleep, and then go right back to snoring.

"For tiny creatures, they have some loud sinus issues," I laugh as I emerge from the tent.

Eldoris joins in my laughter as he stands and starts organizing the camp. We hope it will look like we've all gone to sleep after dinner, and no one will question our whereabouts tonight. I enter my tent and send magic at my mattress, fluffing the blanket so it looks like a person is sleeping beneath it.

"I could have used this in the mortal realm when I was sneaking out of my parents' house," I mutter. "Forget pillows."

"Did you get caught?" Eldoris asks, appearing behind me in the doorway of the canvas tent.

"Nah," I smirk, but my light mood is quickly dampened thinking about my biological parents. "They never cared enough to catch me."

"I'm sure that's not true—"

"It is." I turn and pat him on the arm. "But it's in the past."

When everything is in order, he guides me out of the camp, casting protective spells around the perimeter to secure the sleeping pixies. We trudge through the dark forest until we're far from the camp. The moon is high tonight, bathing the trees in an other-worldly glow and illuminating the odd creatures that seem to meld into the trees.

"Dryads," Eldoris says at my questioning look. "Tree Nymphs. They protect the forest. Don't worry, they're loyal to the trees, not Titania. They won't report our position."

When we finally stop in a small clearing, Eldoris says, "How's your ability to glamour?"

I don't answer with words, but I focus my magic on changing my appearance. I feel myself drop closer to the ground, and my back hunches. My usually blonde hair turns thin and gray, and from my creased brow, I can see my nose lengthen and twist until it appears broken.

When I turn back to Eldoris, he's added height and bulk so he's the size of a mountain and has replaced the tribal tattoos that cover his torso with scars. His eyes are more of a muddled slate-blue, and he made his hair long and stringy in the same color that matches his new black, leathery wings.

"The pockmarks are a nice touch," he says, drawing a meaty finger down my cheek, which I've littered with dark age spots and wrinkled so much that it looks like it's about to fall off. I stick my tongue out of the hole in my missing tooth. He procures a black cloak from thin air, and I wrap it around my frame, flipping the hood up so it hides my new face.

"Remember, we need to split up down there," he says, putting on a cloak of his own. "But you'll be meeting a friend." I nod, and we walk out of the forest and into the meadow. The spot where we glamoured ourselves is close to a hill, which we ascend, the long grasses tickling my ankles.

I'm not sure where I expect the entrance to the tunnels to be, maybe in the mouth of a cave or a tree trunk like the portal, but I don't expect it to be in a freaking gopher hole. That's what it looks like, a gopher hole in the middle of an open patch of grass.

"Do we need a story?" I ask, modifying my voice with magic so the sound crackles over the words.

"No." Eldoris' voice is deeper too, and rough around the edges. It adds to his hardened look. "If anyone asks, kill them."

"Okay then." The Fae have a take-no-prisoners attitude, and I get it. If anyone were to recognize us or put together that we're here tonight, not only do we run the risk of the hellfire Fae knowing we're after them, but we will most likely be in a fight for our lives.

"How do we get down?" I ask, staring at the hole that's entirely too small to fit a person. I'm starting to think we should have tapped the pixies for this mission when Eldoris wraps his arms around my middle so my back is to his chest. He jumps in the air over the hole. And then we're falling and it takes everything I have in me not to scream.

We hurtle down an earthen shoot, kicking up dirt and bugs. My elbow smacks against the edge, sending a root scattering down below us, and whatever was living on that root falling in little buggy spirals. Eldoris uses his fire magic to burn them all to a crisp before they can land in my hair.

After what feels like the longest fall ever, we're deposited onto a rock floor. Eldoris dismounts the slide with ease and places me on my feet in front of him. I can tell by the smile he suppresses that I must look even worse for wear, so I fix him with my deadliest glare.

"Keep that face on," he murmurs, and gestures behind me.

I turn and find what, at first glance, appears to be an underground bazaar. Colorful banners hanging above tables line the hallway and Fae of all types browse with shopping bags slung over their arms. It's what the booths are selling that makes it clear this is not above board.

On Eldoris' urging, I walk through the center aisle, past the first table that has little baggies of glowing powder. A too-thin Fae female lovingly fingers a neon-green bag, but the male manning the booth smacks her hand away and hisses about payment. I watch as she teeters into the corridor in front of us, walking past the vendors selling cases of wine, pills that boast they'll boost your magic, a table that's fashioned to look like a tree stump covered with mushrooms, and a booth of glittering scales.

We reach a fork in the earth-carved tunnel with two wooden arrows pointing in either direction. Words in a language I don't recognize are carved into the wood and painted in a red that looks suspiciously like blood.

"It's old Fae," Eldoris says, regarding the sign. "One says *life*, the other says *death*."

"Ominous."

"This is where we split up." He pulls away from me, heading toward the *life* hallway.

"You want me to go into death?" I hiss.

"It's better than life, trust me. Stop at the second table on the left and say, 'I seek revenge so sweet.' The owner will help you."

"This sounds like I'm entering a bad after-school special."

"I don't know what that means."

"Maddeningly inconsistent," I repeat my earlier barb with a sigh. "Is that the friend I'm meeting?"

"No, he'll find you." Without another word, he disappears down the hallway toward *life*. As soon as he takes a step past the archway that separates it from the main hall, several doors swing open. Female Fae in various stages of undress hang in the hallway, calling Eldoris and offering him time for the night.

Some things look the same in every realm.

I recognize the woman from the faerie dust booth in the second door, her shaking intensifying the longer she goes without the drug. I can't stop watching her. How close was I to becoming that? If Katie hadn't woken me up, if Eldoris hadn't found something to help with my pain...

She notices me staring and gives me a wide smile that suggests she used to be stunning. "I can take care of you, mommy."

Very few sexual things can shock me. Being called mommy by a prostitute while in an old crone glamour is one of them.

Eldoris stops halfway down the hall, looking over his shoulder with a stern glare. I shake my head at the girl, who shrugs, and I turn away, ignoring the knot that's formed in my stomach as I head into death. *Will Eldoris actually fuck a prostitute?* Why does that bother me? I'm the one with hangups surrounding monogamy, I should be glad he's seeking other options. He's free to do what he wants.

Even thinking the words leaves a sour taste in my mouth.

The death hallway is exactly what it sounds like. Weapons, poisons, hit men... basically, everything you'd need to induce death. Unlike the life hallway, no one calls out to me when I enter. Instead, they glare and assess, trying to unearth if I'm a narc.

I approach the second table and find a male with a selection of finely made throwing knives. Each handle looks uniquely carved with symbols of the different courts, and I find myself running a finger over the swirling snow pattern of the one closest to me. I could use a dagger. I don't know how to use it, but I feel like having a weapon is always a good thing.

"You gonna buy something or just stroke it?" the male grunts and my head snaps up. He's a short, squat male, with a balding head and a red nose. I sneer, leaning into my character, and he backs down the slightest amount. "What do you want?"

"I seek a revenge so sweet," I reply, fighting the urge to roll my eyes at the corny secret phrase. His ice-blue eyes widen.

"That so?" he regards me, his eyes scanning over my hunched shoulders and toothless grin. "This way then."

He moves quickly, but I keep up as he dodges other shoppers. He slips between two tables, one boasting 'real human firearms,' which has a table of guns that look like they were made around the Revolutionary War, and a man who stands in front of a sign that says, 'Any Fae, any day. Will kill for money.'

The male knocks on the rock wall, and a hidden slat opens, revealing one giant red eye.

Is that a Cyclops? I suddenly feel very unprepared for my task here.

"Yes?" the eye drawls.

"She seeks revenge so sweet," the male escorting me barks.

"You sure she said sweet?"

"I know what she said."

"Your hearing hasn't been the best."

"*She said sweet.*" The bellow is loud enough to draw eyes our way.

"I said sweet," I reply. The eye blinks once, then the slat closes before the entire door swings open.

"Off ye go," the male says, stepping aside for me to enter the unknown room.

Chapter Twenty
Edina

THE MALE GIVES ME a rough shove through the doorway into a small room that smells of earthworms and stale malt liquor. The walls are roughly hewn in the dirt, with sticks and the occasional vine making its way through, but the floors are wooden and even appear to be relatively clean. The bright yellow fae lights make me squint from the relative darkness I just came through, but I notice there's a blind spot in the corner. I think I hear the sound of clashing swords and smell the faint tinge of brimstone coming from that direction, but I can't be sure.

I hiss through my teeth at the male's rough treatment, but the door swings closed, leaving me alone with the cyclops...who isn't a cyclops at all, but a troll whose eyes are so wide set around his bulbous nose that I could only see one through the peephole. He's massive, at least eight feet tall, and his belly sticks out just as far. He wears a loose tunic that must have once been a bedsheet, a loose pair of linen shorts, and a chunky necklace that looks to be made of bones.

The troll scoops his lush, black hair into a ponytail and gestures at the singular table in the room with two seats. I choose the one not made of stone, instead sitting in the smaller, wooden chair, lest the poor thing becomes kindling.

"You're looking for an army," he says, plopping his large frame in the stone chair and jostling the table as he situates his knees beneath it.

I keep my expression neutral except for the raise of my eyebrow. Eldoris said this is the best way to find out where the hellfire Fae are, to act like we want to hire them.

"What could an old thing like you need an army for?" he scoffs, and I bite my tongue to keep from snapping back. "Suppose it's none of my business." He reaches into the folds of the large tunic and pulls out some papers.

"Don't have many that are willing to work on assignments together," the troll continues, shuffling papers around. I very slowly lower my eyes to peek at the papers as he puts them in two distinct piles. They're dossiers on mercenaries. Another glance tells me there's a section on whether they'll work with others or operate alone. "Course for the right amount of coin..."

His eyes meet mine expectantly. I'm still not sure how money works in Faerie, other than the obvious. Gold coins are worth more than silver, which is more than copper, but what they translate to eludes me. I don't know what things typically cost, let alone the cost of a freaking army.

I decide to sidestep the question. "There's a rumor of a very powerful group working together," I say carefully. "A group with...*unique* magic."

"I have a group of necromancers if you're looking for that sort of thing," the troll says. "Otherwise, I can't help you."

"No?" I let my gaze trail over to the shadowy corner, which definitely gives off the smell of brimstone. "Nothing hotter? I'm looking to start a fire."

The troll's widely spaced eyes widen. "Listen," he says, leaning in across the table. His breath smells like rotten eggs. "Even if I did know of a certain group—and I'm not saying I do—who's to say they're for hire?"

"Everyone is for hire," I remark, leaning into the troll's space. "Now why don't you stop wasting my time with talk of necromancers and tell me where I can find them?"

The troll leans back, testing the limits of the stone chair, and then releases a boisterous laugh that shakes the very walls of the room. "You want their handler?" His face goes red from laughter. "You don't know what you're asking." I remain neutral as he dabs his eyes with the bottom of his tunic, showing off his hair-covered belly. "It's your funeral. Stay here, I'll bring her."

He stands, almost upending the table, and walks directly into the shadowy corner, disappearing into its depths. The hair on my arms rises, and I feel a prickling sensation on the back of my neck. I contemplate running, but we need a lead on these Fae. If I can just find out who their leader is or meet someone so we can sense their magical signature, maybe we can track down the rest.

The longer I sit alone, the longer I'm convinced this is a trap.

And then I get an idea. A terrible idea. An idea so stupid it makes me question my competency and my ability to keep myself alive.

Who am I kidding? Of course, I'm gonna do it.

As quietly as I can manage, I push the chair away from the table and stand, making a beeline for the shadowy corner. The darkness creeps over my body, making my skin crawl. I reach a hand out and find a gap where the walls should intersect. I don't give myself time to second guess this colossally stupid mistake before stepping through.

I expect a portal, but it's just a dimly lit hallway. I cast a ball of light in my hand, just bright enough that I can see a row of closed doorways. The doors are all the same, worn wood with varying scuffs, and the walls are the same roughly carved dirt that was in the small room. It feels like a back alley, like the life and death hallways are for show and this is where the really bad crime happens.

I inch down the hall and pause by the first door. The sounds of sex—and not good sex by the fake moans the female is making—come through the door. I move on as she yells something about how big he is, not even trying to put any emotion in her voice. The next room has the sound of clinking glasses, but luckily has a big enough knot in the wood that I can get the tiniest glimpse inside. It's set up like a bar, but I watch as Fae slam back shots of amber liquid and then do a line from the bar top before slamming their glasses back down on the wood.

A large puff of smoke filters through the last door in the hallway, and I slink closer. Sure enough, when I press my ear to the wood, I hear the troll's voice. "Old crone-type. Came in with a beefy younger male who ditched her for the brothel. He's been holed up with Seraphina since."

Acid churns in my belly, but I push it away. Eldoris sent me to find out information, I'm sure he's doing the same. With a prostitute. Named *Seraphina*.

"How much?" the voice that responds to the troll is female and nasally but sounds...forced. Like there's a glamour overtop of her regular voice making it sound different than it truly is. It would make sense for whoever this 'handler' is to use a glamour. I wouldn't be surprised if most of the Fae who come to the underground use glamour to hide who they are.

"I didn't ask," the troll responds, sounding sheepish. The female scoffs.

"Find out," she snaps.

"But you're not taking jobs—"

"Doesn't mean we can't rob her," the female laughs, and I swear I've heard that laugh before. Even with the glamour.

I turn to retreat to the room I came from when something cold and sharp is placed against my throat and a large hand covers my mouth. "Don't make a sound," a low voice grumbles in my ear. "Or I'll have to tell them you were spying."

I raise my hands in surrender, not wanting to give away the type of magic I have or what I can do with it, and let the male prod me forward. He walks me over to a door on the side of the hall I hadn't inspected and pushes me into darkness. With a swear and a snap of his fingers, a brilliantly bright fae light turns on, making me squint until my eyes adjust.

The sight of the room leaves me breathless.

I'm in a nursery. Ten cribs line the walls, each filled with a mewling baby. A dazed woman walks around, depositing bottles in the newborns' mouths and magically keeping them aloft.

"What is this?" I ask. My captor hasn't removed the blade from my throat, but I almost forgot he was there in my shock.

"Who are you?" he demands, ignoring my request. "Why were you spying on that room?"

"I was making a deal with the people inside," I murmur, my eyes latching on one baby who has blonde hair and brilliant blue eyes. "What. Is. This?"

Using a maneuver Katie taught me, I spin out of my captor's hold, knocking the knife free with only a small nick marring my skin. Luckily, it was a steel blade, not iron. I'm still not sure of the effect iron has on Fae, but I've been told to avoid it. The blade goes clattering to the floor, turning the attention of the female attendant. One look at her tells me she's high. She doesn't even know where she is right now, let alone what's going on here.

I draw a knife of my own from thin air and press it against the throat of the male who captured me. He has sickly gray skin and hair that matches, and his black eyes bore into me. "What does it look like?" he sneers, spittle flying from his yellowing teeth. "We're selling 'em. Been in the business since we discovered other realms."

A pit forms in my stomach. "You're selling children?" I breathe. "To the handler?"

He scoffs. "Nah, she needs older kids for her work and doesn't wanna wait for them to grow up. We're selling them to the mortal realm."

Changelings. These children are going to be changelings.

The male laughs. "Don't look so pious," he says. "You're no priestess if you're down here. We all gotta make a living."

"These are purchased already?" I ask, my knife still pressed against his throat. The male clearly doesn't think I'll use it, but I so fucking will. I just want all the information first.

"Why? Ya looking to buy?"

"Maybe," I muse as I look around. "Quite the operation you have here." Any wariness he has of me melts away as I stroke his ego. "You've been doing this since the portals opened?"

"Yes," he puffs out his chest. "Me and my brothers. Though one passed, killed by a *human*." He spits the word. "Some self-righteous bitch with an inflated sense of ego got him when he was making a drop off. Now there are just two of us. My brother handles the procurement, and I handle the sales. The one there is available. The blonde—"

He doesn't finish his sentence as my blade slices across his throat. His mouth opens and closes as blood pours from the wound, coating my hands. He squeaks, and I step back, letting him fall to his knees. I watch as he staggers for a moment before sinking into a heap on the wood floor, his blood pooling out in a dark red circle.

I look up and find the female attendant looking at me with eyes wide. Her magic has failed, sending all the bottles toppling into the cribs and making the children wail.

"He..." she starts shaking violently. "He's..."

The door bursts open behind me and I banish the knife and the blood from my hands as Eldoris steps inside.

Chapter Twenty-One
Eldoris

I GET ONE GLIMPSE of Edina, crone glamour still in place, with a knife in hand and covered in blood before she banishes the evidence into thin air. I'd be proud of her quick thinking if I wasn't in total shock. The corpse of the murdered male is still leaking blood all over the wood floors and behind Edina is a rail-thin female who is high...or in shock. Probably both.

"Holy shit," Seraphina breathes behind me as she enters the space. She pulls the thin robe closer around her and wrinkles her pale nose at the stench of blood. "What did you do girl?"

"Nothing," Edina and the female answer together. Edina's eyes, even in her glamour, are narrowed and filled with loathing toward Seraphina, who doesn't make matters easier as her fangs dip over her pouty, pink lips.

And that's when I notice the rest of the room, which is filled with cribs and crying infants.

"What the hell is going on here?" I demand.

"He was selling them," Edina says, her voice low and crackly and not her own. For a second her eyes flicker, the sapphire blue intense and imploring. "I couldn't just leave them."

The protective part of me wants to pull her into my arms and erase the pain filling her eyes. This is personal for her. Confronting this male, the one who probably stole her when she was a baby, must have been emotional. The pragmatic part of me is screaming that she just fucked us. I have no idea how we're going to get out of here without help.

Turning over my shoulder, I drop my voice to a whisper. "How fast can you get to the Night Court's Underground?"

"Through the tunnels?" Seraphina asks. "Few minutes. Why?"

"We need Hades," I say. Seraphina swears and cinches her silk robe tighter over her chest. "Remind her she owes me a favor."

She purses her lips but snaps her fingers and disappears from view.

"I thought there was no teleporting between courts," Edina says, and when I look back, her glamour is firmly in place.

"Many of the wards don't apply to vampyres."

"Seems like an oversight."

"Are we really going to talk magical prejudices with a corpse between us and a witness behind you?"

Edina doesn't cower, she simply stands as tall as she can in her imposed body and glares at me. "What did you expect me to do?" she hisses. "Leave them? Walk away and forget that they were being sold to humans who would have no idea how to care for them? Let their parents search for them for decades, or worse, mourn their deaths?"

"No, of course not. But what was the plan? How were you going to sneak ten screaming children out of the tunnels?"

"I didn't get that far, clearly," she throws her hands up in the air.

Seraphina throws the door to the room back open and scuttles out of the way, leaving room in the doorway for Hades, Princess of the Night Court and ruler of the Underground. Most of it, anyway. Wearing a tight black button-down and a gray pencil skirt, her black hair is cut to her chin at an angle that accentuates the sharpness of her jaw. She looks around the room with calculating eyes that are such a dark blue they're almost black, and when they fall on me, she arches one slender brow.

"This isn't worth one favor," she says, pursing her red-painted lips that stand out so starkly from her creamy beige skin. I don't break her stare, but even though she barely clears my chest in her black heels, she's still intimidating.

"Hades—" I start, but she holds up a hand and turns to Edina.

"You did this?" she gestures to the body at her feet. Edina straightens and dips her chin in acknowledgment. Hades then turns back to me.

"I'll take care of this in exchange for the favor you owe me, and a favor from your betrothed to be used at the time of my choosing," she says. "Assuming you're in a position to offer that." There's no doubt in my mind that she realizes Edina is the crone in the room, and I'm not sure why she doesn't reveal her identity, but I'm grateful she doesn't. As much as I trust Seraphina as an informant, I wouldn't trust her with Edina's life. And I certainly don't trust the attendant who's shaking in the corner.

"I accept on her behalf."

Beside me, Edina stiffens the slightest amount. Fae take favors very seriously, and I know she's feeling the weight of that. I also know she would have told me to do it. We don't have another choice.

Hades turns on her heel to the attendant, who is actively trying to become one with the wall. "You," she snaps her fingers, and the female stands at attention. "You know who I am?"

"Yes," the girl mutters.

Hades crooks her finger, and as if she's tethered to a string, she walks forward, stopping a few paces away from the ruler of the Underground. Hades circles her, assessing every inch while the female holds perfectly still. Well, as still as she can when she's vibrating with nerves.

"Name?" Hades asks.

"Minthe."

"That your real name?"

"The closest you'll get to my real name," she quips.

"Smart girl," Hades preens, and the girl straightens imperceptibly. Edina exchanges a glance with me across the room, like she's unsure what we're supposed to do in this situation, and I can't exactly blame her. Hades may be one of the second generation, but she's always kept to herself, choosing to avoid her brothers at all costs.

"You have a choice, Minthe," Hades continues. "I can wipe your memory of this incident, give you enough gold for the next fix of whatever you're on, and we'd go our separate ways." The girl tugs a cracked lip between her teeth. "Or you could work for me. Once it gets out that Titania was running a smuggling ring, or worse, it was happening without her knowledge, I'll take over the entire Underground, and I'll need an assistant. But if you work for me, you're clean. I can't have my people slacking on their responsibilities."

Minthe continues to chew on her lower lip, but Hades just cocks her head to the side and waits. It's so unbearable that I almost answer the question for her.

"I'll work for you," she finally says in a soft voice.

"You'll work for me..." Hades crosses her arms over her chest.

"Mistress," Minthe breathes.

"Good girl," Hades says, a very rare, small smile ticking up the corner of her mouth. Then she turns back to me as if the exchange never happened. "Now, we'll need a way to carry these children into my territory."

"Why can't we get out the way we came in?" Edina asks.

"While I *will* run this section, it currently remains under *other* management," Hades says. "And, if I was caught interfering in the operations of this hallway would be very bad for my lifespan."

"There are carriers," Minthe offers. "For the children. In the storage closet across the way."

"Thank you, pet. Would you mind grabbing those for us?" Minthe blushes scarlet and then runs off. As soon as she's gone, Hades turns to Edina. "You should come up with a new glamour. You too, Eldoris." She jerks a hand at me. "There's a very pissed-off troll looking for the princess here."

"Shit," Edina says, and then instantly transforms from an old crone into...well she looks like she could be Minthe's sister. Her hair is dull and lifeless, her eyes are decorated with purple bags, and her cheeks are gaunt. She looks like every other drug-addled Fae in these tunnels.

Hades nods in approval. "I need you to glamour the children in their carriers to look like shopping bags."

"I've never glamoured someone else."

"Then I suggest you practice as long as you can."

Minthe returns and Edina follows Hades' instructions as we load the ten children into carriers. As soon as the children are quieted and packed up, Edina turns to me with a shopping bag hanging from her arm. "Good," Hades says. "Now the rest."

She quickly glamours the rest of the children so it looks like each of us has a shopping bag in each hand. Hades throws a quick glamour over her appearance, and Seraphina follows her example. "When we leave, act like you're supposed to be here," she says. "If they ask, the bags are full of weapons for the Summer Court Queen."

"Why my mother?" I demand.

"Because everyone knows of your hunt of the hellfire Fae, no one will think anything of you buying extra daggers and swords. Any other court and word would trickle up to higher powers and we'll be back at war again."

It's a valid point.

Very slowly, Seraphina pokes her head out of the room and gives us the sign that the hallway is clear. Hades breezes through and the rest of us follow down the dimly lit hallway. Edina spares a glance at the room at the end of the hall, but the door is wide open and the room empty. When she catches me looking, she subtly shakes her head, and her meaning is clear. *Not here. Not now.*

We make it into the main corridor and start at a brisk pace toward the border between Spring and Night Courts. Hades and Minthe are in front, conversing in low voices, and behind us is Seraphina.

"So, what came first?" Edina asks, keeping her voice low. "The Greek god or the Fae?"

Hades' shoulders tense. "Later," I promise. Hades' cooperation in this plan is important, and I'm sure she doesn't want to hear us gossiping.

"Lame," Edina scoffs, and then her body goes completely tense. "El..." she jerks her head forward and blocking the path that will lead us to Night Court is a troll.

"This is the troll you met with?" I mutter, and she nods.

"What's the meaning of this?" Hades asks as we approach. Edina is visibly rattled.

"A friend of the owner's has gone missing," he responds. "We need to do a sweep of this whole area. Let me check your bags."

"You think your friend is in these bags?" Hades scoffs. "We've done nothing wrong."

The troll clicks his tongue. "But you're obviously hiding something."

"Why's that?"

"The glamour. I can smell it."

"Everyone uses glamour down here," Hades brushes him aside, but he steps his large body in her path. "Let. Me. Pass."

He laughs and bends down so he's looking at her. "Or what?"

Fuck, she's gonna do something stupid. Hades is a strategist ninety percent of the time, but the other ten is ruled by her anger. I need to find a way to get these babies out of here before she blows our cover and we're all completely fucked.

"El—" Edina whispers. "Follow my lead, okay?"

She puts her children down, encouraging me to do the same, and then grabs my arm and slips away before the troll notices we're moving. She hides us behind an abandoned tent. "Quick, back to your original glamour." As she speaks, the drug-addict façade fades and she's the old crone again. "Follow me in three seconds."

And then she slips from the tent. "There you are!" she bellows and marches right up to the troll and jabs him in the belly button. "This is how you conduct business? Leave your customers to rot in a room when they're willing to pay for services."

People watching snicker at the innuendo, and the troll sputters. "You—I—"

"I waited forever for you to return from your 'contact.'" The air quotes are a human thing, I have to remember to tell her that. "Who I'm not even sure exists! And now...Now I won't be spending my hard-earned coin with you. No, sir."

"Mother!" I yell and charge after her, remembering my part in this little play almost a moment too late. When I get closer, I realize Seraphina and Minthe have slipped past the troll with their children and are coming back to secure the ones Edina and I left unattended. Clever girl.

Edina turns and I yank her arm back. "Enough," I hiss. "You don't need to be shouting your association with this—" I sneer at the troll, "—for everyone to hear."

She kicks my shin and I inhale...not from pain but from surprise. "Go back to your whores and let me handle the real business." Even through her disguise, her tone turns bratty, and before I realize what I'm doing, I have her chin in between my fingers, squeezing it hard enough that she looks up at me.

"Behave," I growl. She swallows against my hand, her throat working. And then her lips part and her glamour fades just around her eyes, just enough for me to see her pupils are blown. She scrapes at my hand, and I squeeze lightly.

I release her roughly and check that Seraphina is back behind me, without the children. Minthe and Hades have disappeared down the opposite hallway. "Let's go." I wrap an arm around Edina's bicep and tug her back the way we came. She starts protesting, snapping back into character as we hurry to the entrance and back into the spring air.

Chapter Twenty-Two
Edina

ELDORIS MANHANDLES ME ALL the way through the Underground, up the magical tunnel, and across the hills, which does nothing to quell the random uptick in my libido. I was so damn distracted by him holding me by the throat that my glamour slipped...and I once held a glamour during three hours of sex. Adrenaline. That's all this is. The wires in my brain got crossed because we were in mortal danger and sent a signal to my vagina that it was time to throw a goodbye party.

That doesn't explain why I'm still so turned on I can't think straight.

"What the hell happened?" Eldoris demands. "Seraphina was taking me to where the hellfire Fae were last spotted when we heard you. How did you end up in that hallway?"

Right. Serious moment, Edina. Get your shit together and stop thinking about how good it would feel to have Eldoris' hand around your throat while the other—

"Edina."

"Shit, what?" I stammer. Eldoris has dropped his glamour, and his eyes are drinking me in...but not in a sexy way. In an *I'm-con-*

cerned-for-your-mental-stability way. Which is probably good, since I'm still very much disguised as an old lady.

"What happened back there?"

"Where was the friend I was meeting?" I ask instead. "You left me on my own with almost no information on what to expect, and I saw an opportunity to see the handler—"

"He wasn't in the room?" Eldoris asks.

"Unless he was the troll that just tried to kill us. It was just the two of us."

"I'm here." We breach the wards, and Radley, Prince of the Autumn Court, is standing in the middle of our camp. "I was detained. I just got down there when you were being held up. Figured I should leave before they noticed me."

Eldoris strides over to the male and claps him on the back. "It's all right."

"It's not all right," I exclaim, and both men turn to me. Radley scraps a hand through his thick beard, his brown eyes full of remorse, but Eldoris still looks furious. "And doesn't he like...play for the other side?"

"Sexually? I play on all the sides," Radley winks and if I wasn't all pent up and coming down from the scare of that situation, I'd find that funny. "Politically, I'm on the side of us all not dying in a fiery blaze."

"Radley has been helping me," Eldoris says. "Especially when I can't get away from the army. He's been a mole in the Spring Court Underground."

"Second-generation loyalty and all that," Radley adds. "And if I stay home for too long, my father starts bitching about the fact that I'm unmarried."

I plop down on a log by the fire, which is still burning strong thanks to Eldoris' magic, and push the heels of my hands into my eyes. Exhaustion is catching up to me, but the events of the day still have me feeling jittery. I let my glamour fall, sighing as my spine straightens from its hunched position. I need a bath or a massage...or an orgasm.

"Want to explain how you uncovered a changeling operation?" Eldoris asks, sitting beside me.

"What?" Radley asks.

I quickly catch them up on what happened when I left Eldoris, telling them about the meeting with the troll and how I snuck down the hall to eavesdrop.

"You heard him talking to the handler?" Eldoris asks. "Did you get an idea of who it is?"

"I know like...four Fae in this realm, so no, I do not know who it was. Plus, she was using a glamour."

"You sure it was a she?" Radley asks.

"No, but the troll said he'd get *her* before he left."

Eldoris harrumphs. "I'll sift through your memories and see if I recognize the person. If that's okay."

"Yeah, fine."

"Did you learn anything from Seraphina?" Radley asks Eldoris and the name has me clenching my fist. *Why does she bother me so much?* It's like a hot knife wants to explode from my chest whenever I hear her name. It didn't help that she was gorgeous.

"Nothing of importance," Eldoris says with a shrug that has me narrowing my eyes and mining his words for subtext.

"We should talk to Puck," Radley says, and Eldoris groans. "I know, but it's time. We can't ignore his involvement any longer."

"Why would Puck know anything?" I ask, and Eldoris and Radley exchange a loaded look.

"He runs the Underground for Titania," Radley finally says, not meeting my eyes. "He knows everything that goes on down there."

My stomach lurches. Puck runs the section of the Underground that's been harboring the hellfire Fae and running a fucking child trafficking ring. Even if he doesn't know explicitly what's happening, even if he just collects money, he's complicit.

"He knows everything?" I repeat, staring into the flames. "That's how he knew how to find me." He knew the entire time where I was because he knew the smugglers. He would have had everything to get to me, my age, my parents' names.

When I discovered Puck worked for Titania, I thought she might have sent him to get me as a power play against my mother. I assumed he had just been looking for me and got lucky, or maybe the mating bond helped. I never thought it was because he knew who sold me. Did he...did he help them with my sale? Did he ensure I was smuggled out of the realm without incident?

I want to say he isn't capable of that kind of betrayal, but the truth is, I know nothing about the male I'm mated to.

Pain that's been non-existent since I started taking the tea flares to life in my chest. My stomach churns, my head starts pounding.

"Edina—" Eldoris starts.

"You're back!" Althea and Brigid fly out of their tent in a huff. They whiz around me in a flurry of *we were so worried*, and other sentiments I can't catch because they're speaking so fast.

"Radley said you went to watch the sunrise with your betrothed," Althea says. "We wanted to give you space—"

"But you're back before sunrise," Brigid says, plucking a twig from my tunic. "What happened? Did he try something untoward?"

"You do smell odd," Althea says, sniffing my hair. "It's not quite sex, but it's sex adjacent. Arousal maybe."

"Did you do something sex adjacent? It wouldn't surprise us if you did," Brigid says.

"Not that we're judging!" Althea says quickly.

"By the fucking goddess," Eldoris breathes.

I hold up my hand and both pixies stop hovering around my head. "Nothing sex adjacent," I say. They open their little mouths to ask more questions, but I interrupt them. "How are you feeling?"

"Oh," they exchange sheepish glances. "We're better. There must have been some mushroom in the food that we didn't scent."

"Please don't tell your mother we fell asleep," Althea pleads, her little hands holding my cheeks. "We love being your lady's maids."

"And we love our heads attached to our bodies," Brigid scoffs.

"Your secret is safe with me," I say. "And on that note, I'm gonna get some rest before the sun rises."

I slip past the fire into the tent and release a breath, letting the weight of the past few hours settle on me. It feels like I'm going to explode, my skin feels too tight for my body. I tear at my hair, unwrapping it from its confines and running my fingers through it. I want a drink, to slip into the oblivion that Faerie wine allowed me. To sleep without being plagued by thoughts of the male who doesn't want me and could have had a hand in my sale to the mortal realm.

But I can't. I won't. Tonight, I saw the end of the path I was on, and I won't let that happen to me. I won't let Puck be the reason that happens to me. I just need a distraction.

The sound of Eldoris clearing his throat has me blinking away tears. He slowly slips into the tent, like he's trying to give me enough time to tell him to go away. When I don't, his ocean-blue eyes lift to mine. "Do you need to be alone?" he asks with sincerity that threatens to crack me in half.

A distraction. That's what I asked for, isn't it?

I lock my emotions down, turning everything off, and paste a smile on my lips.

"Are you asking if I need time to rub one out after you tossed me around?" My chuckle is husky and deep, my voice a little more than a purr. Eldoris goes still, all except his eyes, which widen at my switch in demeanor. My hips sway as I close the distance between us, sidling up to him until our chests are touching. He doesn't retreat. "Because if that's the case then I'd much rather you stay."

"Edina," he warns, but his voice has gone thick.

"You liked that," I continue, shoving everything else away and focusing on this seduction. This is the next best thing to wine. Something that will take me out of my mind and put me firmly in my body. "Having me at your mercy." I place a hand on his chest, and the muscle jumps under my touch. "Which is good, that's how I like it too."

He wraps his fingers around mine, simultaneously linking them together as I slide it toward the expanse of bare skin by his collar. "I know what you're doing," he murmurs. His flesh is so hot against mine, I want to sink into it.

"So?" I smirk to keep my lip from wobbling. "You can't claim you don't want me."

"I never said that."

"Then take me." I try to release his hand to reach for my tunic, but he keeps me firmly in place as he leans in closer. My eyes flutter closed as his breath ghosts across my cheek, my ear.

"No," he whispers. I rear back like I've been slapped, and my eyes pop open. "We have a deal, and part of that deal is...how did you phrase it? The slow burn to end all slow burns." I swear under my breath. "Besides," he continues, "you'd just be using me to hide from your problems."

"What's wrong with that?" I ask.

"Would it make you feel better?" he asks, and I glare at him because he's right. Sex would only take my mind off everything for about a half hour, less if it wasn't good, and then I'd be right back where I started, and my plan would be ruined.

But fuck him if he thinks I'm gonna admit he was right.

I toe at the grass with my boot, not making eye contact. "You're probably all worn out anyway."

"What?" When I don't answer, Eldoris takes my chin in his fingers and tilts my head up to look at him.

"By Seraphina," I drawl, putting a little extra ire into my words. "I'm just saying, I could have visited the prostitute and you could have dealt with the troll."

Eldoris' smirk is slow and so wide I catch the glimpse of a dimple beneath his thick beard. "Are you jealous?" he asks.

I scoff. "That you got laid. Not of anything else."

"Mhmm," he intones. "Then I guess you'll be disappointed if I tell you I didn't sleep with her. Seraphina is just an informant."

I purse my lips. "Shame," I say derisively, and Eldoris laughs again. He releases my chin but tugs me into an embrace. I stiffen for a moment before melting into him, my arms coming up around his back as he rests his chin on the top of my head.

The pain in my chest eases and my stomach settles. I don't know why he has this effect on me, like a balm to my nerves. He's almost a better remedy than the damn tea.

"Does this help?" he asks, and I hum in agreement. "Would talking about the changeling operation help? I know it must have been hard for you to see that—"

"I don't want to talk about it." I hug him tighter, sinking into his warmth like a plant seeking sunlight.

Without letting me go, he says, "We'll head to the Spring Court palace in a few days." I nod against his chest. I know this was the plan, there's some kind of festival happening there. But that was before I knew Puck and Titania were behind this. "I hate to ask this—"

"You want me to talk to Puck?" I ask.

"Only if you feel comfortable. If not, I'll do it."

"He doesn't like you," I respond. Even before their altercation in the servants' hallway, I could tell Puck didn't like Eldoris. It must be some lingering effects of the broken mating bond, I can feel his stronger emotions, and his hatred of Eldoris is strong. I'm pretty sure the feeling's mutual.

"I won't make you do anything you're uncomfortable with," Eldoris says.

"Can I think about it?"

"Of course."

I'm not sure how long we stay like that, locked in each other's embrace, but it's long enough that outside tent, birds start chirping and the sun starts to rise.

"Will you stay in here?" I ask. I know he has a tent of his own, but the past few nights have been the best I've slept in a long time. I'm not ready to unpack why that is, but I know having Eldoris nearby helps. He answers by summoning a bedroll beside my mattress.

We talk a little more about the things I saw beneath the tunnel as we get ready for bed, but as soon as my head hits the pillow I drift off. I fall into the same dream I always have. I'm walking down the aisle in the ballroom toward Puck, and he's looking at me like I'm the only person in the world. I watch him realize we're mates. I watch him realize he has to say no, and I hear him say the words, "I'm sorry."

But just as he's about to actively reject me, to say the words that will punch the air from my lungs, a hand closes over mine, and a deep baritone says, "You don't need to stay here for this."

I look up, searching for the voice, knowing in my gut who it belongs to, but I can't see him. Puck is opening his mouth to say the words, but I hold up a hand and start backing up. My fathers are there, and they form a wall around me, shielding me from what's to come.

When I wake up, my hand is reaching off the mattress toward Eldoris, and his hand is reaching up toward me, the only things touching are our pinkies.

Chapter Twenty-Three
Eldoris

EDINA AND I SPEND the next few days keeping up appearances by roaming the Spring Court in search of the hellfire Fae. On the first day, I take her around the Iridis Hills, each one known for its growth of a different flower so the entire area looks like a rainbow from overhead. Next, we stop in a village nearest to the palace and get faerie cakes—cupcakes as she insists on calling them—from a renowned bakery, then to a tavern where some of the patrons teach her an old card game. Naturally, Edina wins, and only later does she tell me she's been playing poker since she was a child.

The evening before we're due at the palace, Radley returns from a trip into the Underground. According to his sources, the monarchs took Edina's idea and moved all Fae families with children into their palaces to keep them safe. From the murmurs Radley heard, this stopped hellfire Fae from recruiting, and they're now hiding somewhere as they plan their attack.

"Any idea on a place that can hide them?" Edina asks. The three of us sit around the fire, snacking on some berries the pixies collected during the afternoon. The sun slowly sinks below the horizon, casting everything in a soft golden glow as the dying rays filter through the trees.

"There are a few places large enough to host an army," Radley says. "One is the Underground, but our intel suggests they didn't linger, only used the tunnels. The rest are in the courts."

"Wouldn't the monarchs know if they were hiding in their court?" Edina asks. Radley's mouth thins so it's lost behind his beard, and he stares at Edina with soft eyes. "You think they're working *with* one of the monarchs?"

"It would make sense," he replies. "If I was a monarch who was mad about the impending alliance between Seelie and Unseelie forces, but also didn't want to anger my current allies, I would hire outsiders to take care of the problem."

"Did you?" Edina asks, but her voice holds no real accusation.

"If I did, why would I reveal my dastardly plan?" he cackles, imitating a villainous voice.

"Besides, the hellfire Fae have been organizing since we returned from the Witch War," I add. "Edina and I announced our engagement and alliance in response to them, not the other way around."

Radley shrugs "Maybe they want to stir the pot. Zahir is the newest," he says, referencing the King of the Night Court. "He could be trying to prove himself."

"Didn't you say that the magical signature smelled like the Night Court?" Edina asks, but I shake my head.

"Hades wouldn't have helped us if they were involved. She may hate her brothers, but she loves her court. Day Court has that big arena in the middle of the desert."

"The late queen was killed by hellfire," Radley says. "They wouldn't do it."

"That leaves Spring," Edina says, running her hands through her hair. "Assuming neither of our mothers has anything to do with this."

"Or they're working solo," I conclude. "We'll need to investigate tomorrow when we go to the palace."

"Be careful with that," Radley says. "Titania is a crazy bitch and won't hesitate to use your snooping as an excuse to go to war, with or without hellfire."

We shore up a few other plans as we finish dinner before Radley leaves to go to the palace, deciding it's in all of our best interests to arrive separately and not give any hints to our alliance.

"Are you tired?" I ask Edina, whose knee is bouncing vigorously. She hasn't mentioned it, and I haven't pushed, but I know she doesn't want to talk to Puck tomorrow. And I know the changeling operation is bothering her more than she let on.

The pixies, who must also sense her nerves, are hovering close by, trying to braid her hair or massage her shoulders, but she just bats them away. "Can we take a walk?" she asks, and the pixies freeze where they are, looking between us with rapt interest. "Alone?"

"But—" Althea and Brigid start, practically salivating to come with us.

"I'll keep her safe," I wink, and their eyes go wide as saucers as I take Edina's arm and we leave the wards surrounding the camp. The pixies won't disobey an order from their princess, so they don't follow, but I do hear little screams of frustration following us into the forest.

As soon as we're out of earshot, Edina releases a breath. "They mean well, but they can be a lot."

"At least that will get the rumor mill churning," I offer, and she chuckles softly as I steer her away from the hills and deeper into the forest. It's a beautiful, warm evening with just the slightest breeze tickling the trees. Even with the ball of magical light illuminating our way, the forest swallows the light, keeping us shrouded in shadow.

"I haven't been this way before," Edina says. "Do you have a destination in mind?"

"Maybe." Edina rolls her eyes but accepts that I want to surprise her. Our conversation flows easily as we walk, Edina telling me more about her childhood, and asking questions about mine. The topics are light, filled with seemingly unimportant details, but each piece fills in the puzzle a little more.

A little while later, and a few mumbled curses from Edina who's tripped over a root, and I hear the sound of our destination. "Listen," I whisper, pulling her to a stop.

"A river?" she asks as she identifies the sound of rushing water.

"Close," I pull her along further, and it starts to smell like the earth after a rainstorm mixed with cherry blossoms. We come to a weeping willow, and I push aside the drooping branches that hide this place from the rest of the forest.

"A waterfall," she says on an inhale. Water streams down rocks that glow with turquoise bioluminescence before emptying into a small pool. Large, mossy rocks sit around the edge, like little benches perfect for viewing the beautiful scenery. To the right side, a pink, flowering tree drops flower petals onto the pool's surface, where they drift peacefully until they get too close to the falls. "It's beautiful."

Edina throws her ball of light into the sky and adds some power, so it illuminates the entire clearing, bathing it in a soft, yellow glow. For a moment we stand, watching the water flow down the rocks, watching it get trapped along one rogue pebble before eventually flowing into the pool and frothing the water into shallow white caps.

"Anything live in here?" Edina asks. "Crazy fae-fish? A rare form of mermaid I don't know the name of?"

"No, nothing's in the water," I say with a laugh. She gives me a wicked smile and whips her tunic over her head so she's just in a mint, lace bra and then kicks off her boots and leggings. Her eyes stay on me as she strips, daring me to do the same before she runs into the shallow end of the pool, kicking up water as she goes. She sinks below the surface and pops up, flinging her hair behind her so it lays in a sleek sheet down her back.

"Come on, El," she calls, and something about the use of a nickname makes my heart jump. She used it before when we were in the Underground, but we were in distress. This time, between her playful tone and the twinkle in her eye, it feels different.

I strip down to my underwear and wade into the water as Edina floats, using her water magic to keep her aloft. The light is just bright enough that I can see the stiff peaks of her nipples through her wet bra, and I sink beneath the cold water before I can stare for too long. *What is wrong with me lately?* I'm behaving like a teenager with his first crush.

When I resurface, I release my horns for the first time in a few days and sigh at the sensation. "Do they hurt?" Edina asks, her skin tinted blue from the light of the waterfall. "When you release them?"

"No, it feels good," I answer, brushing stray water droplets from my face. "Like letting your hair down after it's been up all day."

"What would you know about that?" Edina asks, abandoning floating and sinking so just her head is above water.

"I grew my hair out when I was in the mortal realm. It grew wide," I gesture, showing her how large my curls grew, "But a friend convinced me to straighten it once or twice."

"I can see you rocking an afro," she laughs, and I want to bottle the sound. She's given me chuckles or scoffs so often, but her real laugh is magic all on its own. "Tell me about your time in the mortal realm."

I do, and we spend more time alternating between light conversation and floating in companionable silence. After we've been in long enough to make my fingers wrinkle, Edina propels herself to the edge of the lake on a wave of her own making and plops her dripping body onto a moss-covered rock, tilting her head to the night sky like she's sunbathing in the darkness. I stay in the water, trying to ignore the way the droplets make her skin glisten, how they get stuck on grooves in her wings likening her to some ethereal goddess.

"You can look, you know," she says, catching me in the act. My heart jumps in my throat, but there's no use pretending I wasn't just staring at her. "You're stuck with me for eternity, you might as well see what you're getting."

I fight a smile and swim over. "In that case..." When I stand, her eyes widen as the water slides down my body and lingers over the tattoos inked into my chest.

"What's the story with those?" she asks, speaking directly to my abs, and I don't fight the laugh that bubbles up in my chest from the blatant way she checks me out.

"You'll have an eternity to find out," I tease, which makes her roll her eyes, but she drops the subject. I sit beside her, wincing at the cool temperature of the rock before using my magic to warm it. Edina sighs in contentment at the heat.

"So," she says, nudging me with her elbow. "What's the plan for tomorrow?"

"We're leaving at—"

"I mean, with us." Her eyes glimmer mischievously, and she drops her voice. "With *our* plan."

I lean in conspiratorially. "Well...do you think we should be convincing people we're friends? Or do you think we can move forward?"

"I think we can take it up a notch. What's that? Flirting?"

"Sure. And maybe some..." I pointedly look at her lips before swallowing hard and looking back into her eyes, "...lingering looks."

"Especially when the other isn't looking?" she asks, her voice light and beguiling.

"Perfect," I murmur, and Edina laughs heartily. "And you should keep calling me El."

"I've called you El like once."

"It shows we've gotten closer. That you're comfortable enough to give me a nickname."

"I give everyone nicknames. The Fae you walked in on me with? I called him the Hulk."

I ignore the sinking feeling I get when she says that. "That reference I know."

"I hate you," she deadpans and throws her head back, arching her back as she does and once again drawing my attention to her body. Goddess, she's not even trying and she's posed in the sexiest way, one knee up on the rock while the other is draped along the edge. It draws attention to her long, lithe figure and gives me flashes of what it would be like to be hovering over her in this position, but with her leg over my shoulder instead of on that rock.

Edina coughs, snapping me out of my daze and when I look up, she meets my eyes. Heat crackles between us. Her breaths come in faster, her chest rising and falling, and...*fuck stop looking at her chest.*

Instead, my gaze falls to her lips, like that's much better. She wets them and it takes everything in me not to lean in and kiss her. We have a plan...a plan that is important for reasons I can't think of when she's looking at me like that.

Her eyes flit to the entrance of the clearing like she's looking for someone, and it's like a shock of cold water. Edina wants people to believe this is real because she's hurting, and here I am, salivating over her like every other Fae since she's returned to Faerie. *Goddess, I'm an asshole.*

She must sense the shift in me because she stands and vacates her rock, brushing past me and walking around the clearing to where she discarded her clothes. I see her magically dry herself off before slipping her leggings and tunic on. "We should head back," she says, still facing away.

"Edina—"

"We're on the same page for tomorrow." When she looks back at me, that fake smile is plastered on her face. "Play it just like that."

"Right." I stand and follow, putting on my clothes and boots. This time, the silence between us isn't comfortable, it's awkward and stiff.

We're halfway back to the camp when I can't take it anymore and grab Edina's hand, pulling her off the path and further into the trees. "El—" she squeaks, and I tug her along after me. "Seriously, what the—"

I stop by a flowering tree, the creamsicle-colored petals lazily floating down and landing on the grass, which is almost blue beneath the light of the moon. "I don't like how that went," I say, and Edina's eyes widen. "I'm not going to stand here and lie to you, or shut down, or not tell you what I'm thinking. For this to work, we need to be transparent."

"Okay," Edina draws out the word, prompting me to continue.

"I..." I swallow because saying this out loud is harder than I thought.

"You want me," Edina says simply. "Well...you want my body, but you won't cross that line because of the rules I've set. And you're also a little worried that you're disrespecting me—even though I said you could look all you want. Sound about right?"

I blink, stunned, and she laughs. "We're going to be pretending to fall in love, so you're right," she says. "Communication is important, but you don't have to tell me every time you fantasize about me. It's not a crime."

"No?" I ask, leaning in a little too close.

"No. Besides, if you told me every dirty thought that crossed your mind, then I'd have to do the same." Her gaze is like a warm caress as it travels down the expanse of my torso to my rapidly hardening cock and then back to my face.

"And that would be bad?"

She nods, biting her lower lip. "You tell me." Her voice dips. "Would it make it hard if I told you how badly I wanted you to fuck me against the wall back there, pushing me into the rocks until they bit into my flesh as you relentlessly pound into me?"

Her back is arched again in a strategic move that makes our chests touch without providing too much temptation. Because if she was plastered against me right now, she'd feel exactly how hard that made me.

Wanting to give her a small taste of how wild she makes me, I lean forward as a low grumble builds in my chest. She shivers as my breath ghosts along the slender column of her neck, and she tilts to give me further access.

"Save that fantasy for when the slow burn ends," I murmur.

"Fucking hell," Edina swears and then pushes my chest so that I'm upright in front of her. "This is gonna be fun."

I blink again. This time Edina slides around me as she laughs, tugging my hand with her and leading me back behind the path as my brain struggles to form coherent thoughts.

We walk back into camp with our fingers interlaced, and I'm sure I'm still wearing the same awe-struck expression I had in the forest while Edina practically skips us into the tent...but not before we get a once-over from the pixies.

As I fall asleep, I can't help but think if I was another male, it would be so easy to fall in love with Edina.

Chapter Twenty-Four
Edina

The Spring Court palace looks like something out of the Renaissance. Large towers jut up behind a thick stone wall, the parapets flying multicolored flags that Eldoris told me don't actually mean anything, but Titania thought were festive. The gently sloping hills give way to a crystal-clear moat, and today, the drawbridge is down and Fae in pastels saunter through to the festival inside the walls.

"Spring Court doesn't hold this festival often, at least not where it's open to the public," Eldoris explains as we cross over a field of soft grass that's dotted with clovers. This morning, the pixies presented me with a *Spring Court dress*, which is a pale pink, has a fitted bodice, and a skirt made entirely of tulle. I feel like a ballerina, but I'm grateful the skirt isn't quite as full as is the fashion of Winter Court.

Eldoris, in a robin's egg blue tunic and cream linen pants, extends his hand, which I gratefully take as we cross the wooden planks that make up the drawbridge. The opening in the wall feels more like a tunnel than a doorway and is covered in ivy that's wrapped with faerie lights, giving the feeling of a magical portal into another world. And then it gives way to the grounds.

It's annoyingly pretty. Trees with flowering branches scatter white and pink petals across the meticulously trimmed grass. Children hold streamers and run in between colorful booths strung with flower garlands. Someone is blowing magical bubbles that don't pop, but instead nestle down in the grass and reflect the sunshine in a rainbow of hues.

The lower walls of the palace are covered in rows upon rows of roses in every shade, some of which are closed up in the daylight but I assume bloom at night. Their thorns jut out just far enough to discourage touching without quite being long enough to stab anyone. Up close, I can see the parapets of stone that rise into the sky are also draped in floral strands. Even with magic, I can't imagine the upkeep on grounds like this.

"Where to first?" Eldoris asks. "We can browse the stalls, get something to eat, try our hand at the hedge maze..."

"There's a hedge maze?" I ask and follow his glance around the side of the palace, where there is indeed a gigantic hedge maze. I don't actually see any Fae inside the massive structure, but large poles with colorful ribbons poke up above the greenery, occasionally changing directions. When a shower of pink sparks goes up from the middle, a little swarm of pixies flies in to assist.

I turn my attention to the row of vendors, set up in a way that's not much different from the Underground, but brighter and more festive. "Let's shop." He places a hand on my lower back and guides me forward.

The booths are all wooden, and all have some sort of floral arrangements alongside handmade signs. I poke around a stall that boasts naturally harvested honey while Eldoris slips inside a booth that has leather sheaths stamped and carved with intricate patterns. When I slide up beside him, he shows me the supple leather sheath he's looking at.

"For your dagger," he says, and I can't help the laugh that bubbles up in my throat. I take the sheath from him and place it down.

"Come on," I lace our fingers together and tug him out of the booth. "If you're buying me something, it's gonna be jewelry."

We walk past a few vendors selling food, paintings, woodcarvings, and someone doing in-person drawings with some kind of charcoal—which I try in vain to make Eldoris sit for with me—until we find a small, unassuming booth with a cluster of pretty yellow flowers in the doorway. Inside are glass cases with simple silver necklaces, bracelets, and earpieces like the ones Eldoris wears.

"I can get anything I want, right?" I bat my eyelashes, fingering a necklace that has a sapphire laid amongst an iridescent gem I don't recognize.

"Actually..." It's Eldoris' turn to grab my hand and lead me over to a display case. "What do you think?" There's a hint of vulnerability in his voice, and he gives me a sheepish smile. When I turn to look at what he's found, my breath catches.

On a small velvet pillow are two gold rings. They're simple, unassuming, but they glitter in a way that gold in the mortal realm just doesn't.

"Wedding rings?" I gasp, my throat feeling suddenly very tight.

"More like an engagement ring. In Faerie, all parties who are betrothed wear rings to signal their intention." He swallows. "But we don't have to—"

"Excuse me," I call to the attendant, a petite female who moves with the grace of a fawn as she saunters over. "Can we see these, please?"

"Of course, Your Highnesses." I suppose I shouldn't be surprised that she knows exactly who we are. She slides out the pillow and hands the slimmer band to Eldoris, who turns to me.

"We wear our rings on our left forefinger," he taps my index finger and I extend it. "It's said to be a direct line to the heart."

He slides the band over my knuckle and settles it in place. It's a little big, but then the attendant waves a hand and the band glows molten before shrinking to the perfect size. She hands me the ring and I repeat the process with Eldoris.

"Do you like them?" he asks, and I find myself nodding. The fact that it's not on my ring finger somehow makes it less scary. I always assumed if I got it together enough to get married, I would get a flashy diamond, but this feels right.

Eldoris lights up, giving me that wide smile that brings out his dimple. It should be criminal.

"Then we'll take them," he says, slipping out his coin purse and handing over a buttload of gold.

"You need to teach me how money works," I say as she hands him silver pieces as change and thanks us both.

"Why? You're getting married, let the male handle the money."

"Funny. You're hysterical. Seriously, who knew I was marrying a comedian?"

"Bit of a bonus for you." He smirks and intertwines our fingers together. We continue walking through the aisles, occasionally stopping and perusing through the vendor's wares. I even buy a painting of the Winter Court Ocean for Katie.

"Is that a maypole?" I ask as we round the corner. Sure enough, Fae are holding ribbons around a gigantic pole, waiting for more to come by so they can be dragged into the dance.

"You should go," Eldoris says as I watch with rapt attention as a plump, older female tries to get a little boy to hold the ribbon beside her.

"I don't know the steps," I say.

"They'll show you." He takes my bag and gestures forward.

I make my way over tentatively, but when I approach, a few people begin cheering, calls of, "Your Highness, come on!" and, "We'll show you how it's done," chasing away my fears. I pick up a powder blue ribbon, the texture like silk in my hands, and wait.

The yellow ribbon beside me stays empty even when the music, a jaunty melody played by two flutists, picks up. I'm concerned that with no one next to me, I'll flub the dance, but when I look back, it's not empty. I meet Puck's emerald green eyes and he smiles tentatively before the crowd starts moving, weaving in and out in an intricate dance that takes all my concentration to follow.

ELDORIS

I watch as Edina stumbles through the first few steps, but then seems to get the hang of it and weaves in and out amongst Fae like a pro. Puck seems to always be hovering around her, and I don't like the tightness in my chest that happens when he calls something over his shoulder and she laughs.

"Don't be that male, brother." Devorah appears beside me, in a similar dress as Edina but hers is a buttercup yellow that she's accented with teal jewelry...most likely at my mother's behest.

"What male is that?" I ask, keeping my eyes on my betrothed instead of looking into my sister's knowing stare.

"The jealous type. You have to know Puck will always be around, even if you do marry."

Edina catches my eye and the look she gives me threatens to crack my heart in half. She looks...free. So much freer than she did a few days ago when she was laden with pain and pressure. Now she practically floats.

"Mother here?" I ask, pointedly changing the subject.

"No," Devorah says, and I don't have to be looking at her to feel her stiffen beside me. When I do turn, her entire body is rigid. "Winter Court was too much for her. She's been out of sorts ever since. Last night, she asked for him."

Him being our father. Our human father who's been dead for centuries. She never spoke of him when we were growing up, but Devorah and I deduced he was a slave to some human monarch who wanted magic. That was the agreement the Fae made back then, magic in exchange for humans to breed. It was a dark time in our history.

Sometimes I wonder if she really loved him. Occasionally, she thinks I'm him, and she's always very respectful of boundaries in those situations, which makes me hope the arrangement was more consensual than we thought.

"What have the healers said?" I ask. "Anything new?"

Devorah shakes her head. "I can't keep excusing her absence forever, but she won't step down. When she's lucid, she thinks she can handle it. And I won't get her to agree to losing her title when she's having one of her episodes."

"I know," I sigh, turning back to find Edina cackling at something the woman beside her said. "It's an impossible situation."

"You don't know though," she hisses. "You're never home. And if you marry Edina—"

"You're the one who wanted me to marry Edina."

"I know." Her response is loud enough that a few heads turn, and again Devorah sighs. "I know. But I didn't expect to do this on my own."

"What about Hershel?" Devorah rolls her eyes so intensely I can practically hear them. Hershel has been an advisor to the crown for as long as I can remember, but he's a kind man. Stubborn, and very rigid sometimes, but kind.

"Hershel suggested I kill her," Devorah says. "I fired him."

"He *what*?" I hiss. "*You* what?"

"Relax, the position has already been filled." She jerks her head to the side, where a vaguely familiar male with ink-black hair and fair skin stands chatting up Larisa, who tosses her honey-blonde hair like she's flirting...much to her boyfriend's chagrin. "Hershel's son," Devorah explains when I show no signs of recognition.

"Right."

"Enough about home," she says with a dismissive wave of her hand. Then she snatches my left hand and holds it up to the sunlight, inspecting the brand-new band. "You're still planning on proceeding with this farce?"

"The betrothal is real, Devorah."

"I mean the falling in love part. Because you don't seem like you're pretending."

I look back and find Edina gazing at me. She bites her lip when I catch her, before returning her attention to the dance...just like we discussed. "Maybe we're good actors," I reply.

"Her, maybe. But I know you...we shared a womb—"

"I've begged you not to use that phrasing."

"—and you're in dangerous territory. You have feelings for this girl."

I shake my head. "Am I attracted to her? Sure."

"I'm not talking about that," Devorah says. "I'm talking about the little hearts in your eyes every time you hear her laugh."

On cue, Edina's laugh filters over the din of music and conversation, and it pulls at the corners of my mouth. I shake it loose and turn back to my sister, who's wearing a smug smirk.

"I had my one love, Dev," I say with a shrug. "I don't get another one."

"Who says?"

Her question lingers in the air until a loud trumpet blares, signaling the start of the next event. "I have to go," I say. "Do me a favor and bring Edina to the box. Front row if you can."

Devorah agrees, and I kiss her cheek before heading around to the other side of the palace, not even looking back to find Edina as I go.

See? I'm totally fine.

Chapter Twenty-Five
Edina

Puck leads me to a table laden with multi-colored drinks in large punch bowls. A purple liquid produces smoke, the mist billowing onto the tablecloth like a Halloween party trick, and one that's a vivid shade of pink with a hard white foam on top. When Puck dips his ladle into the pink mixture and pours it into two goblets, the foam parts, and then immediately covers the surface again once he's gone.

"Non-alcoholic," he says, handing me the mixture. I'm not sure how he knows I'm sober, but I decide not to ask. I want him to answer questions for me, so even though my instincts are to pick a fight, I know the smarter move is to hold my tongue.

The drink has a light, citrusy flavor that reminds me a lot of pink lemonade, but there's an undertone of magic that's floral and earthy.

We drink in silence for a moment before Puck finally says, "You look well." I sip my drink in lieu of a response. Puck looks a lot like he did at Winter Court, dark circles under his eyes, his skin too pale, his body just a bit leaner than I'm used to seeing. "I mean, you look happy." He runs his fingers through his hair, which is distinctly more brown than red today.

Again, I don't respond, using every ounce of willpower not to demand answers about the child trafficking ring. But he can't know I was there, so I can't ask those questions.

"Eldoris makes you happy." The shattered bond between us twinges, urging me to soothe Puck, to assure him there's nothing between me and Eldoris.

"Don't do that," I assert, my hand drifting to my chest where the pain is the most acute.

"What?"

"You don't get to ask me about him." My control slips when our eyes meet. "You don't get to ask me if I'm happy or have a say in who makes me happy."

"Why not?"

"Because when you had the chance to be that person for me, you said no." Puck swallows, so I keep going. Around us, the sounds of revelry continue, everyone oblivious to our conflict. "I did some research on the mating bond. Did you know that you don't have to accept it right away?"

"I'm aware," he says.

"You can wait years. Centuries. Sure, the bond will urge you toward each other in the interim, but you don't have to fully accept it at all. You can just ignore its presence. It's why rejected mates are so rare."

"You don't understand," Puck snaps. He downs the contents of his glass and turns to refill it, this time going for a carbonated, electric green mixture that releases bubbles into the air above its bowl.

"I understand that Titania has some type of hold on you," I respond, and Puck's eyes immediately find mine. They're wide, begging me to stop talking. "No one will tell me what exactly happened, but the context clues are there. You *belong* to her, right? She makes you do her dirty work, like running the Underground. Either that or her pussy is magical—"

Puck grabs my arm and tugs me away from the refreshment table and the Fae who mill around it. "Don't touch me," I hiss. He tightens his grip and doesn't stop until we reach the shade of the palace wall.

When he releases me, I slap him across his face. The crack of my hand against his flesh is like a gong. It suspends time and locks the two of us in this unexpected moment.

So much for keeping things civil.

But damn that felt good.

His hand drifts to his reddening cheek, his eyes widen in disbelief.

"Next time you touch me without permission, I use magic and I aim lower," I hiss, calling an icicle to my hand and aiming at his crotch in case the message wasn't clear.

Puck is panting, but his eyes are more alive than I've seen since the night he rejected me. He dips his chin in understanding. "I'll leave you alone, then." He turns to go.

"Wait," I call, cursing my short temper. "I need to know what you know about the hellfire Fae."

Puck very slowly turns. "I'm not saying I know anything, but if I did, why would I tell you?"

"Because you still owe me," I seethe. "One slap doesn't make us even, and you damn well know it." Puck releases a low breath, squeezing his eyes shut and the pain he's feeling hits me in the center of the chest. I breathe through it and wait for him to gesture for me to continue.

"My sources say the hellfire Fae hid in your section of the Underground, and I want to know where they are now."

"They arrived a few days ago," he whispers. "I informed Titania of their arrival, and she dealt with it."

"What does that mean?"

"I don't know," Puck says. "When I asked, she just said it was handled."

The word *handled* hangs heavy in the air. It can't be a coincidence that the troll said he was speaking to the Fae's handler.

"Is Titania working with them?"

Loud trumpets interrupt us, and I watch as Puck visibly shuts down. "It's time for the joust," he says, swiping a hand through his hair. "If I hear anything, I'll let you know."

I watch until Puck retreats around the side of the palace and then I sink back against the wall, letting the cool stone seep into my skin.

"That was brilliant," Devorah says, appearing beside me from thin air. I shriek and scurry away from her, but she just laughs and fixes her yellow dress. "Sorry for startling you, I just assumed you knew I was here."

"You assumed I knew you were invisibly eavesdropping?" I ask, one hand against my chest as I try to catch my breath. She considers that but then nods emphatically. "How long were you here?"

"Long enough to hear you threaten his manhood," she cackles. "Seriously, brilliant."

"Glad you approve," I chuckle, the initial shock of her appearance gone.

"Eldoris sent me to find you. You're sitting with me for the joust. Come on." I pry myself off the wall and she links her arm through mine, tugging me in the direction of the drawbridge. As we walk, I look around for Eldoris, but Devorah keeps heading forward. "He'll meet us there. Don't worry, you're going to love the joust. So much more fun than the human version."

"How is it different?" I ask.

"You'll see."

We pass the drawbridge, moving away from the hedge maze and around the side of the palace. "The grounds are huge," I remark. I know the grounds in the Winter Court are big too, but they're mostly taken up by forests or groves of the faerie fruit trees. This is all open, with nothing but sunshine and grass and a few patches of well-placed flowers.

"Yes, yes, Spring is lovely," Devorah monotones. "Wait until you see the summer palace. It straddles two terrains, it's spectacular."

I don't tell her that Eldoris already took me to the beach. That moment feels special. Too private to use in our trickery.

We continue following the crowd around another parapet and a large arena comes into view. In the center is a worn, dirt path that currently has Fae on horses performing tricks for the audience. There are two giant poles with rings at the top on either end and in the center is a wooden barricade that divides the two sections.

Most of the crowd is standing, jammed in along a wooden railing, waving colorful banners or flowers, or holding out sugar cubes for the horses, but Devorah leads us past them to a wooden structure situated center stage. There's an identical structure across the way, and I see a familiar blonde head of hair ducking into the doorway to ascend the interior staircase.

"Is that my mother?" I ask, and Devorah shrugs a slender shoulder.

"Probably, that's the Unseelie side." She pulls me through the doorway, and we make our way up a rickety staircase that's only lit by the stray rays that make it through the wooden slats.

"I'm Unseelie, you know," I say, and she waves me off.

"Yes, but you want to be on this side, trust me."

When we crest the top of the stairs, we're dumped into a small seating area that's open on all sides but has a roof overhead blocking the harshest of the sun's rays. The seating is arranged like bleachers, with Titania on the highest level and Puck by her side, his arm locked in her death grip. Seated in the middle is the Day Court King, Larisa, and her boyfriend, and their advisor, who gives me a leering look, which stops almost immediately when he sees my ring.

"Best investment ever," I mutter to Devorah, who laughs and tugs me to the very lowest row of seats, which happens to be the closest to the jousting arena. A male is currently doing a one-handed handstand on a horse's back as it gallops around the worn dirt path and the audience is going crazy, tossing flowers at his feet as he passes by and waves.

"Why are we in the front row?" I ask as a very tall male with ink-black hair and the most ridiculously corded arms I've ever seen sits beside Devorah.

"Oh, that's quite the insult," Devorah says, loud enough that she's heard above the cheering and conversation in the private box. "Titania is angry because my mother isn't here. Otherwise, you and I as *princesses*," she practically yells the word, "would be beside Larisa, His Majesty would be beside Titania, and Ayelet, Puck, and Little Hershel here would be in this row."

"My name is Ari," the male beside Devorah says, extending his hand. "I'm the new advisor to Summer Court. It's lovely to meet you, Princess." He takes my hand, across Devorah's body and leans down to kiss it. Devorah releases a puff of air from her nose that's about thirty seconds away from a growl.

"Why did you call him Little Hershel?" I ask, trying and failing to hide my amusement.

"Hershel was the previous advisor," Ari says. "And my father."

"Gotcha."

The male atop the horse takes a standing bow on its back and then gallops into a tunnel that no doubt leads to some sort of stable. "Here we go," Devorah says, sitting forward just enough that I can no longer see Ari, and I find myself chuckling until I hear the sound of hoofbeats.

"What the hell is that?" The breath leaves my lungs as I see the creatures entering the ring. Half-horse, half-human, they hold bows in their hands, quivers strung along their muscular torsos. They each have a rider who is in full medieval-style armor wearing a banner that represents one of the courts.

"I thought you had centaurs in the mortal realm." Devorah says. We do have centaurs in the mortal realm. In fact, the last time I saw a centaur was on the opposite side of a battlefield.

I distantly register that they're introducing the centaurs and their riders, but I don't hear them until they call a familiar name. "—Your Prince of the Summer Court...Eldoris and his centaur, Phillipe."

I don't even realize that I'm on my feet and crossing to the edge of the stadium seating until I feel the bite of the wood beneath my fingers. Devorah is calling me, but I'm zeroed in on Eldoris, riding on the back of a centaur who has his bow strung and the tip of the arrow raised over his head entirely too close to my betrothed. It doesn't matter that he's wearing so much metal that it would take a chainsaw to get through.

"No," I say, shaking my head. "No, he can't...why is he out there?"

Devorah appears beside me, placing a hand atop mine. The wood beneath my fingertips is frozen, and I release my white-knuckle grip and shake them out to warm them up as I will my magic back inside. I haven't lost control of my magic in forever.

"Eldoris has been riding with Phillipe since they were both kids," Devorah says. "He's not in any danger."

"So, Fae don't die during these jousts?"

"Well..."

"So, what do you think?" Eldoris' rich voice croons as he stops by the box. He lifts his visor when he sees me, his eyes serious. "What's wrong?"

"It appears, our dear Edina is worried about your safety," Devorah answers.

Eldoris scoffs, but when he looks at me, sobers. "Is that so?"

"He'll be fine, Princess," Phillipe says, his voice deep and gruff and his smile easy. "I'll keep him safe." It doesn't make me feel any better.

Eldoris' eyes flash with understanding. "A friend of yours died from a centaur arrow, right?" he asks. I don't answer, so he extends his hand until I lower mine into it. He's wearing thick gloves, so I don't feel his skin, but I can still feel the heat radiating off him. "I'm not going anywhere, Edina. Feel this armor? It's designed especially for this. It looks like human armor, but it's spelled. I'm practically indestructible."

With his other hand, he removes his helmet. He's wearing a covering over his head in the brilliant turquoise of his court that makes his eyes pop even more than they usually do. He leans down and kisses my knuckles, and my heart does this uncomfortable squeezing that I shake off as nerves.

When he releases my hand, he stands as much as he can in the saddle and cups my face in his gloved hand. It's so large with the glove on that it spans the entire length of my face, and it makes me chuckle. "There she is," he murmurs, and on some instinct I don't understand, I lean forward and kiss his cheek. "Relax. Have some popcorn, and watch Phillipe and I destroy the competition!" he says the last part loud enough that the crowd to the right side of our setup hears and releases a chorus of cheers. I laugh a little as Eldoris releases me and they ride off to the other side of the arena. Before he slides his helmet back on, he tosses me a wink.

"Oh, you're both so screwed," Devorah says, and when I look at her questioningly, she just shakes her head and sits.

I feel Puck's eyes boring into me, but I ignore it and take my seat. We're so close in proximity that despite the tea I'm taking, I can still feel fragments of our bond. It's like he's whispering something to me from far away and I can't quite read his lips. There's pain there, but there's something else mixed in.

I rub at my chest like the simple action is enough to silence the splintered mating bond. I want Puck to hurt; that was the whole point of this. I want him to feel as shitty as I felt when he rejected me.

"You all right?" Devorah asks, not so subtly looking at me and then over her shoulder. "If you want to go to the other side..."

I shake my head, because at that moment, the announcer, a Fae sitting in a booth similar to ours but at the long end of the arena, begins to explain the rules. I went to a Renaissance Faire once when I was in the mortal realm, so I have a general idea of how this works. The goal is to knock the other rider off his centaur by using a lance, a long pointy stick. Centaurs can also knock the riders off with a well-placed arrow, but their main goal is to attack the other centaur, hoping that an arrow to the leg or chest will be enough to cause them to buck their rider off.

"It sounds violent," I whisper to Devorah as two riders, Day and Night Court judging by their colors, take their positions on either end of the arena on opposite sides of the metal bar. They each raise their lances to the ready position.

"It is," Devorah says, and grabs two giant paper containers full of popcorn from a brownie who comes around offering. She hands me mine and I sniff. It smells sweet...and floral, and not at all what I was expecting when Eldoris said popcorn. "Lavender and honey," Devorah supplies, taking one dainty kernel and popping it in her mouth.

I'm tempted to shove a whole handful in my mouth just to buck her propriety, but I take one as well since I have no idea how lavender-honey popcorn will taste. It's not terrible. It melts on my tongue and reminds me almost of kettle corn in its sweetness.

"Here we go," Larisa claps, shifting forward in her seat as the centaurs begin to gallop while simultaneously firing arrows. The jousters ignore the magical missiles aimed at them and lower their lances, taking aim at their opponents.

The crash is so loud it makes me wince. It sounds like a four-door getting hit by a semi, there's the initial crash, and then a crunch as the Day Court's lance dents the Night Court rider's armor. The lance snaps and a piece flies off. Meanwhile, the Night Court's lance stays intact, but Larisa is cheering as the centaurs round the corner and retake their positions.

"I don't get it," I say. "Isn't the goal to knock the person off?"

"Yes, but there are different levels of points," Devorah explains. "Breaking a lance is more points than just a regular hit. Also, an arrow that sticks is worth more than one that simply bounces off."

I nod, resigning myself to not understanding the rules. I cheer whenever anyone gets a hit, much to the chagrin of Larisa, who thinks that since I'm in the Seelie box, I should be rooting for the Seelie rider.

After the Day Court rider dislodges the Night Court rider, it's Eldoris and Phillipe's turn. They're facing off against Autumn Court, so I don't even feel guilty when I join the crowd around us chanting my betrothed's name.

When they're about to ride, an awed hush falls over the crowd, thousands of Fae all holding their breath in anticipation. My hands wring together in my lap as Phillipe charges forward and releases arrow after arrow, distracting the Autumn Court rider so thoroughly, that he's late in lowering his lance. "Watch, watch, watch!" Devorah exclaims, grabbing my hand as Eldoris rams his lance into his opponent's chest, and since he is already distracted, the rider goes flying.

"Holy shit," I breathe, as the crowd goes wild, tossing flowers at Eldoris as he takes his helmet off and waves to the crowd. "He just won in the first round."

"I told you there was nothing to worry about!" Devorah says, tugging me up to the railing as Eldoris slows just enough to place a flower crown that he caught on my head. His gloved finger trails down my cheek, and he says something, but it's too loud to hear. He's off before I can ask him to repeat himself.

We spend the rest of the tournament eating color-changing faerie floss—cotton candy—and drinking that foamy pink lemonade while we watch the other contestants. Before the final match, the riders do tricks with their lances, catching rings from impossibly tall poles while their centaurs charge at breakneck speeds.

Eldoris wins the tournament and is crowned the victor and given a sash and a intense flower crown that's comprised of vines that wind into spikes. When the ceremony is over and everyone disperses, they open the gates to the arena so the crowd can meet the riders and their centaurs. Devorah drags me along after her to Eldoris, who still sits astride Phillipe and speaks very seriously to a young male who is telling him all about his jousting lessons. Eldoris laughs and encourages the boy to keep talking until he sees me.

"Is it true you won the lost princess' hand in marriage?" the boy asks. I've heard that some call me the lost princess—or worse the human princess...which is just incorrect—but I've never heard it in person.

"That's exactly how it happened," I say, making the boy jump, and his mother starts apologizing profusely as she bows. "No need to apologize,"

I assure her. "I was pretty lost. I'm very lucky a vampire found me and brought me home."

"A vampire?" the boy exclaims and starts asking me a million questions, but before I can answer one, the mom thanks us all and ushers him away.

"I won your hand?" Eldoris asks, sliding off Phillipe and walking over to me. He's taken off his armor and is just in a tunic in Summer Court turquoise.

"I like the sound of that better, don't you?" I ask, and because we're supposed to be in the flirting stage, I run my hands up Eldoris' chest, fiddling with the collar of his tunic. He hums, and the deep sound sends vibrations into my hands and through my entire body.

"Did you enjoy the show?" he asks, one hand falling to my waist.

"You were okay," I shrug.

"That so?" he asks, and I swallow hard. "Glad I could entertain you." His eyes are fixed on my lips, and almost imperceptibly he drifts closer. My hands shift around his neck so I'm playing with the sweat-dampened curls at the nape of his neck.

This isn't real. We're faking it.

"All right, love birds," Devorah says too loudly, and too close. I turn and she's practically hovering over my shoulder. The look Eldoris gives her is one of pure ire. "Time to get settled in our rooms."

Eldoris drops me, and I laugh, threading my fingers through his. "Come on, El," I purr in my most over-the-top-sexy voice. "Time to go to our room."

Chapter Twenty-Six
Eldoris

THIS IS AN INSULT.

I stare around the single room that the Spring Court attendant put Edina and me in, and I seethe. At least the bed is large. Unfortunately, it takes up so much room that there's only a sliver of space on either side before there's a wall. A wooden wardrobe is jammed into one corner, making it almost impossible to walk around the bed, and the bathroom door is directly next to the headboard. Add in the tacky, floral wall decorations and the dark green carpet—not wood like the rest of the palace, but imported shag carpet from the mortal realm—and the thing is an eyesore.

Edina, seemingly unphased by this atrocity, rolls over the edge of the bed so she can get to the bathroom.

"No," I assert, and reach down the mental link to my sister. *What does your room look like?*

A shit box, she replies instantly and sends me a picture of a similar-looking room only with a smaller bed so there appears to be more space. I wasn't sure if we were slighted because of Titania's hatred of Edina or my mother's absence. Now I have confirmation it's the latter.

"The fuck is this?" Edina asks, exiting the bathroom and brandishing a chamber pot.

I send a mental picture to Devorah, who laughs and says, *at least I have running water.*

"That, my betrothed, is a chamber pot." Edina's eyes widen, and then she shrugs.

"I guess that explains the bucket next to the bathtub." She retreats into the bathroom and when she emerges again, performs a cleansing spell on her hands.

I haven't moved from the doorway. I'm not quite sure how to process this, and knowing it has something to do with my mother's absence makes things worse. Devorah and I need to make a plan on how we're going to handle this, but I've been so wrapped up in everything with the hellfire Fae and Edina that I've let some balls drop. I need to do better.

"Hey." Edina appears in front of me, ice coating her hands as she touches me. The fire I unknowingly called to my fingertips sizzles out. *I haven't lost control of my magic in ages.*

I stare at the place where our hands are linked, the cool touch of her skin grounding me, and I release a breath. "Wanna tell me what's really going on?" Edina asks softly. She bends until I'm forced to meet her gaze. "This can't be all about a room."

Sighing, I debate how much to tell her. Sure, we're betrothed, but that doesn't provide me with loyalty. Not yet. And we've only been a team for a few days.

For some reason, I trust her anyway.

"My mother is fading," I tell her. "It's a disease, one the healers don't have a cure for. Something is attacking her brain, her memory mostly, but it's only a matter of time before it affects other things. Her motor function, her speech."

"That's why she hasn't been coming to events," Edina says.

"If the other courts find out, they'll capitalize on the weakness. Try to invade. Devorah is set to take over, but we need my mother to step down when she's lucid."

"And when she's lucid, she thinks nothing's wrong?" Edina surmises. A look of determination crosses her features, and then she pulls me into a hug, wrapping her arms low around my waist and resting her head against my chest. "I'm sorry."

"Not your fault," I reply, and fold her into an embrace. It's starting to feel so natural, holding her like this, tucking my chin against the top of her head. And it releases some of the tension. "This room is because she's not here. Devorah's is similar but with running water."

"Other than the chamber pot, I don't see a problem. This place is basically its own palace!" She pulls away and gestures wide with her arms, but because there's literally no space, when she steps back, she trips and goes flying backward onto the mattress. She laughs at her misstep. "Bed's comfy, at least."

A hint of a smile crosses my lips as I take the position beside her, lying on my back and staring at the cracked ceiling. But she's right, the bed is comfortable.

"You can't control what the other courts do," Edina says after a moment. "Or what room they give you. But if you and Devorah need help, you should talk to my mom."

I sigh. I've pondered it, especially now that we're aligned. "It's still a risk."

"But telling me isn't?"

I roll on my side, propping my hand under my head, and she mimics my pose. "No, it's not."

"Shucks, El. You're gonna make me blush," she quips, but her cheeks pink despite her teasing. "Okay, well, if we can't do anything about *that*," she gestures wildly, "We can do something else."

Whatever she's thinking makes her eyes glow in excitement. "What?" A barrage of ideas of what we could be doing crosses my mind. Things that have my heartbeat quickening and my cock stirring.

"We can sneak around and see if there's any evidence that Titania is helping the hellfire Fae." *Right. That.* A completely platonic, productive thing to be doing. *Goddess, I need to get it together.*

"Might I remind you, your sleuthing left much to be desired?"

"I blame that whole situation on Radley," she snorts. "Come on..." she drags the word out for about ten syllables. "This time we won't separate, it'll be fine."

"Where would we even start?" I ask.

"Glad you asked." She snaps her fingers, and her pixies appear, looking worse for wear. Their colorful hair is askew, and the purple one looks like she's been dunked underwater.

"We searched the towers, Your Highness," Althea starts.

"There are five," Edina informs me as if I've never seen the palace before.

"Three are occupied," Brigid says. "The east tower seems to be for guests of this event. The south tower is where the Spring Court families with young children are housed for their safety. This tower was protected with Seelie Guards on every floor..."

"We had to use the pipes to get around," Althea whispers.

"*You did nothing*," Brigid shouts, shaking out her wet locks for emphasis.

"Brigid," Edina scolds gently, and Brigid shuts up while Edina waves a cleansing spell at her, and I add a drying spell for good measure. She could have done both of these herself, but I expect arriving soaking wet was meant to prove a point.

"Then there's the west tower," Brigid continues, fluffing out her hair and flashing me a smile that feels more like a threat. "That's where Titania's rooms are."

"And the central tower?" Edina asks.

"It was empty," Althea shrugs. "Some levels were locked, but we didn't magic ourselves inside. We wanted to wait for you."

"In case we tripped an alarm," Brigid says.

"Not willing to take the fall for your princess?" I ask, and Brigid's eyes narrow to slits.

"How dare you—" she starts to fly toward me, but the other holds her back. Her little arms reach forward like she's going to strangle me.

Edina hops up from the bed. "Thanks, ladies," she says, grabbing my hand. "Come on, we're going to the central tower."

I'm momentarily stunned by how comfortable I've gotten with Edina holding my hand and dragging me around, but she doesn't give me time to process as she tows me out of the room and down the hallway like a seasoned pro. "How do you know where you're going?" I ask as she slips into the main hallway.

"I have an awesome sense of direction. It's the New Yorker in me," she says, nodding at someone who is fascinated by our linked hands. Edina smirks but keeps her eyes forward as she beelines straight toward a dilapidated door.

I cast a quick spell that unlocks the door and feel around for any magical signatures that suggests the area is warded, but we appear to be lucky. With a hard twist of the antique doorknob, the wooden door swings open. We slide in quickly, closing it behind us with a resounding click, and plummet into darkness.

Edina beats me and casts a magical light, illuminating a spiral staircase comprised of thick drab stones draped in cobwebs. Edina takes a step toward the staircase and then jumps back with a yelp. Hanging on a web at the foot of the stairs is a giant black spider. The insect lifts all eight eyes in a challenge, daring us to cross it.

"Maybe not," Edina says.

"You took on a Fae male who had a knife and ran an illegal business, but the spider is too much?"

"Say what you will, but I know my limits." The spider clicks its pincers like it's laughing, and her body shudders. "Yeah nope, hard pass."

"Hang on." I take hold of her hand. The palace in Spring Court has wards that restrict Unseelie Fae from teleporting, but they're surprisingly lax when it comes to the Seelie Courts. I assume it's because the previous king, Oberon, was a trusting fool and Titania has such an inflated sense of ego that she hasn't updated them.

I imagine us at the landing of the stairs right above us. The familiar squeezing that comes with teleportation wraps around Edina and me and then we're at the landing, looking back at the spider sentinel. "You may proceed with your mission." The spider starts clicking its pincers again as we start up the stairs.

The first few floors are sparse. One has nothing but rooms filled with plates and other dinnerware stacked in high piles that look ready to topple. The next has some rooms that clearly haven't been in use for ages. It isn't until the sixth story that we encounter a locked door, and Edina's eyes light as she unlocks it, and we step inside.

The room we find is the first that isn't clogged with dust. It's simple, with cream walls, a four-poster bed, and a writing desk, but the bed is unmade, and there's a damp towel hanging off a chair.

"Quickly," I say as Edina crosses to the desk and starts shuffling through papers.

"These look like depositions," she says, and I stand behind her, reading over her shoulder. The entire stack is indeed statements from Fae in the Underground. The picture on top catches my eye.

"Minthe," I murmur, and in giant red letters, it says "MISSING."

"This is about the changeling ring," Edina says, abandoning the papers in favor of opening drawers. "I guess that answers our question about that."

"It's not enough to have the other monarchs take action though," I sigh.

"But if she knew about that..." Her thought is interrupted as one of the drawers springs open and bursts into flames.

"Fuck. We gotta go, now."

"What is that?" Edina asks, water forming in her hands as she prepares to douse the flames.

"Don't," I yell, stopping her in her tracks. "It's a very specific ward that self-destructs if anyone other than the caster tries to open the drawer. If you use your magic, they may catch your signature. We have to go, right now."

She drops her magic and follows me to the door, stepping in front of me as I usher her out into the dark hallway. Instead of going down, Edina sprints up. "Top floor," she says, slipping out of my hold so I can't teleport us both.

"Let me get us out of here," I say as we pass by the next landing and head up another story.

"I have a feeling," Edina calls without turning around. I follow her and we run up five more flights of stairs until the staircase ends at another old door. Edina unlocks it before we even reach the last step, and it pops open, waiting.

We crash into the room, shutting the door behind us and panting. Adrenaline courses through me, but we're not out of the woods yet. We need to teleport back to our room immediately before anyone thinks to come to look for us.

"Oh my goddess," Edina gasps, and I look up, taking in the room for the first time. It's a huge circular space that's packed with sleeping bags. That in itself wouldn't be damning, but the walls are all scorched, covered in black soot.

"Is that from—" Edina starts, and I know where she's going with her question. I throw a fireball at a clean patch of wall. It connects but leaves no residue behind.

"They were here," I say. "Titania is working with the hellfire Fae."

Chapter Twenty-Seven
Edina

TITANIA IS HELPING THE hellfire Fae.

As much as I wanted to villainize the woman who is sleeping with my mate, I didn't think she'd do something like this. Even when all evidence pointed to her, I was hoping we were wrong, that they were working on their own.

I stare at the scorch marks on the walls, the bedrolls crammed into every inch of the floor, and the curtains that darken the high tower room. All we know about the hellfire Fae is that they were eradicated by my mother centuries ago, but the magic to create that power somehow survived. Until they showed up in the mortal realm with a small army, we thought they remained extinct.

How long has she been harboring them? And what is she planning that requires an army that's not associated with the other Seelie Courts?

"We have to go," Eldoris says, also transfixed by the evidence before us. "Our magical signatures are all over this tower. If they don't follow us, but go to our room and we're not there—"

"We need to bring evidence," I say, staying just out of Eldoris' reach. If we don't give them concrete proof Titania is helping the hellfire Fae, the other courts won't act. They'll pretend to be concerned, and say they're handling it, but they'll drag their feet.

Or they'll tell her our accusation and give her the reason to attack. I'm not sure I can handle another war. One was enough.

"We have our memories," he says, wrapping his arms around me. "That'll have to be enough." The scent of his magic, sandalwood and the salty tang of the ocean, wraps around me, squeezing as the tower room fades away.

When we land back in our atrocious guest room, we topple into the bed because of the lack of space. "Pretend we're taking a nap," he says, throwing back the comforter.

He barely kicks off his shoes before an angry voice starts yelling at the pixies. The muffled voice is male and contrasts sharply with the high-pitched timbre of our guards. They yell and hiss and insist that Eldoris and I are sleeping and not to be disturbed. "Change in plans," he mutters. "Lie down, and I'll confront whoever's at the door."

I strip out of my dress. "Give me your shirt," I tell Eldoris, and he doesn't fight me, he just whips off his tunic, revealing his broad chest. He tosses it to me, and I slide it on before climbing under the covers. The voices grow louder, more insistent.

"Ready?" he asks, and I nod, clutching the comforter close as Eldoris throws open the door.

"What's going on?" he bellows.

Framed in the backdrop of hideous floral wallpaper, huffing incredulously is Puck. He looks between me and Eldoris, registering my attire as I rise up on my knees. I watch as something possessive distorts his features at seeing me in another male's clothes. His jaw ticks; his eyes flare. "Is something wrong?" I ask innocently.

Puck's gaze travels to the bare expanse of my thighs peeking out from Eldoris' tunic and I'm not even sure he realizes he does it, but Eldoris shifts slightly, blocking me from view and drawing attention away from me.

I move forward and lay my hand on his back, covering a tattoo of a cresting wave that's made of the same tribal marks on his chest. It spans across both scapula and the length of his spinal column. It's beautiful, and I've somehow never seen it before.

"Can we help you with something?" Eldoris asks.

"Have you..." he trails off, eyes narrowing. I can practically hear him thinking. On the one hand, if he asks us about the tower and the guards were wrong, he'd be admitting to hiding something. Even if the guards are right, there's no concrete proof. Especially not if they don't want to open the tower to an investigation.

Puck's features shift into a smile I've never seen before. It's so fake it almost hurts. "My apologies for waking you," he says smoothly. "But it appears there's been a grave mistake." My heartbeat picks up, and I subtly call my ice to the hand that's blocked by Eldoris.

"This room wasn't meant for you," Puck says with a chuckle. "Titania sends her deepest regrets for this oversight. We'd like to move you to a suite right beside your mother, Edina."

It takes a lot not to roll my eyes.

Eldoris relaxes a fraction. "Thank you. Just let us get dressed—"

"Of course," Puck says, another smarmy smile on his face. "I'll be right outside to personally walk you to your real accommodations."

He turns to go, and Eldoris says, "Oh, Puck." Puck pauses, shoulders tensing but doesn't turn back around. "Devorah is also in an unsatisfactory room. Another oversight, I'm sure."

Puck gives us his profile, but I can see a predatory glint in those green eyes. "You visited her room?"

Eldoris taps his temple. "She showed me." Puck deflates, and leaves, promising to rectify the situation. When the door clicks shut, Eldoris follows it with a blast of magic, a shield that will let us speak freely.

"We need to talk to your mother," he says. "She needs to know what we saw."

I agree, shucking off his tunic and passing it back to him. "Good call, by the way," Eldoris says stepping close enough that I can feel the heat radiating off his body. My breaths stutter. "Wearing my shirt. He was so distracted he didn't even notice—" he runs a hand through my hair, and my eyes drift closed at the contact. But when he pulls back, I shriek.

Eldoris is holding a very tiny spider and its accompanying web. He laughs as I immediately douse myself in cold water, ensuring no other creepy crawlies are lingering on my skin. Shivering and soaking wet, I glare at my betrothed as he wrenches open the old window and places the spider on the sill. The little bastard scurries off as if he were the one wronged here, and I glare until Eldoris closes the window again.

"WE NEED TO WAKE her," Brigid whisper-shouts. I'm too warm and comfortable to give in to their antics. I finally had a dreamless sleep last night, and I'm relishing every single second of it. I snuggle further into the bed, hoping they'll eventually get the hint and leave me alone.

"Look how cute they are," Althea coos. "Leave them be. We'll just tell the queen—"

"You're going to tell the queen you won't wake her daughter because she's *cuddling*?"

Cuddling?

I crack my eyes open to be greeted with the sight of a chest rising and falling beneath me. The arm behind me shifts, drawing me impossibly closer.

When the hell did I end up in Eldoris' arms?

After we were given our new room yesterday, we tried to meet with my mother to tell her everything that happened, but according to her advisor, Cornelia, she and my fathers were occupied for the evening. All evening. If they weren't my parents, I'd be impressed.

I remember spending most of the night on edge, having to socialize with everyone as we pretended nothing was wrong and Titania isn't out to get someone. And I remember Eldoris trying to comfort me before bed. I must have cuddled up to him in the middle of the night.

Is this why I didn't have any nightmares?

"Wouldn't be the first time we pulled her out of a bed she was sharing," Brigid intones.

"This is different!" Althea insists. "Cornelia thinks they're falling in love."

"Only because you keep spinning stories."

Very slowly, so as not to disturb him, I extract myself from Eldoris. The second I move, the two pixies zero in on me. Althea turns as pink as her hair and Brigid's eyes narrow, suspicious that I was listening in. I sit up and give her a look. "If you don't want me to overhear, don't gossip about me in my room." She makes a dismissive sound low in her throat but has the sense to look a little sheepish.

"Your mother wishes to see you," Althea says, flying closer to me. She eyes Eldoris' sleeping form. "Only you."

"That's ominous," I grumble, but stand and cross to the wardrobe. This room is so much nicer than the closet that was our previous room. The walls are a pale, sage green and the floors are old wood that's been treated with magic to feel soft on your bare feet. It's smaller than my suite at home, with only a sitting room, bedroom, and bathroom, but it's comfortable and homey. And there's running water. Thank the fucking goddess.

"She said to come as you are," Brigid says, zipping in front of me and handing me a long, silk robe. The material is cool against my skin, chasing away the remnants of the warmth I felt in bed.

Does Eldoris even realize we were all cuddled up?

I mentally shake myself and let the pixies lead me down the hall. I can't focus on that right now, or dwell on why it felt so damn good, not when I'm about to walk into the lion's den. Althea and Brigid open a door a few paces from ours, and I enter a sitting room with enough couches to accommodate a dozen people. It's a larger version of our sitting room but done in pastel blue tones rather than green.

My fathers, Five and Four, are sitting on a floral loveseat, Four's arm around the back while Five leans into him, resting his head on his chest. From what I've gathered, they're the only two of my fathers in a relationship with each other as well as my mom.

"Morning, darling," Five says when he sees me. He gestures to the coffee table has a silver tray and a stack of mugs. "Coffee?"

"Please." Four kisses Five's temple before they both shift and Four starts preparing my mug. I flop down in the chair beside them and run my fingers through my hair, untangling it as I go. "Mother summoned?"

"She'll be out in a moment," Four responds. He dumps a ton of sugar into the dainty coffee cup and hands it to me. "You look good. Better."

"I'm sober," I say. "And the tea Eldoris found is helping with the pain from the mating bond." I take a sip and grimace. Five laughs at me. "What is that?"

"Flavored coffee," Four responds simply.

"Flavored with shit," I mutter and put the mug down.

"Close," Five responds. "Flavored with lavender."

"I don't understand the hard-on this court has for lavender. The popcorn was decent, but some things are sacred."

"I couldn't agree more," my mother's cool voice intones from the doorway.

She seems softer today, her usual façade missing. She's in an identical robe to mine, but hers is blue instead of pink, and she holds the top of hers together so it bunches under her neck. Her blonde hair is loose, with just the hint of a wave. It's so much like mine this way, without the elaborate pinned curls and accessories she usually wears.

"Thank you for coming alone," she says, and the rest of my fathers slide past her and into the sitting room, taking up seats like they've been assigned. At a glacial pace, she crosses the room, all eight sets of eyes in the room on her as she moves to the largest couch and sits between Astor and Two. She crosses her legs at the ankle and accepts a cup of coffee from Four. "We wanted Eldoris to have plausible deniability."

She stirs the coffee, a silver spoon clinking against the edges of the mug. For a moment, I just watch the eight of them in their companionable silence. Two has extended an arm around my mother's slim frame, and Astor's hand sits on her knee. Six and Seven are offering coffees to everyone who doesn't have one.

They're just so relaxed. Happy.

I know I should be here, that I was invited. That this is my family. But I feel like an outsider looking in.

As if he senses my discomfort, Seven places a hand on my back and starts rubbing in small circles. The motion releases some of the tension that's been there since I started using my wings, and I sigh into him.

"You discovered something," my mother prompts. "The changeling ring—"

"How did you know about that?" I ask. Eldoris and I haven't told anyone we were even in the Underground, let alone about the back tunnels.

"Hades was concerned," Six says, his green eyes piercing. "She said you killed the male responsible."

"Good," Four grunts. "We thought your human friend took care of him, otherwise we would have continued our search."

I look into my disgusting coffee mug, debating on sipping just so I have an excuse not to talk about this. "There are apparently three of them," I say to the brown liquid. "Katie killed the first in the mortal realm, I killed the second here. There's one more, the one who steals the children."

"I'll let the guards know," my mother says. "We'll find him."

"But that's not why I asked you to meet." I switch topics as swiftly as I can. My fathers, while well-meaning, have tried to get me to speak about my adoptive parents before, and I have a feeling they were angling back there again. I cut them out of my life for a reason, I have no desire to dig up sour memories.

"Hellfire Fae have been staying in the central tower," I continue. "I found evidence they were there and am willing to have my memories examined to prove it."

My mother's eyebrows arch, and my fathers all lean into her in subtle ways. I catch them up on everything we learned from the Underground and our own sleuthing in the central tower. They're all perfectly still until I finish.

"This complicates things," my mother says when I've finished my story. "I need to take this to the Unseelie Courts."

"Not the others?" I ask.

"Their armies are intertwined," she says. "Even if they wanted to attack Titania, they would need to find every soldier from Spring Court and imprison or discharge them. That wouldn't go unnoticed. No, they can't know we're moving on this."

"And will you move on this?" I ask, leaning back in my chair. "Because last time I came to you about aid in a war, you took your sweet time."

My mother waves me off, ignoring my qualms. "Things take time," she says. "You and Eldoris will need to continue to be on your guard, but no more searching for the hellfire Fae. You should stay within the wards of our court..."

"We're due at the Autumn Court right after this event," Three says, and my mother sighs heavily.

"Right, right. Then, Edina, you'll need to keep calm about this information until we can act on it. It may not happen on your timeline, but we'll do things as quickly as we can."

I shrug. The lack of urgency is something I'll never get used to, but I can deal with it for now.

"Now," my mother says, her face breaking into what I think is supposed to be a smile but ends up more like a wolf's grin. "Tell me how things are going with your Faerie lessons."

"You mean the information Eldoris is teaching me?" She nods. That's not where I thought she was going with this at all. "Umm...they're fine, I guess. I'm learning."

"Since we have time this morning, I thought maybe your fathers and I could help fill in some of the gaps pertaining to the Winter Court. Would you like that?"

They all look at me expectantly, and it's so sincere and sweet that I'm a little stunned. "Sure," I say, and they all spring into action. Seven runs into the bedroom saying he has books in the suitcase, Four summons a blackboard, and Five says he's going to order breakfast and some real coffee.

The distance I felt just moments ago evaporates in an instant, and for a minute, I let myself sit amongst the chaos of a family. The first time I was in Faerie, I realized their love for me. They did everything they could to find me to no avail, the way they worried the entire time I was away. I lost sight of that through my heartache, and I went back to feeling alone when I didn't have to. I have an entire support system right here, ready to jump in and teach me remedial things about our court just so they can spend the morning with me.

That's pretty fucking special.

Five hands me a large iced coffee, overflowing with whipped cream, and I hum happily as I sip the sugary goodness. "Thanks, Quintin."

The entire room freezes and all eyes land on me. "I—" Quintin stammers, running a hand through his long hair. "You called me by my name."

I can't help but notice the way his eyes start to tear and his face falls. "Did you...not want me to?" I ask. All my fathers exchange glances.

"It's just...we thought the numbers were signs of affection."

"The way you give nicknames to everyone," my mother adds.

"You want me to keep calling you numbers?" I ask incredulously, and they all nod enthusiastically. I swipe my hand down my face to hide the laughter bubbling up in my throat. "Okay then."

Quintin—Five—rushes over to me and wraps me in a bone-crushing hug that brings tears to my eyes. The rest of my family steps into me, each of them touching me in some way as they join our giant group hug.

When we break apart, my mother lays one hand on my cheek, her eyes glistening and her features soft.

"Can I still be called Astor?" Astor—who I've never called One—asks. It makes the rest of us laugh, which puzzles him greatly.

At that moment, I make a vow to not let anyone take this away from me again.

Chapter Twenty-Eight
Edina

AFTER THE CONVERSATION WITH my mother, I was surprised when Devorah called us to her room to tell us Winter Court is sending troops to the border between Summer and Spring Courts. She was rightfully confused, but we caught her up on the situation, and then she was grateful for the extra aid. Eldoris also subtly advised Radley to convince his father to fortify his border with Spring Court. He's convinced that if Titania attacks, it will be one of the two.

"It would make the most sense," he explains. "Both share a border with Spring Court and conquering either territory would make it easier to get to the rest of the realm."

"You think she's going to try and rule the entire realm?" Devorah scoffs. "I spoke with some of the vendors yesterday, she's barely holding Spring Court together."

"All the more reason to be desperate. She'd do anything to hold onto power."

"If she wants to make a splash," Devorah's new advisor Ari says, "she'll attack Autumn Court when all the Noble Fae are in attendance."

"We need to be on our guard," Eldoris agrees.

As soon as we have a plan in place, and Devorah has assured Eldoris that their palace is safe, we decide it's best if we leave Spring Court. Puck is still incredibly suspicious and watches me like a hawk every time I'm not sequestered in my room.

Since we're not due to arrive in Autumn Court for a few days, and since Eldoris still has a job to do, he takes me to the Seelie army base, which is in the area between the three Seelie Courts. I was expecting an area with tents and campfires and such, but it's a full-blown city. The portal lets us off in the training building, which has large areas for sparring as well as classrooms teaching strategy to those looking to ascend ranks.

But outside the building...

"It's New York," I marvel as I spin along a crowded concrete sidewalk with buildings that reach into the sky. Fae on wings zip in and out of the upper stories, some swan diving until their wings pop out and they fly into a lower window. Each building has its own personality with different colored bricks or elaborate painted murals and Fae of all sizes crowd the walkways, hurrying to get wherever they're going.

We leave the initial hub of army-related buildings and cross a bridge that arches over the Padauk River. "This is the residential section," Eldoris says. The streets turn from concrete to cobblestones, and trees pop up along the sidewalks. "These buildings are dormitories." Each dormitory is short and squat, about five stories compared to the others with ten or more. On the first floor of each is a different business; a coffee shop, a bakery, restaurants, tailors, and so many more. The dorms eventually give way to rows of three-story townhouses. "This is where the soldiers with mates, partners, and families live. Officers also live here."

"Do you have a townhouse?"

"I commute," he says. "But the house on the end of the street is empty. That's where we'll stay."

The townhouse in question is a perfect blank canvas. The floors and banister are all a rich, cherry wood, the walls are painted a simple cream, and the rest is just waiting to be customized. Eldoris summoned the essentials we'll need for our stay here, but as I tour the house, I can't help but decorate in my mind. The small room on the second story with the built-in bookshelves would make a great office, the bay window needs some pillows so you can sit and spy on your neighbors, and the room that attaches to the master is a perfect nursery.

Fuck me, where did that come from?

It would also make an amazing walk-in closet. Yeah, let's go with that.

The pixies meet us a bit later and proceed to follow me around when Eldoris spends the rest of the day working. They help me find a library, where I spend most of the day keeping up with my studies on court politics, and I even figure out how money works.

In the few days we spend on the army base I can almost imagine I'm back home. I'm not doted on or watched like a hawk. I'm able to buy things for myself, sit in cafes with other Fae, and go out to dinner with Eldoris. He even takes me to a club one night.

I'm ashamed to say that I pout when it's time to return to court life.

"I have something that will make it easier," Eldoris says as I'm lingering in the townhouse. "I promise it's worth it."

We portal back to the Varesen Forest, and immediately head in the opposite direction of the palace. "I did love the lake," I say once I figure out where we are. "But I'm not sure that's worth..."

I drift off because we're not by the lake that Eldoris took me to. One second, we're walking through lush greenery, and then next, leaves are falling around us in an array of oranges, yellows, and reds. The temperature dips slightly, brought in by a crisp wind that makes the leaves swirl and dance in little cyclones.

I straddle the line between the two courts, marveling at the change.

"Welcome to Autumn Court," Eldoris smirks as I stand in amazement, catching a leaf as it flutters down in front of me. We walk slowly so I can take in everything. The slant of the light makes the colors pop so much more than they do in the mortal realm and even the brown, dead leaves on the forest floor seem to glow.

It's not far of a walk to the palace, which blends beautifully into the area that it surrounds. I've only ever seen Winter and Spring Courts' palaces, which are designed to stun and stick out from the surrounding terrain. They're elevated with tall spires, and the coloring is designed to pop. But Autumn Court's palace looks more like a sprawling estate. It's made of a beige-colored stone with a blue roof that blends into the evening sky. And it's no higher than two stories, but it goes on for the equivalent of blocks. I take to the air and fly up a bit to get a better look. The estate is in a giant U shape, with both wings extending back as far as I can see.

"Goddess help the people in the back rooms," I say, landing beside Eldoris in a cluster of fallen leaves. I avoid the giant pile beside me since I jumped in a pile earlier and ended up disrupting a colony of some sort of Fae I'd never seen before. They were tiny like pixies, but they didn't have wings or sharp teeth, and they all looked like old men. When I asked Eldoris, he said they were leprechauns. I laughed it off as a joke, but I'm pretty sure he was serious.

"Usually the servants," Eldoris says. "In Autumn Court, only the servants can teleport, so they're given the rooms farthest away."

We make our way inside, get assigned another suite—this one done in pretty shades of gold and red—and get ready for another party. "Should have stayed at the base," I mutter as the pixies dress me in a peasant-style dress that's all the rage in the Autumn Court. It's lightweight cotton with a square neckline, long flowy sleeves, and ruching in the bodice that's super flattering. The dusky rose color flatters my complexion, which has some of its sun-kissed glow back.

"It's not proper for the heir to the throne to live in an army base," Brigid huffs.

"I think that was a joke," Althea says, looking to me for confirmation.

I give her a thin smile that appeases them both and let them continue dressing me, wondering if I can convince Eldoris to buy that townhouse so we can have an escape from court life.

"YOU SHOULD GIVE ME a nickname," I say to Eldoris as we walk down a long, carpeted hallway to the main part of the palace. Magical orbs of light flicker from sconces positioned within elaborate wainscotting, providing just enough light to see by.

"What?" Eldoris asks, eyeing me like I'm crazy.

"That's what people do when they're flirting." Another confused look. "Like a pet name."

"A pet name."

"I'm not crazy, this is a thing," I huff flapping my flowing sleeves in frustration. "Did you call your mate by her name?"

He gets a quiet, wistful look on his face. "No, I called her..." he breaks off, his throat working as he swallows down the emotion.

"You don't need to tell me," I tug his hand and pull him off to the side of the hallway. "But I think if we're moving to the next phase..." The next phase is more physical contact in addition to our flirting. Little touches, hugs, holding hands, that sort of thing.

"It makes sense," he says. "What will you call me?"

"I call you El," I say simply. "That should be good enough to appease people. But you only ever call me by my full name, so a pet name is required."

"Okay, I'll think on it," he says, and we walk toward the lounge where the cocktail party is held.

The room reminds me of a ski lodge complete with a giant stone fireplace that makes the room a little too warm. It's a casual affair, with people milling about and talking in small groups. There's no throne or dais or dance floor, just large armchairs and wooden coffee tables.

"Welcome," Radley booms, greeting us with two glasses of steaming liquid. "Here, cider. Spiked and non-spiked," he says, handing us the drinks. He tugs us out of the doorway and over to the corner where Izar, Prince of the Night Court, is leaning against a built-in bookshelf.

"Thank the goddess," Izar says, lifting his glass in a salute. Eldoris and I take a sip of the cider, the warm liquid fizzing on my tongue. Radley drinks his so fast I'm not sure how he doesn't burn his mouth.

"That kind of day?" Eldoris asks and hands Radley his drink for him to down.

"I've been home for three hours and have been asked five times when I'm planning on procreating," he intones.

"No marriage?"

"I think he's given up hope on me."

Izar laughs at Radley's expense and the three of us launch into an easy conversation. We hide in that corner for a long time, long enough that the passed hors d'oeuvres turn into passed desserts. Eldoris snags a tart from one of the waiters and holds it to my lips.

"You have to try this, kitten."

I choke, full-blown sputtering that does a decent job of hiding my laughter because a crumb is quite literally trying to kill me. When I get it together and am able to sip my drink, Eldoris looks mortified, and Izar and Radley are clearly trying not to laugh.

"Did you just call her kitten?" Radley asks.

Eldoris chuckles low and smooth, clearly having regained his composure. He pulls me flush against his side and says, "It's because I make her purr—"

"Will you excuse us for a second?" I grab Eldoris' hand, leaving the duo hunched over in hysterics.

I head straight for the open door to a brick patio. The air is cooler out here, the wind fluttering the magical lights as if they're candles. I pull Eldoris into a corner that's hidden in shadow, farthest away from anyone else.

"Kitten?" I laugh, finally allowing myself to break. "Of all the nicknames you could have chosen—"

"I panicked," he says, and I lean against the wall of the palace as he stands in front of me. "All I kept thinking was pet names—names of a pet—and kitten just came out. But we'll walk it back, say we were just fucking with the guys."

"It's okay," I sigh dramatically. "In the mortal realm, it's more of a...private pet name."

"Ahh," he says, taking a step closer to me so I can feel the heat of his body. The contrast to the cold stone behind me has my senses in overdrive. I place a hand on his chest, but whether it's to pull him closer or keep him at a distance, I'm not sure. "So, the purring comment probably wasn't the best."

"Not so much."

He hums and leans in to whisper in my ear. "I'm sorry, kitten." It sends a shot of pure lust right to my core and I release an exhale that sounds more like a breathy moan. When he pulls back, I tug my bottom lip between my teeth, and his eyes track the movement. And it strikes me how much I want Eldoris to kiss me.

We discussed how our first kiss should go. Somewhere private yet accessible so someone can catch us without it looking like we're trying too hard. Hiding in a dark corner of a party is the perfect space.

But that's not why I want him to kiss me. I just want it. I want *him*. All the flirting, the caresses, waking up in his arms—which I've done every damn day since that first night—it all has me primed and desperate for him.

I shift my hand, slowly sliding it up his chest before slipping it around the back of his neck and playing with the soft curls back there. Eldoris leans in, propping one arm on the side of the wall, caging me in. His other hand brushes the hair from my face and skims along my jaw.

"Do you want this?" he asks, his thumb brushing across my bottom lip. The question feels loaded. He's not asking me as the male fake falling in love with me. He's asking me as Eldoris. At least I think he is. I hope he is.

"Yes." My chest is heaving. My muscles are too tight, too hot. I need this kiss like I need air in my lungs. I need some form of release from the tension that's been building.

Eldoris swallows, and dips his head, moving too slowly. Normally, I'd meet him halfway. I'd take what I want from him. But something in me is hesitating. I want him to initiate this, to admit that this pull isn't just on my end. He avoids my lips and kisses the corner of my mouth. I whimper as he moves to the other side and repeats the action. I apply pressure on the back of his head, urging him forward.

My eyes drift closed. Our breath intermingles.

"There you are." Devorah's voice makes us spring apart like teenagers caught in the act. My heart pounds the haze of lust clears, and I realize what was about to happen. Eldoris and I were about to kiss, and it was about to mean something.

That scares the shit out of me.

I laugh breathlessly while Devorah is talking a thousand miles a minute, but I don't hear her, and Eldoris is looking at me instead of his sister. He looks torn between telling her to fuck off and being grateful that she interrupted. I know, because I feel the same.

"Hello, did you hear anything I just said?" Devorah says, once again snapping us out of our trance.

"No," Eldoris says honestly.

"There's an attack. The hellfire Fae are at Summer Court's borders."

Chapter Twenty-Nine
Edina

I'M NOT SURE HOW the party is going on like normal, how everyone can go on drinking and laughing as if nothing is happening. The only one who looks as though they're doing anything is my mother, who is quietly relaying orders to her pixie.

Eldoris walks straight over to a male in an army uniform, but Devorah grabs my arm and steers me toward a door off to the side of the fireplace. "Trust me," she says and pulls me into a small library. "Here." She summons a navy blue tunic and a pair of black leathers and hands them to me. "You're not fighting anything in a peasant dress."

"You underestimate me," I say, but shuck off the dress. "I fought in a bridesmaid dress once."

"Not in the jungle."

As soon as I'm dressed, she hands me a pair of socks and boots. "You're not changing?" I ask as I slip them on.

"You don't want me on the front lines." There's a touch of sadness in her tone. "I'd be a liability."

I don't press for more, and as soon as I'm fully outfitted, she opens the door and leads me back into the party. I scoop my hair up into a ponytail as we walk over to Eldoris and the officer. My mother has joined them, her face fixed in a cold mask.

"Looks like it's a small force," the soldier is saying. "Just a handful, but they're wreaking havoc."

"The vegetation should be too wet to burn," my mother says.

"The hellfire is strong enough to combat the moisture, Your Majesty."

Lovely.

My mother clucks her tongue but doesn't say anymore. Her eyes soften when they meet mine, but it's so fleeting I'm sure no one else noticed. "We trust your ability to handle this, General. Keep us apprised of your efforts."

"Your Majesty." Eldoris bows at the waist, and I give a half-assed curtsey as my mother returns to the party, her pixie, Cornelia, in tow. Everyone else in the lounge has started taking notice of us, but they don't comment, or offer any help. They simply whisper amongst themselves.

"Ready?" Radley says, appearing beside the soldier. He's changed into a russet tunic that has a leaf embossed on the breast. "I figure you'll need someone to suck the oxygen from the flames." As if proving his point, the air around us gets thinner, like we suddenly scaled a mountain.

"Thank you," Eldoris says, and then places his hand on my lower back, before addressing Devorah. "You're going to the palace?"

"Unless you think I shouldn't," she says, and Eldoris shakes his head. "It's safer there."

"Unless we get invaded," Devorah scoffs. Then she and Eldoris have some sort of mental conversation that I'm not privy to before she nods earnestly. "Let's go."

We rush out of the lounge and down the main corridor to the long hall with all the rooms. "The portal is at the very back of the property,"

Radley explains, extending sharp-edged, brown wings. "It'll be faster if we fly."

He scoops Eldoris into his arms, bridal style, and I fight the urge to laugh as my wings extend through two tiny slits in the tunic. Devorah extends hers, which are much softer around the edges and iridescent like mine, but when they catch the light, look like flames, giving the impression she's a phoenix.

I fly after Radley, over the heads of the servants and party guests, and after what feels like forever, we approach the portal door, which is open and emitting the swirling bluish-purple mist. Radley lands, and I follow his lead, entering the portal on my legs. Then we're hurtling through the enchanted walkway, zooming past elaborate doors.

"This is it," Eldoris says, gesturing to the door quickly approaching. "As soon as we land, I'll teleport us to the front lines."

"Don't die," Devorah calls as she continues past us, and we jump off the walkway and through the open entrance into a dark cave. Just like he did when we visited the beach, Eldoris wraps his arms around me, grabs Radley's hand, and teleports us out of the cave and further into the Wyld Jungle.

The air is weighed down by humidity, making it hard to breathe. Sweat instantly beads on the back of my neck as we land amidst the vibrant green vegetation. The trees hang low, and the plants on the ground grow high, closing in around us and making visibility difficult. Radley lands in a nest of vines and has to kick his way free as Eldoris and I head toward the plumes of smoke.

"The Padauk River is just ahead," he says. Impossibly, the air gets thicker, and the smell of smoke mixed with burning flesh burns my nostrils. It's a scent I hoped to never experience again but know intimately.

The Padauk River is the boundary between Summer and Spring Court. It's a wide river with an unforgiving current, that has never been breached by attackers. But then again, Spring and Summer have rarely been in conflict with each other. The water churns, swirling up sediment from the bottom and turning the water brown, except where there are white-capped rapids.

But the river is clear. There are no boats, no brave souls trying to swim across its width, and the blasts of white-hot fire seem to be coming from the trees themselves.

The soldier who briefed Eldoris arrives beside us. "General, they're in the jungle." He points behind us to the trees, where lines of soldiers have retreated and shoot blasts of magic into the canopy.

"Front lines mean the river," Eldoris snaps, and the soldier looks properly chastised. We run back through the jungle, slowly picking our way through.

A fireball streaks across the sky and lands in the middle of a group of soldiers. The flames take out the Fae standing in the middle before slowly inching outward, jumping high and igniting vines and leaves that then drop scalding embers on the heads of other soldiers. The screams, the scent, it all tugs at my memory in the worst way.

Instinct takes over, and everything I learned fighting in the Witch War comes back in full force. I jump forward and use my water magic to extinguish the flames with a hiss. The soldiers sigh in relief and return to trying to shoot down the Fae hiding in the trees.

I scan the area, searching for other Winter Court soldiers. Arguably, our magic is the most effective against hellfire. The other Fae can focus on taking out the enemy, but once the magic is cast, they need water. I find them peppered in with other soldiers, working with the Seelie Fae to keep the flames at bay.

Eldoris calls me, but I'm already springing into the air, looking for an area that doesn't have a Winter Court soldier. Night has fully fallen, adding to the visibility issues, so I fly toward the light. After almost flying into the mouth of a ridiculous snake that will haunt my nightmares forever, I find a blast site and put out the flames before landing on the ground behind the soldiers. "Did you see where it came from?" I ask, shouting over the din of bomb-like sounds as more hellfire crashes into the ranks of the army.

"It's too dark to tell," he says. "But it looks like they're in the trees."

"I need someone with light magic," I call, and a female with hair so blonde it's almost white steps forward. "Can you fly?" She shakes her head. "Come on then."

I pick her up and fly up to the middle of the trees, in between the canopies. We need to take away their high ground. Others realize what I'm doing and take to the sky, ready to take down attackers as soon as they're spotted.

"Which way is the river?" I ask, and she points. I spin in the air, and as soon as I'm situated, the girl releases a pulse of her power.

Light magic is blinding, and I squint against the initial blast as the glittering silver and gold magic illuminates the canopy. It crashes directly into some of the hellfire Fae perched in the trees and knocks them over. Some are quick enough to get behind the trunk or drop low to their branches, but their locations are uncovered, and the other Seelie attack.

"More light," I tell the girl, and she pulses out the magic again. The Seelie Fae are fast with their attacks this time, aiming for the kill. More fall.

"I need my hands," I tell her and fly her over to a branch so thick she can stand with one foot in front of the other. One Fae is directly in front of us, I can see his silhouette hiding behind the tree trunk just across the way. "Now."

The female releases another blast of light, and this time, I follow it with a wave of water that douses the fire the hellfire Fae gathered. They start retreating, and I hear Eldoris bellow an order to not let them get across the river.

I'm about to join the pursuit when the hellfire Fae across from me emerges from behind a tree trunk. A ball of white-hot fire sits in his hand, casting shadows that make his grinning face look sinister. With a bellow, I launch a series of icicles at him, but he melts them with a sneer.

It happens faster than I expect. One minute I'm sending more icicles at him, the next there's a blinding light streaking toward my face. I duck, but I'm not fast enough and the fire connects with the edge of my wing. The pain is instant and so intense it makes me heave. Then I'm falling as the hellfire starts creeping inward, eviscerating my wing. I cast ice over it as I tumble toward the earth and stop the spread just as it reaches my other wing.

I try to flap them, but one wing is out of commission, so it only makes me spin in circles as I drop like a rock through the branches of the trees. I hear my name being called, but I can't tell from where as I try to use my magic for a spell to cushion my fall. I reach for a branch and miss, but it hits my injured wing, and my vision goes black.

I'm going to die falling out of a fucking tree.

Of all the ways I could die, this one sucks the most.

I hit an air current and bounce, flipping so I'm falling face down instead of backward. I'm so delirious with the pain and everything looks so similar in the dark that I have no idea how far I'm falling. "El—" I squeak out as I'm sure I'm close to the end.

Something warm cradles me, guiding me gently to the ground and setting me down with a soft thud as I fall into the abyss.

※

"Princess, you with us?" A gruff voice calls. Everything is too bright behind my eyelids for the nighttime. Where could I possibly be?

"You need to chew this." I blink open and see a woman holding a bright red mushroom to my lips. The sky is still dark, or maybe that's just the way it always is in the jungle, but I'm surrounded by a ring of Fae with light magic pooling in their hands.

"Open," she orders. "We need to repair your wing and it's going to hurt. Take the mushroom."

"No drugs," I say. "Sober."

"All well and good, but this isn't habit forming, and trust me, you're gonna need it." The woman pushes the thing into my mouth when I open it to protest, and I find myself chewing. The mushroom works fast, and my head starts to feel light and floaty.

"I can't feel my body," I mumble, but I know I said a few words wrong, which makes me giggle. A wave of exhaustion overtakes me, and my head lolls forward.

"Princess, I need you to stay awake," the female says.

"Mmmkay," I say as I start to slip back into darkness.

"Princess, eyes here." I blink and the female's form comes more into view. "My name is Marjorie; can you say that?"

"Marcy?" I ask.

"Close enough," she says. "We're going to heal your wing. It's going to hurt, even with the mushroom, but I need you to stay with me, okay?"

"Okay, Marvell," I murmur.

Then I pass out.

Chapter Thirty
Eldoris

MY HEART STOPS. My lungs seize. Edina falls from the sky and we're too far apart; I won't get to her in time. Uselessness renders me immobile, and I just watch as she plummets toward the ground.

"I've got her," Radley says, casting a torrent of air at the space where she's falling. She hits his pocket of air and bounces. "Shit, hang on." He flies up and then sends a gentler breeze that cradles her like a hammock and slowly brings her to the ground.

And then I'm running, using spells and fire magic to cut down any trees in my path, uncaring that I'm destroying the jungle. I need to get to her.

I'm vaguely aware of my lieutenants calling out orders to follow the retreating hellfire Fae as they scatter like ants back into the pits they've crawled out of. I don't pay them any mind but keep my shield tight to my body just in case one of them lingers, planning to ambush me. The only thing on my mind is Edina.

There are shouts up ahead, and soldiers frantically scurrying around. I follow the commotion, straight toward a small clearing where the healers are stationed. The clearing is chaos as soldiers drag their friends in to be examined. The scent of burning flesh permeates the air, mixing with the scent of the plants. Off to the edge, tarps are laid out like sleeping mats for the dead.

A circle of healers surrounds one stretcher, brilliantly bright healing magic pouring from their hands to the patient. I can't see within their ranks, but in my gut, I know she's there. I approach slowly, not wanting to distract them from their work, and one healer shifts slightly so I catch a glimpse of yellow-blonde hair.

All at once the light is extinguished, and the healers open their circle to let me in. Edina lies on her stomach as one of the healers wraps her wing in thick gauze so quickly that I can't see the damage. The other one looks mostly unharmed, the swirling pattern shining iridescent, marred only by a dark, singed part at the bottom edge. Her skin is pale, and her eyes are closed, but her body rises and falls with her breathing.

My vision shutters, and for a moment, I'm looking at my mate, Dark Magic spreading up her ebony skin. Her brown eyes close, and I'm powerless as she slips away from me.

"El?" The soft, melodic tone of her voice makes me inhale sharply, and I blink away the vision of my mate to find Edina opening her eyes with great effort.

I crash to my knees beside her and press a kiss on her forehead. "Thank the goddess," I breathe against her skin, not wanting even that little bit of separation between us. Her lids blink extra slowly.

"I fell out of the sky," she murmurs.

"I saw." She huffs, trying to blow a rogue piece of hair from her face, only to have it land in the same place. I tuck it behind her ear, lingering to cup her cheek, and she gives me a dopey smile.

"They gave me drugs," she whispers, a crease forming between her brows. "I told them I didn't need it, but they said—"

"It's okay, kitten," I say, the nickname rolling off my tongue easily and without thought. "You don't need to explain."

"I told them I'm sober," she says, grabbing my hand. "They said I needed it, and I won't be addicted. And my wings hurt so much."

"Shh," I murmur, petting her hair. "Everything will be okay." She nuzzles into the contact and sighs in a way that's very close to a damn purr.

A small female in a healer's uniform comes over and gives Edina a pat on the head. "Macy, look, it's my fiancé," Edina coos, and then frowns. "That's not right. That's a human term."

"You can call me whatever you want as long as you're okay," I say, the band around my heart tightening again as Edina winces at something the healer does to her.

"Be-troth-ed," Edina slurs. She tries again. "Be-trooooo-thed." She extends the word for too many syllables and then makes herself giggle. "It's a funny word."

The healer chuckles and then turns to me. "We gave her a mushroom for the pain. Her right wing took the worst of the damage, but that magic of hers saved her life. She'll need one more round of light magic therapy in the morning, but then she won't even scar." She fixes Edina with a stern look. "Absolutely no retracting your wings or teleporting tonight, and I'd refrain from flying for a few days."

"Aye aye, captain," Edina salutes, and the healer frowns at me, confused. That's probably not her rank and Edina's turn of phrase was misunderstood, but I don't bother to clarify.

"I'm taking her to the palace," I inform the healer instead, and she purses her lips, but agrees.

"I can walk," Edina announces, and pushes off the stretcher. She barely gets to a seated position before she starts to flop over, but I'm there and she lands cheek-first into my chest. "Mmm, you're so warm." She grapples with the neckline of my tunic, seeking skin, and tries to pull it low enough that she can rest her head there, choking me and snapping the threads in the process.

"I'm gonna carry you, is that okay?" She just reaches up to play with my hair, venturing dangerously close to the base of my horns. It's not something we've discussed, but horns are very sensitive, and usually only touched in private. "Edina..." I warn, and her eyes flick to mine. The sapphire blue is almost eclipsed by her pupils, and she gives me a sheepish grin that tells me she knows exactly what she's doing.

"You can carry me," she says and proceeds to hold her arms straight out like a child waiting to be picked up. I scoop her into my arms, winding her legs around my waist so she's hanging onto my front like a koala, and her injured wings aren't rubbing against anything.

She nestles into my neck, breathing me in with long, greedy inhales. I walk in the direction of the portal, navigating the uneven terrain as Edina tells me all she did during the battle. I know most of it, I couldn't take my eyes off her as she streaked through the sky like some water-wielding goddess.

"And I got the fire out, but it tore a hole in my wing." She twitches the wing for emphasis. "So, I was falling, watching the ground come faster and faster, and couldn't do anything but spin in a circle thanks to my other wing. Then the air was helping me. Was that the goddess? I don't know enough about her, but would she save me?"

"I'd like to believe she would," I say. "But the air was all Radley."

"I need to send him a bottle of wine or a fruit basket or something to thank him." She pulls back, her face gravely serious. "Will you remind me? I'm high and I don't know if I'll remember on my own."

"I'll remind you, kitten," I assure her, and she settles herself back into my chest.

My heart is still pounding a million beats per minute, adrenaline is still coursing through my body. I hug Edina tighter.

"I like it when you call me kitten," she murmurs, her hands tracing the tattoos exposed from my ripped neckline.

"I thought you hated it."

She shakes her head against me. "I never said that." I feel her smile. "I said it was a name you should use in private. It makes me think of all the dirty things you could be doing while you call me that."

My steps falter and I have to pause my trek. She laughs against me, the sound lower this time and filled with promise. I know she makes things sexual as a defense mechanism, but that statement just felt so honest. Not at all contrived like her usual innuendos. It was almost...innocent.

"We'll revisit that statement when you're not high."

"Yes please," she purrs, and the sound has blood rushing to my cock.

We get to the cave that houses the portal and step inside. As soon as we're on the walkway, I assess Edina, looking for signs of distress from moving at the breakneck pace down the ley line. "You okay?"

"Mmm," she mumbles and says something else into my neck, but I can't hear her. Before I can ask her to repeat it, our exit is up and I'm jumping through space, trying hard to keep Edina still so as to not jostle her wings.

The portal entrance in our palace is kept secret, only those who know of the entrance can see the doorway from the portal, and as such, it remains unguarded on the inside. We step into the secluded hallway of the sandstone palace, but I barely register the familiar halls as I carry Edina to my room. I send a mental message to Devorah to let her know I've arrived, and to ask her to send the healer to us in the morning.

We reach my rooms, and I walk straight to the bedroom, bypassing the small library that serves as my central sitting room. I was never one for formal spaces, so I had the oak bookshelves built into the walls and stocked with the rarest history books I could find. Part of the problem with the Fae is that history is approximate, so I collect tomes from every court on one incident since each account is vastly different. I find it fascinating.

I'll have to add some books that Edina will enjoy.

When we enter the bedroom, I quickly slide open the thick curtains and open the window. At the scent of the salt water, Edina hums in happiness. "We're at the beach."

"Yes. Our palace overlooks the ocean."

"I like the ocean," she sighs, nuzzling back into me.

"I'm going to put you to bed now," I say, flinging back the navy comforter on the side Edina prefers. She whimpers and tightens her hold on me. "You need rest."

She grumbles again but releases her death grip and I sit her on the edge of the bed, dropping to my knees to help remove her boots. I'm assessing how best to help her change from her tunic when she procures an icicle and slices it down the center so the entire thing falls off both her wings and her arms. Then she flops face-first into the pillows in just her lacy bra.

I hover for a moment. There's still a tightness in my chest, like someone has wrapped their hands around my heart and keeps squeezing. I should go to Devorah, ask if she thinks I need a healer or something. There's no physical reason I should be feeling like this.

I keep replaying her falling from the sky, and once again I'm frozen while I try to decide what to do. "El?" she calls sleepily, patting the bed beside her, searching for me.

I clear my throat. "I'm here."

She turns her head and sighs when she finds me. I kneel beside her so we're at eye level. "Will you stay with me while I sleep?" she asks. I can't say no to her, not when she's hurting.

I change out of my tunic and leathers, slipping into sweats and a soft t-shirt. The second I get under the covers, Edina curls into my side, her bare skin cold even through my shirt. I wrap my arms around her and pull her closer and she hums in contentment.

"I like it here," she says.

"Summer Court?"

She shakes her head. "Here," she nudges my chest with her nose. "I sleep here every night."

I chuckle, "I know." I've come to expect her drifting toward me as she sleeps.

"You do?" She sits up, her blue eyes wide and shining. "But I roll away in the morning."

"You don't have to," I say. "I like you here too."

Her hand splays on my chest, and she starts tracing the lines of my tattoos by memory. "We fit well together," she says, and as if to prove her point, her body molds perfectly to mine. Our legs intertwine, fusing the last little bit of space we've been keeping. "I..." she starts and then tightens her hold on my shirt. "I haven't fit into many places."

"Edina—"

"It's true," she says softly. "I never really fit in the mortal realm, or with my family. And even with my bio family...it's not the same. But here..."

I swallow hard because fuck if I don't feel the same way about her. It's just so easy to be with her. Even when we're fighting outside forces or putting ourselves in ridiculous positions with this fake relationship, we fit together seamlessly. In a short time, she's become my best friend.

"I feel it too," I murmur, and cup her face, tilting her chin up so she looks at me. Her eyes are shining with tears.

"It scares me."

"Me too." I kiss the tip of her nose. "But I'm not going anywhere."

"Promise?" The question is so small, her voice fragile and it makes me want to wrap her in my arms and protect her from the world. When Edina is feeling strong, she's incredible. But this Edina? Vulnerable, open and honest Edina may be my favorite.

"Promise." She sighs happily and lies back on my chest. "Don't roll away in the morning," I say, holding her as tight as I possibly can without touching her wings.

"Okay, baby." She cracks herself up. "I don't know where that came from. You're like a million years older than me."

"A million is a stretch," I tease, pinching her side and making her laugh. "But you can call me whatever you want."

"Oh, you don't want to give me that kind of leeway," she laughs. "We'll see how I feel when I'm not high on mushrooms."

"Deal."

Chapter Thirty-One
Eldoris

EDINA QUICKLY FALLS INTO a peaceful sleep, but I stay awake all night. She doesn't have any nightmares, hasn't since she started sleeping on my chest, but occasionally she winces when her wings flutter in her sleep. Every time I close my eyes, I see images of her falling. The tightness in my chest is constant, painfully contracting with every shallow breath I take.

I almost lost her, just like I lost Arella.

The sour taste of bile rises in my throat, but I swallow it down. I promised Edina I wouldn't leave, that she wouldn't be alone. How can I keep that promise when I can't assure her safety? My thoughts spiral, sinking down that dark path I walked after my mate's death. The feeling of impotence and uselessness overtakes my mind and fills it with doubt.

By the time the sun rises, I can't stand it anymore. I haven't taken a full breath in hours, and the short choppy motion jostles Edina. Gently, I slip out from under her and bolt from my room in search of the one person who knows how to calm me down. The halls are a blur, fading at the edges of my vision. The normally soothing décor of our home does nothing for my agitated state. The soft cream walls and sandstone floors are dizzying instead of providing their usual soft reassurance. The sea glass mosaics on the walls all look the same as I run past them and finally reach my sister's office.

I don't bother knocking on Devorah's door but fling it open. It's a small and cluttered room, the built-in shelves crammed with papers and other important-looking missives. Her desk is large cherry wood, a total contrast with the coastal vibe of the rest of the palace, and she keeps the curtains drawn, so it's somber in here.

Ari leans over her shoulder, a little closer than appropriate, while they're looking at some documents. The two of them jerk their heads up at my entrance, and he jumps back.

"Sorry," I say aloud, but through our link, I ask, *Am I interrupting?*

"It's fine," she replies. She doesn't need to ask me if something's wrong, she's always been able to read me with a single look. "Could you give us a moment, little Hershel?"

Her advisor purses his lips but bows and exits the office. Devorah gestures to a black leather wingback across the desk from her, and I take a seat. She summons two cups of espresso for us both and I take mine but don't drink. My hands are shaking, and my heart may actually burst if I add caffeine to my panic.

"Edina almost died," I say. She nods knowingly. "And ever since...it's like I can't breathe, Dev. My chest hurts, my head is pounding, I keep—" I suck in a breath through my teeth as emotion overwhelms me.

"She's okay," Devorah says, abandoning her cup and moving to stand in front of me. I lean forward, propping my elbows on my knees and pressing the heel of my hands into my eyes as my sister starts rubbing lines up my back.

"It's completely normal that you're feeling like this," she soothes. "It brought up old trauma."

"No, it's not supposed to be normal," I say a little too forcefully. "I'm not supposed to feel..." I rub my chest, which has started throbbing again. "She's not Arella."

"I know," Devorah says. "And Edina is well. The healers said she won't even have a scar."

"I need to end it," I say, and my sister's hand pauses as the shock of the words penetrate the air.

"You don't mean that."

"It's the only way. I can't do this again."

"Stop." Devorah drags out her powerful voice, the one she uses when she's playing her role as princess, not one she's ever used with me. She grabs my chin and forcibly lifts it to meet her eyes. "You are not going to break off your betrothal because you're scared."

"I'm not—"

"You are. And I'm going to tell you why, but when I do, you need to not jump down my throat. You need to listen and absorb the information." I motion for her to continue. "You're falling for Edina."

"I—"

"Sit and absorb, remember?" she says, giving me the eye. Then she continues, "I know you don't think you're capable of loving anyone since Arella, but that's bullshit. You're falling for Edina, and that scares you. And you probably feel guilty because, in your mind, you're being unfaithful."

"Aren't I?" I ask.

"No." She leans forward and places her hands on mine. "I want to show you something. Arella asked me to take a message for you before she died. She said I could only show it to you when it looked like you wanted to move on but were holding yourself back. She was very clear on that, so if you don't think you're falling for Edina, I'll hang onto the message."

"You're blackmailing me with a message from my dead mate?" I seethe.

"She was my best friend," Devorah snaps. "You better fucking believe I'll honor her last wishes. So, you tell me. Are you ready to hear it?"

"I could say yes even if I don't agree with your assessment."

"You could, but you won't. You wouldn't disobey her wishes any more than I would."

She has me there. I grind my teeth but nod. "Show me."

Devorah leans forward and I open my mind further than I usually do for our link. Like a film screen, a memory floats to the forefront of my mind, propelled there from hers. I see it all from her point of view, through her eyes.

As my sister, I sit behind her desk shuffling papers around looking for a note. I feel her heart rate skyrocket as she thinks about the order for more uniforms for the army, and how I asked her to complete the form four times and now she can't even find it.

I pull out of her mind enough to give her a raise of my eyebrow. "It was a long time ago."

Back in the memory, the door to the office slams open, and Arella storms in, her dark braids tied back in a haphazard bun. She's wearing fighting leathers, a regular occurrence when we were on the battlefield, but unusual when we stayed in the palace. It's then I notice the small gold necklace hanging outside her tunic.

This is the day she died, I mentally say to Devorah. She doesn't respond as the memory keeps playing.

Seeing my mate like this, like she's real and I can reach out and touch her, it's like a punch in the stomach. I can't move closer, because in the memory, Devorah stays seated. But I want to. I want to run and hold her and convince her to stay here and not come with me to the attack of the Night Court. If she just stayed...

Arella has a thin sheen of sweat coating her warm brown skin and her eyes flit around the room wildly. "What did my brother do?" I hear myself, as Devorah, ask. She shakes her head, sending more hair from the bun, and opens and closes her mouth before steeling her spine and putting on her determined look.

"There's an attack at the borders," she says, and the statement is so similar to what we experienced today that it has my heart pounding. "Night Court, we think. There's dark magic."

Devorah swears and runs her fingers through her hair. "Can you see anything?"

Arella swallows. While she had fire magic, like me, her greatest strength was clairvoyance, she could see the future. It's very rare amongst Fae but doesn't discriminate on the type of Fae or type of magic. Most hide their abilities to keep from being used by royals, but Arella always shared it willingly. She'd remind us that the future is fickle but would give readings on battles, alliances, and anything else we could need.

The fact that she's quiet about it now speaks volumes, and Devorah realizes this.

"What is it?" my sister demands in that no-nonsense tone. Arella purses her lips, and Devorah sighs and crosses around the desk, just like she did with me today. "Ar," she softens. "You can tell me anything."

Arella meets her gaze, a tear brimming on her lashes. "I think I'm going to die today."

Devorah sags back against the desk. I feel the wood against her back, biting painfully, but not nearly as painful as the clear and calm way it felt hearing Arella say those words. She wants to argue, she wants to lock Arella up just like I did, but my mate opens her mouth.

"And I need to leave a message with you, for Eldoris."

I feel Devorah's desperation cool slightly, and when I look down, her hands are shaking. "You won't see him?"

"I will," Arella says, tears flowing freely now. "But...this is for later. For when..." A low growl builds in her throat, but she shakes it off. "For when he's falling in love again."

Devorah agrees. She's still thinking of ways to prevent this, hoping to find a way to spare me this pain and, selfishly, to save her best friend.

Arella places a calloused hand in Devorah's, and I jump. *I can feel her.* I shouldn't be able to feel her in a memory like this. Her hands are cold, and the callouses from all her training bite Devorah's soft skin. I always loved her callouses and the fact that her hands were worn from the elements.

When she looks into Devorah's eyes, I feel the switch. She's looking at me. One last tear rolls down her cheek and then she smiles widely. "Hello, my darling."

The wind is sucked from my lungs. I haven't heard those words, that soft tone, the way her R rolls slightly in so long. "If you're seeing this..." she pulls a plump lip between her teeth to keep it from wobbling and then starts again. "If you're seeing this, that means I'm gone. I'm sorry I had to go and that we didn't have enough time together, but know that I love you so much, and will always love you.

"And if you're seeing this, it means that you've found someone you love. Or, more likely, are trying not to love in honor of my memory." She squeezes my hands the way she always had, the way that was so comforting. "My darling, please don't deprive yourself of love for my benefit."

The impulse to brush off her words is strong, but this is someone who knew me better than anyone, and so she anticipates it. "I'm serious, Eldoris. I want you to be happy. I want you to live a long life filled with laughter and light and, goddess willing, a family."

Her light laugh is half a sob. "I'm not sure how things work once we pass on, but if I have any say, I'll send you someone to love. Someone with a sense of humor, who could keep you on your toes, and won't let you get sucked into the politics of court, but instead can make fun of them alongside you."

I'm not breathing. She describes Edina so perfectly it's like she *did* send her to me. That is until she says, "She wouldn't be too pretty though, I'm not sure my ego could take it." Her laugh is warm and joined in by Devorah.

"But please, my darling, if you feel love again, embrace it. Don't let the fear of what happened to me stand in the way, and don't let my memory be a wall for you to hide behind.

"And when it's your time, hopefully in thousands and thousands of years, I'll greet you with open arms. Both of you.

"I love you."

She blinks, and when she looks back at Devorah, it's my sister she's seeing. Devorah isn't the messenger anymore, she's herself. And she's sobbing.

"Don't go," she pleads.

Arella pulls her in close, squeezing so tightly it feels like she's wringing out the tears from my sister's body. "If I don't go, if I change fate in that way, it won't just be me who dies today."

Understanding dawns in Devorah's mind and mine, and I feel her chest crumple. When my mate died, power erupted from me in a powerful wave that destroyed the opposing army and sent the rest retreating. If not for that, who knows what would have become of our court.

She sacrificed herself for us.

She pulls back and I bathe in her brown eyes, drinking in every inch of her while she's here alive. "Make sure it's real," she says. "When you tell him, make sure she's the one. No need wasting that message on some floozy." They both laugh and Arella cups my sister's face before kissing her cheek. "I have to go."

Devorah wraps her arms around herself as my mate smiles and walks out the office door.

The memory fades and I crumple, huge heaving sobs wracking my body. But it's the kind of crying that's cleansing. It's letting go. I need to let go of my mate and open my heart to the possibility of a future.

Devorah wraps me in a hug, and together we cry, releasing the pain of centuries with our tears.

Chapter Thirty-Two
Edina

I'M NOT THE KIND of girl to pout when she spends the night with a male and he's gone in the morning. I'm not the type to sit around and wonder what the hell happened while I was sleeping, or if I said anything while I was on pain meds that made him up and bolt without so much as a note. After he specifically told me to stay, to not run away.

So, when I wake up alone, in a ton of pain from the fucking hole in my wing, I don't do any of those things. Instead, I head straight to the mirror in my room and call Katie.

"Hey, Tinker Bell," a deep male voice croons as the picture solidifies, and I fight a groan. It's not that I don't love talking to my vampire friend, I just don't have the mental capacity for his banter this morning.

Vlad has always reminded me of an old Hollywood movie star. His blonde hair is always impeccably styled, swooped back and away from his clean-shaven face. He's always dressed formally, though today he's lost the suit jacket and is only in a pinstripe vest and a blue button-down that brings out his eyes. When the picture comes into focus, he flashes me a dazzling grin, the fine points of his fangs descending over his lower lip.

"Where's Katie?" I ask, giving him the best smile I can muster.

His chuckle is deep and full of enough subtext that I understand exactly what he means when he says she's "in a meeting." If I had any questions about my best friend's status, they are squashed when I hear a breathy moan in the background.

"Are you sitting outside their bedroom, creeper?" I quip, with just the tiniest edge.

"No, I'm sitting in my office. They're in her office. She forgot to re-soundproof the room after she sent me the mirror."

"You could go to another room."

He waves me off, like listening to two of his friends fuck on a desk is more of a regular occurrence than it should be. "You look like shit."

I glare, although he probably has a point. I didn't shower because I wasn't sure if I should get my wing wet, so I'm still covered in dirt from my fall on the jungle floor. I run my fingers through my knotted hair and pull out a green leaf.

"Nice," Vlad smirks. "Tell me that's from some wild forest orgy."

"You really are an old perv. What's wrong? Not happy with wifey?"

"You're feisty today," he says, not rising to my bait. Instead, he watches me curiously. I hate that he can probably read me. Vlad always had an uncanny ability to know what I was thinking, but he doesn't push it. Instead, he says, "I'm coming out there soon."

"Really?" The lift in my voice is a tad desperate, but Vlad is someone I consider a close friend, and I could use a friend right now.

"Coming out for a little Night Court shindig. I think it's in a week, your time."

"We'll be there," I say, and then immediately wince.

"We?" There's a string of curses in the background followed by a male grunt. "I think that was the finale, so tell me quickly."

"There's nothing to tell. You know I'm betrothed," I say. Even if Katie didn't tell him, Vlad has spies everywhere and knows everything. Expecting him not to know something is just setting yourself up for failure.

"That's not why you look like you got hit by a truck."

"She what?" The sound of my best friend's voice, still a little breathless if we're being honest, is both a relief and makes me jump. She grabs the handheld mirror from Vlad, and I get a full shot of her cleavage.

"Holy titties, Batman," I laugh, and she holds the mirror higher so I can see her pinking cheeks. "Are they bigger?"

"What's the matter?" Katie asks, ignoring me.

"That's just not fair. I think I lost a cup size with the whole not-eating thing, and you gained one. There has to be a spell that will let you give me your excess."

"I'll get right on that," she deadpans. "Stop deflecting. Why do you look like you got hit by a truck?"

I sigh dramatically. "I got in a little firefight, that's all," I say, and flash my bandaged wing. Katie runs a hand through her mussed sex hair.

"A hellfire fight?"

I wince, and she gasps, all the color leeching from her face. The mirror starts shaking, blurring her image.

"Woah," Vlad says off-screen, and then his arms are around her, guiding her into a chair. He disappears and then a second later hands her a glass of water. "You have to be careful," he murmurs. Katie waves her hand, and everything goes silent, but the picture clears enough that I can see them arguing.

"Hello? What was that?" I demand.

"Nothing," Katie responds and then goes silent again. I can't tell who wins the argument, because Vlad goes off-screen but Katie doesn't look victorious. "I was trying to get Vlad to go out there and be your bodyguard. But he's *needed here*." She says the last words in a very poor attempt at Vlad's voice.

"No, why did you almost pass out?" I ask.

"Low blood sugar." I frown at her blatant lie, but I know my best friend enough to know she won't be pushed when she doesn't want to share. I'll ask Vlad when he gets here. "How are things going with your fake dating trope?" she asks.

"Making Puck miserable," I smirk, a little satisfaction bleeding into the words. "He bailed on the last event." I catch her up on all the steps we've been taking to slowly progress our relationship, watching as her color slowly returns as I tell the story.

When I get to the part about nicknames, she says, "Wait, you call him El, but what does he call you?"

"Kitten."

"Hot," Vlad says, smushing his face next to Katie's.

"No...it's..." I stammer because when he whispered it in my ear, it was sexy as hell. Katie and Vlad exchange a look that makes me scowl. "Oh, shut up."

Our laughter is interrupted by a knock at the door. "Edina, are you decent?" Astor calls from just outside.

"Not remotely," Vlad answers, and if I could, I'd slap him through the mirror. Astor is the most literal of my fathers and won't understand Vlad's innuendo. I call him in, and on his heels is the Winter Court healer, Eirwen. His hair is stark white, and his skin is so pale it appears the only color on his body is the pale blue of his eyes.

"Astor, you remember Katie and Vlad," I say, gesturing to the mirror. They all exchange quick pleasantries before Eirwen insists he needs to look at my wings.

"I'll see you soon, Tinker Bell," Vlad says.

Katie tugs her lip between her bottom teeth and tears well in her eyes. "Love you," she eeks out.

"Love you most, but why are you crying?" I ask. "I'll talk to you soon and see you before you know it!"

"I know, I'm sorry, I just..." she blinks rapidly as the tears start to fall. "I just miss you."

"I miss you too, babes."

I remove the spell from the mirror, watching as my friends' image slowly disappears and is replaced by my reflection. Vlad was right, I look like shit.

"When did you get here?" I ask Astor as Eirwen directs me to lie on my stomach with my wings up.

"Eldoris sent word this morning and said it was safe to travel. He thought we'd want our healer to look you over, so we just arrived. Your mother and fathers are getting settled in their suite and they'd like to have breakfast when you're done if you're feeling up to it."

"Did Eldoris say when he'd be back?" I wince as the bandage sticks to the wound. Eirwen is clicking his tongue about 'battle healers,' and then gets to work. His magic is cool against my inflamed wing, and I sigh and sink into the pillows as he starts his work.

"No," Astor says simply. "But I'm sure he's attending the boating luncheon today."

"Boating luncheon?" I ask.

"At the lake on property," Astor says it like I should know exactly what he's talking about. "It's a Summer Court tradition." I'm too tired to push for more, and somehow, the fact that Eldoris called my family to take care of me hurts more than it should. It feels like he's pawning me off.

But I'm not the type of girl to get bogged down in things like that, so I ignore that uncomfortable itching in my chest.

EIRWEN WAS ABLE TO finish healing my wings, and after a shower and breakfast with my family, I headed back to the room to get ready for this 'boating event.' I was hoping it would be a yacht or a dinner cruise or something, but it's a rowboat. I have no idea what's supposed to happen on said rowboat, but any hopes that it's a race are dashed when the pixies dress me in a maxi dress.

"You're all set, Princess," Brigid says, and Althea is cooing over how I look as she encourages me to the full-length mirror.

"Damn," I breathe when I see my reflection. This is what I would wear all the time if I was allowed to dress myself.

The thin straps lead to a deep V that dips all the way to a tie at my waist before gently flowing to the floor. There's a large slit by my thigh and two cut-outs by my rib cage. I love the turquoise color, and how the pixies left my hair down in simple, beachy waves, but have given me a large sunhat. I pluck a pair of sunglasses from the vanity beside me and put them on while stepping into flat, gold sandals that wind around my ankles and up to my calves.

"Let's do this."

They lead me down halls that are made of large, misshapen, sand-stone-colored rocks. Every so often, the stones give way to archways that overlook the ocean. Some are left wide open to allow the breeze to flutter in, and some are covered in multi-colored sea glass. Vases with tropical flowers sit atop tables in the corridors, bringing hints of the jungle into the palace.

At the end of a long hallway, we reach a set of glass double doors that are thrown open. I don't realize how close the jungle is to the palace, but it's literally up against the building. There's a patio, and then the greenery begins.

"This is the front of the palace," Althea says, leading me off the stone patio past the mingling Fae, and onto lush grass. "The Summer Court palace doesn't have a wall like ours does. Instead, the Fae take sentinel in the trees." I crane my neck up, looking at the tangle of branches and vines, and sure enough, guards are stationed in the trees, keeping watch over the palace.

We walk down a clear-cut path lit with torches, which is convenient because the second we step beyond the tree line, the thick canopy makes it harder to see.

"The beach is on the other side?" I accurately guess.

"You'll see that at dinner tonight. It's a beachside barbeque."

It strikes me as too normal. Going to a barbeque on the beach isn't something that should happen in Faerie, right?

Althea flies up beside me. "He thought you might like it. That it might remind you of your summers in the Maldives." I catch her eye and she winks conspiratorially.

"That's—" We spent hours talking about the things I missed from the mortal realm, but I always kept things light. I certainly didn't mention my adoptive parents or the island they owned or the fact that summers there were the highlight of my childhood.

I swallow around the lump that's formed. My anger is threatening to dissolve, but I cling to it like a life raft.

Althea beams, her pointed teeth flashing. "He's a good one," she whispers, and then flies back beside Brigid, leading me forward once again.

The path opens to a clearing with a large lake surrounded by torches that cast firelight on the surface of the opaque water. The sun is more visible here, but it's still shaded, so I hand my sunglasses to Althea and look around. The shore is lined with row boats, some filled with Fae, some waiting to be claimed. I find my mother with Seven, while Four and Five wait in boats across the lake. The rest of my other fathers are farther up the shoreline, chatting with other dignitaries I recognize from the many parties.

"There," Althea points her little fingers to the left around the bank of the lake, where Eldoris is laughing with Radley and Izar. I almost don't recognize him. His thick beard is gone, not even a hint of stubble. He looks youthful and excited and...free. I can see his dimples— plural apparently—from across the lake.

As if he feels my gaze, his eyes find mine and everything else fades away. It's a sensation that's happened once in my life, and yet it's totally different. I can't explain the change, but it's there. It's as real as the sunlight on my face, and the wind in my hair.

I don't know how long we stay like that, staring at each other from across the shore, but Radley waves a hand in front of Eldoris' face. Eldoris ignores him and beelines toward me. My heart is pounding, my brain is whirring, trying to figure out if I should bring up his absence this morning. But doing that would admit that he hurt me, and I'm not ready to examine why that is.

"Hey, stranger," I say as he approaches...apparently not able to keep it cool at all.

"Edina..." he trails off, drinking me in like he's dying of thirst. "You look... You're..."

"The ends of those sentences better be 'stunning.'"

"It's not good enough," he says, wrapping his arms around my waist. I stiffen for a moment before I realize people are looking and place my hands on his chest. "You're breathtaking."

I give him a small smile, and then focus on my hands so I don't have to see that look in his eyes that's incredibly close to sincerity. But he's not having it and tilts my chin up. "I'm sorry I left this morning."

"Oh, were you gone?" I deadpan. "I didn't notice."

"Kitten..." his voice is low and warning and, fucking hell, it sends shivers down my spine and has heat pooling in my core. "I wouldn't leave you if it wasn't important." I bite my lower lip, and he swallows. "I had a bit of a panic attack."

My feeble anger drops to zero. "Why didn't you wake me?"

"You needed rest. You're healing. I just needed to talk to my sister."

"Do you...Do you know what brought it on?"

He nods. "Your injury brought up some old trauma."

"Oh fuck, El." I pull him into a hug, and he goes so willingly. I didn't make the connection that seeing me hurt would bring up the trauma of his mate dying, but it must have been so similar for him. Unable to help, that terrible feeling of watching someone you love hurt.

He nuzzles into the crook of my neck, and I press up on my tiptoes so I can do the same, breathing him in and letting that sandalwood and salt scent calm me. His lips are warm as they press against my skin, and I groan into him as sparks ignite where he kisses.

"I'm sorry I worried you," I murmur, and he shakes his head, nuzzling in further.

"I'm sorry I wasn't there for you. It won't happen again." When he pulls away, he doesn't go far, just enough that we can look at each other. My hand brushes against the bare skin on his cheek. It's so smooth, that I want to feel it everywhere. "You like it?" he asks, and my fingertips skate down to the dimple I've only ever caught glimpses of.

"Maybe," I shrug. He leans his forehead down against mine and my eyes flutter closed. His nose brushes against mine. He's so close, I can feel his breath on my lips.

A ship bell clangs, breaking the moment, and I can't help the whine that escapes my lips as Eldoris straightens and turns back to the lake. "That was the last call," he says. "Come on, we can talk in the boat."

"What exactly are we doing in this boat?"

"You'll see."

NOTHING. THE ANSWER IS nothing.

We're literally rowing around the lake. Some Fae have books with them and are just floating along the surface without rowing at all, some are sunbathing in the shade, and some have picnics. Eldoris and I have none of these things. I catch him up on my conversation with Katie, healing with Eirwen, and breakfast with the family pretty quickly. And then we're rowing. On a flat surface. In silence.

"Explain the significance to me again?" I ask.

"Of the boats? It's just a relaxing day on the water."

I blow out a breath, looking around again at everyone who seems to be thrilled. I'm bored out of my mind, and counting down the minutes until we can go back to shore.

Eldoris starts laughing, and when I turn back, his entire face is lit up. "I never got it either," he says. "I usually skip this event and go surfing."

"You're telling me we could be surfing instead of on this fucking boat?" I whisper-shout, and Eldoris laughs again.

"You want to be seen as a couple? This is what couples do."

I look around again and see that the majority of the Fae in the boats are couples except a few. "Care to make this more interesting?" I ask.

"I'm intrigued," he smirks.

I stand, causing the boat to rock slightly, but I control the water around us, so we stay level. Then I climb behind Eldoris and perch on the bow. The boat tilts up in the air a little, and Eldoris moves like he's about to stabilize us, but I hold him still. "You trust me?" I ask, leaning forward so we're cheek to cheek.

"Not even remotely," he scoffs.

"Smart male." I dip my fingertips in the water and then shove back. The wave I create has us catapulting forward. I adjust my power, controlling the water until our speed evens out and our little rowboat turns into a speed boat.

Eldoris tilts his head back into my lap and laughs heartily as I guide us around the lake, increasing our speed. Larisa shrieks as the wave from my magical boat gets her wet, and Eldoris waves his apology as we zip off to the other end. I make a large circle right as we reach Radley and Izar, who look as bored as we were, and add a little extra oomph to the magic, so the wave cascades over them.

They cackle as we take off, and then we're hit with a blast of air that has us going even faster. I whoop in excitement, turning to thank the males when Eldoris screams my name. I turn back just as we collide with a buoy in the center of the lake. It normally wouldn't be big enough to upend us, but with the speed, we hit the object and fly off the back of our boat as it gets caught on the metal.

I scream as I land on my back, sinking below the surface with Eldoris right on top of me. He rights himself pretty quickly and I follow suit, my gorgeous dress tangling around my legs as I kick back toward the surface. I emerge with a sputter.

And then I'm laughing so hard I can barely breathe. I'm not even sure why I'm laughing, except that it feels so good to completely let go. For the first time since I emerged, I wasn't thinking about my perception. I wasn't trying to get a rise out of someone or break the rules for the sake of breaking them. I was purely enjoying myself.

Eldoris' arms wrap around my waist, and his eyes shine in the filtered light of the trees. Wet hands brush wet strands of hair from my face, the smile on his face unrestrained in the same joy I feel. I don't want to lose this moment, the feeling of doing something just because I want to. So even though it's not an ideal time, and it's not what we agreed on, I lean forward and kiss him.

It's light, barely a brush of our lips together. Brief enough that if he didn't want this, that could be all. But when I go to pull away, Eldoris seizes control. He wraps one arm around my waist, tugging me flush against his body, and threads the other through my hair, using his grip to tilt my head the way he wants. His tongue flicks a bead of water on my bottom lip, and I open for him. He makes a sound low in his chest that vibrates against mine, pebbling my nipples and making my core clench.

I can't get enough. My hands rove everywhere, starting at his jaw and then slowly sinking into his curls before I decide I need to feel his skin. I slip my hands beneath his button-down, relishing the feel of the warmth of his chest against my cold hands. The kiss grows more frantic as he pulls me closer, and I feel his erection through the fabric separating us. I roll my hips and groan at the feel of him.

"Fuck, kitten." His voice is ragged and deep and makes me whimper and pull him into another searing kiss. Everything around us has fallen away. We're the only two people in the entire universe.

Until we're not. Someone catcalls, and while it's not enough to get me to stop, it's enough to bring us back to the moment. We break apart, our breathing short and shallow. "That's not how I planned it happening," Eldoris says, and a laugh bubbles up from my throat. He kisses me again, soft this time, and somehow that's even better. "But there are selkies in this lake, so we should get to shore."

"Shit, yeah," I say, not sure what a selkie is, but I hear his tone. Our boat, however, will not get us back to shore, since it's quickly filling with water. "Hang on." I wrap my arms around Eldoris's waist again and kick forward, using my magic to propel us to the shoreline, where Devorah is waiting with two large towels and a smirk on her lips.

"I think I like the dress even better wet," Eldoris murmurs in my ear as we stand and walk on the shoreline. I look down, and my dress is not only clinging to my skin in a sopping mess, but it's see-through.

"At least I wore panties," I tease. I did not, however, wear a bra and my nipples are so hard from the kiss and the cold that they're *very* visible. Eldoris is momentarily transfixed before I wrap the towel around my chest and use a spell to dry off.

Still wet, Eldoris steps into me and cups the back of my head. "In case anyone missed it," he murmurs and pulls me into another kiss.

This one leaves a sour taste in my mouth as I realize to him, this is all still an act.

Chapter Thirty-Three
Eldoris

EDINA IS ANIMATEDLY TELLING a story, but I don't hear it. I'm too distracted by how fucking perfect she looks, and the memory of the way she tastes. By the goddess, *that kiss*. That kiss was the kind of thing people write sonnets about, and it still wouldn't be enough to describe it.

When I saw Edina in my colors—Summer Court's colors—looking like an angel, any last shred of resistance shattered. I want to keep her. I want to *worship* her. It felt real when we kissed. It didn't feel staged or acted, it felt so genuine that it seared itself on my very soul. But just because I had this revelation doesn't mean that Edina feels the same way. It could have been a well-crafted ruse on her part. Even though we plotted something different for our first public kiss, she could have changed her mind.

The fact that it might not have been real to her makes my chest hurt.

We need to talk, but we haven't been alone since we left the lakeside to change for dinner.

The fire from the barbeque has long since been extinguished, and the sun has set, leaving a clear view of the stars. They seem brighter tonight, closer, as if they too want to join the party. The large wooden table is covered with empty plates and dwindling wine glasses, but no one seems in a rush to leave. Everyone is enjoying the easy conversation and the stories. It's the most relaxed I've seen this crowd. Even my mother seems in good spirits, hanging on every word of the stories Edina tells about the mortal realm.

Everyone laughs at the punchline of Edina's story, and I stretch my arm along the back of her chair, my thumb barely grazing the skin of her bare arm. She gives a small shiver and lays her hand on my thigh. It's such a simple motion, one I'm sure almost no one else can see, but it feels so natural like we've been beside each other for centuries instead of weeks. It's easy... comfortable.

It feels like coming home.

"Did you catch that," Edina gossips in my ear, and I follow her gaze across the table. Fae are starting to sink into their partners, the affection more overt than it was when we sat down, but she's looking at my sister, who is in a very close conversation with her advisor. His body crowds hers, and she leans into it, the two of them shutting out everything else in the world.

"Get it, Devorah."

I shudder in disgust. "We should go before I see anything that scars me for life."

"Poor baby," she coos, patting my chest. I snap my teeth at her nose, and she laughs before snuggling into me. "We can go."

"So, Eldoris," Ayelet—the Advisor from the Day Court—says, trying to summon the control to command an entire room. "Any luck snuffing out our little hellfire problem?"

Edina stiffens, and her hand tightens on my thigh. I'm not sure if it's a warning for me not to rise to his challenge or if she's holding herself back from doing the same thing. "Unfortunately, the Fae from yesterday's attack escaped, and we're unsure if that was their entire force."

Ayelet scoffs. "And yet, you're here? Throwing a *party*?"

"Would you rather lead the army?" Edina hisses, causing Ayelet to balk.

"It's okay, kitten," I soothe, trying to calm her.

"No, it's not." She turns her full fury on the advisor, and his orange skin turns to a pale yellow. "If you have any suggestions, we'd be happy to hear them, but considering you're sitting here—at this *party*—passing judgment instead of at a strategic meeting, I have to assume you have none."

"I meant no offense, Princess," he mumbles. Edina looks like she's about to press, but then stops, and gives him a sickly-sweet smile that's somehow more terrifying than the anger she was just displaying.

"And you'll be happy to know," I cut in before Edina can unleash whatever is behind that smile, "that we have a team following any who have retreated. Hopefully, we'll know their hideout shortly."

Some of the table has started listening in, even though they appear like they're not, and I see a few looks of approval. There's no other odd behavior, which is unfortunate. I was hoping my declaration might reveal anyone working with Titania and the hellfire Fae, but I'm pretty sure she's acting alone. She never did play well with others.

I wait a few more minutes for the conversation to ease and go back to trivial topics before leaning into Edina's ear and asking if she wants to leave. She nods quickly, and as soon as we stand, everyone else disperses, glad to be heading back to their private rooms for the evening.

Edina and I walk in silence since we're being followed by her pixies, but as soon as we reach the door to my suite, she stops and turns to them. "Thank you, ladies. I'm all set for the night." They exchange looks, but eventually bow their heads and fly off in the direction of their rooms down the hall.

Finally alone, I gesture for Edina to enter before me. We need to talk, but the conversation we're about to have feels like navigating a landmine. Edina ignored me for the better part of two mortal years because she was convinced I was in love with her. And while I feel the urge to tell her of these developing feelings, I need to do so in a way that will make sure she doesn't panic.

Not that I'm even sure what this is. With Arella, our love grew subtly over our entire childhood. It never wasn't there. It was like jumping with wings already unfurled.

This feels like getting shoved off a skyscraper. It's fast and intense and I'm unsure how to handle it.

I close the door behind me, still figuring out what the hell I'm going to say, when Edina is on me, her lips pressed against mine.

All thought disappears from my brain as I seize control of the kiss and she goes pliant in my arms. *Fuck, I love that.* She's not afraid to take the reins, but when I start to lead, she follows so beautifully. I spin us so she's against the door and lift her, her legs immediately winding around my waist as I grip her ass and keep her close.

She sighs, and I take advantage, sliding my tongue between her lips. It's a perfect dance that heats my blood and has my cock standing at attention between us. Edina groans when she feels it and works her hips, using me for friction. There are layers and layers of clothing between us but even this feels fucking fantastic. I can't even imagine how perfect it's going to be when we actually come together, when I get to feel her contracting around me.

She breaks the kiss, panting heavily, her eyes a little glassy and her lips swollen from the kiss. We just stare at each other for a moment before

Edina chuckles, unwinds her legs from my waist, and drops to the floor. "Thanks," she breathes. "I was just...checking."

She slips out of my grasp, and saunters over to the bed, her body swaying with the motion. "Checking," I repeat. She gives me her profile, looking coquettishly over her shoulder as she says, "Yeah."

And then she slips into the bathroom, leaving me completely shell-shocked and so hard I'm aching. The plan to go into this conversation with a cool head is obliterated, I follow her, knocking on the door. "Checking for what?"

She opens the door, still in her dress, but holding it to her chest because she's already unzipped it. I'm not sure why it matters, she's never covered up in front of me before. She tugs her lip between her bottom teeth, but not in the way she does when she's being strategically sexy. This is vulnerable. "Checking for what, kitten?" I ask, softer this time. I cup her cheek in my hand, my calloused fingers brushing against her smooth skin. She leans into the touch, closing her eyes as she relaxes.

"That it was real," she whispers.

Every wall, every defense I've built around my heart to keep this girl out, shatters. I thought I had no reservations when I came in here, but now...there is nothing, not a damn thing, separating us.

I kiss her again, sweeter this time. I keep it light even though my cock is begging me to ramp up the volume, especially when she whimpers and melts against me. "It's all real," I say, letting her infer the rest.

If I'm being honest, the only people Edina and I have been fooling have been us, because we thought we were faking it. But it was never fake. Maybe it's because we've always been attracted to each other. Maybe it's just the chemistry we have or the friendship we've built.

"This is real," I murmur again, this time against the sensitive skin beneath her ear. She shivers when she feels my hot breath, and then I move slowly down the slender column of her neck, kissing and biting her golden flesh.

Edina drops her dress when she threads her hands through my hair, baring herself to me fully. I move further down, my tongue drawing a line to the hollow of her neck before I bend to get to the bare flesh of her breast.

"This is real," she echoes. I bite gently, but her resulting moan has me biting down harder the next time. I lose control of my horns, and they pop out, extending back. Edina's hands instantly find them and wrap around their length, squeezing. It's like she's gripping another part of me, and I swear as I suck her nipple into my mouth.

"Fuck." She uses her grip to drag me closer. "El," she pleads as I swirl my tongue around the perfect pink bud. Her skin flushes, and her eyes are more black than blue with how turned on she is. "El...we still need to take it s-slow."

"Fuck them," I say, pulling up and holding her chin in my hands. If possible, her eyes grow darker. The scent of her arousal, that sweet sugary scent mixed with a hint of rose, is everywhere, mixing with my own scent in a heady concoction.

She's right on the edge of this cliff with me, wanting this as badly as I do.

But the last thing I want is for her to make this decision in a haze of lust. Tilting my head back on a groan, I release a heavy sigh. "You're right."

"I was about to say you were right," she laughs.

"I know." I take a step back, putting some distance between us. "We should see your plan through. Which means—"

"—slowest burn ever," she grumbles, and I can't help but laugh in our shared misery. Then she takes a step toward me, and unbidden, my eyes skate over her naked body. "But we can still kiss, right?"

In response, I pull her back into me, kissing her until we're both breathless. She hums in contentment when she steps away. "I need a cold shower," she says, and I grunt in agreement. My cock is still trying its damnedest to escape my pants, and I'm not sure how I'm going to sleep next to Edina without taking care of this.

"You first," I say, and she bites her lip again in a completely unselfconscious way this time as she saunters back into the bathroom.

Of all the ways I expected this conversation to go, that was not one of them. And I'm not complaining one fucking bit.

Chapter Thirty-Four
Edina

Do you know what television characters in a slow burn never talk about? How fucking horny they are.

Seriously, this is actual torture. It's the ultimate edging, and I'm not a fan. After that kiss...*kiss plus*? I'd refer to it in bases, but I don't know the base equivalent for making someone almost come by rubbing their horns. Anyway, after that kiss plus, I had to get myself off in the shower. I'm pretty sure Eldoris did the same thing because he was in there for a lot longer than necessary.

And this was day one.

I couldn't anticipate the sparks that were flying when he kissed me in the doorway of the bathroom. Every touch, every kiss, every place he licked or bit was on fire. I've never had someone almost give me an orgasm by sucking on my nipples, but he had me right there.

Sex with him is going to be fantastic. And right now, I can't remember why I was so insistent that we wait.

"Morning," Eldoris murmurs, kissing the top of my head before gripping my chin and tilting it up so he can claim my lips. And that's exactly what it is...claiming. It isn't rushed or frantic like our kisses were yesterday, it's soft and exploring and has my entire body turning to mush.

"Fuck, when you make those sounds..." he growls against my lips and shifts us so he's lying on top of me, his body a welcome weight.

"What sounds?" I pull away, only for him to bite my lower lip which makes me moan.

"That," he chuckles and kisses away the hurt. His tongue dips back into my mouth, teasing and playing and doing everything so perfectly that all I can think about is that tongue between my legs.

"We have that meeting with your mom, kitten," he murmurs.

"Fuck it," I wrap my legs around his waist and grind into him. "Let's just stay here and make out all day."

"If we stay in bed all day, we're not just making out," he grumbles. *Yes, please.* "We can't miss this one. They're deciding what to do about Titania."

He's right, I know he's right. But waking up like this, with lazy kisses that set my body alight is just too fucking perfect.

"Morning," Brigid calls from the doorway, not bothering to knock as she bursts into the room, finding Eldoris, shirtless, on top of me. She gasps and then turns as if to avert her eyes, but Althea slams right into her, spinning her back around.

Althea's eyes go wide. "A very good morning indeed," she sing-songs.

Eldoris throws off the covers and shows them that he has pants on and that I'm fully clothed as he calmly greets them. Althea visibly pouts.

"I'm gonna shower," Eldoris says, spinning in a way that hides his erection from my lady's maids before he silences my laugh with a sweet kiss and then disappears into the bathroom.

"Did you—" Althea starts.

"They didn't," Brigid answers.

"But look how she's glowing!" Althea flies over to me and starts stroking my cheek with her little hand.

"It's not a sex glow. It's..." Brigid pauses to think.

"Sex adjacent?" I taunt, and she narrows her eyes. "Okay, Brigid, what's the deal? Do you not like Eldoris? I know you're not a prude; you've participated in some of my orgies."

"She ships you with Puck," Althea answers, moving along to stroke my hair.

"I do not!"

"How do you even know what that means?" I chuckle, but I'm ignored as Brigid flies over and smacks Althea so hard that she slams into the headboard. Once she shakes her head loose, she charges Brigid and I barely escape the bed before the two of them start tearing at each other with their talon-like nails.

"No biting," I call as Brigid bares her teeth. After another few minutes of watching them scrabble, I grab a tunic and leathers, dress, and do some minimal makeup. When I'm ready and they're still fighting, I head into the sitting room to have my morning tea while I wait for Eldoris.

I grab the steaming mug from the coffee table and head to the windows. Eldoris's room is on the side of the palace that faces the beach, and from the bay window, I can watch the surf crash against the shoreline. It's a beautiful day, of course, and I'm trying to figure out if we'll have time after the meeting to go for a swim when Eldoris emerges in low-slung pants, his torso still damp from his shower.

"There's a brawl in our bedroom," he says. I don't even think he notices he does it, but the word *our* sticks in my brain and makes my stomach feel all floaty. That...or the fact that he's wet and shirtless. *It's probably the latter.*

"What are your tattoos?" I ask, my eyes tracing over the marks. "They look tribal."

"From my father's tribe in Africa. I had to do some digging, but once I found them, I thought, 'there is nothing more beautiful than this.' So, I found someone who could ink them to my body."

I close the distance between us and place my hand right over his heart, where there is a series of four circles in a cluster with a small line at the top of each. It stands out from the surrounding angular shapes and lines. "And this one?" I ask.

He swallows. "It means commitment."

"You didn't want love? Or family or something?"

He places his hand atop mine. "Not at the time," he smirks. "At the time, commitment was the thing I honored the most." I realize he isn't going to elaborate, so I busy myself with tracing the lines that snake up to the base of his neck. "Ready for the meeting?"

In a way, the hellfire Fae attacking Summer Court's borders was a blessing, because when they retreated, they went straight into Spring Court. My mother called a meeting of the Unseelie monarchs, and oddly, they all agreed. They asked me and Eldoris to be there as well, but not any of the Seelie monarchs. My mother's exact words were, "We'll involve them once we're sure they'll go against Titania."

We head down the hall to my mother's suite, which has a dining room that we'll be using for the meeting. When we enter, everyone is already there, waiting. The three monarchs sit at the table while their advisors and the princes and princess, stand behind them.

"It's about time," Zahir, the King of the Night Court, says. Behind him, both Izar and Hades roll their eyes at their brother's antics.

"Hush, Zahir," my mother says. The male runs his fingers through his thick white hair. "We're not on a schedule today." Zahir grumbles under his breath but doesn't make any further comments. On the other side of the table, standing behind his father, Radley winks at me.

I feel the familiar tingle of a magical shield being slid into place around the room, creating a bubble around us so that no one will even realize we're inside. Knowing my mother, the magic will mask everything, sound, scent, even heat signature. If someone opens the door, they'll find an empty room.

"I've called this meeting," my mother continues, "because we have reason to believe Queen Titania is harboring the hellfire Fae."

"That's quite the accusation," King Oakley of Autumn Court says, scratching his graying beard.

"I don't make it lightly," my mother says. "General, if you please." She leans back in her seat, the picture of calm despite the topic at hand.

"I sent a crew after the retreating Fae," Eldoris says. "They fled directly over the river and into Spring Court territory."

"That's true, I saw that as well," Radley offers.

"There's also been whispers of them using the Underground to travel. When we visited, we spoke with a troll who believed they were available for hire."

All heads turn to Hades, before Eldoris quickly adds, "The Spring Court section of the Underground."

"I thought you took that over," Zahir scoffs at his sister.

"Titania is holding on with an iron grip," she replies. Her words are calm and unaffected, but the rigid set of her jaw says other things. "I have nothing to do with her dealings."

"We know," my mother says. We agreed to leave out the evidence we found in the tower, just in case it got out that we were snooping. The Fae will use any excuse to go to war, but they also will use any excuse to pawn a war off on someone else. If they heard we trespassed in Titania's tower, they could say it's an issue between Spring and Winter and withhold aid.

"Why would she want her hands in this?" Oakley grumbles.

"My opinion is that she hopes to become Queen of all Faerie," my mother states, again in that cool and collected voice. "Titania has shown signs of searching for more power for ages. For a time, I believed she was searching for personal power. She became obsessed with the way the Fae gave magic to humans and spent quite a bit of time in the mortal realm."

"That technique doesn't work Fae to Fae," Zahir says. "It only worked on humans."

"I'm aware. The only way to enhance one's magic is what's being done by the hellfire Fae."

"You think she's trying their methods?" Eldoris asks. "Are we sure it works on other forms of magic?"

"We don't know," my mother says. "But she may be using these Fae to fight her battles as well as studying them."

"It's smart," Hades says. "She's using an unclaimed army to do her dirty work. It makes it hard for us to attack Spring Court because we have no tangible proof."

"I'm working on that," my mother says. "And while the ultimate outcome will be war, this meeting is about other tactics."

"You want us to stop trade with Spring Court?" Oakley asks. My mother gives him a curt nod.

"And I want a blockade around their borders," she says. "If Titania asks, we can tell her it's because of the retreating Fae, but I want to restrict their use of portals and other ways into the other courts."

"Is Eldoris keeping their soldiers?" Zahir asks. "Or are they being sent home?"

"I'll send a battalion home," Eldoris says. "Not all of them, so it's not suspicious, but enough that it looks like we're searching the court for these Fae."

Zahir and Oakley exchange a look, and then each turn to their advisors. They speak in hushed voices for a moment before reconvening.

"Izar will send some of his ships to the river to block that border," Zahir says. "And we agree to let the Unseelie army blockade the borders."

"We agree as well," Oakley says.

"I'll cut off their access to the Underground," Hades says.

"Will you need soldiers for that?"

Hades scoffs. "I'll handle it."

"Done," my mother says. "Thank you, Your Majesties, it's been a productive meeting. You are now free to enjoy your day."

Eldoris and I hang back while we wait for everyone to clear out of the dining room. As soon as they're gone, my fathers come in bringing breakfast trays. "We invited Devorah and Queen Talia to breakfast as well," Five says as he sets down a giant tray of pastries. "They'll be here in a moment."

"Did you have questions before they arrive?" my mother asks.

"What are we supposed to do while we wait for Titania to go crazy under the blockade?" I ask. "That's the goal, right? That she uses the hellfire Fae to break through?"

"Yes, the goal is that she strikes first, so all five courts can fight back and crush her." How my mother says things like that with a completely straight face is beyond me. "As for what we do now, we continue life as we did before. We attend the parties on schedule, or we go home and wait. But either way, the next phase is all about patience."

I huff, and Eldoris slides an arm around my waist. "You're good at being patient," he murmurs in my ear. "Aren't you, kitten?"

"It's a fucking virtue," I grumble, and he laughs and kisses me, completely obliterating my bad mood.

Chapter Thirty-Five
Eldoris

EDINA SIGHS LOUDLY, PURPOSEFULLY. I've ignored the first four sighs, but I turn my head this time. After the meeting, we changed, headed to the beach, and have been here ever since. I assumed she'd be thrilled since that's all she's spoken about all morning, but now it seems my betrothed is bored.

"Yes, kitten?" I drawl, lowering my sunglasses. I can't help but drink in Edina's body in her little white bikini, the contrast against her rapidly tanning skin striking and so fucking sexy.

"I'm hot," she whines.

"We could go in the water."

"We already did that. Let's go to base and people-watch at the cafe."

"Lying low means, no trips to an army base."

She harrumphs, flopping back onto her towel dramatically. When I chuckle at her response, she crawls across the small strip of sand separating our towels and straddles my waist. "I'm just not used to relaxing." She leans down and kisses my neck, giving me a whiff of her hair, her usual scent mixed with the salt of the ocean.

"And I'm guessing if I told you to read a book that wouldn't go over well?" She glares in response, and I pull her down to kiss away her pout. I love how she melts into the kiss, into me. The ultimate sign of her trust. It's heady and makes me want to do absolutely filthy things to her.

"Stop," she pleads, pulling away. "I can't think when you're thinking like that."

"Like what?" I recapture her mouth briefly before she pulls away again.

"Whatever you were thinking to make your cock this hard." She rocks back into me.

"Okay." She stops, sliding off me and back onto her towel for some much-needed space. "The number of cold showers I'm going to need by the end of this slow burn," I grumble, and Edina's eyes light before she douses me in her ice-cold water magic. I sputter as she laughs and scrambles to her feet. "Oh, you better run," I call. She runs through the sand a few steps before her wings pop out and she tries to fly away, but I'm fast and I wrap my arms around her waist and tug her back to earth.

Edina squeals as I turn her in my hold and start tickling her, taking her down into the sand as I go. Our laughter mingles together, combining with the crash of the waves in the background and the caws of the gulls, creating the perfect melody.

"Okay, I give!" she bellows, and when I don't stop, she says something that sounds a lot like, "Watermelon."

I switch my assault and kiss her instead, and quickly her laughter fades, changing to a long, sexy moan. When I pull away, she takes my bottom lip between her teeth, trying to draw me back in, but I stay firm. "I have an idea of something to do."

"Me?" she says, sinking back into the sand, which is now coating her hair and sticking to her skin.

"Whenever you give me the green light, kitten," I say because I know that even though she jokes, she wants to stick to her plan. She doesn't want people to think I'm another notch on her bedpost and, in her mind, to do that, we need to take things slow.

I respect that. I'm just going to be very well acquainted with my hand.

"If we want to get there in time, we need to hurry. And change," I say, standing and offering her a hand.

"I'll get the sand off," she offers and then throws another deluge of water at me.

A LITTLE WHILE LATER, we emerge from a portal near the border between Summer and Day Court. My court is the most diverse, terrain-wise, with three distinct sections. The Wyld Jungle takes up the most space and stretches from Spring Court's boundary to the beaches, but in the corner where Summer and Day intersect, is the start of a mountain range. The lower peaks in our court are home to dragon hoards.

"Did you say dragons?" Edina asks.

"You've seen dragons, right?" I ask. They exist in the mortal realm, though they usually keep to themselves, but I know they fought in the Witch War. Edina gets that far-away look she gets when she talks about the war, before shaking it loose and taking my hand in hers.

The jungle thins until the ground grows dry and cracked, the rich soil fading to dust that's easily kicked up by our feet. With the heat from our court and the constant sunlight in Day Court, the mountain range bakes into a warm terracotta color.

We walk around the base of the structure until we come to the mouth of a cave. "Stay here," I say, and inch toward the dark opening. Dragons are amenable creatures, but in general, you don't want to sneak up on them. And I didn't inform this one that we were coming.

"Yeah, okay," Edina scoffs. Casting a ball of light in one hand and an icicle in the other, she takes the lead. "Should we call or something?"

"No need," a deep disembodied voice says from the darkness, making Edina freeze as the sound echoes across the chamber. I chuckle because that's very much like my friend, and his need to be theatrical.

"Hello, Shesha," I call, and a broad male with olive skin emerges. His rippling muscles are covered in different forms of gold, necklaces that drip down his torso, a band that winds from his elbow to his shoulder, and bracelets that snake up his forearm. You can barely see skin. His dark hair is long and unbound, and adorned with little winking gems.

"Oh my," Edina breathes, her eyes firmly stuck on Shesha's penis, which is out and tipped with a golden stud.

"That's new," I say, and my friend laughs with his whole body.

"I want to get gems down the underside too, but the mate disapproves." Shesha and his mate have been together since before I was born and have ruled over this hoard ever since that time.

"Give her our love," I say, and Edina finally snaps out of her stupor enough to introduce herself.

"Of course, I know you, Princess," Shesha says, his lime green eyes glowing slightly as if he's assessing a threat. "My son, Ormr, spoke fondly of you after your night together."

Edina's eyes go wide. "Um, right. Tell him I said hi?" she squeaks. Shesha looks at me, and when he sees this information doesn't upset me, his eyes return to their normal green hue.

"What can I do for you both?" he asks, and I smile widely.

"I was hoping I could persuade you to give us a ride."

Edina gasps and looks at me with surprise and excitement. Shesha tsks. "And what would persuade me to do that?" he asks, but his smirk gives him away.

"My eternal friendship."

"I already have that."

"Ahh," I snap my fingers, and Edina chuckles. I withdraw a large aquamarine gem from my pocket. "Will this suffice?"

"If he says no, I'm taking that," Edina says, but Shesha is fast and has already snatched the gem from my hand.

"I accept your offer." Out of the shadows, a female dragon in her Fae form appears and takes the gem from Shesha. She begins taking off the chains but stops when he emits a low growl and waits for him to remove every strand of jewelry from his body. When he's done, she disappears into the darkness of the cave and Shesha claps his hands together.

I pull Edina back just as Shesha's eyes begin to glow that electric green again, and his body expands. Bones pop, skin stretches, and inky, midnight-blue scales appear. Wings, large and leathery, emerge from his back and he drops to all fours. Opening his giant snout, he tilts his head to the sky and releases a wave of ultraviolet fire. Edina is transfixed as it colors the sky and then is in instant laughter when Shesha tilts his head down and huffs smoke that surrounds her. "Ready?" he asks, his voice deeper and booming against the side of the cavern.

I gesture to Edina, who releases her wings and flies up and onto the dragon's back, leaving me to clamber up on my own. Using his front leg for purchase, I heave myself onto his back and settle myself right behind Edina, who looks around for somewhere to hold onto. I take her hands and place them around a small spike at the base of Shesha's head. "Hold here."

"And what will you hold onto?" she asks, and I wrap my arms around her waist, and rest my head between her unfurled wings.

"Better hold tight, kitten."

Her laugh turns to a squeal of delight as Shesha starts walking, his giant muscles flexing beneath our thighs as he gets us used to movement on his back. Once neither of us has shown signs of distress, I feel his back legs prep and then we're shooting straight up into the sky.

Edina is screaming and lifts one hand off the spike to raise it in the air like it's some kind of thrill ride, which I guess it is. The wind rushes around us as Shesha spins and ascends higher and higher. He catches some kind of air current, and it feels like we're on a rocket headed straight to the moon.

Finally, after what feels like hours, he evens out and starts lazily flying toward the ocean, where the sun is starting to descend. We fly in a sherbet-colored sky, occasionally passing through fluffy white clouds that leave us damp.

Edina sags into me, an awed smile lighting up her gorgeous face. The golden light picks up tiny flecks of silver in her sapphire eyes, and I find myself completely entranced as she looks over her shoulder at me. "This is a pretty romantic date, El," she says, letting go of the spike completely and placing her hand atop mine.

"Well, I have to up my game, now that I know I'm competing with a dragon."

Edina's eyes grow serious. "I don't even remember that," she mutters. "It's like a chunk of my life is just missing. How could I forget sleeping with a dragon?"

I kiss the tip of her nose. "You did what you had to."

We sit in comfortable silence for a while as Shesha floats over the water. When the stars begin to emerge, he makes a wide arc and starts heading toward Day Court, which is shining like a beacon in the night sky.

"So, the sun never sets in Day Court?" Edina asks. I nod against her, at some point she put her wings away so she could nestle in closer, and I'm enjoying the feel of her body pressed against mine. "And Night Court is always dark?"

"It becomes less odd when you think of them like Alaska," I say. "Spending months of the year in all daylight or darkness."

She nods in understanding. "And they share a desert?"

"Correct. What's the name of that desert?" I ask, letting a little bit of my teacher's tone emerge. Edina's shoulders shake.

"I can't remember, professor," she says in a breathy voice. "But I can't fail this class. Is there something I can do for...extra credit?" I pinch her side and when she turns to me, the playful mischievous gleam in her eyes is intoxicating.

I am so gone for this girl.

I kiss her because I can't do anything but kiss her.

Shesha drops us off on the beach by the palace, and we both thank him profusely. As soon as he takes off into the sky, Edina wraps her arms around my neck and kisses me, murmuring her thanks against my lips. "I can't wait to see what you come up with tomorrow when I tell you I'm bored."

I swat at her ass, and she laughs as we walk back to the palace with our arms wrapped around each other.

Chapter Thirty-Six
Edina

THE WHOLE, "FAE DON'T worry about time," thing is super disorienting. It's like being on a vacation, all the days start to jumble together and you're not sure if it's Monday or Wednesday, or if you spent two days lying by the beach or four.

Eldoris and I spend our days in a haze of lingering kisses interspersed with royal events...where we sneak off to kiss more. I never really understood the appeal before. Kissing was fine, but it was always the prelude, the opening act I needed to sit through to get to the main event. But since it's now the *only* event, I'm learning that I actually fucking love it. And I love that I can tell exactly what kind of mood Eldoris is in by the way he kisses me. When he's sleepy, his whole body melts into mine. When he's feeling sentimental or romantic, he strokes my hair. And when he's really fucking horny, he holds me by the throat, which turns me on to no end.

It's how he's kissing me now. We were on our way to our room in the Night Court when we passed an alcove framed by two white marble columns. Eldoris abruptly grabbed my hand and tugged me into it, pushing me flat against the wall. One hand leans against the pillar at our side, the other braces against my throat, his thumb ever-so-slightly pressing down on my pulse point. He's solid against me, meanwhile, I'm writhing and trying desperately to gain friction between our pelvises, but whenever I gain traction, he tightens his grip and holds me immobile.

I'm so wet I can't stand it.

"Tonight." Eldoris' promise sends shivers down my entire body. Tonight is some kind of event that's not sponsored by the royals, in fact, the kings and queens are specifically not invited. No one will tell me exactly what it is, but Eldoris said that no one would think twice about finding out we had sex afterward.

And as much as I want to say, 'screw it,' and not wait, the anticipation is making everything that much hotter.

"Get a room," a familiar voice drones. Eldoris chuckles, clearly recognizing our intruder, and pulls back to give me a view of my vampire friend.

Vlad is in one of his signature three-piece suits, this one is pinstripe and has a matching navy tie. His blonde hair is impeccably swept back and his smile is wide, fangs popping down over his lower lip as he sees me. I squeal and maneuver out of the alcove and launch myself into his arms.

"I missed you too, Tinker Bell," he chuckles, spinning me around. When he sets me down, he holds me at arm's distance and looks me over. I'm wearing a gauzy set of harem pants and a matching crop top that I was given in Day Court, where Eldoris and I spent the past few days, with my hair tied back.

"You look good," he says finally finishing his assessment. "Much better than the last time I saw you."

"Thanks," I deadpan, but I know he means it out of love. The last time I was in the mortal realm, I'd catch him staring at my jutting bones with concern etched on his face.

Eldoris walks up beside me and shakes Vlad's hand before sliding his arm around my waist. "I'll meet you back at the room," he says and kisses my temple. I tug him back and kiss him in earnest, hard enough that he groans when he pulls away and his dark gaze is promising me all sorts of wonderfully dirty things.

When he walks off down the hall, Vlad lets loose a low whistle. "Was that for my benefit?" he asks. "Because I'm aware of your...arrangement, so there's no need to put on a show just for me." He winks one of his ice-blue eyes, and then takes my arm and steers me in the opposite direction of my room.

"It wasn't for your benefit," I say with a smirk, keeping my eyes forward even when Vlad turns to me with a wide, toothy grin.

"My darling, Edina," he croons. "Might it be that you're developing feelings for a boy?"

"He's not a boy," I shoot back. "And no, of course not. He's just a good kisser."

Vlad hums and steers me out of a set of thick marble columns onto a small patio beneath the night sky. The Night Court is mostly desert, but because the sun never rises, it's cooler in temperature. Not that it bothers me because it's still warmer than Winter Court. We walk over a white patio that's slick with grains of sand to a railing, where I can just barely see a rushing river in the distance, the only source of water in The Night Court. I'm pretty sure it's been magically protected to keep it from drying out in the desert conditions, but it rages straight through the endless sand, creating a fertile riverbank where most of the crops in the court grow. From here, I can see the signs of the vegetation.

Vlad points one finger at a very dark shape in the distance. "See that?" he asks, and I squint, but can't make out anything more than a shadow. "That's vampyre territory. An entire species clustered in one oasis in the middle of a desert."

"Makes sense, with the lack of light," I murmur. Unlike vampires in the mortal realm that can't be in sunlight, vampyres in Faerie can, but they still don't like it.

"I'm supposed to go there to see my maker," Vlad says, his face briefly serious. "But he's insufferable."

"Aww, like daddy like son."

Vlad snaps his teeth at me, but his smile gives him away. "You ready for tonight?"

"No one will tell me what it is," I say. "I'm guessing an orgy."

"Wrong," Vlad says, making the sound of a buzzer. "But it'll be a fun time."

"As long as I get laid, I don't care."

Vlad throws his head back and laughs. "Keep pretending it's only that."

"It is!"

"Mhmm, If Eldoris got called to the front lines, would you fuck me?"

"Been there," I sneer, and again Vlad laughs. "Besides, I'm going for *in love and only want to sleep with one male*, not *so horny she'll fuck anyone*."

"Thanks," Vlad scoffs and puts his arm around me. "Just admit you're in love with your fake love, and I'll leave you alone to get ready."

Love?

The word is like a slap in the face. Is that what this is? No. What Eldoris and I have is...easy. It's fun and sexy. There's no angst, there's no hurt. Love isn't this simple. What we have is friendship and attraction. It's not love.

Right?

I shove Vlad off me, determined not to let him see how much he rattled me. "How's Katie?"

"You'll see her soon. Your trip is due, right?" It's the only reason I've been able to keep any sort of timeline here. I leave for the mortal realm in three days.

"There was something up the last time we spoke; she's been ignoring my calls since. Is she okay?"

"She's fine." The wind picks up in the distance, disturbing the sand and pushing it into large drifts. It dissipates as it reaches us, briefly tickling the loose material around my legs.

"What aren't you telling me?" I ask.

Vlad sighs and swipes his hands through his hair. "Think, Tinker Bell. What's something she would want to tell you in person? Something that makes her irritable, tire easily, and would be noticeable if you saw her in the mirror?"

Holy shit. My eyes go wide as the realization crashes over me.

"She wants you to be surprised when you get there, so I hope you're better at feigning surprise than you are at hiding your feelings for Eldoris."

"I'm supposed to look like I'm falling for Eldoris," I hiss. "It's the plan."

"I call bullshit," he scoffs. "Come on, you need to get ready for tonight."

"Will you give me a hint about what to expect?" I plead as we make our way back off the patio and into the halls.

"No way in *Hades* would I give it away," he waggles his eyebrows.

"Are we going to the Underground?" I ask, and he shrugs in a way that tells me we definitely are. "It's probably something stupid, like an Underground wine bar that the Fae think is all scandalous."

Vlad laughs. "How wrong you are."

⁂

ELDORIS

The shower spray is ice cold and I'm still rock hard. Don't get me wrong, the intimacy of kissing Edina, holding her, and everything else we've been doing has been amazing, something I never thought I'd have again, let alone want.

But I'm ready to combust. And there's a certain amount of pressure that comes with tonight, our first time. If it's bad—or if I come within seconds of being inside her—it'll set a tone, especially since everything else has been so great.

Swearing, I turn up the temperature of the water and wrap my fist around my throbbing cock. I hiss at the sensation and slowly drag my fingers up the underside before catching the bead of precum at the tip. I rub it into the sensitive head before pumping my hand up and down my length. This can be fast, there's no reason to drag it out.

My eyes drift closed as my hand increases tempo, and my mind conjures the image of my favorite fantasy. Edina kneels before me, her pretty pink mouth open and waiting. She's panting, but she stays in that exact position, sapphire eyes on mine as I work my length. I imagine fisting my hand in her hair and dragging her closer, watching those full lips that have been teasing me wrapping around the head—

"Oh fuck," I grunt, the thought of her hot mouth on my cock almost enough to have me spilling myself right then and there. I pump faster, tingles starting at the base of my spine. My muscles clench, tightening as my orgasm dances just out of reach.

A small gasp has my eyes flying open and looking to the doorway where Edina is standing, watching with rapt attention. Her eyes are wide and her mouth is in the exact O I'd been daydreaming about.

I go completely still, my hand still gripping the base of my shaft as we both pant. "I—" she clears her throat, trying to organize her thoughts, but she still appears dazed. I have no idea what to say, what to do. I just remain frozen under the water, torn between telling her to leave and begging her to get in the shower with me.

After an eternity, Edina finally says, "Why did you stop?"

She puts the towel in her arms on the edge of the bathtub, and I watch, completely mesmerized as she walks over to the glass doors and slides them open so I'm completely visible to her. She drinks me in, and as her eyes reach my cock, it's like a lightning strike.

I slowly start to work myself again, and she whimpers, tugging her bottom lip between her teeth as I fuck my hand. "I knew your cock would be perfect," she rasps, her voice raw and filled with lust. She clenches her thighs together, and I wonder if she realizes her hand is braced against her throat.

All my control snaps. "Join me," I command. "Sit on the bench."

She takes off her pants, staying in a small, lacy thong and her crop top, and steps inside. Following my orders, she takes a seat on the bench at the back of the shower, directly facing me, and scoots back so her back rests against the tiles. She bends her legs and puts her feet on the edge of the seat baring herself to me before she scrunches the top so it lies above her tits. Without prompting, she moves her thong to the side so I can see her pretty, pink, glistening pussy.

"Is that for me, kitten?" I ask, and she nods before running one finger through her slickness. "By the goddess, you have no idea how badly I want to taste you."

Her laugh is breathless as she dips her fingers inside her opening and uses her other hand to rub circles around her clit at the same pace that I jerk my cock. "You have no idea how many times I've come to the thought of your mouth on me," she rasps, her eyes briefly closing in pleasure before she zeroes back in on me.

"Tell me."

"Twice a day," she says and then chuckles. "Why do you think I take so many showers?"

"I thought it was a human thing," I mutter, and her breath turns into a lusty moan that zings through me. "Keep making sounds like that and I'll come."

"Good," she says, a challenge in her eyes.

"You first, kitten."

Her fingers start moving faster, her pace turning erratic as she chases her orgasm. Everything in me is coiled tight, ready to snap. I was ready to come before she came in here, but now I'm dancing on the edge.

"That's it." I'm not sure if I'm speaking more to her or myself, but I can tell she's right there too.

"Fuck, El." Her hips thrust up to meet her fingers as she adds another and plunges them deeper. "I need—" she starts, but I already know what she needs. I've become so attuned to her needs over the past few weeks, that I know before she even asks for it.

I stop what I'm doing and cross the short distance to her. Her eyes are so dark they're practically black as I reach for her neck, and she presents it to me.

I barely touch her, just the slightest press of my fingers against her pulse, she explodes, her orgasm coming in hard. Her scream echoes off the tiles in the bathroom and keeps going when I release her throat and move to rub her hardened nipple between my fingers. I watch her pussy flutter around her fingers as she rides out the wave of pleasure.

When she's spent, she extracts her fingers, glistening with her arousal, and holds them out to my lips. I descend on her like a man starved, sucking them into my mouth as her unique flavor bursts on my tongue. "I knew you'd be sweet," I murmur around the digits, licking every drop from them in a way that has Edina squirming again.

I kiss her, hard, leaning over her lithe body and grabbing my cock again. This time, I can't hold back. I'm pumping furiously as her tongue licks the seam of my lips, tasting herself.

She's so fucking perfect.

"Come for me," she says. "Please, El, give it to me. I need it."

That breathy plea does it. My abs clench and my toes curl as I groan out my release, ropes of come spilling into my hand. Edina breaks away from our kiss to watch, which makes me come harder.

"Wow," she breathes when I'm finally done. Then she grabs my come-covered hand and sucks one finger into her mouth and all the way down her throat.

"Fuck." Her eyes don't leave mine as she releases it with a pop, leaving the digit clean. I can't do anything but stare in awe.

"You taste good too," she gives me a satisfied smirk that has me hardening again. I think, as long as I'm with her, I'll be in a constant state of arousal.

I snag her wrist as she stands and haul her under the water with me. I steal her squeals with a kiss under the spray of the shower.

I will never get enough of her.

Chapter Thirty-Seven
Edina

MY BODY IS ON fire.

Just the touch of Eldoris' hand on the bare small of my back sends sparks flying throughout my body that all pool in my core. And the way he keeps looking at me, like now that he's had a small taste, he wants to devour me, has me clenching my legs together.

We're both in all black tonight, but Eldoris has left his shirt open, showcasing those tattoos that I want to trace with my tongue. I'm not sure how I'm expected to behave tonight when just that little moment in the shower is enough to have me begging for more. Never in my life has masturbation been so exciting.

Eldoris leads me off the patio where I spoke with Vlad earlier and onto the sand. The palace is made of white marble that seems to collect the moonlight and gleam on its own, a beacon in the dark desert. We walk around the circular exterior between two marble columns where Eldoris presses a hand to one gray stone amongst the white. A hidden door emerges, revealing a descending staircase lit with a soft, red glow.

"Secret society? Fight club?" I've been making guesses about what I'm walking into all night, but Eldoris is being frustratingly vague. He won't even tell me when I'm wrong, so I've eliminated nothing.

"You know, if she doesn't like the nickname, Hades really shouldn't be so on the nose with her décor," I muse as we pass a magical torch that's lit with red fire. The steps are dark stone, and my heels click loudly as we wind down and down in a spiral.

"You wanna tell her that?" Eldoris asks.

"She terrifies me." When I look over, Eldoris is unabashedly checking out my legs, which I have to say, look fantastic in the black mini-dress I'm wearing. "See something you like?" I ask.

"Yep." He pushes me against the wall and kisses me, his hand possessively cupping the back of my head. "And it's all mine," he growls against my lips.

Well, shit.

I like that entirely too much.

He doesn't hold back, thrusting his tongue into my mouth before gently sucking on mine. I don't know how long we kiss on the staircase, but I know at least one other pair walks past us. When we break, my lipstick, which I very purposefully didn't set with magic, is smeared all over his lips, staining them red.

"Fuck." He runs his thumb along the corner of my mouth, no doubt where more lipstick has smeared.

"I wore the red for a reason." My eyes drift down to his erection, so he picks up the implication. "You're sure you want to go to this?"

He chuckles, and pulls me back off the wall, steadying me when my knees buckle. "You'll enjoy this."

"Not as much as other things," I grumble.

We continue down, and the white marble walls of Night Court turn black, making it appear darker even though the light is the same. When we finally reach the bottom, a vampyre is standing before an archway. His pale skin is almost translucent, and his dark hair is so black it blends into the wall behind him, but even with the odd lighting, I can see his red eyes and the blood staining his fangs and lips.

"We're guests of Hades," Eldoris says smoothly. The vampyre nods to him, but then sizes me up, his eyes drinking me in slowly. When he finishes his perusal, he chuckles and motions for us to be on our way. Eldoris keeps a hand on me at all times, whether he's holding my hand, his arm wrapped around my waist, or on the small of my back.

We walk down a surprisingly finished hallway. It's painted matte black with the marble floors and red torches that were on the staircases, but after Spring Court's Underground, I expected it to feel like I was...well, underground. Instead, this feels like the back hall at an exclusive club.

When we approach a door with a golden door knocker in the shape of a three-headed dog—swear to the goddess— Eldoris halts. "If you want to leave at any time, you just say the word and we'll go. And if you want something, I need you to promise you'll ask for it."

"Do I need a safe word?"

Eldoris shakes his head. "Not yet, anyway," he winks.

Fuck me sideways.

He knocks on the door, and we wait for a long moment before it magically creaks open. Every hair on my body stands at attention, the anticipation and arousal a heady combination as I wait to see what's behind the door. We walk into a room that's so dark it takes my eyes a moment to adjust, but when they do, I can see clusters of small, plush booths along the walls, and in the center...

"That's a bed," I say, noting the king-size bed atop the unlit stage with a slotted headboard and two posts at the foot. It's decorated with clean white linens and is otherwise unremarkable...unless you count the female strapped spread-eagle to the center. "Is this a sex show?" I try to keep the crazy excitement out of my voice.

"It is," Eldoris says, and tugs me into a booth with a view of the center of the bed.

"Best date ever." If I wasn't trying to play it cool, I'd be skipping and clapping my hands.

Once we're seated, a female in a simple black dress comes and takes our drink order before heading off. As soon as we're alone, Eldoris slides in close and puts an arm around my shoulders. I sink into him but keep the contact light, wanting to be able to look around the room.

"I would have put money on an orgy," I murmur, and Eldoris chuckles. I notice the only source of real light is a spotlight illuminating another stage with a throne. Hades, in a red silk blouse and pencil skirt, sits atop it, her chin-length black hair even sharper than it was a few days ago. She's toying with a leash in her hand, and some clever craning around the edge of my booth shows me that leash is attached to a collar...on Minthe, who's dressed in white lingerie and kneeling on a pillow at Hades' feet.

"The word *assistant* means something very different in the mortal realm," I mutter, recalling the position Hades said she had available for Minthe, and Eldoris chuckles while nuzzling into my hair.

"Oh, she's a real assistant. I spoke with her when I requested this booth," he says. "She must really like her. Hades rarely takes on a new sub."

"Know from experience?"

Eldoris shrugs. "We're both dominant, but we did a group scene together once."

"Damn, that's hot."

His chuckle is low and deep. "Glad you approve, kitten."

Something about how he says the nickname has me recalling how he said it in the shower, and instantly I'm filled with white-hot need. I don't even remember moving, but suddenly I'm straddling Eldoris' lap. He buries his head in my chest, breathing me in and placing open-mouthed kisses up my breastbone to my neck.

"That's new," he mumbles. "Hades hired sirens."

I'm not listening, I'm too focused on how good the rough texture of his pants feels against my core. "Did you say sirens?" I ask, still seeking friction. Eldoris grabs me, but instead of encouraging it, he holds me still. Some of the haze clears, and I realize what happened. "Sirens," I repeat.

"Sirens," he says, and turns me so I'm sitting across his lap instead of straddling him. "It's like at the symphony, they're increasing everyone's lust." He points into the darkness, and I can see the faint outline of booths with other couples. Most are in a similar position as Eldoris and I, but one female is already lying on the table with her legs around the male's head.

"Oh, this is gonna be a good night."

Another spotlight turns on, illuminating the female in the bed. She makes a show of jerking her restraints and whining around the ball gag in her mouth. Everyone starts shifting so they can see the show, and I catch sight of Vlad sitting at an open table closer to the foot of the bed.

I hold my breath as a male appears, wearing nothing but a towel around his waist. He steps onto the platform and trails a finger down the female's arm as the entire room watches with bated breath. He whispers something. She nods eagerly. And he begins slowly, reverently, removing the small scraps of lingerie she has on. The anticipation is enough to have my core clenching, an already steady throb present between my legs. I become very, very aware of every place Eldoris and I are touching. My side plastered to his chest, my ass balanced on his thigh, his warm palm flat against my knee.

The male on stage takes a long time to undress his partner, but when he's done, he moves with fervor. His mouth is everywhere, her neck, swirling around her nipples, licking his way down her torso. When he reaches her sex, the room collectively groans.

Eldoris starts drawing circles on my thigh, inching up ever so slightly. By the time he's toying with the hem of my dress, the male on stage has his partner on the precipice of orgasm. Her gag obstructs her sound slightly, muffling words that sound a lot like 'please,' and, 'fuck.'

Just when I think she's about to come, the male pulls away and she screams as she's denied her release. Eldoris somehow mimics this and slides his hand back down my leg, but I'm having none of that. I grab his wrist and slide it back to where it was without taking my eyes off the stage. His responding chuckle rumbles through me, making me vibrate with need.

I expect the male to return to his partner, but instead, he sits beside her on the bed, removing her ball gag and kissing her. He's stalling. Waiting for something.

While they kiss sweetly, my gaze snags on Hades, who now has Minthe in her lap. She still wears her unaffected mask as she watches the performers and appears to be ignoring the female in her lap...but her hand is between Minthe's legs, moving at a pace that has her sub shaking and moaning so loudly that she's stealing attention.

"Fuck," I breathe as Hades casually tips Minthe over into orgasm, removes her fingers, and sucks them clean. I'm completely riveted, ignoring whatever the main couple is doing on stage and watching Hades as she murmurs something that has Minthe sliding back down into her kneeling position.

"Crawl," Hades orders, and Minthe responds by dropping to all fours and crawling off the dais while Hades holds her leash. She crawls across the empty space between platforms, and then up onto the bed where Hades jerks her to a stop right over the bound female.

"Make her come."

Minthe's mouth descends, causing the female to scream in pleasure while the male begins playing with her nipples as he kisses her. Hades watches from the foot of the bed, the leash dangling from her fingertips.

I'm panting. I can barely think, as I watch the three of them writhe together on the bed. Another blast of lust hits the audience as the female is worked up again, and my mouth drops open as shadows leak from Hades' hands to remove the male's towel. The magic wraps around his cock, and he groans as he continues his ministrations, the shadows jerking him off at a furious pace.

"You like that?" Eldoris murmurs in my ear just as his knuckles brush my very damp panties. When I don't answer, the contact disappears. "Do you like that, kitten? Watching all of them worship her?"

"Yes." I'm rewarded with a finger sliding beneath the edge of the lace. It's still not where I need it, dancing around my lips in a delicate, teasing touch.

"Is that something you want?" he asks. "To invite others into our bed?"

I lick my lips as I think of how to respond to that question. I enjoy being with multiple partners and, if the rumor mill is anything like I think it is in Faerie, Eldoris knows this is how I spent many nights here. But do I want others in our bed? Monogamy was never something I wanted or thought I was capable of. Is this the happy medium I've been looking for?

"Sometimes," I decide. "Like a special occasion maybe. But only when we're together, I don't want..."

"You want them to join us, not replace one of us?" he asks, and I nod. He hums in approval.

"Is that something you want?"

"What do you think?" He shifts me so I feel the strain of his erection against his trousers, and I moan... loudly. "I like the idea of fucking you while you're gagging on another male's cock or buried in a female's pussy."

I think I could come just from his words alone.

"But not tonight," he says, biting my earlobe and making me wince. "Tonight, you're mine."

"Yes, please."

I've completely lost track of the stage as Eldoris and I somehow decide what fidelity looks like in our future marriage. I would laugh at the fact that we cleared a pretty big hurdle during a sex show if I wasn't so turned on that I couldn't think past the hand beneath my skirt and the rock-hard cock under my ass.

There's an earth-shattering scream, a low guttural moan and when I turn back, Hades is bent behind Minthe, eating her out from behind. Her shadows have seeped everywhere, playing with the male's cock, surrounding the female's breasts, and thrusting inside Minthe's ass. All three subs come together, and there are quite a few sounds from the audience as others finish with them, but not mine. Eldoris has barely touched me. I get the feeling he doesn't want to share my orgasm tonight.

The spotlight on the stage goes out, and I see Hades moving around the female, untying her from the bed as Minthe helps clean up the male, whose come is all over his stomach, and a little on the female's hip. When she's freed, Hades scoops the female into her arms and leads the others out a door behind the throne.

"They'll do aftercare behind closed doors," Eldoris explains. As soon as the door closes behind Minthe, the house lights brighten the space. Still dark and red, but now the entire room is bathed in a soft glow rather than the darkness that was cast when the spotlight illuminated the stage.

Many Fae are shifting, righting clothing, and fixing mussed hair or makeup now that we're in a more visible light. I bury my face in Eldoris' shoulder and giggle as he slides his hand out from beneath my dress. "Now what?" I ask. "We all go home?"

"Kitten, that was just act one."

Chapter Thirty-Eight
Eldoris

EDINA SAGS AGAINST ME, feigning exasperation. "I don't know how much more of that I can take," she murmurs, placing a kiss on my jaw. I'm in complete agreement. I'm ready to take her on this table right now and we've only watched the opening act.

"Say the word and we'll go," I reply.

She looks like she's seriously considering saying the words, but instead asks, "What's the next act?"

Vlad approaches our table and slides into the booth with us. If looks could kill, I think Edina would have staked her vampire friend for interrupting, but if he sees the look, he ignores it. "Not bringing my progeny was a huge fucking mistake," he grumbles. Edina's annoyance turns to a bark of laughter from her place on my lap. "Now I need to go home after the show. I was planning on hiding in Faerie for a bit."

"Do my ears deceive me?" Radley asks as he approaches our booth. His long hair is bound, but still mussed, and I have a feeling the female in his booth—the one who looks well and truly fucked—is the reason he isn't sporting a painful erection like the rest of us.

"Are you off the market, Vladimir?" Radley continues, sliding in beside the vampire.

"By all means, join us. Not like we were having a private moment," I deadpan.

"Thanks," Radley says, helping himself to my untouched drink.

"Can't say the same for you, can I?" Vlad quips back at Radley. "Not married with a gaggle of babies yet?"

"Fuck off with that," Radley says, but there's no real ire in his words. We've all known each other too long to take anything personally.

Vlad flashes Radley a toothy smirk. "I have a vampire baby, yes. She's...batshit crazy." In my lap, Edina scoffs. Vlad's face softens. "But I'm so damn in love with her."

"That's oddly sweet," Radley says. Then clears his throat and points across the room. "Think I can get the siren who keeps fucking with everyone's libido to sleep with me?" Everyone dissolves into easy laughter.

"The siren is act two." Larisa's haughty voice cuts through the din as she and Behar approach the table beside Radley. "Hades gave me a rundown of the performers last week. She didn't mention the new girl though, her new pet. She must be infatuated with that one to get involved in a scene."

"Hades usually stays on her throne and uses her magic," I explain to Edina.

"That shadow magic was hot as hell," she murmurs. "I assume fire doesn't work like that?"

"Fire play, Tinker Bell?" Vlad asks, breaking our little private bubble. "I'm impressed."

Edina shrugs. "I'll try anything once." I nestle into the crook of her neck, biting the soft flesh there before swirling my tongue along the same spot. She arches to give me further access, which I take greedily.

Vaguely, I register a feminine scoff, but I don't pull my lips away from Edina's skin. She's like a drug, one taste and I can't get enough. Another scoff and Edina's sigh turns from sweet and sexy to frustrated.

"You have something to say, Larisa?" she asks, and I pause.

Behar grabs her hand, but Larisa shakes him off. "You're not fooling anyone," she sneers. "Honestly, the whole act is getting old."

Edina's body goes ramrod straight in my lap, and around us, the others look down and away.

"Act?" Edina asks, her voice like a samurai.

"You're only getting married for an alliance between your courts. This," she gestures between us, "isn't working."

"Larisa, enough," I snap, holding Edina close to me. She's vibrating, though I can't tell if it's with anger or fear that Larisa has discovered our initial intentions.

"Eldoris, you're better than this," Larisa continues. "And it just makes you look petty, Edina. Like you're trying to make Puck jealous."

"Don't you dare say another word about my betrothed." My voice is low and rough as it tries to escape past the knot in my throat but judging by the way everyone's eyes snap to me, they hear me just fine.

"I—"

"Leave," I assert.

"No," Edina says. It comes out soft, but there's an edge to her voice, one I've never heard before. It's worse than anger, she's fucking furious. She scrambles off my lap and out of the booth with more grace than anyone else in a mini dress would be capable of and stands opposite Larisa, towering over her short stature.

"You're right," she says, affecting a sickly-sweet smile that looks poisonous. "We're obviously faking it." I know it's just the group with us that goes silent, but it feels like the entire room is holding its breath.

"Our marriage was arranged, you're right about that. And there's no way that two people who have been through similar trauma could possibly bond when thrown together in a situation like ours. There's no way they could become friends, and because there's a level of physical attraction, start to develop feelings for each other. No, that's impossible. Much more likely that they've been faking every kiss, every touch, every skip of a heartbeat when the other walks in the room. It's much more likely we're pretending to be in love than actually falling."

Edina stares Larisa down, her face fixed in an icy mask that rivals her mother's.

"I—" Larisa starts.

Edina turns on her heel to make her exit but runs straight into Puck. His arms reach out to steady her, but she shakes him off. I'm out of the booth and behind her before she even gets her footing.

"Hey," he says, looking between the group of us. Edina's cheeks are pink in her anger, Larisa looks thoroughly chastised, and Vlad and Radley are watching the exchange with rapt attention. Radley has even procured a bowl of popcorn. "What's going on?"

"How did you get out of the Spring Court?" I demand, wrapping my arm around Edina's waist as she fumes.

"I came straight from the mortal realm," Puck says, his brow creasing. "I have a meeting with Hades. Why?"

"El, I want to leave."

"Wait," Puck says, reaching for her again. She smacks his hand away so loudly that other people turn to look. "Edina, I need to talk to you."

"No," Edina says, leaving no room for argument. She grabs my arm and tugs me out of the room, leaving Puck calling after her. When we reach the hallway, she says, "I don't want to stay here. Can we go back to Winter Court?"

"Of course." I guide her in the direction we came. More people are coming down the stairs now, ready for the main event of the evening, but Edina and I swim upstream as we ascend to the main level.

"You can teleport here," I tell her when we're back out in the night air. "You remember where the portal is?"

Edina's icy magic envelops us, and we teleport right to the portal door. In a mere moment, we exit the ley line into the freezing temperature of the Winter Court wastelands, and Edina teleports us again, right outside the palace gates.

She doesn't stop as we make our way through the palace. She doesn't look at me, or talk, she just silently charges ahead until we reach her rooms. The familiar white color palate welcomes us as we enter the sitting room. I send a flame into the fireplace, igniting the wood already there.

Edina doesn't turn on any light, she just paces the length of the sitting room, back and forth. Back and forth. Every time I think she'll stop, she completes another path around the room.

"Edina—" I start. When she turns to me, her mask is gone. She's open, completely vulnerable, and wearing her heart on her sleeve. The firelight flickers, dancing across her features and illuminating the cracks in her armor.

She's too far from me, an entire room and a fainting couch between us, and I long to close the distance, but I'm afraid to move too quickly. This feels delicate. A night I thought was going to be all about sex has turned into something much more momentous.

"I need you to tell me that this is real again," she pleads, her voice unsteady. I take a step closer, and when she doesn't retreat, I very slowly close the gap between us. She watches me the entire time, eyes wide and hands shaking.

"Yes." I grab her hands and place a kiss on her knuckles. She shudders, her shoulders sinking in relief, and folds her body into mine. "Did you mean what you said to Larisa?"

She nods. "I don't know how to do this," she murmurs against my chest. I squeeze her tighter, promising without words that I'm here, that I'm not going anywhere, and that she's safe with me. "I'm freaking out a little."

"Better than the panic attack I had," I admit, and she jerks her head up, meeting my eyes.

"The one you had at the Summer Court?" she asks. "It wasn't about me getting hurt?"

"It was because my betrothed, whom I was falling in love with, was hurt." It slips out like it's the most natural thing in the world.

I'm not sure when exactly I fell in love with Edina. Maybe it was when she jumped into a pile of leaves in Autumn Court with child-like abandon. Maybe it was when she flew straight into danger to keep other Fae from dying. Maybe it was when she picked herself up off the floor, despite being in excruciating physical and emotional pain, and agreed to sacrifice her freedom for the good of our courts.

Or maybe it was all those little things plus a million other mundane moments added together.

"*Was* falling in love?" Edina asks. "Like it's over?"

I thread my hands through her hair, playing with the silky strands. "I am so fucking in love with you, Edina." Her breath hitches, but I keep going. "I was walking around in a fog, drowning in my despair and self-pity for centuries. You woke me up."

Her throat bobs, as my hands cup her cheeks. "I don't expect you to say it back, not right now. I had time to process and a person to process it with. But we've always been honest with each other, it's what makes us work, so I wanted to tell you."

Even in the dark, I can see her eyes shining. The silence between us stretches, brimming with possibility. For a second, I'm worried I've pushed her too far. Edina has made it clear she fears commitment, but after hearing the things she said to Larisa, I hoped that changed.

"El?" she says softly, sliding impossibly closer. She kisses my neck where my tattoo ends. "I've never been in love, I'm not sure what it's supposed to be like. But," she moves higher, kissing just under my ear. "I want you. All of you. The dark and the light. The good and the bad. I want to celebrate with you when we're happy, but I want to be there for you when you're scared."

I'm perfectly still as she kisses my cheek and stops until our lips are a hairsbreadth apart. "If that's love, then I love you too."

Chapter Thirty-Nine
Edina

ELDORIS CLOSES THE GAP between us, smashing his lips against mine. It's one of his possessive kisses, the kind where he keeps me as close as he possibly can like he can fuse the two of us together. His tongue tangles with mine in long, deliberate strokes, claiming every inch of my mouth.

I'm so fucking in love with you, Edina.

The words replay on a loop in my mind, shattering every defense, every wall, every hardened armored shell that surrounded my heart. Having that admission of his love fills cracks I didn't know existed. It makes my heart feel simultaneously light and like it's going to explode right out of my chest.

His hand brackets my jaw, lightly resting against my throat as he starts walking us toward the bedroom. My hands rake into his hair, tugging until he's snarling against me. We only make it a few steps before he hauls me into his arms, his hands gripping my ass hard enough to bruise in the best way. I register the sound of the door slamming and the magic of a shield being slid into place.

"You went for the good shield," I laugh, barely lifting my lips off Eldoris'. He spins us so my back lands against the doors. His mouth drops to my ear, his teeth dragging across the lobe before he sucks it into his mouth. My moan is breathy and wanton, and results in him rocking his erection against my core.

"I've waited too long to get inside you." His voice is deep and thick with arousal. "I'm not stopping because some meddlesome pixies breach your shields."

He pulls me off the doors so he can unzip my dress as he lavishes my neck with little bites and open-mouthed kisses. I tear at the buttons of his shirt, my fingers flying over the material as he struggles with my zipper. "Tear it," I command. There's a satisfying rip of fabric before it falls enough to expose my breasts. Eldoris is on them like a man starving, sucking my nipple into his mouth and making me writhe seeking any friction I can get.

We're all sensation. Hot mouths on cool skin. Calloused fingers and silken hair. I push his shirt off and drop to my feet so I can lick his tattoos like I've been dying to. I trace the lines and circles that decorate his shoulders, his neck, his chest, not even needing light to know their path. His horns extend. My wings unfurl.

When Eldoris' teeth scrape against my nipple, I lose it. "I need you inside me." My command comes out like a plea as I reach for his zipper. "Now."

Eldoris groans into my skin. "We have all night," he says. "And there's a lot I want to do to you."

"No," I pull his chin so that his crazed eyes meet mine. I know I must look the same, lust overriding every other emotion. "We can do all that later. Right now, I need it hard and fast. Please, El."

He carries me to the bed, throwing me on top of the white fur comforter where I land with a bounce. My torn dress is still on, bunched around my waist, and Eldoris doesn't even take off his pants, he just undoes the zipper, letting his cock spring free before he's following me onto the bed and covering me with his weight.

My panties are shoved to the side and the head of his cock notches my entrance, but he teases me, dragging it through my slit and brushing against my sensitive bundle of nerves. When I moan appreciatively, he does it again.

"You're soaked for me, kitten," he murmurs.

"Which is why I said no foreplay," I pant, and dig my nails into his hips to try and get him where I need him. We've had so much foreplay, between the shower and the sex show, and every single time he's kissed me. I'm one light breeze away from spontaneously combusting. I need him inside me more than I've needed anything in my entire life. It's so all-consuming that I can't even process what Eldoris is whispering in my ear.

"You're not listening to a word I'm saying," he says, and sits up enough that he can grab my wrists. He pins them to the bed above me with one hand.

"Not a single word," I arch into him like a cat in heat.

"I was saying," he drawls, returning his mouth to that spot on my neck that instantly makes me wetter. "I don't want to rush this. I've wanted you too much for too long to—"

"Oh my god, El, please fuck me!" I'm aware the whine in my voice makes me sound like a total brat, but I'm going out of my mind waiting for him. He turns feral, and finally, he slams into me in one long thrust.

"Fuck," we swear in unison, drawing out the word so it's more of a moan than an actual word.

As if that one thrust unleashed him, Eldoris starts fucking me hard and fast. His hands around my wrists are a delicious pressure as I lie completely at his mercy.

"You're so fucking perfect," he growls, his voice coated with lust. "So warm and tight. Fucking made to take my cock."

"You. Same." My brain is all muddled from the intense pleasure coursing through my veins.

"I'm made to take my cock?" he smirks, and I nip his bottom lip between my teeth.

"No, your cock is made to fill my pussy."

He releases my hands to cup my face. "See what I mean?" he chuckles. His thumb brushes my bottom lip and I suck it into my mouth, swirling my tongue around the tip until his eyes roll back in his head. "Perfect."

Eldoris shifts so he's lying almost flat on top of me, and the new angle somehow stimulates my clit while his cock hits my G-spot and makes me see stars. His breath is hot in my ear as he continues driving me higher and higher. "I want you to come on my cock, kitten." He ruts into me at a brutal pace. I fucking love it. I love being used by him like this.

"I'm so fucking close. Don't stop, please don't stop," I beg.

"I'm right here, I'm not stopping," he says, but the way his jaw clenches says something else. Then he pulls up just enough that our foreheads are touching. "Look at me," he commands. My eyes, which have closed at some point, flutter open and I'm ensnared in his gaze. His pupils are blown, the black almost eclipsing the ocean blue that I love so much.

"Choke me," I plead. It's something I love, but I don't ask partners to do it often. It's too dangerous if they don't know what they're doing. But I trust Eldoris with my life.

His pace stutters at my request, and then his hands bracket my throat.

"Tap my arm if you want me to stop," he says, and then he's squeezing. My body coils tight, right on the precipice as my breaths are stolen and my vision turns fuzzy. His forehead presses to mine, and all I can see are his eyes, the ocean blue eclipsing everything else. Just when I'm about to tap out, he releases my neck. Oxygen floods my lungs and I shatter.

"That's right," he grunts. "Milk my cock."

My orgasm is intense, not a gentle ebb and flow, but like being hit by a freaking tsunami. There's no floaty feeling when I'm out of my body. No, I'm present the whole time. I feel every thrust amidst my ecstasy, and soon one orgasm rolls into another, pulling me along in a riptide.

"It's too good, kitten. You're gonna make me come." Eldoris grits.

"Come inside me," I breathe, and those words are his undoing. His cock swells inside me and he shouts my name like it's a prayer. My inner walls squeeze every drop from him as I continue spasming around his cock.

Still in a frenzy, Eldoris pulls out of me and climbs off the bed, kicking off his pants in the process. I squeal as he yanks me to the edge and drops to his knees. His mouth closes around my clit, making me buck off the bed in surprise. His fingers sink inside me, shoving any of his come that spilled out of me back in. It's so dirty and erotic that I'm right on the edge again.

His hands are skilled, knowing exactly how to work me as his mouth sucks and licks and drives me fucking wild. I grab his horns, and he growls. The vibrations on my clit have every nerve ending in my body sparking. I start stroking them the way I would stroke his cock while using them to keep him right where I want him.

I'm arching up off the bed, my legs shaking over Eldoris' shoulders as I see him reach for his cock, jerking himself off in time with my hands on his horns. The sight of him being so turned on while he devours me makes me come again. My orgasm is silent this time as my body trembles and shakes as I detonate into a thousand pieces. He works me through it, and only after I'm completely spent does he stand and furiously jerk off his cock.

I slide off the bed onto my knees, opening my mouth and sticking out my tongue as I wait for his release. "Fuck, kitten," he grunts, and I close my eyes right before thick ropes of come hit my face.

ELDORIS

I shudder through my orgasm, coming into Edina's pretty mouth and spilling a bit on her cheeks and chin. There's something so sexy about seeing her covered in my release. When I pulled out earlier and saw my come leaking down her thighs, something inside me snapped. It was this primal need to keep it inside her, to mark her as *mine*.

Everything about that was perfect. The sounds Edina makes, the fact that she slips into mortal realm colloquialisms when she's out of her mind with pleasure, the way she tightens around me as she comes like she can lock me inside her and keep me there forever.

When I'm spent, she blinks up at me, giving me a sexy smile before licking the tip of my cock. She pulls the head into her mouth, sucking me dry. "Insatiable little thing," I murmur as she takes me to the back of her throat and releases me with a pop.

The icy kiss of her magic swirls around me, cleaning me up. She does the same for herself and the comforter and then climbs back in bed, scooting back until she's at the head. She pats the spot next to her and I'm helpless to do anything but follow her. I get settled and pull her into my side. She molds perfectly into me, sighing when she nestles into my chest.

Every time she shows me a different side of her, I fall a little bit more. but this satiated, content Edina is officially my favorite.

"That was—" Her body convulses in an aftershock, and I pull her closer. "El," she pleads, and I feel her start to tremble as she comes down from the high.

"I know, kitten." I place a sweet kiss on her temple, and then slowly work my way down her jaw, to her cheek, her nose, to her lips. She giggles, but her body is still shaking softly. "I've got you."

I rotate us so we're on our sides and I can draw her as close as possible. When she's wrapped in my arms, she sighs and her body relaxes, melting into me. I rub soothing circles up her back as I keep her close, relishing the contact. She's cool to the touch. Even sweating, she's colder than most Fae, so I manage to untuck the comforter and wrap us in it so we're cocooned.

"That was intense," she breathes, not lifting her head from the position under my chin.

"Very," I agree and kiss the top of her head. When I feel her lips move into a smile against my skin, I can't help my responding grin. "This whole night was intense."

"It feels like we were at the sex show ages ago," she chuckles.

It really does. There's been too much that's happened since then, but none of it matters, not when Edina is in my arms. We lie like that for a while, holding each other tight, fitting together like two puzzle pieces.

"I have a surprise for you," I murmur.

"Is it the fact that you're hard again?" she asks with a satisfied smirk. And I am. Somehow, my cock got the idea that because I was close to her, it was time for another round.

"Not much of a surprise, I'm always hard around you." Her laugh is light and lilting and fills me up. "I bought the townhouse."

She jerks away from me, searching my face for any sign of a lie. "The townhouse at base?" I nod. "Why?"

"You were happy there. I'd do anything to make you happy."

"I—" Her mouth opens and closes, and finally she decides on kissing me. She pours her gratitude into the kiss and rolls on top of me. "No one has ever done anything like that for me," she murmurs against my lips. "Thank you."

Sitting atop me, she strips the ruined dress off over her head and tosses it to the floor. "We can take our time now," she says, and slowly, torturously, lines me up with her entrance and slides down until I'm fully seated inside her. Her head tilts back and a breathy moan slips through her lips. I could listen to that sound forever and never tire of it.

I swear and take her in as she rides me. All the time we spent in the warmer courts has given her skin a gorgeous, golden glow that looks so natural on her. She might be a Winter Court princess, but she was meant to be in the sun.

My fingers skim over her ribcage, which is much less visible than the first time I saw her topless. She stills, simply watching as I reach her breasts and take them both in my hands and squeeze. As I roll her nipples between my fingers, she matches my movements, rocking her hips in long, luxurious strokes, tossing her head back when she finds a rhythm that feels good.

She's a fucking goddess like this, riding me, taking exactly what she needs, using my body.

I drop my hands back down to her hips and thrust up into her, making her squeal in surprise and fall forward. She catches herself on my chest, her hands pressing into my muscles as she engrains herself on my heart. The pace increases as she rides me in earnest, and I match her thrusts.

"We're supposed to take it slow," she teases, pushing back against me and taking me so deep I see stars.

"I don't think it's possible. I crave you too much."

This time, when she comes, I manage to hold off. When she's spent from her orgasm, I roll us and fuck her so hard the beautiful bedframe breaks.

Chapter Forty
Edina

ELDORIS AND I STAY in the room for the next three days, unable to keep our hands off each other. We've ignored everyone who's come to our door and skipped every scheduled event. The realm could be burning down for all we know, but I can't find it in myself to care.

I never really got the point of keeping the same lover. I was more interested in the thrill of the chase, and the passion that comes with knowing you only have one night. I always assumed sex with the same person would get boring, even when friends told me otherwise.

I get it now.

Eldoris knows me so well that he seems to know exactly what I need before I can figure it out myself. I thought our first time was mind-blowing, but each and every time it just gets better and better. And I love learning what makes him moan, what turns him feral, and what makes him instantly explode. It intensifies the experience so much.

At some point, we extended the shield to the entire suite, and have since fucked on every surface. Today we're christening the fainting couch in the sitting room.

"Remember when I walked in on you with that male?" he says, slamming into me from behind. His pace is brutal, punishing, and I relish every single thrust.

"The Hulk," I chuckle. "The one who kept stroking my hip instead of my clit."

My laugh is forgotten as Eldoris reaches around and starts rubbing the apex of my thighs... the one they actually mean in romance novels.

"I felt like such an asshole that day," he says, his breath hot in my ear before he bites down. The spike of pain has me pushing back to meet his thrusts. "You were going through something, but all I could think about was sucking these perfect tits."

"You should have, I might have actually come." He tweaks my nipple and I yelp until his thumb rubs it in circles, the pain turning to pleasure. I love it when he laughs while he's turned on. It's such a low, sexy sound. Between that and the way he's playing my body like his favorite instrument, I'm so close.

"Wait," he says, sensing my impending orgasm. I whimper at his command. "Unfurl your wings."

"What?"

He gently smacks my clit, making me jump. "Do it." I release my wings, and he slows his pace marginally and removes his fingers from my clit. I instantly miss the contact and unabashedly whine for him to put them back. "Trust me."

A feather-light touch drifts across my skin at the edge of my wings. "Oh," I gasp as he travels up my wings, dancing over the swirling pattern with both hands as he continues to pound into me. It's like he's simultaneously hitting every erogenous zone in my body. It's better than anything I've ever felt.

"Oh god," I whimper.

"Goddess."

"Maybe I'm calling *you* a god." I start shaking, my orgasm teetering right fucking there. I can barely breathe. And then his mouth licks a line up my shoulder blades, right where my wings connect. "D-definitely calling you a god." The entire world fades, the entire universe pinpointing to the spot where his mouth and his hands are on me.

"Come."

One word is all it takes for me to explode, screaming out my orgasm as I topple over the edge. I come so hard I think I black out. And through it all, Eldoris keeps playing with my wings, building me up even as I'm falling.

"Coming again," I manage before I can't speak anymore. All I know is pleasure. His touch is a wildfire, igniting every inch of me. The third time he brings me to climax, I drag Eldoris off the cliff with me as he roars his release so loud the room quakes with it.

I flop forward over the arm of the couch, my knees unable to hold me anymore. Eldoris sags against me, giving me his weight while simultaneously holding me up. He places chaste kisses along my shoulders and my neck, wiping the sweat-drenched hairs on the back of my neck out of his way.

"You are welcome to play with my wings anytime," I pant, and he places his forehead on my shoulder as his body shakes in laughter. He slips out of me and cleans us both up before scooping me into his arms and flopping onto the couch while still cradling me.

An abrasive knock on our door startles us. "Open up, buttercup," Vlad's voice calls. "Time to get shit done."

"We could ignore him," I offer.

"Today's the day you're supposed to go to the mortal realm." I groan at Eldoris' reminder. It's not that I don't want to go. I miss Katie so much that my chest aches. But for the first time, I have a reason to want to stay.

With a dramatic sigh, I summon robes for us to slip on, and Eldoris drops the shield around the room. No sooner than we do, Vlad bursts into the room.

"It smells like sex in here," he says, wrinkling his nose before flashing us a toothy smile. I roll my eyes.

"What did you think we've been doing all week? Playing Scrabble?" I deadpan, resuming my spot on the couch, tucking my legs under me and sinking into my betrothed's open arms. "What do you want?"

"Two things," he says, his tone glacial considering he was just banging down our door. "I thought you'd be interested in the drama that happened at Hades' place after you left."

"Always."

Eldoris starts running his hands through my hair, and I practically purr at the contact. I love that he knows how much I love that.

I summon an armchair for Vlad to sit in. "Well," he says dramatically, crossing one leg. "Puck told you he was in the mortal realm, right? He supposedly went right after the joust on some errand and had no idea the extent of Titania's alliance with the hellfire Fae. Then he interrupted Hades during the second scene and begged her to let him into the Spring Court so he could find out what was happening."

"I bet she loved that," Eldoris scoffs.

"Oh yes, very accommodating, our Hades." Vlad chuckles. "They made some sort of deal, and she escorted him past the blockade."

"That's intense," I say. "What's the second thing?"

"Hm?" he asks, with a devious smirk. "Oh, Katie's in labor."

"*What!?*" I jump to my feet, ignoring the fact that Eldoris is tugged along with me since his hands are tangled in my hair. "We have to go, we're going right?"

"You might want to wait," Vlad says. "I only stopped by and the language I heard was enough to terrify me into hiding. Again."

"Coward," I tease. "I'm going, you both can wait..."

"I'm right behind you, kitten," Eldoris says, placing a hand on my lower back. Vlad groans dramatically and tilts his head to the sky.

"Fucking breeders," he grumbles. "Come on, let's go experience the miracle of life."

I halt. "Experience it from the hallway though, right? I love Katie, but I don't need that image in my head for all eternity."

"One hundred percent," Vlad shudders.

We teleport directly to the portal and step into the swirling mist. When we emerge in the hall of her house, it's eerily silent. "That's ominous," I murmur. "How far along is she? I thought she wanted me to be surprised that she was pregnant." Vlad shrugs, and I pinch the bridge of my nose at his ignorance.

We walk down the halls toward Katie's bedroom. "Wait," Vlad holds out a hand, and I hold my breath. "There." As soon as the word leaves his mouth, I hear the faint mewling of a baby, which immediately ratchets up in sound.

I sprint down the hall, the slap of my bare feet against the hardwood the only reminder that I'm in a silk robe without shoes on. Up a marble staircase and down another hallway, this one carpeted, and we finally arrive at Katie's room at the same time the healer— an older man with white hair and kind blue eyes—emerges.

"You have good timing," he says, eyeing my wardrobe with confusion. "She had a feeling you'd be here soon and said to send you in."

"How are they?" I ask, taking his hand as he extends it.

"Perfect," he beams, and I catch the hint of a tear in his lashes. "Early, but the baby is healthy, and Katie did beautifully."

"Thank you," I murmur, and push past him, not bothering to knock.

Sitting propped up against pillows, with her mate's arms around her, my best friend looks exhausted and sweaty, but holy hell is she glowing. In her arms is a pale yellow blanket that she doesn't even look away from when we come in.

"E," she hiccups, and I walk over and slide into bed beside her. I put my head on her shoulder, and Katie tilts her head to meet mine. "I'm sorry I didn't tell you. I thought I had more time and I wanted it to be a surprise."

"You're forgiven," I laugh amidst tears, and kiss her cheek before looking down at the baby in her arms.

"Her name is Lorraine," Katie says, meeting her mate's eyes. He's looking at my best friend like she hung the moon and the two share a chaste kiss that's so full of love it makes my heart swell.

Lorraine has a smattering of dark hair atop her head that matches the color of Katie's mate. But the shape of her nose, the way her brow furrows is all Katie. "She looks just like you, babes."

"Except her eyes," she says, and as if she hears us, Lorraine blinks her amber eyes open. They're the perfect blend between Katie's and her mate's. They're gorgeous. Katie leans in, resting her nose against the baby's, and her eyes drift closed again. "Do you want to hold her?"

"I can wait," I say because she clearly doesn't want to let her out of her arms, but she shakes her head and transfers her to my arms. The baby fusses for a moment as I get her positioned, but I make soothing sounds and bounce her a bit until she settles.

And then she opens her eyes again.

"By the goddess," I whisper as this little creature instantly wraps me around her finger. "Hi, Lorraine," I coo, and she blinks two long, slow blinks. "I'm your Aunt E."

"Actually," Katie says, drawing my attention. "We were hoping you'd be her godmother."

Tears brim in my eyes, and I have to swallow around the lump in my throat before I speak. "Is it because you want her to have a Faerie Godmother?"

Eldoris' low laughter from the doorway has me looking up. He managed to put real clothes on before coming into the room. When our eyes catch, my stomach does this crazy flip. It's the way he's looking at me like he's glimpsing our future. And, surprisingly, I don't hate it. Actually, I really like the look in his eyes.

"I'm telling you this right now...I get to plan your bachelorette party," I tell the baby. "I know it's not for a while, and you may even choose to never marry, which is fine, but ask your mom, you want me to plan at least one big party." Katie laughs and wraps her arm around my waist.

"Next time, you tell me right away," I say, fixing her with my best stare. "Nine months is nothing in Faerie. I'll be here for everything. Each morning sickness episode, every mood swing."

"I didn't have many mood swings."

Vlad coughs loudly, and she glares at him.

"We'll tell you next time," her mate promises. "And the time after that. And the time after that."

"Pup, you're writing checks my vagina can't cash," Katie laughs and he shuts her up with a kiss.

The baby squeaks, and after a moment of trying to calm her, Katie takes her back and says she's probably hungry. With one final kiss on my best friend's cheek and one on the top of my goddaughter's head, we excuse ourselves from the room to give the new family some alone time.

Before I leave, Katie snags my hand and says, "Do you know how Eldoris was looking at you just now?" she asks.

"Like he wants to put one of those little suckers in my not-so-fertile Fae womb?" I ask, causing her mate to laugh. "Would it surprise you if I said I might be okay with that?"

"Really?"

I shrug. "The breeding kink is kinda hot."

"I know, right?" she whisper-shouts. "Like, the feminist in me wants to hate it, but..." The two of us giggle as quietly as we can without jostling Lorraine.

"You look really happy," Katie says, squeezing my hand.

I lean in conspiratorially. "I'm a romance novel cliché." She squeals in delight, making the baby let out an actual cry. "I'll tell you the sex details when you're not lactating."

"Appreciated. Love you."

"Love you...second most," I say with a glance at her daughter.

"I can deal with that."

I leave before Katie whips her boob out, softly closing the door behind me and tilting my head back against it, listening to my goddaughter cries from between the walls. I'm sure that sound will get old fast, but right now it's better than a siren symphony.

Eldoris stands across from me, leaning against the opposite wall, watching me with hungry eyes. A million things pass between us in the blink of an eye, and I know we'll have to have an actual conversation about them at some point, but for now, I let myself sink into the moment. I can see myself having a family with this male. It's another item in the long list of things that simultaneously excite and terrify me, but I'm learning to roll with it.

"Are you staying?" Vlad asks. I honestly forgot he was in the hall.

"There's no way in hell I'm leaving right now," Not yet, this is too important for me to miss. I turn to Eldoris. "Will...can you stay with me? I can show you the joys of binge-watching trashy TV, and take you to meet Joe, and if the baby gets too loud, we can go to Katie's summer house—"

"Princess?" a voice calls, and I turn to find Astor frantically running down the hall. His usually pale skin has gone gray, and his eyes are wild, unable to focus on anything.

"What's wrong?" I ask, pushing past Eldoris and Vlad to go to my father. He bypasses my hands and pulls me into a hug, something I can't remember him ever doing.

"Something's happened in the Spring Court."

My breath stalls, my heart is beating too fast. "What?" I squeak. "Is it the hellfire Fae? Did they attack—"

"All we know is that it's something at the palace, and it's something big," he looks past me toward Eldoris and the door we just came through. "I'm so sorry, but we need you home. It's an unknown threat, we need you in the palace."

I swear, but nod. They need to make sure I'm protected, and while the chance of a hellfire Fae attacking me in the mortal realm is slim, there's still a chance. In the fortress that is the Winter Court palace, the chances are a lot lower.

Eldoris comes to my side, wrapping an arm around my waist. "Katie will understand," he murmurs. When I look at Vlad, he just winks, promising in his way he'll keep me updated, and will tell Katie why we had to leave.

"Let me put real clothes on and we can go."

Chapter Forty-One
Edina

ASTOR TELEPORTS US FROM the portal directly to the front gates of the palace. All the guards immediately have magic in their hands, icicles sharper than daggers ready to strike when we land. We raise our hands and soon the main guard, Bylur, rushes down from the battlements to confirm our identities.

"Let the princess inside!" Astor bellows, magic in his own hands. I swear he wasn't this protective when we fought in a war, I'm not sure why he's so afraid now.

Bylur gives the soldiers a signal and quickly motions for the gates to be opened. We're ushered ahead and told not to linger on the grounds, but to go straight inside. The halls are a mess of servants running around in a panic, readying the palace for battle. "We don't know what happened at Spring Court?" I ask, because the way they're reacting, it sure seems like they know something.

"The only thing we know is that something happened at the palace," Astor says over his shoulder as he leads Eldoris and me to the throne room. That's why everyone is taking this so seriously. It's not a random attack on an outpost or even one of the civilian towns. For whatever reason, someone turned on the palace.

The throne room is empty except for my mother and fathers, who are currently using magic to fortify the windows. My mother releases a sigh of relief when she sees me, but then goes right back to her ministrations.

Althea and Brigid zoom in and are uncharacteristically silent as they take up defensive positions around me. Even Eldoris is keeping unusually close.

"You know I can fight, right?" I tease, but his smile is tense.

"I still have no intention of losing you, which means I'll protect you at all costs."

I wrap my arms low around his waist, and only then does he relax and hug me back. I know how important protecting me is to him, and if I can help in any way, I will.

After a moment, Bylur enters the throne room and sinks to one knee. "Your Majesty, someone is at the gate requesting an audience," he says.

"Who?" she demands.

"Puck of the Spring Court." His eyes nervously shift to me. "He says he needs to speak to Her Highness."

"Not now," my mother answers. "How did he get past the blockade?"

"They let him through, Your Majesty," Bylur says nervously.

"Why?"

The door clangs open, and every Fae in the room gets ready to attack as Puck walks in, hands raised in a placating gesture. In one of his hands is a severed head.

Althea screams. Eldoris swears.

The only part of the head I can see is a mess of reddish-orange curls.

"This is why," Puck says, a slightly feral glint in his eye. His tunic is covered in drying blood, but I can't take my eyes off the severed head. He notices me looking and says, "Oh, here."

When he turns it around, there's no doubt the head belongs to Titania. The look on her lifeless face is one of pure shock. Her lips are open in a forever-silenced scream, her green eyes open and wide.

My mother recovers first. "What did you do?"

"I couldn't stand by anymore," Puck says. "She cursed me and she was destroying our court. Aligning with the hellfire Fae to take over Summer Court was the last straw. She wouldn't have stopped there. It was never going to be enough. So, I killed her."

The confession sits for a moment, and then my mother nods once. "All right then," she says.

"*All right then?*" I demand, completely shocked. "He committed murder, staged a fucking coup, and all you have to say is '*all right then*'?"

"For now," my mother says with a casual air of elegance. "I'll send word to the other monarchs to come for a meeting to induct our new interim King of the Spring Court. I'm sure we'll have to look over the laws pertaining to this kind of situation, but I'd expect a swift coronation thereafter, Puck."

And without another word, she turns and leaves the throne room with my fathers trailing behind her.

Puck takes a step closer, and I step back. "Edina, please. I need to talk to you. To explain." His face becomes so earnest, that I almost consider it. Then he says, "Alone."

"No," I respond simply.

"We'll umm..." Althea starts, motioning to Titania's head.

"We can take that, Your Majesty," Brigid says, addressing Puck by a fucking title.

"He's not a king!"

"He will be," Brigid shrugs, her purple eyes lighting.

"We'll make sure the guards return it to the Spring Court if you'd like," Althea says. Again, it strikes me as incredibly odd that no one is bothered that they're talking about disposing of a head. It's like they're offering to take his luggage.

Puck thanks them, and when they leave, he looks imploringly between me and Eldoris. "Please," he says. "Just a moment, and if you never want to speak to me after that, I'll understand."

I exchange a glance with Eldoris. "I'll stay right outside," he says, pulling me into him and kissing my temple.

"I won't hurt her," Puck swears. He's fidgeting, tugging on the hem of his blood-splattered tunic like he's just now realizing it's covered in gore. We ignore him.

"Just send Bylur," I sigh. "I'll meet you in our room."

Eldoris squeezes my hand and leaves, the door echoing in the giant chamber as it clangs shut. Puck paces back in forth in front of the dais, wringing his hands or running them through his auburn hair.

"Anytime now," I deadpan, putting my hands on my hips. His green eyes meet mine and he sighs.

"Can we sit?"

I don't even want to hear his damn story, but clearly, he's going to be heard, so I sit on the edge of the dais. Puck swallows and continues his pacing as he starts to speak.

"Titania is dead," he says.

"I got that message when you placed her head at my feet," I say. "What does this have to do with us?"

Another drawn-out sigh. "Everything."

I scoff. "You're claiming what? She possessed your body when you rejected the mate bond?"

Puck shakes his head, his hair falling in front of his eyes. He pushes it back with an exasperated huff. "I was magically tied to her," he says finally. "She controlled everything. I couldn't—"

My heart jumps and constricts painfully, and I'm not sure if that's a natural reaction or if I'm feeling some of what Puck is feeling through the bond. "Start from the beginning," I say, softer.

He nods and then sits cross-legged on the floor before me, looking up into my eyes as he tells me the tale.

"Spring Court was different when Oberon was king," he says. "But when he married Titania, everyone started noticing changes. Higher taxes, less freedom to come and go as we pleased. It was subtle, so most Fae didn't notice until it was much worse.

"I was the emissary to the mortal realm." His expression grows wistful. "I loved it there, and the people there loved me...most of the time. I had a penchant for pranks back in the day that sometimes got me in trouble, but mostly the humans thought it was funny.

"One day, someone I—let's say teased—found out what I was and slipped iron into my drink. Have you come across iron since you emerged?" I shake my head. "It's painful when it touches your skin, but when you ingest it, it weakens you. I couldn't move, I could barely breathe.

"They wrapped me in iron chains and threw me off a cliffside." My eyes widen, and Puck takes that as encouragement. "It wasn't a far drop, but the iron made me sink, fast. And because of the iron in my system, I couldn't fight. I resigned myself to my fate—a little pissed that was how I was taken out, but accepting nonetheless—when a siren pulled me from the water. In their monster form, iron doesn't hurt them as easily.

"When he deposited me on the shore, Titania was there. She said she was the one who bid the siren to save my life, and that I owed her a favor. She wanted me to kill Oberon."

"I've heard rumors she killed her husband," I say, and Puck's shoulders deflate a little.

"She had me do it. The Fae take favors very seriously. My choice was to be indebted to either her or the nameless siren, and I was convinced since sirens are Unseelie, that request would be worse."

"Worse than murder?"

Puck shrugs. "There was still iron in my system, it made me groggy. I'm not saying it was a sound decision. In fact, I know it wasn't, because the second I killed Oberon, Titania had me surrounded by Spring Court guards. She accused me of treason and sentenced me to a life of service. She performed a spell that tethered me to her, not physically, but mentally. Anytime I fought against her, my body revolted, like I was being tortured from the inside out.

"Mostly, she had me do grunt work. She let me handle the Underground, made me befriend the second generation so she could stay current on the other ruling families' gossip, and other small things around the Spring Court. It wasn't bad. Until..."

"Did she...did you two—" I swallow, trying to get the words out, but Puck shakes his head.

"She wanted everyone to think we were fucking. It was easier to explain my loyalty if they thought we were having sex, but she never crossed that line.

"After a time, her requests became more sinister. She forced me to aid a changeling operation. She had me investigate rumors of hellfire Fae returning. She offered me up for experiments for them to test their twisted magic on me."

I want to reach out and touch him, but I don't. I stay frozen. The primal Fae in me wants to reattach Titania's head, bring her back to life, and then rip it off again for the way she abused my mate. But I remain silent.

"I think the experiments helped actually, because her spell weakened. Suddenly I could think for myself again. I could feel myself returning to normal, but they were rare moments, like pockets of clarity. Until I met you."

Puck's eyes meet mine again, I didn't even realize he was staring at the floor until the contact is back. "I was sent to find and bring you to Titania. And I was going to do that...until we kissed. I returned to myself enough that I was able to take you to the treehouse, and then we made love and it was like...I was me again. You brought me back to myself."

"You wanted me to stay," I say softly, and Puck's smile is sad.

"I was hoping the reason I had such clarity around you was that you were my mate. And I was hoping, if you emerged with me and we accepted the bond, it would override the spell Titania placed on my mind."

He looks away again. "She found out I had you and didn't bring you in and recast the spell. That night at the ball, when I realized you were my mate, I couldn't accept the bond fast enough. I hoped she'd let us leave, and leave you hanging, but..."

My brain flashes back to the moment he said no, the pained look on his face, and his apology right before he rejected me. I swear and wrap my arms around my middle, trying to digest this new information.

Because how can I hate him now?

I can't.

I don't.

"How did you break free of it?" I ask.

"She sent me to the mortal realm after the joust," he says. "But she forgets, I have friends there. I found the descendant of a witch I knew back in the Renaissance, and she was able to remove the curse completely. She used some kind of blood magic, crazy-intense stuff, but it worked.

"When I came back and learned Titania had allied with the hellfire users, I asked Hades to sneak me back into court. Titania thought I was still under her spell, so she didn't suspect anything when I went to her bed and killed her."

I feel like I'm not quite in my body when Puck leans forward and takes my hands. "We can be together now," he says. "We're fated, Edina."

Are we?

A few weeks ago, I would have said yes. I hate myself for it, but I would have run into his arms.

Now I'm not so sure.

I'm about to tell Puck that when he says, "I know how badly I hurt you, and that I'm not deserving of a second chance. But if you'll let me, I promise I will spend eternity making it up to you." Again, I open my mouth to answer, and he cuts me off. "Don't answer me now. Think about it. I'm heading back to the Spring Court in a bit, once I speak with your mother and get her to call off the blockade. But when I go back...I'd like you to come with me so we can start figuring things out."

This time I don't bother trying to answer, I just nod, stand, and leave Puck alone in the throne room. My brain is whirring as I go back to my room. Puck didn't want to reject me. Titania was magically holding him hostage. Puck killed Titania so we could be together.

But I'm in love with Eldoris.

And as far as I'm concerned, that overrides a broken mating bond.

I run down the long hall and burst into the door. "El!" I call, ready to tell him everything, ready to tell him that even when given the choice of being with Puck, I don't want it.

But Eldoris isn't there. "El?" I call again, and he emerges from his bedroom across the sitting room. The one he's never actually used. "What—"

He gives me a wide smile, but it doesn't reach his eyes. "I stayed in the hall for a bit. I heard what Puck said."

"I know, it's crazy. I knew Titania was certifiable, but that's—" His throat bobs and his smile slips. My stomach drops. Something isn't right. "That's not what I was going to tell you."

"You don't need to." He crosses the room and takes hold of my hands. "I understand."

"Understand what?"

"Your mate wants to be with you, and has a perfectly reasonable, and tragic, reason why he rejected you in the first place." He pulls me into a hug, but I go ramrod straight. "And you deserve to know what that feels like, kitten. You deserve to have the unconditional love of a mate. I would never take that away from you."

It's one blow after the next. He's repeatedly knocking the wind from my lungs.

He's leaving me.

"You said you love me," I whisper, hating how small my voice sounds.

When he pulls away, he's beaming again. "I only want you to be happy."

But he doesn't say he loves me. Now that I think about it, he only said it once. Maybe he was just swept away in the moment and didn't mean it.

He told me from the very beginning that he wouldn't be able to love me.

I should have listened.

I can't hear beyond the pounding in my ears. I can't breathe. I can't form the words to tell him I want him. My chest feels like it's caving in on itself.

He's leaving me. Just like everyone leaves me.

I pull away as much as I can, but Eldoris keeps his hands on my biceps, rubbing what would normally be comforting lines, but now makes me want to throw up. When he stops, assessing me, I put up every wall I can, erecting them around my heart.

"Well," my voice breaks a bit, but I clear it, "thanks for pretending with me."

It's a low blow, and it's enough to get Eldoris to jerk away from me. "Kitten—"

"I should go," I say, pointing back to the doors. "I'll see you around, Eldoris."

I turn and flee the room before I can see his face, only stopping when I get far enough from the room that I'm certain he won't see. I take a shuddering breath and release it. I won't cry, even if it feels like I'm breaking.

I square my shoulders and keep walking, returning to the throne room, where Puck is still waiting for his audience with the other monarchs. When I enter, his face lights with hope.

"I'll come with you," I say, happy my voice is solid and unwavering. "I don't trust you yet, and I'm not sure anything will completely repair what was broken, but...I'm willing to try."

ELDORIS

I'm doing the right thing.

It doesn't matter that it feels like someone reached into my chest, squeezed, and then left the pulp in my ribcage. It doesn't matter that everything in my body is screaming at me to run after Edina, wrap her in my arms, and never let her go.

I can let her go to Puck. I can let her know the love of a mate, and what that security and happiness feels like.

I can do that because I'm in love with her, and when you love someone, you want the best thing for them. You want their happiness over yours.

So, I wait in her room for long enough that I know she won't be in the halls, and then I leave. I walk with my head held high, without making eye contact with the pixies who flutter around and try to get me to tell them what happened. I ignore the buzz of servants for the entire walk through the castle, its surrounding grounds, and the entire trek through the winter wastelands. I keep moving through the portal as it spits me out into the hallway of my palace, past Devorah's office, ignoring when she calls me until I reach the door to my bedroom.

It's only when I'm inside, and the room still smells faintly of Edina, of rosewater and sugar, that I realize I can't stay here.

A tear beads in the corner of my eye as I cross to the closet and find it filled with the dresses she wore while she was here. My fingers trail over the fabric, tracing the fine material that looked so good on her. In one sweep, I pull the clothes together and banish them. I throw a cleansing spell around the room, removing her scent even if I can't completely remove her memory.

She won't be gone from me forever. She'll always be my friend.

And because I love her, I can stand beside her when she gets her happy ending.

I just wish it was with me.

Chapter Forty-Two
Edina

Later...Goddess knows how long (about two Fae weeks maybe)

My spoon clangs against the teacup loud enough to pause the incessant chatter of the females I'm taking tea with. We're set up in one of the many gardens that exist on the palace grounds. This one is full of bubbling stone fountains and other statuary of various creatures in Faerie. The one behind my current guests is a centaur with a massive marble penis that hangs so low it touches the plot of daisies at its base.

When we got back to the Spring Court, Puck was quickly thrust into the role of interim king. While technically he staged a successful coup, that sort of thing hasn't been done in Faerie. And when things don't go exactly to plan in this realm, everything takes longer than it should. Until the monarchs decide on how to handle it, Puck won't be coronated, but he still needs to undo the wrongs Titania committed.

As his mate, I've stayed in the palace with guards surrounding me at all times and am in charge of winning over the courtiers. I hate every second of it, especially since they all adore Puck, which makes the task pointless.

I sit here and make polite conversation, and with each minute that passes, I die a little more inside.

The sweating carafe of wine is calling me, begging me to slip into its embrace and let it take away some of the pain. This court is breaking me. Okay, maybe it's not the court. It's this life that I never asked for but somehow found myself accepting.

It just felt like a waste not to try with Puck. He is my mate; I should be craving him the way I was before I became betrothed to Eldoris. But it feels *wrong*. Every time I see him, I wish he were someone else. And then I feel guilty because Puck didn't do anything wrong, so I should be giving him more of a chance.

I only want you to be happy.

I squeeze my eyes shut to banish the image of Eldoris saying goodbye, but it stays there, ever present in my mind.

"We were just saying how wonderful it is that Puck is disbanding the Underground," one of the females, a petite blonde with blushing pink skin, says. That's a gross exaggeration. In actuality, Puck promised the Spring Court section to Hades in exchange for getting him past the blockade the night of the sex show. But sure, let's go with *disbanding the Underground*.

I nod, my jaw clenching.

"So," the other female, a tall brunette who's built like an Amazon warrior, leans in and draws out the word for ten syllables. "Have you started planning a wedding?"

I choke on my sip of tea. Althea and Brigid, who are always hovering close by, fly over and pound on my back, surprisingly hard for their little fists. When I'm finally done hacking up a lung, I thank them.

"No," I respond sternly, hoping that's the end of the conversation.

It's not.

"You'll have it here, I'm sure," the blonde says. "Spring is much more suited to a wedding than Winter."

"Oh, but how will that work?" the brunette asks, feigning horror. "You're in line for Winter Court's throne. How could you marry the Spring Court king?"

"I'm sure they'll figure it out," Blondie says, placating the Amazon.

"Ladies." Puck's hand on my shoulder makes me flinch, but it's small enough that the females don't notice. When I look up, Puck's eyes are serious, so he definitely felt it. He covers up quickly and flashes the females a winning grin. "Might I steal my mate away for the afternoon?"

The females stand and give little curtsies, preening with *of course* and *I'm so sorry we kept her so late.* I force a polite smile as they walk away, their skirts rustling as they flee the garden, escorted by two guards. The guards are everywhere since Puck wasn't sure which of the courtiers and advisors he could trust. So far, all has been quiet.

When they've gone, Puck sits in the seat closest to me, and I find myself enraptured by the roses in all colors blooming by the table. I trace their vines, find their thorns, and study their petals as servants clear the females' plates and bring a new one for Puck. I can feel his gaze on me the entire time, but I don't acknowledge it.

"You've been avoiding me," he murmurs.

"Not at all," I lie.

"We're still bonded, gorgeous. I can feel you hiding from me."

Fine, I've been avoiding him.

When we first arrived, Puck brought me to *our* bedroom, not Titania's master suite, but one of the guest suites. He said we could make it ours until the king and queen suites were demolished and redecorated. I told him I wasn't ready to share a room with him, and he sullenly took another one across the hall.

"Edina," he says softly, laying his hands atop mine. I force myself to look at him, but I don't bother hiding my feelings.

I miss Eldoris.

I miss him every morning while I drink my tea. I miss him whenever one of the courtiers says something silly and I want to make fun of them with someone. I miss him at night in my bed, not in a sexual way, though I miss that too. Mostly, I miss falling asleep in his arms.

But he didn't want me.

When I spoke to Katie about it, she tried to convince me that Eldoris must love me a lot for him to step aside, but I know the truth. He didn't love me at all. If he wanted me, he would have fought for me.

"I know you've been sad," Puck says. "And I know you miss Eldoris." I don't answer.

"I wish you would talk to me," he continues. "I'm here, and I know things are awkward right now, but they won't get any better if you keep avoiding me."

I sigh. I've been wallowing in my grief. But he's right. If I'm going to give him a chance, I need to actually give him a chance.

"Okay," I whisper. Puck's face lights up, and he flashes me that dazzling smile.

"I'd like to take you somewhere," he says. "Somewhere special."

He takes my hand and extends his wings, urging me to follow. We spring into the air, soaring over the rainbow Iridis hills toward the Varesen forest.

We're going to the treehouse.

It's a weird sense of déjà vu, flying beside him, anticipation tying my stomach in knots. But as we soar over the treetops, I'm not thinking of the night he brought me to Faerie. I'm thinking about flying into the sunset on the back of a dragon. I push the memory aside. I prefer flying with my own wings to flying on the back of some beast anyway.

When we land on the balcony, Puck's face looks freer than I've ever seen it. He's light and unburdened, despite his new responsibilities. His reddish-brown hair catches the light, making it look like there's a halo over his tresses. He catches me looking and beams, dimples flashing before he pulls me into him.

My breath catches. This is it. You can do this. You can let him kiss you. *You can get your fucking happy ending.*

He doesn't kiss me though; he simply pulls me into a hug and the breath releases from my lungs in a whoosh of relief. My arms circle his waist as he holds me tighter, and suddenly I'm crying. I haven't cried since coming back to the Spring Court. Not through the nightmares that have returned, not through the mornings I woke reaching for Eldoris. I've kept the tears at bay this entire time.

"I know," Puck whispers against my hair, and I continue to sob into his chest. His hold is firm, keeping me locked in place as the tears keep coming, and my whole body trembles.

"I'm sorry," I get out, my throat thick.

"You don't need to apologize for anything," Puck insists, not relinquishing his hold on me. "Nothing about this is your fault."

It feels like it is. I'm here, with my mate, someone who just a short while ago I would have done anything to be with, and I can't stop thinking of another male. I don't blame Puck, he clearly had very little choice in the destruction of our relationship, and I can't blame Eldoris for sticking to his promise not to fall in love with me. He gave me fair warning. So, who else is there? Who else can I blame?

"Let's go inside," Puck says, and when I pull away from the cage of his arms, I realize the sun has set, and the world around us is dark.

He guides me directly to the large couch that overlooks the forest, the same one he fucked me on the first night we met. Everything looks exactly the same, treehouse bachelor pad chic. Even the forest outside the windows looks the same, and yet I feel so different. The last time I was here, I was so excited. Now it's like the enthusiasm has been leeched from my body.

He disappears only for a moment to grab a large, crocheted blanket. Wrapping it around my shoulders, he gives me a gentle squeeze before moving into the kitchen. "I know you're sober, but do you want water? Tea? Hot chocolate?"

"Is the chocolate combined with some kind of floral?" I ask, wrinkling my nose. Puck chuckles.

"Removing the floral flavors from food will be my first decree," he teases. "This is from the mortal realm."

"Sold." I watch as he moves around the kitchen, boiling water, and again another memory of Eldoris bringing me the tea that helped with my pain comes unbidden to my mind.

I clutch the blanket a little closer. The silence between me and Puck is weirdly comfortable. There's no pressure to share what I'm thinking or to delve back into the meltdown I just had.

When the hot chocolate is made and topped with marshmallows, Puck sits beside me, stretching his arm on the back of the couch so it's behind me, but not holding me. "I think," he says slowly like he's chewing on each word. "We should kiss."

I arch an eyebrow over my mug. "If you give me some bullshit about true love's kiss…"

He laughs and takes the mug from my hands and places it on the coffee table. "No, gorgeous. But…I don't know, I can't explain why I think it's important, but I think we should try."

I tug my bottom lip between my teeth. "I'm trying, Puck," I promise. "I just...I don't know how to describe what I'm feeling."

"You're hurting," he says simply. "You're mourning the end of a relationship. I get that, believe me, I do."

I want to ask more, ask if he lost someone when he was cursed, but I don't. If he's not forcing me to open a painful wound, I won't force him to open one either.

"Okay," I say after a beat. "Let's do it, rip off the bandage."

"That's one way to think of it," he glowers, and I find myself chuckling. His hand cups my cheek, a thumb brushing a soothing line along my skin.

I lean forward, placing my hands on Puck's chest, feeling the muscles jump beneath my touch. He leans in further, and gently kisses me. Barely a brush of his lips against mine before pulling back to check in with me. I nod, and he kisses me again, harder this time.

And I feel nothing.

No electricity, no spark. No desire to take the kiss further. Not a damn thing.

Puck pulls away, his brow furrowed. He opens his mouth, then closes it. "Huh," he says.

"Can I—" I don't finish the thought, but he nods, and I climb into his lap, straddling his waist. I run my fingers through his silken hair, and his eyes close in contentment as his hands fall to my hips. I close the distance and kiss him again, taking the reins. My tongue playfully traces the seam of his lips until he opens for me, and our tongues tangle together.

Nothing.

He tightens his hold, rocking me forward, and I'm very aware that he's very unexcited. A hysterical laugh bubbles up my throat as I grind over his flaccid cock, and soon I'm laughing so hard that I need to pull away and bury my head in his chest. Puck's laughter joins mine, a low rumbling that embodies the frustration I'm feeling.

"We used to be good at that, right?" he asks, and I nod through my hysterics. "My brain was muddled, but I remember our first kiss being—"

"Electric," I say, sitting back a little, but keeping my hands looped around Puck's neck. "Like coming home."

"Yeah," he says. "But the mating bond is still there, I feel it."

And then I realize what's happened. I groan and climb off Puck's lap, returning to my hot chocolate, the marshmallows having long since turned to foam on top of the liquid. "What does the bond feel like to you?" I ask around a sip.

"Like a tether," he says simply.

"You sure about that?"

Puck's eyes go wide. "It's...yes, but it's splintered." He swears. "You think the physical intimacy part of the mating bond died when I rejected it?"

"It makes sense."

He swears again, abandoning his hot chocolate and returning to the kitchen. He grabs a bottle of Faerie wine from underneath the counter, uncorks it, and drinks directly from the bottle. "But we're fated," he says after he downs the majority of the contents.

I sigh. "Maybe...maybe fate just isn't enough."

"Then it's my fault," Puck says with a swear. He runs his fingers through his hair until it sticks up at an odd angle.

"Maybe it's both of us," I offer. "The fact that I'm in love with another male right now probably isn't helping." When he looks up, the crushed look in his eyes is enough to have me going to him. "Or maybe, we're not fated to be together romantically, but we're fated to be friends."

Puck scoffs. "That sounds like a line, gorgeous."

"It can be a line and still be true," I smirk. "And if it makes you feel better, I never stay friends with exes, so this basically makes you the most important person in my life."

Puck laughs and walks back over and wraps me in a hug. "I'm sorry," he says.

"Yeah, me too." I breathe in his scent, and I realize it's not nearly as comforting as it used to be. It doesn't make me feel like I'm at home. It's not the scent of the ocean and sandalwood.

"Goddess, this hurts," Puck says, scrubbing at his chest.

"Did you drink the tea I gave you?" Puck shakes his head and drinks more wine. "It still hurts with the tea, but the pain is more manageable."

Puck stares into his wine glass. "I think you need to reject me."

"Did you not get that from what I just did?"

"Magically," he says, his eyes welling with tears. "The blood witch that broke my curse had some grimoires. They were in ancient Russian so it took me a long time to decode them all, but one had information on mates. It focused on creatures in the mortal realm, but I think...it might work with us.

"It said if both mates reject each other, it will be a complete death of the bond."

As soon as he says the words, I realize he's right. I don't know how I know, maybe it's instinct, but I know in my gut that's the way things have to go.

I swallow hard, but I take his hand, linking our fingers together. And then I repeat the words that have plagued my nightmares for three mortal years.

"I renounce our mating bond. I renounce the ties that bind us. You are not my mate, Puck of the Spring Court."

It's a flash of blinding pain. It feels like my heart is breaking into a thousand pieces. Puck screams in pain, I start sobbing. The splintered tether between us bursts, exploding in a burst of magical light.

And then it's over. The bond is gone.

Puck and I find each other's eyes and I sink into his embrace, the two of us crying, mourning what we could have had if things had been different. When the tears have subsided, we pull away from each other and Puck gives me a chaste kiss.

"Now what?" he asks, and a wet laugh escapes my lips.

"I'm gonna go home," I say.

"You're not going to him?"

I shake my head. "I guess I can tell you this now, but we were just trying to make you jealous."

"Bullshit," Puck says.

"Well, that's the way it was supposed to be. I was stupid and fell for him, but he's not in the same place."

"Again, I call bullshit." Puck takes my hand in his. "I've seen the way he looks at you. If you love him, you should go to him." He finishes and makes a weird face like he's tasting something sour.

"That was weird," I say.

"Yeah, I'm not sure we're at the 'romantic advice,' part of our friendship."

I chuckle, and after putting my empty mug back down, wrap my arms around Puck's neck. It's the most platonic hug I've ever experienced and sends us both into another fit of giggles.

"Right," I say when we've both stopped laughing. "You go run your court. I'm gonna go home and start learning to run mine."

I'm about to leave when there's a knock at the sliding glass doors. A female in the Seelie Army uniform enters at Puck's urging. She looks panic-stricken, her wings fluttering so wildly I'm surprised she's not hovering like a hummingbird.

"Your Majesty. Your Highness, so sorry to disturb you," she says with a bow. "But it's the hellfire Fae. They're attacking the Summer Court again."

"Where?"

"Our border. They went across the river."

"Shit," Puck swears, swiping a hand down his face. "Eldoris will think we're behind this."

The female squeaks. "He said to tell you, 'I know you didn't authorize this, but get your ass—'" she whispers the word, afraid to offend, "'—down here and help us fix Titania's mistake.'"

"Damn," I swear. "Did they send anyone to the Winter Court?"

My answer comes in the form of my mother, who lands on the balcony dressed in her fighting leathers. "We're using your court," she informs Puck. "We'll attack from behind, surround their forces, and take them all out. Edina, get changed."

Puck bristles at the order but nods his agreement. I run into the bedroom to change, and when I emerge, my mother and Puck are in a serious conversation that cuts off as soon as I enter. "You told her?" I guess, and Puck winces.

In a rare show of emotion, my mother rushes me and wraps me in a tight hug. I collapse into her, burying my head in her shoulder. She smells like cinnamon and spice and reminds me of Christmas in the mortal realm. She strokes my hair as I stay in her arms, accepting her comfort. "I love you so much," she says, and my tears from earlier threaten to resurface.

"Love you too, Mom."

"You know Eldoris loves you too, right?" she says, not breaking our embrace. I open my mouth to argue with her when she cuts me off. "He's been a mess since you've come here. Won't stay in the palaces, won't return to the army base. We think he's been living off the land."

"And he's been a nightmare to work with," the female officer says, her eyes immediately going wide like she's surprised she said that.

"Told you." I glare, but Puck only smirks. "I'm gonna go help your betrothed on his side of things."

"He's not my betrothed anymore—" he fixes me with a look, and I sigh. "Keep him safe. Fire doesn't do shit against hellfire." He mock-salutes me and flies off, taking the female with him.

"Do you want to talk about it?" my mother asks.

"There's a battle going on, can we maybe not focus on my love life?"

My mother waves a hand. "We'll get there." *Fae and their lack of urgency.* "When you see him today, if you still have feelings for him, tell him." Her smile turns from gentle to evil. "And then make him grovel."

It surprises a laugh out of me. "Let's just go save his life first."

Chapter Forty-Three
Eldoris

EVERYTHING IS ON FIRE.

It's fitting since I blew up my life that my court would also be engulfed in flames.

When Devorah heard I told Edina to go to her mate, she smacked me on the back of the head and told me I was making a mistake. She wanted me to go to the Spring Court and apologize until Edina came back to me. I didn't do that. I slept in the jungle on the front lines—not even summoning a tent because it reminded me of our camping trip—and snapped at everyone who dared to talk to me. Radley and Izar eventually camped near me and warned off anyone who came close.

Then we were attacked. The hellfire Fae came out in full force, incinerating everything in their path. They must have been holding back during their first attack because they're damn near unstoppable this time. Radley thinks Titania urged them to use caution since she didn't want to take over a court that was all ashes. The hellfire Fae have no such qualm.

The Unseelie Army—not just the battalion Gwyneira sent, but the entire army—have joined us, trying to contain the enemy to the edge of the jungle closest to the Padauk River. They all have a stake in this battle. If the hellfire Fae win today and topple our monarchy, nothing is stopping them from attacking the other courts.

The air users are doing their best to choke the oxygen from the flames, but the hellfire is spreading too quickly. Not even regular water magic is a match for it, as evidenced by the Winter Court battalion that's been practically demolished. Objectively, fire is the weakest element against this particular foe, since it can't hurt them. I've been using some offensive spells, but nothing is as strong as my raw magic, and it's only so effective.

We need Gwyneira and Edina.

Selfishly, I hope Edina stays away, no matter how much she's needed. I don't want her getting hurt in this mess.

Puck arrived a bit ago, despite having been absent from battles for ages. He hasn't strayed far from my side, like an annoying earth-wielding shadow, springing up and blocking fire from hitting me with manifested rock formations. Even worse, he smells like Edina, which makes me want to punch him in the face even though he's saving my life.

Radley lands next to me and quickly folds up his wings. I think he's still scarred from seeing the hellfire consume Edina's wings. "The pixies reported back," he says. When a group of pixies arrived wanting to help, we sent them beyond the front lines, since they could get close without drawing too much attention. Despite their size, they are strong enough to take down a troll, and vicious enough to try. They took out an entire section of hellfire Fae before they couldn't get any closer.

As if summoned, Althea and Brigid appear, hovering over Puck's head.

"We overheard their leader," Althea says, her magenta eyes fixed on me.

"This is all of them. If we can get them all today—"

"Easier said than done," I remark as a ball of hellfire streaks toward us, and all we can do is drop to the floor while the pixies shriek and scatter.

The hellfire hits the tree behind us, and Radley quickly sucks the oxygen from the air surrounding it, reducing the fire to embers, but not before the tree starts to teeter.

"Run," he yells, but Puck's vines wrap around the tree, holding it upright until he can manipulate the wood. When it's stable enough, he releases the vines, and the tree is back to normal.

I still want to punch him.

"He went that way," Althea says, gesturing to the retreating form of our attacker.

"He's the leader," Brigid adds, shaking out her purple hair until it lies back in place.

I take off in the direction they pointed. The entire group yells after me, but I know this jungle like the back of my hand, and I'm quick on my feet. Even flying, they won't catch me before I catch the hellfire Fae. I don't have a plan, other than destroying him for what he's doing to my home.

He sees me taking chase and starts wildly throwing fire over his shoulder, but his aim is shit. All he's doing is igniting the trees around me, not even ones that are close enough to hurt me. The Winter Court soldiers appear from the vegetation, putting out the individual fires as fast as possible.

"General, wait for someone to go with you—" one yells, but I'm already gone. They'll be too slow, and I'm not losing him.

The trees start to thin, and I burst onto the sandy riverbank. The full moon is bright overhead now that it's not hidden beneath a canopy of trees, and it perfectly illuminates a hellfire-wielding firing squad.

A line of Fae with white-hot flames pooling in their hands stares me down, poised to strike. "Fuck," I swear. I turn to flee back into the jungle, to get help, but two launch their hellfire. The magic sales past my head and ignites the trees along the river, engulfing them quickly until I'm staring back at a wall of fire.

I'm trapped.

The male I was chasing, a slimy-looking fucker with pale skin and dark hair, balances a fireball in the palm of his hand and sneers at me. "Well, well," he clucks his tongue, "if it isn't the halfling prince. Just who we were hoping to see."

"That so?" I ask, holding my head high. They may have me penned in, but I'm certainly not going to go down sniveling.

"A coup is only successful if there are no heirs remaining to take the throne," he sneers, baring his black-tinged teeth.

"If you think the people of this court will accept your rule, you're delusional," I goad, trying to distract him while I search for some way out of this predicament.

"Agree to disagree."

Time seems to slow as he launches the fireball at me, and the rest of the Fae behind him follow suit. The attack forms a perfect arc of fire, blocking me from all exits, including the river. I enact a shield around myself, not that I'm sure it will hold up amidst that level of power.

The air around me ripples in the heat. Smoke from the trees burning behind me stings my lungs and I squint against the brilliant light coming off the fire. I square my shoulders and lift my chin, determined to go out with my head held high.

Love you, I send mentally to my sister, who is safe inside the palace. *I'm sorry.*

Eldoris! she shrieks in my mind. *Don't you dare. Don't you dare leave me.*

I think I hear a voice calling my name, but it's drowned out by the roaring of the flames as they quickly approach. I expected my life to flash before my eyes in the face of certain death, but I only see two faces. Arella looks at me fondly, but there's a twinge of disappointment on her face.

Then I see Edina, surrounded in a tempest of snow and ice, looking like an avenging angel descending between me and the fire. The mirage lands before me and ice blasts from her fingers, her chest, and her open mouth. Power explodes out of her in all directions, dousing the fire behind me and the fireballs streaking toward us. The temperature around us drops as the jungle hisses in relief.

She turns to me, eyes blazing in anger, and douses me in a torrent of cold water. I sputter and gasp, swiping the water from my eyes. She's still there, beautiful in a navy tunic and her hair tied back in a braid. Wisps of blonde hair float around her face as she stares at me incredulously.

"Are you trying to get yourself killed?" she demands. *She's here.* This isn't some end-of-life vision. This is real. "Why are you here by yourself? There's a whole-ass saying about fighting fire with fire."

"That's a mortal thing," I mutter, which was definitely the wrong thing to say.

"Are you fucking kidding me?"

I want time to stop so I can run to her, but her attention shifts to the enemy surrounding us still gaping in shock at their failed attack. Just like we hadn't seen the extent of their magic, they haven't seen all that Edina can do. I fought beside her in a war, I know exactly how formidable she is.

Her eyes flare electric blue as icicles emerge from her knuckles like claws. She pauses, waiting for something. The hellfire Fae ready themselves for an attack, but Edina just grins.

The water behind them swirls into a whirlpool. As if controlled by the same brain, they turn to face the new foe. Gwyneira bursts from the center of the pool, the water holding her aloft as she uses the river water to create weapons of ice that spear through them.

Puck emerges from the jungles, the pixies hot on his heels, panting from exertion.

Edina flicks a whip of water at him, the crack resounding even with the sounds of the battle raging on the river. "You said you'd watch him."

"I saved his life like eight times. It's not my fault he ran."

She makes a sound close to a growl, and with one final glare at her mate, takes off to fight alongside her mother. Puck's eyes light with mischief when he finds me staring at him, and he uses a wall of sand to block an incoming attack.

Edina is a force to be reckoned with. She's quick with her magic, making decisive strikes. Sometimes she opts for injuring, especially in the few face-offs where her opponent is savvy. Her ice forms thin shards that slice into important arteries, distracting the Fae as they try to cauterize their wounds so she can take them out. She's just as good as her mother, who is living up to her legendary status.

As if their arrival has spurred on the rest of the army, our forces drive the rest of the hellfire Fae back to the river, delivering them to Edina and her mother, who work in tandem with powerful waves of water and ice that douse the hellfire and then kill their wielders.

At some point, Edina tosses me a sheathed dagger and says, "Make yourself useful," with a hearty cackle. I stay near her, orbiting around her like she's the sun and attacking anyone who gets close.

Puck pulls me away from the fight when there are only two hellfire Fae remaining. Edina and her mother corral them, fighting until they're back-to-back. "Now," he says, and we rush forward so the Fae are surrounded. A secondary circle forms around us in case we fall. Radley and Izar are across the circle, Hades is to the right, and even Larisa is here.

"Any final words?" Edina asks, water dancing around her in a flame-like shape. It licks up her legs, mocking the enemy as she controls it.

"You think this is it?" the leader says. "As long as there's a way to get more power, someone will always find it. You may have bested us today, but I guarantee this won't be the last of the enhanced elements that you see. History repeats itself. Just like with Queen—"

Edina fills the male's mouth with water choking his words. His gurgling is the only sound as we wait with bated breath for her to finish him off. She lets him suffer for a little longer before encasing both males in impenetrable ice. Gwyneira joins her, and together the ice becomes so cold that it starts smoking. The Fae scream within their confines as their skin burns and turns mottled blue and purple.

Finally, when the pressure becomes too much, their bodies explode, icy chunks of Fae blasting into the air like a geyser. Edina throws up a shield around our army, protecting them from the carnage raining down. A pointed ear lands on the shield right above my head and falls to the sandy riverbank.

"Gross," Edina says, wrinkling her nose. Her mother sighs, but the corners of her lips turn up in the hint of a smirk.

There's a hushed awe from our army that erupts into thunderous cheers. *We won.* Somehow, for the second time in recent history, the Fae courts banded together against a common foe and won. Soldiers from both sides clap each other on the back. Radley keeps walking up to random Fae and kissing them on the lips. I send a message to Devorah to tell her the news and can feel her relief, as palpable as my own through the link.

Edina and her mother embrace, and when she breaks away, she turns to me fire blazing in her eyes.

"Good luck with that," Puck murmurs, clapping me on the back before disappearing into the crowd. Confusion wars with the other mixed emotions I feel at having Edina before me.

She stands before me, silent, her brows arched, and her arms crossed over her chest. Her eyes bore into mine as she waits. I know what I want to say. I want to lay my heart at her feet and beg her to come back. I want to tell her how desperately I need her.

I want to tell her how much I love her.

But I can't say any of that. I let her go for a reason. I want her to be happy.

So, I just stare back, a lump caught in my throat keeping me from saying something I'll regret.

We've garnered an audience as many of the Fae who were celebrating notice we're locked in this silent conversation. Whispers of curiosity ripple through the crowd. Out of the corner of my eye, I see Althea smacking Brigid excitedly, hissing at her to watch.

"For fuck's sake," Edina grumbles and erects a wall of water around us. There are audible boos as we take away their entertainment for the evening. Someone outside our bubble starts organizing the forces. I think I hear Puck order the earth users to help restore the jungle, but I'm too focused on Edina.

"One of the best things about our relationship is that we were honest with each other," she says. Her usually melodic voice is hardened, and I hate that she feels like she needs to block herself off from me.

"Yes," I agree. She steps in closer.

"If you could ask me one question, and know I was answering honestly, what would you ask?"

There are a million questions I could ask her, but I settle on the most important one. "Are you happy?"

She shakes her head, and a tear slides down her cheek, freezing as it goes until a ball of ice plunks into the sand. "No." I fight the urge to take her into my arms and hold her and make it better. "Ask me why."

"You could just tell me."

"I could, but my mom told me to make you work for it."

"Work for what?"

"This ravishing creature before you." She holds her arms out wide, her small smile reaching her eyes. It makes me chuckle. *It's impossible not to smile when Edina is smiling at you.*

"Why aren't you happy, kitten?" The nickname slips out, but it makes her breath catch.

"Because I'm in love with you." She says it like it's the most natural thing in the world. Like she's stating the color of the sky or the fact that it's cold in the Winter Court.

"And," she continues, "because you pushed me away instead of fighting for me. You made a decision for us without consulting me. If we're going to make this work, you can't do that anymore. We're a team."

Mist from the wall of water rains over us, dampening her hair and making it stick to her face. "I know you thought you were doing the right thing, that you just wanted me to be happy. But I'm happy with you."

"What about Puck?" I ask, my body unconsciously drifting closer to her. *I'm in love with you.*

"We're done," she steps into me, resting her hands on my chest. The gold of her ring glints under the moonlight. I haven't taken mine off either. "I rejected the mating bond."

"You what?" I ask, and she takes my hands in hers, linking our fingers together.

"It's gone. There's no more pain. We're officially untethered. It was fucked up anyway. We kissed and it was like kissing a sponge." A growl reverberates in my throat at the thought of his hands on her, of his mouth kissing her lips.

"Before you sent me away, do you know what I was going to tell you?" she asks, leaning in a little closer. I'm barely breathing, barely moving. I'm afraid if I shift an inch, it will shatter this illusion and I'll be back to the misery of a life without her. "I was going to pick you."

"You were?" I ask my voice barely a whisper. "And now? After I sent you away?"

"I still want you." Her hand drifts up to my cheek and her fingers rake through the beard that's grown back in her absence. "I *choose* you."

It's like a dam breaks. My hand snaps out, cupping the back of her neck and hauling her against me. She leaps into my arms and crushes her lips to mine. My whole body reacts, my arms winding around her and hoisting her up to a better angle. My heart wants to burst through my ribcage, beating erratically even while the rest of me relaxes because she's back with me, where she belongs.

"I love you," I say against her lips. She sighs at the words, and I use the opportunity to slip my tongue inside her mouth.

As quickly as I start the kiss, she ends it with a sharp tug on my horns. When I meet her eyes, her shields are down, complete vulnerability shining through those gorgeous blue eyes. "I thought you didn't want me."

"That's—" I swear. "Fuck, no. That's not what I meant at all." I hug her as tight as I can. "I love you more than anything in any realm, and letting you go was the hardest thing I've ever done, but I will never make a decision for us again. We're a team."

"Good."

I kiss her again, and this time it's frantic and dizzying. I can't get enough of her. I want to make up for lost time by worshipping her in every way possible. "I will spend every day on my knees before you to prove how much I want you."

Her moan is breathy as she draws me back in and grinds against mine.

A cheer goes up from the crowd and my eyes drift open. Edina buries her head in my chest as she realizes her magic slipped, and now everyone can see us, soaked from the mist of her water wall and wrapped around each other. Althea is in the front, celebrating with wild jerky movements, and even Brigid has a small grin on her face. Puck is beaming beside Radley and Izar, who are whooping louder than anyone else in the crowd, and Edina's family looks on with pride. The only person missing is Devorah, but she's screaming in my head about her advisor not letting her out of the palace and demanding to know what's happening.

"This is so fucking cheesy," Edina laughs into my skin.

"Absolutely awful," I hold her tighter, not letting her go.

"Will you hate me if I make it worse?" She kisses my neck before dropping to her feet.

"I could never hate you."

"Good." She takes both my hands in hers. "El?"

"Yeah, kitten?"

"Will you marry me?"

Edina

A Little Way Down the Road

"YOU ARE SO PERFECT," Eldoris whispers, kissing my shoulder, then my neck, and then gripping my chin to tilt my head to him so he can claim my lips.

After Eldoris and I got married, we moved out of the palaces and into our townhouse. It didn't go over well with either of our families, but they eventually adjusted with the caveat that we have to move back into the palace when my mother finally gives up the throne. Since I never see that happening, I agreed quickly.

Althea and Brigid zip around our heads, one redoing my hair while the other slides a new robe over my shoulders. Despite the fact that it meant leaving court, they came with us when Eldoris and I moved, and have become such an important part of our lives. But I've never been more grateful for them than I am today.

A soft coo has us pulling apart and looking down at the bundle wrapped in a soft white blanket. "I'm sorry, were we ignoring you?" I say, my voice light as the baby girl in my arms fidgets and tries to get comfortable. She surprised us all by arriving early, and she came so fast that the healer hasn't even arrived yet. I'm very lucky my lady's maids knew how to deliver a baby.

Our daughter blinks her eyes open at me, and a joy so deep, so profound fills my chest, lighting me up from the inside. "Hi, sweet girl."

"You're perfect too," Eldoris says to our daughter, running a finger gently along her cheek.

There's a soft knock at the door, and Vlad pokes his head in, his toothy smile wide as he steps through the doorway. "Look what I found," he says, and steps aside, revealing a tall, lean male with yellow-blonde hair, golden skin, and ocean-blue eyes.

"It's been so long!" I bemoan, dramatically placing a hand on my chest. "You don't call, you don't write. This is how you treat your mother?"

Joseph, my oldest son, rolls his eyes emphatically in a move that's been passed through generations. When he was old enough, he became the Winter Court's emissary to the mortal realm and has since stayed there more often than not. I'm convinced he has a lover there, but he won't say anything about it.

"I've missed you too." He comes over to the side of the bed and kisses my cheek.

Another knock, and this time a female with pale skin and dark brown curls walks in, her sapphire blue eyes ignoring everyone else in the room and zeroing in on the bundle in my arms.

"Yes! I knew it was a girl, pay up!" Arella, my now middle daughter, squeals, holding her hand out until Vlad places a purse of coins in it. She shoves it in her pocket and then kneels at the foot of the mattress like she did when she was a child. "Hi, baby sister."

"Notice how she doesn't care about me," Joseph scoffs.

"Maybe if you came home once in a while, I'd recognize you," Arella says coolly. Joseph snaps a water whip at her, and she feigns shock, calling fire to her fingertips.

"No fireballs around the baby," Eldoris admonishes. She gives him a sheepish look but banishes the fire and then turns back to me.

"Can I?" she asks, and I very gently transfer her sister into Arella's arms. "Wow, Dad, she looks just like you." And she does. Our daughter has the same coloring as her father, with the same hint of dark curls, but her eyes are sort of a mix, like a stormy ocean sky.

"Does she have a name?" Joseph asks as the baby grabs his finger. My eyes lift to my vampire friend, who has moved to a chair in the corner of the room, content being here but not intruding.

"Her name is Kathryn," I say, and a fond smile crosses Vlad's face. He stands, rebuttoning his suit jacket, and crosses to the bed, motioning for Arella to give him the baby.

"Kathryn," he murmurs, holding her aloft for a moment before tucking her into his arms. "You have some big shoes to fill, kid."

The baby takes that exact moment to spit up, right onto Vlad's suit. He wrinkles his nose and passes her back to me. "She already has her namesake's sense of humor," he deadpans, making everyone in the room laugh as Joseph takes pity on the vampire and uses his water magic to clean him up.

Another knock sounds, and when the door swings open, it reveals my mother, all seven of my fathers, and Devorah. Saying our bedroom is modest in size is generous, but they all manage to shove into the room, speaking a million miles a minute, greeting Vlad and my grown children before surrounding the bed to fawn over the newest addition to our family.

Eldoris places his arms over mine as I hold our daughter and looks into my eyes. "I'm the luckiest Fae in all the realms," he murmurs, before placing a gentle kiss on my lips.

But looking at our crazy family, I disagree.

That title belongs to me.

The series continues with Puck's story in...

Of Vines and Rivals

An enemies-to-lovers Fae romance
Spring 2024

Want to know more about Edina's time in the mortal realm and her best friend Katie?

You can find them both in The Made from Magic Series: a complete urban fantasy romance trilogy!

About the Author

Marianne A. Scott has been writing since she was a kid. When she was always singing, those stories appeared in song form, when she majored in acting, they appeared as screenplays, but novels and short stories were what she returned to when inspiration struck. Each and every story was driven by characters and love, and, most of the time, the hope that there was something fantastical about this world that we humans just haven't discovered yet.

When not writing, you can find her with her Kindle and a latte, sitting opposite her husband in their New Jersey home. In her other life, she teaches tiny humans how to sing, passing along her love of musical theater to the next generation.

Want first dibs on all future ARCs, special sneak peeks, and more? Join my Reader's Group or sign up for my Email List.

All links can be found at www.marianneascott.com

Also by Marianne A. Scott

The Made from Magic Series
Made from Magic
Made to Conquer
Made to Rule
A Court Where I'm Freezing My A** Off (Made from Magic #2.5)

The Fae Romance Series
Of Ice and Heartbreak
Of Vines and Rivals (Spring 2024)

Acknowledgements

First and foremost, I'd like to thank all of you who have made it this far. Thank you for helping me realize this dream.

To the best husband in the entire universe of the world, thank you for always supporting me, and for always comforting me when the imposter syndrome hits. Thank you for being a sounding board when I need to talk through plot points, even when I don't listen and just need to talk at you. Thank you for taking care of all the behind-the-scenes things I wasn't prepared for when I went into self-publishing.

To my amazing parents, thank you for being excited every time I tell you page read numbers and Amazon rankings. You're my biggest cheerleaders and I thank you so much for your never-ending support. And for John, thank you for reading and providing me with up-to-date texts to let me know what you think. PS: I hope you all collectively skipped some sections.

To my writing partner/sounding board/plot-hole canon Rachel, thanks for listening when I talk about this series every single week during our chats. Thank you for every note, every hour spent listening to me dissect the magic system only to scream "There's a spell for that" when I couldn't answer your question, and every creativity check-in.

To all those who have helped me along the way, including my amazing editor Samantha at Samantha Reads Spicy who made me sound way smarter than I am, Cassidy at Townsend Works for listening to my ramblings about the cover and turning it into something truly stunning, Amanda at Eternal Geekery for taking a potato of a map and turning it into a real-life world, and Kelsea R for being an amazing sensitivity reader and providing insightful notes that I will take with me through all my future projects.

When I began writing this series, I found myself suddenly needing names for landmarks. As someone who typically writes Urban Fantasy, I was overwhelmed. Thank you to everyone who offered amazing names for forests and rivers and everything in between on my Instagram and Facebook posts, but a super SUPER special thank you to the following for helping me bring this world to life: Samantha Newsome (Padauk River), Carol Bennett (Etherealia Meadow), Rachel Betancourt (Varesen Forest), Elizabeth Grimme (Dorchas Desert), Pradhyutha (Atavi Forest), Sarena (Allagi River), Kelsey Lynn (Oraiste Mountains), and Jillian Melko (Immutavi Ocean).

Thank you to my family who are literally the most supportive people in the entire universe. I'm seriously so lucky to have you all rooting for me. I hope you know how invaluable your support has been.

Last but not least, thank you to the amazing readers who have taken a moment to reach out and tell me how much you love these books and characters. You have no idea how much your comments brighten my days and keep me going through the worst of the imposter syndrome. A huge mega shoutout to the readers in GrossBooks 2.0, for your overall positivity and willingness to talk about all things book-related!

Made in the USA
Las Vegas, NV
05 February 2025